A Shot
to Die For

Also by Libby Fischer Hellmann
An Eye for Murder
A Picture of Guilt
An Image of Death

A Shot
to Die For

Libby Fischer Hellmann

Poisoned Pen Press

Copyright © 2005 by Libby Fischer Hellmann
First Edition 2005

10 9 8 7 6 5 4 3 2 1

Library of Congress Catalog Card Number: 2005903227

ISBN: 1-59058-185-7   Hardcover

Poisoned Pen Press
6962 E. First Ave., Ste. 103
Scottsdale, AZ 85251
www.poisonedpenpress.com
info@poisonedpenpress.com

Printed in the United States of America

For Deane and Steven
Playmates, support group, and all-around
extraordinary siblings

Acknowledgments

Among the folks who gave me their time, expertise, and stories were Helen Brandt at the Lake Geneva Historical Society, who clued me into *Newport of the West, 1870–1920* by Ann Wolfmeyer and Mary Burns Gage; the wonderful Pam Showalter-Blades; former Lake Geneva mayor Spiro Condos (aka Speedo); Pam Rawlinson; Mary Welk; Mike Black; Dave Case; Teri Mathes; Reba Meshulam; and Captain Ralph Bauman (aka Homer) of the Lake Geneva Police Department.

Also, someone I should have acknowledged long ago is Cindy Clohesey, who has graciously allowed me to "borrow" some of her best lines.

As always, The Red Herrings, who meet at Scotland Yard, deserve cheers. There is no better writing group in the universe. Thanks, too, to Michael Dymmoch and Barb D'Amato, who helped me out of a hole. And Roberta Isleib and Deborah Donnelly ("Sex" and "Lies"), without whose daily encouragement "Videotape" would be permanently out of focus.

A special acknowledgment to editor Nora Cavin, whose perceptive comments and suggestions were the reason this book came to be finished at all.

And, once again, my thanks to my Berkley editor, Samantha Mandor, whose grace and talent are unmatched; Barbara Peters, whose eye is unerring; and Jacky Sachs, the best agent in the business.

Finally, one last, loving tribute to my friend Susan White, the "Susan Siler" in my books. She will live forever on these pages.

Eight children were at play, seven sisters and their brother. Suddenly the boy was struck dumb; he trembled and began to run upon his hands and feet. His fingers became closed, and his body was covered with fur. Directly there was a bear where the boy had been. The sisters were terrified, they ran and the bear after them. They came to the stump of a great tree, and the tree spoke to them. It bade them climb upon it, and as they did so it began to rise into the air. The bear came to kill them, but they were just beyond its reach. It reared against the tree and scored the bark all around with its claws. The seven sisters were borne into the sky, and they became the stars of the Big Dipper.

N. Scott Momaday,
The Way to Rainy Mountain

Chapter One

"What do you mean you're not coming? You were supposed to meet me! We had a date!" With each syllable, the woman's voice slid up the register toward hysteria.

I slowed. I was walking toward the Lake Forest rest stop—an oasis, we call them here—just off the interstate near the Wisconsin state line. The woman was talking on her cell phone about thirty feet away, but her voice carried clearly. "How could you do this to me? After all our plans! You knew I'd be stranded!"

A man with a buzz cut and horn-rimmed glasses stood near the entrance, his hands in his pockets. He stepped aside as I approached.

"Look. I can't talk long. I borrowed a cell." There was a pause. "Mine's out of juice."

A tall, striking woman who appeared to be somewhere in her thirties, the woman on the phone wore a white T-shirt, khaki miniskirt, and sandals. Her shoulder-length hair, held off her face by a wide headband and a pair of shades, was a glossy black. Blue highlights glinted when she moved her head.

I went inside the building, which since its multimillion-dollar renovation, looked more like an airport terminal than one of the antiseptic fast-food places that used to commandeer pit stops on the highway. Donuts, pizza, coffee, and Chinese food beckoned me from cheerful kiosks, and it took all my resolve to resist them. I was tired, having spent the day scouting locations for a video about the Lodge, a luxury resort in Lake Geneva, Wisconsin. I'd stopped in for a cold drink before heading home to Rachel, my fifteen-year-old, who was in the midst of a what-am-I-going-to-do-all-summer-since-I'm-too-old-for-camp crisis.

I bought a Diet Coke, eyed the Krispy Kremes, and quickly headed back outside. A Thursday evening in the third week of June, it had been a hot and humid day. Now, though, a cool front was pushing through, and a breeze was chasing away the heat.

The woman was still on the cell. "I know. I'm sorry, too. I hate it when we fight." There was a pause. "I realize that. It's just—well, this has been a shitty day."

The man who'd been standing near the entrance had his back to her as though he was trying not to listen to her conversation.

"I can't. My cell is out of juice," she repeated. "Okay. Thanks. I'll be waiting. Please come soon." The woman disconnected and looked around. Spotting the man at the entrance, she walked over and handed him the cell. "Thank you. You've been very kind."

The man pocketed the cell. "No problem. I hope everything works out."

"I'm sure it will." She smiled. "Hope you catch some big ones."

The man raised his hand and started across to the parking lot. The woman went inside. I looked at my watch. Almost seven. I wondered if Rachel had eaten. Maybe I should go back in and pick up a pizza. For now, though, I lingered outside with my drink, letting the cool breeze wash over me.

I was just about to go when the woman came back out, carrying a drink. She walked over to a three-foot-high brick wall that ran between the building and the parking lot. Turning her face into the wind, she lifted her hair off the back of her neck.

"Feels good, doesn't it?" I said.

She nodded.

It had been hot in Lake Geneva, the breeze that usually keeps things cool apparently AWOL. For over a century, wealthy Chicagoans had escaped the blistering Midwest summer at the "Newport of the West," where they built luxurious estates and fueled a culture of privilege and class that rivaled anything on

Martha's Vineyard or Nantucket. Though the resort's exclusivity had faded over time, tourists still flocked to it, a fact that had not gone unnoticed by developers. The Lodge's owners snapped up their property as soon as it became available, proving once again that as landmarks turn populist, they become marketable.

Now, though, I was twenty miles southeast, at the only rest stop between the North Shore of Chicago and the Wisconsin state line. Access ramps led from the highway to a paved surface the size of a football field. The building that housed the food court occupied the middle of the tarmac and hung over both sides of I-94. Parking lots flanked with gas pumps sat on both sides.

The young woman sighed. "I guess it'll turn out okay after all."

I looked over. "Bad day?"

"You don't know the half of it."

The door to the restaurant opened, and an elderly couple came out. The man, his thick white hair neatly parted on the side, carefully avoided eye contact with both of us. His companion, a seventyish woman with a wide-brimmed straw hat, tightened her lips when she saw me. I wondered what I'd done to annoy her or whether she was just the kind of person who disapproved of everyone. The young woman flashed me a sympathetic smile. I smiled back.

As the couple made their way to the parking lot, four red-faced kids in tanks and shorts pushed past on their way into the rest stop. They smelled of sweat and sun block and seemed oblivious to everything except themselves.

"I couldn't help overhearing. I hope your ride gets here soon," I said.

The young woman tipped her head. "Me, too. I've lost the whole day."

"I hate fights."

"It was—stupid."

"They usually are."

"It should never have happened."

I nodded. The breeze was so refreshing I hated to leave. I slung the canvas bag that doubles as my briefcase onto my shoulder and joined her at the wall. As long as we were both hanging around, I might as well be nice. She perched on top, her legs dangling in front. Close up, she was stunning, her black hair thick and wavy—without a hint of gray, I noted enviously—her skin olive-gold. She had wide, jade green eyes, and those legs would pass what my father called the "Betty Grable" test with flying colors.

I pressed down on the tiny web of varicose veins above my knee, willing them to disappear, but they popped back out when I lifted my thumb off my skin. I sighed. "What's your name?"

"Daria." She swung her legs back and forth like a kid.

"I'm Ellie. Where are you from?"

"I live in Lake Geneva."

"Small world. I'm producing a film up there."

"A film?"

"Well, a video. At the Lodge. Do you know it?"

"The old Playboy Club?"

"That's the one."

Daria nodded. "I know it well."

The Lodge had been built by Hugh Hefner in the early sixties and was a popular Playboy resort until his empire collapsed in the eighties. It passed through several sets of hands after that, each owner removing more traces of its glamorous X-rated past. Now it's such a G-rated facility that a bronze statue of a father with a little boy on his shoulders greets guests at the entrance.

I scanned the cars heading up the ramp on our side of the rest stop. A silver Beamer slowly turned in, followed by a green pickup with a camper shell. "Is that your ride?" I pointed to the Beamer.

Daria shaded her eyes and looked. As the car passed, we could plainly see a couple in the front seat. The woman in the passenger seat motioned to an empty space in the parking lot. As the Beamer swerved into the spot, Daria seemed to deflate. "No."

I hoisted my bag farther up my shoulder. "Well, don't worry. I'm sure your boyfriend will be here soon."

She was about to say something when the pickup that had been behind the Beamer passed us. It slowed to a crawl, and the window at the back of the camper shell slid open. The movement triggered a prickly feeling at the back of my neck.

I turned to Daria. She stared at the pickup. I was about to ask if she recognized it when I heard a loud crack. I whipped around. The pickup's engine revved, and it tore out of the ramp. I turned back to Daria. A crimson design exploded on her shirt. She fell forward off the wall and crumpled to the ground.

Chapter Two

"Sniper!"

That was the word on everyone's lips even before the state police showed up. It took me a while to realize it, though. I felt as if I was inside a freeze-frame. There was no sound. Movement halted. Even the air currents stopped.

Except for the blood. I don't know how long I stood over Daria, watching the crimson design expand. The red kept spreading, eating up the material, blossoming like one of those time-lapse sequences in nature films. I couldn't tear my eyes away.

Then a face popped up in front of my field of vision. Then another, and another. Mouths opened, lips moved. I saw expressions of concern. Someone took my arm, and guided me away from the wall and the explosion of red. The silence yielded, and I began to hear words.

"I'm all right." The words were coming from me.

"No, you're not," a voice said. "Sit down." A man took my arm. "Make room," he ordered sharply.

The crowd parted to let me through. I squatted on the curb. Someone shoved a water bottle into my hand. The crowd regrouped around me. "Not again!" "How is she?" "Did someone call the police?" "Are you getting a pulse?" "Did she see the shooter?"

A man bent over Daria, his back to me. After a moment, he straightened. "She's gone."

I heard murmurs, a cry, several intakes of breath. "Are you sure?" someone asked.

The man got to his feet and turned around. "I'm a doctor." He checked his watch and then came over to me. "What about you? How are you doing?"

I looked at Daria's body. "I'm alive."

⌐⌐⌐

Sniper!

I saw it on the face of the first cop on the scene. The cruiser raced up the ramp and swerved to a stop. The officer jumped out, leaving the engine on and the roof lights flashing. Young and eager, he was wearing a khaki uniform and the wide-brimmed campaign hat Illinois state troopers have worn since World War One. When he saw Daria, his face paled and his body went rigid, and for a minute I thought he was going to throw up. Then he seemed to realize that people were looking to him for guidance. He threw his shoulders back and planted his hands on his hips, an Eagle Scout with a gun on his hip. The only tip-off to his feelings was a muscle in his jaw that kept twitching.

Once he'd determined who I was and that the pickup was gone and no one was in imminent danger, he radioed from the cruiser, nodding several times as he spoke. Then he went to the trunk and fished out a megaphone.

Knots of people had gathered on the tarmac, some around me, others in the parking lot, still others in front of the building's entrance. "All you folks go inside," he bellowed through the megaphone. "And don't touch anything. More troopers are on the way, and they're gonna want to talk to all of you."

The crowd started to thin. I got to my feet and started toward the building, but the trooper held up his palm. "Not you. You come with me."

He led me over to the cruiser. "The detective wants to talk to you."

"How long do you think that will be? I'd like to go home. My daughter's—"

He cut me off and opened the rear door. "Hard to say."

Reluctantly I slid in. I'd been in patrol cars before; this one wasn't much different. A radio, dash lights, a minicomputer beside the driver's seat. I settled myself in the back seat, pulled out my cell, and called Rachel.

"Hi, sweetie. How are you?"

"Bored." Her voice was sullen. "I IM'd everyone, but no one's around. They're all at camp. Or Europe. Everybody's *someplace*. Except me."

If I didn't know better, I might think she'd developed a case of "North Shore-itis," a common affliction of teenagers who've been raised in affluence and feel entitled to everything. But Rachel is a level-headed girl. Most of the time. "You were the one who said you were too old for camp."

"Yeah, well, there's nothing to do."

I'd been trying to warn her since March this might happen, but any suggestions about getting a job, starting the community service project she'd committed to last spring, or even—perish the thought—summer school had gone unheeded. Like the grasshopper, my daughter was certain *something* would work out without her having to lift a finger, and she'd done nothing to prepare for summer. Ordinarily I might have let loose with an I-told-you-so, but given where I was and why, being right didn't seem important.

"Why don't we talk about it when I get home, okay? I'm calling to say I'm going to be late."

Silence. Then, "You said we could go to the movies tonight."

"I'm sorry. Something happened."

"You're working late…again," she groused.

"Not exactly."

Thankfully, she didn't pursue it. "When will you be home?"

I took a quick look at the clock on my cell. "Eight or eight thirty, I hope."

"Jeez." She sighed heavily. "Well, I guess I'll call Daddy and see what he's doing."

I forced myself not to react. I've been divorced from Barry nearly ten years, and while our relationship wasn't outright hostile, Rachel was savvy enough to use it as leverage. She'd been playing us against each other for years, and it didn't help that I was susceptible to guilt trips, especially where she was concerned. More than once I'd wondered whether my child-rearing skills—or the lack of them—were creating a future ax murderer. Or worse, a politician. But I'd deal with that later.

"Just let me know where you end up," I said evenly.

Not long after that, several cruisers, the paramedics, and an unmarked car arrived in a blaze of lights and sirens. Two troopers herded the remaining gapers back into the building. Another secured the area around Daria's body with crime-scene tape. Another watched the paramedics as they tried to take vital signs. The doctor hovered over them.

A dark van from the Northern Illinois Crime Lab pulled up. Two evidence technicians got out and retrieved large duffles from the back. At the same time, a few roadway maintenance trucks lumbered through the oasis and parked across the ramps, closing the oasis to traffic. One of the evidence techs snapped pictures, while the other took out paper, plastic bags, and markers. There was a subtle harmony to their work, as if each one knew his part and was performing it well.

Their familiarity was probably the result of experience. This was the second sniper attack—or drive-by, or whatever you chose to call it—in the Chicago area this year. The first had occurred in April at a highway rest stop on the South Side. The victim, a nurse named Pam Blades, had been coming out of the oasis with her teenage son. She was shot twice by someone from a slow-moving pickup. She died immediately. Police mounted an intense investigation, but three months later, the shooter was still at large. They did recover a bullet fragment that indicated the shooter had used a high-powered rifle, but whether he was a psycho, a weirdo bent on revenge, or even a terrorist, no one knew.

Now, an older man got out of an unmarked, moving with such a sleepy gait that I wondered if he'd been napping. Smallish, with thin blond hair, he was dressed in chinos and a navy blue golf shirt, and his gut hung over his belt. Fumbling his car keys into his pocket, he conferred with the paramedics, technicians, and the trooper who'd been first on the scene. Then he stuffed his hands in his pockets and stared at me.

⌐⌐⌐

Sniper! I thought. That's what it had to be.

The sun dipped behind the trees along the roadway, streaking the clouds with pink and purple. The photographer packed up his camera; the other tech lit a cigarette. The coroner's rep, who'd been parked in a white van at the edge of the tarmac, wheeled a gurney with a dark plastic body bag to where Daria lay.

The man in the navy shirt ambled over to the cruiser and blinked. I rolled down the window.

"Miss Foreman? I'm Detective Lieutenant Walter Milanovich." His voice was surprisingly soft, in contrast to his world-weary appearance. "How 'bout I buy you a cup of coffee."

As I slipped back inside the building, the elderly woman with the straw hat, who'd been waylaid by the shooting, was inside as well. She pursed her lips again as if it was my fault Daria had died and ruined her day.

Milanovich motioned me to a table in front of the Starbucks booth and a few minutes later brought over two lattes. He had ruddy cheeks and a pink forehead. His eyelashes were even paler than his hair, making his blue eyes appear abnormally large. I had the impression they wouldn't miss much.

He sat down. "So, tell me what happened."

I did.

He blinked. "She was having a fight?" He dumped three packs of sugar into his latte.

I nodded. "With her boyfriend, I think. But they made up."

"How do you know?"

I told him what I remembered of the conversation on the cell.

He blinked again. "She was using a borrowed cell?"

I nodded.

"Can you describe the man who lent her his cell phone?"

I thought back. I'd hardly noticed him at all. "He was—average."

He looked as if he'd expected me to say that. "Can you be more specific?"

"He had a crew cut, I remember. Maybe a buzz. And horn-rimmed glasses."

"Hair color?"

"Brown, I think. But it was short."

"Build?"

I shrugged. "Medium?"

Milanovich shot me a look. "Eyes?"

I thought about it. "I didn't notice. But he was wearing jeans—oh, wait. When she returned the phone, she said to him, 'Hope you catch some big ones.'"

Milanovich raised his eyebrows. "Big ones?"

"Yeah. Big ones. Like fish. I had the impression he was going fishing."

"Peachy." Milanovich looked down and made a note. "There's only about a thousand lakes in Wisconsin." He looked over. "You happen to notice what kind of car he was driving?"

I shook my head.

"You didn't see him drive away?"

"No. He walked around a corner. I didn't see his car."

He blinked again. "Now, you say she lived in Lake Geneva?"

"That's what she said."

He gazed at me with those sharp, oversized eyes. I couldn't help thinking of a large fish. "Did she say where?"

"No."

He took another sip. "What direction was she traveling?"

"I assume she was heading into Chicago."

"Why did you assume that?"

I went over it in my mind. Now that I was thinking about it, I realized I didn't know. We were on the southern side of the rest stop, but Daria hadn't indicated where she was going or what she was doing. "Well, now that you mention it, I guess she could have been heading back to Lake Geneva."

"She never told you where she was going? What she'd be doing when she got there?"

"No."

"Didn't you ask?"

"It wasn't that kind of conversation."

Milanovich blinked.

I ran my tongue around my lips. "But she did say she'd lost the entire day. I got the idea that whatever she'd planned didn't happen."

He blinked. "And you say you didn't know the woman."

"That's right."

"But you overheard her fighting with her boyfriend. And then you talked to her at the brick wall."

"Yes."

An edge had crept into his voice. Where was he going with this? He was about to say something but was cut off by the arrival of the coroner's rep, a middle-aged man with a thick gut, beady eyes, and a five o'clock shadow. "I'm done here, Lieutenant," he announced.

Milanovich rose from the table and motioned the man to follow him. They regrouped a few feet away from me. "What have you got?" He lowered his voice, but I could still hear him.

"Not much." The man reminded me of a three-dimensional Homer Simpson. "The entrance wound wasn't that big, but the exit wound more than made up for it."

"Consistent with a high-powered rifle?"

Homer nodded. "It's a safe bet."

"Chest wound?"

"Straight through the heart, ribs, backbone, and out the other side."

Milanovich blinked. "No one's found any shell casings or fragments yet, but we have dogs on the way."

"The night is still young."

Milanovich ignored him. "Anything else?"

"Just the obvious."

"What's that?"

"The guy's a hell of a shot."

The detective shifted. "You're doing her tomorrow?"

Homer nodded.

"I'll call you."

The coroner retreated, rubbing his hand across his chin. Milanovich came back and sat down. "So. You never saw her before."

"That's right." I said, for the third—or was it tenth—time.

"But you heard her fighting with her boyfriend."

"Yes."

"And then they made up."

"Yes."

"And he said he was coming to pick her up."

"I assumed that from what she said."

"Which was?"

"Which was something like, 'Thanks. I'll be waiting. Please come quickly.'"

"Anything else?"

"What do you mean?"

"Did she say anything else?"

I was quiet for a moment, trying to remember. "Yes. She did. She said her cell was out of juice."

"Again? Didn't you say she'd said that before you went inside the oasis?"

"Yes. She said it twice."

"So she repeated herself?"

I nodded. "The man whose cell she was using was a few feet away. I figured she wanted to get off so she could give it back."

"So she repeated that her cell was out of juice."

I sat straighter. Something about him was different.

He set his cup down on the edge of the table and folded his hands. "Let's back up. You were here…what…getting a cold drink on your way home. The woman…Daria…" He paused. "…a woman you'd never seen before seemed to be in distress, and you stopped to chat."

He'd stopped blinking. That's what was different.

"Then she goes inside, comes back out, and five minutes later is shot dead. Not even three feet from you."

He watched me as if I was some kind of mildly curious lab specimen. I started to miss the blinking fish.

"Look, Detective Milanovich. I didn't know the woman, but she was clearly upset. At least at first. Then she calmed down. I was just trying to be pleasant. That's all."

He settled back in his seat, still appraising me. Then he blinked. "Okay. Tell me about the pickup." His burst of energy had vanished; the world-weary fish was back.

"It was green. With one of those covers on the back. A black cover."

"Could you tell what make or model it was?"

My friend Fouad has a red Dodge Ram, but that's the sum total of what I know about pickups. "It wasn't a Dodge Ram."

"How do you know?"

I explained.

"What about the camper shell. Could you tell what material it was?"

"No."

I remembered a mention of a green pickup from the first sniper attack. "The pickup in the April sniper attack was green, too, wasn't it?"

He didn't answer. "Go on."

"The truck came up behind the Beamer and slowed down. Then it passed us, and the back window slid open."

"The back window of the camper shell?"

"That's right."

"Did you see who was in there?"

"No. I didn't see anyone."

"What about the driver?"

I thought about it. "No. I think—I think the sun visor was pulled down."

"You didn't see anyone in the driver's seat?"

"I saw a body. But that was all."

"Couldn't tell whether it was a man or woman?"

I thought about it, then shook my head. "I just wasn't paying attention. I'm sorry."

He looked at me, then nodded briefly. "And you didn't see anyone through the windows?"

"Nothing."

"Couldn't tell how many people were in the pickup?"

"By the time the window slid open, it was too far away."

"That's a 'no,' I take it?"

"Of course it's a no," I said in a prickly tone. "But there had to be at least two, right?"

"What makes you say that?"

"Well—common sense."

He stared at me.

"One person to drive, the other to shoot."

"I thought you said you couldn't see the driver."

"I couldn't. I'm just—never mind. I didn't. I'd turned around to Daria by then, anyway."

"Why?"

"I was saying I was sure her boyfriend would be there soon."

"Did she tell you his name?"

I shook my head.

"Did she describe him? Tell you what he did? Where he worked? Anything like that?"

"No. All she said was that she hated it when they fought."

Milanovich nodded. "Okay. So you're telling her that he would be there soon."

"Right. I was facing her."

"And you heard something."

"A crack. But loud. Almost like an explosion. Then the pickup's engine revved, and the tires screech, and—"

"Lieutenant!" One of the troopers hurried toward us, breathing hard. A man and woman followed behind. I recognized the couple from the Beamer. The trooper yanked his thumb at the couple. "We got a partial on the pickup!"

Chapter Three

I drove home watching darkness bleed across the sky, staining everything blue-black. The lights at the front of my house were on, and their cheery illumination made me think Rachel was home. But as I walked in from the garage, a deep silence caromed around the walls.

I went up to the kitchen, feeling lonely. After today, I wanted to see Rachel. I wanted to hug her, feel the beat of her heart, her warm skin against mine. Instead, I found a note propped on the kitchen table.

Rode my bike to Dad's. Spending the night.

I live in a small three-bedroom colonial in a sleepy village twenty miles north of Chicago. My ex-husband has a condo less than two miles away. I kept the house after the divorce, although I'm not sure now it was such a great idea. I'm always lining the pockets of plumbers, electricians, and appliance repairmen, while Barry takes his girlfriends on trips to Alaska, Honduras, and Banff. Tonight, though, I was grateful for my refuge.

I poured a glass of wine and headed upstairs, recalling the events at the rest stop. Once the deputy at the oasis burst in with a partial description of the pickup's plates, Milanovich's interest in me waned. After questioning the couple from the Beamer, he told a deputy to get the description on ISPERN, the Illinois State Police Emergency Radio Network, and pass it on to Wisconsin, too. The media arrived soon afterward, and the troopers who'd been interviewing customers at the rest stop reported in as well. Juggling two cell phones and a growing pile of notes, Milanovich glanced at me with weary resignation.

"You can go home. I'll be in touch."

I'd hurried to the car, trying to skirt the news cameras that were staked out at the edge of the crime scene. I thought I'd been successful, but when I turned on the TV, I saw shots of myself scurrying to the Volvo. You couldn't see my gray eyes or the lines around them, but the cloud of dark, wavy hair that refused to lie straight no matter how much conditioner I use was clearly recognizable. I'd lost a little weight recently and was still making grateful obeisance to the calorie gods; unfortunately, the ten extra pounds the camera adds obliterated my gains, or losses, as it were. Still, you could tell it was me.

I groaned. My father never misses the ten o'clock news.

The coverage thus far was the breathy "I'm-on-the-scene-of-carnage" type that every reporter yearns for. Between stand-ups by a sharp-featured blonde who'd mussed her hair just enough to suggest she'd been working hard rather than waiting for her cue in the truck, I saw B-roll of Daria's body being loaded into the coroner's van. There were also sound bites from some of the people who'd been inside the oasis. The reporter called them eyewitnesses, though they'd been nowhere near Daria when she was shot. But who cared about stretching the truth? This was the second murder on the highway during the peak travel season. With luck, the story would throw Chicago travel and tourism into a panic. The reporter concluded with a plea from the police for the man who had lent the victim his cell phone to come forward.

I clicked off the remote, got into bed, and stretched out under a clean, cool sheet that still smelled like fabric softener. I turned off the light and was hovering at the edge of sleep, dreaming about the fortune I could make marketing fabric softener as aroma therapy, when the phone rang.

Sighing, I rolled over. "Hi, Dad."

"How did you know it was me?" He sounded disappointed.

"I'm psychic."

"You have that caller ID, don't you?"

"No. But I probably should."

My widowed father is eighty-two and lives in an assisted-living facility in Skokie, a few villages south. He spends his days playing cards with the boys, steering clear of lusty grandmothers who think he's cute, and trying not to worry about me. He claims the last is a losing proposition, since I'm reckless and stubborn and loath to ask for help—a trait, he assures me, I inherited from my late mother, not him. It evens out, though, because I spend just as much time worrying about him.

"So there I am watching the ten o'clock news with Frank," he said, "when all of a sudden, there's this picture of someone getting into a white Volvo. And Frank says to me, 'Jake, that's Ellie, isn't it?'"

"Ummm."

"I start to look out the window but then Frank says, 'No, Jake. On the TV.' So I turn around and sneak a look. And you know what I said?"

"What?"

"I said to Frank, 'You're wrong. That couldn't be my daughter on the TV.' When Frank asked why, I said, 'Because my Ellie doesn't put herself in jeopardy like that. She has a daughter to raise. A career to manage. A father to look after. She wouldn't be anywhere near a sniper. It's got to be someone else who just looks like her'." He paused. "Right?"

"Well..."

"Don't tell me." He sighed. "What happened?"

Over the years I've learned to parse my father's seemingly contradictory statements, and I had no problem translating: "I-don't-even-want-to-think-about-what-God-*forbid*-might-have-happened-to-you-now-come-clean-and-don't-leave-any-thing-out."

I told him everything.

"So who is—was this woman?"

"I don't know."

"But you were a hairsbreadth away from her. Do you have any idea how close you came to being killed yourself?"

"I—I guess Hashem was looking out for me."

"You don't make it easy for Him." I could have sworn I heard him shake his head. "Do the police think it's the same guy as before?"

"Hard to say what they think. The detective was kind of like Columbo on Xanax." I told him about my interview. "But they have part of the pickup's license plate this time. I'm surprised it wasn't on the news."

He cleared his throat. "You—you're not involved anymore, are you?"

It was a rhetorical question. "The detective did say he'd be calling me back. But other than that, no."

Rachel called almost immediately after I'd hung up with Dad. "Are you okay, Mom?" She sounded worried. "We were just watching the news. You should have told me when you called."

"I'm fine, sweetheart. I didn't want you to worry."

I heard Barry's voice in the background. And then a female voice. Not Rachel's. Soft. Muffled. Rachel spoke. "Mom, you don't mind if I spend the night at Dad's, do you? They—he said he'd make sure my bike is locked up. I'll ride it back tomorrow."

Rachel keeps clothes and an extra toothbrush at Barry's, so it wasn't an inconvenience. And given what happened today, it probably wasn't a bad idea.

"Sounds like a plan."

"You're sure it's okay?"

I assured her and hung up, wondering who the female voice belonged to. Barry has been a member of the girlfriend-of-the-month club for years. He'd been seeing a divorcee with two young kids last winter, but that was six months ago. He'd probably been through six new ones since then.

I was just about to turn out the light when the phone trilled again. I thought about letting it go—this was beginning to remind me of one of those public television telethons—but I grabbed it in case someone was offering me a pledge.

It was Susan Siler, my closest friend. "Tell me that wasn't you on the news."

"No can do."

"Oh, God, Ellie. Are you okay?"

"I'm fine."

"Rachel wasn't with you, was she?" Susan gets right to the core issues.

"No, thank God."

"What happened?" I went through it for a third time.

"Do they think it's the same guy as last April?"

"If they do, they're not saying."

"How come you just happened to be there?"

"I was coming back from Lake Geneva."

"Are you sure?"

"About what? That it was a copycat attack, or that I was coming back from Lake Geneva?"

"Well…both, I guess. But there were other people at the rest stop. Why were you the one in the middle?"

"I wasn't the only one. Some other guy let her borrow his cell phone. I was just making small talk."

"Where's the guy with the cell phone?"

"I don't know. He left before it happened. They're trying to find him."

"Hmmm."

"Don't do that."

"Do what?" she asked.

"Give me that cryptic 'hmmm.'"

"Was I doing that?"

"You were. And I know what you were thinking."

"What?"

"You're deploring the loss of life and the escalating amount of violence in society, but you're too idealistic to admit it."

"That sounds like your agenda." I didn't contradict her. "So what happens now?"

"The cops will try to track him and bring him in. The sniper, that is."

"You won't be—helping them, or anything?"

This was the second time someone close to me had asked. "No."

There was a relieved silence. "Did you see him?"

"The sniper? No. The pickup was too far away. And I was looking at Daria when it happened. By the time I turned around, the truck had taken off." I yawned. "Susan, I'm beat. How 'bout we continue this over coffee tomorrow morning?"

"I'm working." Susan works in an art gallery three days a week. She paused, then made a small worried sound. "Ellie, does he know that?"

"Does who know what?"

"The sniper. You said you didn't see him. But...does he know you didn't?"

"How would I know? And why does—?" I cut myself off. If the sniper thought I'd seen him—even though I hadn't—it wouldn't be difficult to identify me from the news reports. Maybe even find out where I lived.

No. That wasn't going to happen. "Susan, I'm going to sleep."

Chapter Four

But I didn't. I lay awake most of the night, rescreening the murder at the rest stop. I'd assumed a sniper wouldn't revisit a place or a person he'd already hit. It would be too dangerous. If he did pop up again, he'd strike a new target, wouldn't he? Isn't that one of the reasons it's so difficult to track them? Still, that didn't stop the Greek chorus of family and friends wailing through my head. I thrashed under the sheet until it was hot and wrinkled and the edges had come away from the mattress.

There was another reason I couldn't sleep, the same reason I hadn't been sleeping well for weeks. David Linden, my lover who lives in Philadelphia, wasn't. At least not for the time being. Last winter he'd become involved with another woman. She professed her love, wheedled a large chunk of money out of him, then dumped him. Both David and his uncle had been victims of her scheme.

Once he realized how she'd manipulated him, he begged me to forgive him. I did, in a way, and over the next few months we tried to make peace. We spoke on the phone regularly. He'd even flown in last spring, and we met for dinner at one of those trendy new restaurants that serve American cuisine like some exotic newly discovered fare. We chatted about inconsequential things, skirting the real subject on our plates. After dinner he went back to the Four Seasons, and I drove home alone.

We'd have to talk, but for now something was holding me back from a full-fledged reconciliation. Alone, in the small hours of the night, I could admit what it was. David and I were fundamentally different people. We'd met while uncovering long-held secrets that involved both our families. We'd connected because—well—I was never quite sure why we connected. That we were attracted to one another was undeniable. And at the time the ties between our families seemed to suggest a relationship was inevitable. But there had been problems from the start, problems I'd been afraid to confront because of what we might discover about each other. Who knew where a conversation about trust and betrayal would lead?

An hour later, with sleep still eluding me, I got up to check the locks on the doors and windows. Thirty minutes later I checked again. After the third round, I decided the silent house was laughing at me, so I did what any other lonely, dysfunctional woman would do in my position. I polished off the rest of the wine.

⌖

I fell into an exhausted sleep around five and woke up a few hours later, haunted by a dream about shotguns that unfurled like the tongues of snakes. Feeling thick and slow and cranky, I threw on a T-shirt and shorts and went downstairs to make coffee. In the kitchen the message light on my answering machine was blinking. Probably a reporter. I ignored it and took my coffee out to the tiny patch of planks I call a deck.

The backyard was a rich carpet of summer. The grass was soft and green, the brown scrubby days of August a long way off. My peonies, columbines, and irises were flourishing, but the miracle of the season was my climbing June rosebush. I'd bought it four years ago, and it had been dormant ever since. I'd been ready to replace it with clematis vines when it suddenly burst into bloom. Now dozens of healthy pink blossoms were threaded through the trellis. I gazed at them, sipping my coffee and imagining myself in an English walled garden.

The familiar clank of a loose suspension broke my reverie. I walked around to the front of the house just as a red Dodge Ram pulled into the driveway. A dark, slender man whose hair and mustache were more gray than black slid from behind the wheel.

"Good morning, Fouad," I said.

Fouad Al Hamra emigrated from Syria almost forty years ago. He's been my landscaper since Barry and I were married. After my divorce, he took pity on me and has been trying to help me acquire a green thumb. More important, though, Fouad is my friend. He risked his life two years ago to save mine.

"Ellie." His dark eyes were wide and worried. "You are safe?"

I nodded.

He wore grass-stained painter's pants, and his shoes were caked with mud, but he carried himself with his usual grace. "It's a bad business, these attacks." He shook his head. "How did you come to be there?"

I explained.

He listened quietly. When I had finished, he murmured, more to himself than me, I thought, "What is the English expression? 'There but for the grace of God go I'?"

I nodded. Fouad's Muslim, and I'm Jewish, but he has a spiritual bent that is decidedly ecumenical. As for me, I'm not sure whether God does exist, but I'm not willing to put money on it either way. "What does the Koran say about fate?"

"Fate?" His brow furrowed. "The concept is very different in Islam."

"How so?"

"We do not use the word 'fate.' The Sunnah, which is like your Talmud, says that Allah prevails everywhere. Not a leaf stirs without His Will. And since Allah has power over every thing, He must know and determine everything. The concept is known as '*al-qada' wa al-qadar*'...."

"So there is no free will?"

"Not exactly. The freedom we have is granted to us by Allah and we should use it to submit to Him freely and willingly."

"Hold on. Either there is free will or there isn't."

"We believe there is a destiny to everything, Ellie." His eyes twinkled. "Even if we must nudge it along now and then."

He crossed the tiny yard to my vegetable plot. We'd built it last month, edging the sides with railroad ties. We'd turned the earth, enhanced it with manure, and planted radishes, cucumbers, and beans. The next day, in a frenzy of optimism, I'd added tomatoes. I'd been monitoring the seedlings, watching them sprout and thicken and marveling at the wonders of nature.

Now Fouad examined them. "You have not been watering." I felt like I'd been scolded.

"I have. But yesterday, I didn't get a chance, and well, you know...."

He went back to the pickup. Rummaging around in the bed, he pulled out a yellow sprinkler that had seen better days, brought it over, and attached it to my hose. He nodded at me to turn on the water. A few jets spurted out sideways, but most of the spray landed on the plants. I could have sworn they bent gratefully toward the water. He nodded again and surveyed the rest of the yard. Either it met with his approval, or he had something else on his mind. He turned to me.

"How is Rachel?"

I told him about her crisis of leisure. He smiled but again I could see an anxious look embedded in it. "What's wrong, Fouad?"

He didn't answer right away. Then he folded his arms. "Ahmed." His voice was tight.

Fouad's son was about to start his senior year at Johns Hopkins. A premed student, he'd been interested in neurosurgery, although Fouad said that changed whenever he started a new rotation. He was an excellent student and was already being courted by several prestigious medical schools.

"What about him?"

"He wants to go to Iraq."

"Iraq?" I felt a chill. "Why?"

Fouad reached into his back pocket for a small pruner and squatted down beside the columbine. He didn't move, and the pruner dangled from his fingers. "You know Ahmed's mother, Hayat, is Iraqi," he said at last.

"Of course."

"We met here in America. Well—since the war, Ahmed has been—voicing strong opinions about the situation."

"He's not alone."

"But in Ahmed's case, it's more—extreme. He feels he should be over there." Fouad straightened up. "He says Iraqi blood flows through his veins, and it is time he did something for his 'countrymen.'"

I bit my lip. I could understand Ahmed's need to prove himself. To define himself as separate from his parents. But the thought of a child going to a place a shade short of anarchy was every parent's nightmare. "What does he want to do?"

"He met a girl, the daughter of an Iraqi expatriate. She is also a premed student. They want to work in a hospital together."

A girlfriend yet. "Have you met her?"

He shook his head. "Hayat is not comfortable with the idea. For all her American ways, she is very traditional when it comes to her children's lives."

"What are you saying? That she wants an arranged marriage for Ahmed?"

Fouad shrugged.

"Oh boy." I studied the columbine. How much of Ahmed's desire to go to Iraq was genuine, I wondered, and how much was wrapped up in his girlfriend? He was twenty-one, an age when children often do the opposite of what their parents expect. Pursuing a relationship over his parents' tacit, or not so tacit, objections—even fleeing to Iraq because of it—sounded like the sort of rebellion a son might wage.

At the same time, though, working in a hospital wasn't, intrinsically, a bad thing. It was altruistic. Idealistic. The kind of goal you'd join the Peace Corps for. And a hospital is supposed to be a safe harbor. Theoretically. "How long does he want to stay?"

"A year." He ran his hand over his head. "I'm afraid, Ellie...for his—their—safety." Fouad looked as if his heart was about to break.

I shook my head. "No. You're afraid they won't come back."

It took him a while to answer. "Yes," he whispered.

"What does Hayat say?"

"She and I have not" —he paused— "come to an agreement. She still has family there."

"Who might persuade him to stay permanently."

He pressed his lips together.

Suddenly I felt relieved that Rachel was still a teenager. "What about this girlfriend's parents?"

"We do not know them."

"Well, why don't you—"

A horn beeped, and a shiny white SUV pulled up to the curb. The driver was a woman with long, blond hair. Two tow-headed kids peeked out of the back. Rachel opened the passenger door, jumped out, and went to the back of the car. The woman got out, too, and raised the hatch. She was wearing a lime green tank top and white shorts, which revealed a lot of smooth, tanned skin. Together they extracted Rachel's bike and set it on the ground. They were about the same height, and from the back, with the woman's straight blond hair and Rachel's blond curls, they could have been mother and daughter, even sisters. My dark hair pressed down on my head like a weight.

Rachel wheeled the bike halfway up the driveway, then turned to wave. The woman smiled, waved back, then climbed back into her car. As she drove away, the two little kids waved frantically through the window. Rachel waited until they were out of sight, then walked her bike into the garage. "Hi, Mom."

"Hi, sweetie." I gave her a hug. "Who was that?"

Was I imagining it, or did I see a guilty expression cross her face? "Julia. And her kids."

It took a moment to connect the dots. Julia Hauldren was the woman Barry had been dating last winter. Six months ago. This had to be an all-time record for him. "Why did she bring you home?"

Rachel shrugged. "It was on her way. She lives a couple of blocks away."

I remembered. Susan had told me she lived nearby. But that prompted more questions. Had she spent the night at Barry's along with Rachel? Or had she come to his place that morning? I couldn't see Barry tolerating two little rugrats running around his condo—neither child looked older than eight. Then again, beautiful women can make men do all sorts of strange things. And Julia was clearly beautiful.

Rachel waved to Fouad and went inside. I turned around, but he was bent over the columbine, removing the extraneous plants. I squatted down to help, hoping to finish our conversation, but he went silent. I knew better than to force him to talk. I started pulling up chickweed, thinking about Fouad's son and Barry's girlfriend and how difficult it was to embrace change. Within seconds a layer of dirt had collected under my fingernails. I should put on gloves.

I was on my way to the garage when the phone trilled. A moment later Rachel called through the window. "Mom, phone for you. Detective Milanovich."

Chapter Five

I picked up the phone in the kitchen. "Hello, Detective."

"Ms. Foreman? That your daughter who answered the phone?"

"Yes."

"Sounds like a nice kid."

"She is." What did he want?

He cleared his throat. "Got a couple of questions for you."

"Okay."

"You know anyone by the name of Flynn?"

"Flynn? No. I don't think so. Why?"

He was quiet.

"Was that Daria's last name?"

"Yep."

"Daria Flynn." I repeated it softly. "I don't recognize it. How did you identify her?"

"Her mother called the Lake Geneva Police after she saw the news. They lived together. The daughter didn't come home that night. Didn't call either...." His voice trailed off.

I closed my eyes, unable to imagine the pain of learning that your child has been killed.

"Ms. Foreman, I know you said you didn't know her. But I keep wondering—didn't you say you were making a film up there?"

"Yes. I told you about the video for the Lodge."

"You ever go to any fancy restaurants during your breaks?"

"Fancy restaurants?"

"That's right."

"I don't have much of an expense account. Burger King and McDonald's are more my style. Why?"

"The Flynn girl worked at a place called the Grandview."

"The Grandview? Isn't that in the Geneva Inn?"

"That's the one."

The Geneva Inn was the only hotel actually situated on the shores of Lake Geneva. Most of the shoreline was privately owned. The town elders—in an effort to preserve the lake if you listened to some, or keep it exclusive if you listened to others—had restricted the number of boat slips available to property owners. With only one slip per twenty feet of shore, it made no sense for a resort to build; they'd have precious little water access. But the Geneva Inn was an elegant bed-and-breakfast with a spectacular view of the lake. It also housed a five-star restaurant that drew customers from as far away as Chicago and Milwaukee. Boat slips weren't a priority.

"I've never been there," I said to Milanovich. "But I've heard it's exquisite. Was she a waitress?"

He didn't answer for a moment. I pictured him blinking. "No. She was one of the cooks. Excuse me. Chefs."

I swallowed my surprise. To be a chef at one of the finest restaurants in Lake Geneva took talent. And hard work. I hadn't realized there was that much substance to Daria Flynn. I'd pictured her as a woman who, by virtue of her beauty, was used to "winning" fights and getting her own way.

"You're sure you never ran into her?" Milanovich asked.

"Detective, I've told you—several times—that I only laid eyes on her for the first time at the rest stop."

He didn't reply.

"Oh, come on. You can't—" I cut myself off. He was a cop, and cops are trained to investigate anyone close to the victim at the time of their death. I qualified. Then again, if he had checked me out, he'd know who I was. And that I'd been involved in murder investigations before. I started to pace. "Detective, is there something else you're trying to get at? Because if there is, just come out with it. I'll try my best to help."

He drew a long, uneven sigh. "As a matter of fact, there are a couple of"—he paused—"anomalies. Maybe they mean something. Maybe they don't."

"What kind of—anomalies?"

"Well, for starters, it seems there was only one shot fired. Why only one?"

I remembered Homer Simpson's comment. "The guy was a good shot?"

He cleared his throat. "Maybe. But then why was the Flynn girl the only victim?"

There had been only one victim during the first sniper attack, I recalled. Why would it be so noteworthy this time? "Detective, I'm not sure I understand the question."

"You were standing right next to her, Ms. Foreman."

Now I got it. "In other words, why am I still alive?"

"Ms. Foreman, do you have any enemies that could do something like this?"

I stopped pacing. "Do you think someone was trying to kill *me*? And missed?"

"I don't think anything. I'm just asking questions."

First I was a perpetrator, now a victim. My head was spinning. I glanced over my shoulder. Rachel was in the hall listening, her head cocked to the side. I'd been in some dangerous situations in the past. It was possible someone was bent on revenge or some form of vigilante justice. But that assumed I was someone who mattered enough to harm. I wasn't. I was just a video producer with a daughter, a father, and perhaps, a disproportionate amount of curiosity.

"I did some checking," Milanovich went on. "You have a 'relationship' with the local police. They know you."

That much was true. "And that means...."

"Maybe nothing," he admitted. "But the fact remains that you were standing next to her. You were the last person to talk to her. I just keep thinking there may be a reason for that."

"And I keep telling you I don't know what that could be." I paused. "Detective, I'm not an investigator, but it seems to me there are a lot more reasons to link Daria Flynn's death to the sniper attack last April than to me. Female victims, both shot at a rest stop from a green pickup—"

"We are aware of the similarities."

Of course they were. "Well, if there's anything else you can tell me, something you haven't remembered about the pickup or the incident or the girl, you'll call, right?"

"Of course."

"By the way," he added. "Expect a call from the Walworth County Sheriff's Office. Maybe the Lake Geneva Police, too. We're working the case with them. I've filled them in, but they'll probably want to follow up on their own."

"Can't you tell them what I told you?"

"I did. But they're Wisconsin. We're Illinois."

"Cheeseheads versus Flatlanders, huh?"

There was a beat of silence. "Good-bye, Ms. Foreman."

After dinner, I took a glass of wine out on the deck and swung back and forth on my glider. I'd splurged on it last spring, knowing as soon as I tried it out in the store that I would buy it. It was made from redwood and had a green cushion, and its gentle motion has a soothing, almost primal feel. I rocked and sipped my wine and watched the sun retreat across the backyard, glazing everything with splashes of rosy gold.

I'd thought the murder of Daria Flynn at the oasis was linked to the first sniper attack in April, but from the tone of Milanovich's questions, I gathered he wasn't so sure. I could even empathize; I was not only a witness but a possible suspect. But I have a love-hate relationship with cops, and I wasn't eager for more questions.

I thought back to my conversation with Susan. If I'd just refrained from chit-chatting with Daria, I wouldn't be involved. All I had to do was buy my drink and head straight out to the car. I would have been long gone before anything happened. But making conversation is part of my nature, and given a similar situation, I'd probably do the same thing again.

The phone rang inside. I slowed the glider.

"Got it," Rachel yelled out.

When a minute had passed with no summons, I started up again, thinking about Daria Flynn. Had she told her mother what time she'd be home? How much time passed before her mother began to worry? Yes, Daria was an adult, but a mother never stops worrying. What did she do? Read? Wash dishes? Or did she turn on the television, preferring its empty chatter to the silence of the house? What did she think when she heard that a woman from Lake Geneva had been killed? Did she assume it was some other person? Or did she know, in the pit of her stomach, that the victim lying on the tarmac was her daughter?

The sun fled, and the evening light bathed everything in muted shades of green. My mother died from pancreatic cancer. If she were alive, though, she never would have spent time in a glider with me. She was always too busy doing errands, taking care of the house, saving the world. When I was little and had the mumps, it was my father who spent the week at home with me in an old black rocker. Sometimes he'd tell stories. Sometimes he'd sing—not often, happily, since his voice is somewhere between an angry frog and a badly tuned bassoon. But most of the time, he didn't talk at all. He just sat there with me in his lap and rocked.

I slapped at a mosquito emboldened by the deepening dusk and went inside. Rachel had commandeered the couch in the family room, sprawled like Cleopatra on an immovable barge with her possessions spread out around her. Her long legs dangled over one armrest, her mop of curly blond hair against the other. The cordless was glued to her ear and the sound of her conversation floated just over the noise from the TV. I kissed the top of her head.

Chapter Six

Vegetable soup. When the wind blows across Mac's studio from south to north, the smell of whatever they're making at the food-processing plant down the block makes my mouth water and my stomach growl. This morning the rich, hearty aroma of vegetable soup hung in the air, as if a giant pot was simmering on the roof of the building. I parked and inhaled deeply.

Mac, aka Mackenzie Kendall, III, owns a video production studio tucked away in an industrial section of Northbrook. We've known each other twenty years and worked together for twelve. A talented director, Mac has all of the downtown expertise but none of the downtown prices. He also has Hank Chenowsky, one of the best editors downtown or anywhere else. The shows he's edited have won so many awards that the row of plaques on the walls might be intimidating, were I the sort of person to pay attention to those things.

As I pushed through the door, a buzzer sounded. A conversation stopped, and I heard a rustling sound. Seconds later, Mac appeared, coffee mug in hand, a section of newspaper under his arm, and reading glasses on his nose.

"Ellie. Your ears must be burning." In his torn jeans, T-shirt, and Harachi sandals, he looked like an aging hippie, a fact that gives him great pleasure but exasperates his affluent WASP family.

"We were just talking about you." He turned to the shiny new coffee urn and filled his mug. "Grab some and come on back."

I got myself coffee and followed him into his office, a small comfortable room with two narrow floor-to-ceiling windows, both of which had been replaced last year, thanks to me.

Hank, a twenty-something youngster with long pale hair, even paler skin, and the hands and soul of an artist, lounged in a chair reading another section of the *Trib*. He looked up as I came in. "Well, if it isn't the indestructible Ellie."

"Excuse me?"

He snapped the newspaper, then folded it in half. "Dodging bullets, leaping tall buildings with a single bound. They ought to name a doll after you."

"Wonder Woman." Mac sat down at his desk. "No. Buffy."

Hank pointed the newspaper at me. "That's it! Ellie the Bad Guy Slayer."

"No." Mac shook his head and sketched a movie marquee in the air. "Ellie the Warrior Princess!"

Hank shook his head. "No. It's Double-O-Seven in skirts. Foreman," he rumbled in a mock British accent. "Ellie Foreman."

These were the men I trusted to work magic with my shows? "When did you say you graduated from high school?"

"Ooo. A direct hit!" Mac chortled.

I fluffed out my hair, making sure it fell in front of my face. "If anyone, it's Grace Slick. But you're both too culturally challenged to appreciate her."

That prompted more guffaws, which subsided only when the buzzer sounded from the front.

"I'll get it." Hank laughed his way out of the room.

I sat in the empty chair. Mac swallowed a last chuckle and took a breath. "Sorry. Sometimes you can't stop. You know."

"It's okay. I needed it."

"Me too." Mac squared his shoulders. "You holding up? You've been through a lot the past couple days."

"It wasn't that bad—compared to some of the things we've weathered." I motioned to the newspaper Hank left. "They're saying the two attacks are related. That it's the same guy."

Indeed, the media were already highlighting the similarities in the case: young women exiting an oasis on I-94, the shooter in a green pickup with a camper shell. There'd been a stream of articles in both papers, and a talk show was promo-ing a special later today featuring eyewitnesses from both scenes. I'd had a couple of calls on my machine. I hadn't returned them.

Mac shrugged and looked at my feet, then the door, then the windows—everywhere, it seemed, except me. I waited until I couldn't stand it anymore. "You don't agree?"

"You know me too well." He ran a hand through his beard, which he'd grown to hide the scar running down his left cheek. Unfortunately, the beard grew in everywhere except around the scar.

"What's up?"

He raised himself up on his desk. "You know I still keep up with a few of the guys at the station, right?"

I nodded. Mac and I met when we both worked in the news department of a local television station. We'd left around the same time—I went freelance; he started Kendall Productions.

"So, I'm having a beer last night with Brian Stuckley. Remember him?"

I dredged up vague recollections of a skinny, quiet, nerdish guy. "He was on the desk, wasn't he? Three to eleven."

"That's him."

"I remember. So what?"

"Well, he's news director now."

Figures. The nerds will inherit the earth.

"He remembers the restaurant where you found rat droppings and called in the city inspector. Who refused to give the place a citation. You tried to tell us he'd been paid off but you couldn't prove it. Remember?"

"I remember." It had been one of my more underwhelming moments as an investigative producer. In fact, the frustration of not cracking the story—and changing the world according to my master plan—was one of the reasons I left TV news. I crossed one leg over the other. "Sooh..." I said, stretching the word. "Other than fond reminiscences, what did Brian have to offer?"

Mac leaned forward. "He told me the cops ran a partial of the pickup's plates at the rest stop." He paused. "They got a hit."

"And he knows this how?"

"Ellie...."

"Of course. News director. Sorry."

Mac nodded. "Turns out a Jeep was stolen about a month ago."

"A Jeep? But—"

Mac cut me off with a raised palm. "The owner's a construction worker. He was working in Schaumburg when it happened. In broad daylight."

Schaumburg, a western suburb undergoing rapid development, was in the throes of suburban sprawl. More significant, though, it was nowhere near Lake Geneva. Or me.

"Someone switched the plates?"

Mac nodded again.

I recalled my latest conversation with Milanovich. He must have known that before he called me, but he didn't say anything. Not that it would have made much difference. Unless he'd found a connection between the construction worker and Daria. Or someone else involved in the case. Like me.

"Ellie." Mac looked over nervously. "Brian wasn't supposed to tell me that, you know?"

"Not to worry." I uncrossed my legs. "Someone steals a license plate, slaps it onto a pickup that's used in the murder of a woman I don't know and didn't meet until five minutes before she died. What am I gonna do with the information?"

Mac just looked at me.

I swiveled in the chair. Then I stopped.

"What?"

I leaned forward. "Tell me something. If you're a sniper, and you've already killed one person, and you know the cops have ID'd your pickup, why would you steal a set of plates and slap them on the same truck you already used? Wouldn't it be safer to rip off a different truck, one that looked nothing like the first one?"

Mac folded his arms. "What are you saying?"

"Why did the shooter use the same truck but different plates?"

"How do I know? Because he wants to establish a pattern? Let people know he's behind all of them? So he uses the same method to draw attention to himself. Isn't that what the shrinks say?"

"The profilers, you mean." I started swiveling again. "But if you're really trying to hide your identity, it wouldn't make sense, would it?"

"Neither does picking off people at a rest stop."

"How much do you want to bet that's where Brian goes with the story? That's what I'd do."

Mac shrugged.

"There's something else, too."

"What?"

"The detective working the case seems interested that there was only one shot fired. And that it hit the woman dead on."

"So?"

"Is that what happened the first time?"

"Only one person was hit. The nurse."

"But how many shots were fired?"

"I don't know."

"Me neither." I swiveled some more. "So what kind of gun would you use?"

"For what?"

"To kill people from a distance."

"There are all sorts of high-powered rifles. And assault weapons. With a tripod and a scope, any one of those babies could do the job."

"What kind of baby?"

"For starters, something like an M16," he said helpfully.

"The ones they use in the army?"

"Or a commercial version. Why? You thinking of packing some heat?" He stroked his beard. "Actually, with your record, it probably wouldn't be a bad idea."

"Sure. Me and Annie Oakley. No. I was just thinking—do you think the shooter was a vet?"

He snorted. "Military...mob...it could be anyone. Those pieces aren't hard to use. Even you could learn to shoot one in about an hour."

"I could?"

"All in a day's work. Clean the house, cook dinner, and brush up on your marksmanship."

"I must have missed it on 'Here's Martha.'"

"It was a good thing."

I looked through Mac's windows. A docile summer sun was climbing through a sky so uniformly blue it looked like someone had splashed a bucket of paint across it. A huge garbage truck lumbered by and stopped, its high-pitched whistle warning it was backing up. A woman climbed out of a red Toyota, carrying a Dunkin' Donuts bag. Life looked normal. I wanted mine to be, too. I turned to Mac. "Okay. I'm done with this. Let's talk video."

"Good." Mac pulled out his notes. The Lodge had just finished extensive renovations, and our shoot would begin next Monday. We would continue on and off for two weeks, culminating at a black-tie gala to celebrate the resort's official reopening. We would tape all the amenities at the resort, including the private airstrip and the bunny hill for skiers. The Lodge would provide employees for cheerful sound bites, and we'd interview some guests. I was trying to nail down one or two townsfolk to add "color"—perhaps a few recollections about the resort's Playboy days.

Mac brightened. "Hey, maybe we could interview some former Bunnies."

"In your dreams." Despite thirty years of feminism, the mention of anything connected to the Playboy era still triggers a Pavlovian response among men. Forget Samoa; Margaret Mead could have had a field day analyzing Hugh Hefner's effect on the male psyche. "I was thinking more along the lines of people who own those huge estates."

Lake Geneva first came to public attention after the Great Chicago Fire in 1871 when a few industrialists built temporary homes—they called them "cottages"—while their city property was being restored. Once the railroad linked the two places, more Chicagoans followed—Chicagoans with names like Wrigley, Pullman, and Sears. Between 1880 and 1920 dozens of estates went up on the shores of the lake.

"Don't you want to see what the robber barons did with their fortunes?"

Mac didn't answer.

"Oh." I smacked the palm of my hand against my cheek. "I forgot. That wouldn't be some of *your* relatives, would it?"

For a moment, I couldn't read his reaction. Then he laughed. "As a matter of fact, one of my uncles or cousins has a place up there. I haven't talked to him in years."

Mac was estranged from most of his family. Not only were they appalled that he had abandoned his affluent lifestyle for something as tedious as a real job, but they'd never forgiven him for marrying a girl from Chicago's West Side, and raising two children as—dare it be said—Catholics.

"Hey. I was just kidding."

"I'm not. Maybe I should give him a call."

I shrugged. "It's not worth deepening the family feud. We can always grab guests at that black-tie gala. They'll all be wearing tuxedos and smoking cigars—they'll look the part."

Mac drummed the pencil on his desk. "Let's see. Rich Chicago industrialists in tuxedos extolling a luxury resort in their backyard. Are we going for a little visual irony here, Ellie? A touch of Studs Terkel class-consciousness, perhaps?"

"I can get away with it." I grinned. "After all, I am a super-hero."

Chapter Seven

I stopped off at Sunset Foods on the way home to buy shrimp from Stan the Fish Man. Sunset is one of the last upscale but locally owned supermarkets on the North Shore. It's a place where service and quality still matter, and Stan is one of the most knowledgeable people I know when it comes to seafood. He's one of the sexiest, too, and I drove home full of fantasies about grilled shrimp in a lemony-garlic marinade. The problem was I couldn't remember if I had any skewers. I vaguely recalled an adventure in the culinary arts last year involving shish kebob on skinny wooden sticks, but I couldn't remember where I'd stashed them. I was absorbed in a mental search when I turned the corner and spotted an unfamiliar car parked in my driveway.

I pulled up behind a gray Saturn with Wisconsin plates. A pine air freshener hung from the rearview mirror, and the car looked unusually clean, but the beige upholstery was faded in patches, as if it had been parked in the sun too long. I turned off the engine and got out.

Two women climbed out of the Saturn. The woman who'd been in the passenger seat was delicately built, almost frail, with gray hair pulled back in a tight roll. Her face was pinched, and her head was curiously flat on the sides, as if it had been squeezed in a vise, but there was a stately bearing about her. The other woman, the driver, was younger, about my age, and tall. As she lifted a pair of shades, my stomach pitched. She wasn't as slender, and her dark glossy hair was threaded with gray, but the resemblance was unmistakable.

"You're Daria Flynn's sister."

She nodded. "Kim Flynn. And this is my mother, Irene." She walked around to the passenger side, pulled out a cane, and held out her arm, which her mother took. "Could we—talk to you for a few minutes?" Kim asked after she'd helped her mother position the cane. "If it isn't inconvenient."

Kim had the same thick hair and green eyes as her sister but somehow just missed being pretty. Her features were harsher, her forehead broader, her eyes smaller. As if to make up for it, she wore long earrings with her jeans and shirt, and a collection of silver bracelets flashed at her wrist. Irene was dressed in a fussy white blouse and dark trousers.

"Not at all." I opened the door to the Volvo and retrieved my bag of groceries. "Please. Come in."

Irene walked haltingly, and Kim kept a firm grasp on her arm. I unlocked my front door. The silence told me Rachel wasn't home. For some reason, I was relieved. I led them into the living room, which I rarely use. As Irene shuffled to the sofa, the scent of lavender trailed after her. I tried not to react. My former mother-in-law used to douse herself in lavender. I never liked it.

Kim helped Irene sit down on one end of the couch and then took a seat on the other. I put the groceries in the kitchen, and sat in the black leather Eames chair Barry insisted we buy when we moved in even though we couldn't afford it.

"I'm curious," I began awkwardly. "How did you get my name?"

"The police asked us if we knew you," Kim said. "And then I found you on the Internet." She frowned. "I hope that isn't a problem."

Milanovich probably asked them if they knew me the same way he asked if I knew Daria. And my name and number are listed. "No problem. I'm sorry for your loss."

Irene regarded me with an almost regal chilliness, as if my condolences were her due.

Kim nodded. "Well, Mother needed—we both need—well, it was all so sudden, you see—"

"I understand."

"I'm sure you don't, my dear," Irene cut in. "Understand, that is." The skin on her face looked brittle, almost shellacked. She moved stiffly. "But we—I—you are a mother, aren't you?"

I nodded.

"Did Daria say anything at the end? Anything at all that would explain it? We just have so many questions—we don't understand—and we need to, you see...." She broke off.

I swallowed. I knew she wanted some closure, some affirmation of Daria's life. The problem was I couldn't find any meaning in the random, violent murder of a beautiful young woman. Nevertheless, underneath the intensity and sorrow, Irene's expression was hopeful, even expectant.

I chose my words carefully. "She was upset when she was fighting with her boyfriend, but she calmed down when they made up. She went inside and bought a drink, and when she came back out, we started chatting. You know, about the heat, the crummy day she'd had. She seemed...well...happy he was coming to pick her up."

Irene sat ramrod straight, not saying anything. Kim fidgeted as if the couch was the wrong size for her.

"By the way, how is he bearing up?" I asked.

They exchanged glances. Then Irene said, "This—this boyfriend. Did Daria tell you his name?"

"Excuse me?"

"Her boyfriend. His name."

I felt uneasy. Had Daria kept her love life a secret from her mother? I looked at Kim. Her expression was unreadable. "She—she didn't mention it."

Irene nodded as if she'd expected me to say that. "She never told us she had a boyfriend, you see. The first we'd heard of it was on the news reports."

Was she was having an affair with a married man? Is that why she never said anything? Did she know that her choice would be unacceptable to Irene?

Irene went on. "Kim says we can't know for certain. She says Daria might have been seeing someone but just never got around to telling us."

"Or didn't want to," Kim added.

Irene shook her head. "That just doesn't sound like Daria. She told us everything. We were a close family. And Daria was always so busy with her job. Where would she find the time for a boyfriend?"

I tried to change the subject. "She was a chef, I understand?"

"A sous-chef. Second in charge. But she had the lion's share of responsibility." The echo of a smile crossed her lips. "She took up cooking as a youngster. She came by it naturally—my family opened the first Greek restaurant in Lake Geneva. Best place in town for a good meal. Flynn is my husband's name," she added. "But Herbert—he's gone now."

First her husband, now her daughter. "I'm so sorry."

"Kim's pretty much running the place." She looked at Kim. "Since my—my illness."

"Mother had a stroke six months ago," Kim explained. "She's doing much better, but she can't work like she used to."

That explained her fragility. And the shuffling gait. I opened my mouth to offer another apology, but Irene cut me off.

"But Daria…she—she worked so hard. Up at the crack of dawn to hunt for fresh produce. She'd drive to the fish markets in Chicago and Milwaukee almost every day. Once she even drove all the way to Iowa for some beef. Then, after the restaurant closed, she'd be planning menus for the next day. She worked until midnight most nights." She leaned forward. "That's why we were so—"

"Puzzled." Kim offered. "Puzzled about the boyfriend."

"Not that she couldn't have," Irene added. "She was beautiful. She could have had any man she wanted. She took after me."

I looked at Kim. Her expression was blank.

"But no one like that came to the funeral. You'd think if she had a boyfriend, he'd have had the decency to show up." Irene's mouth tightened. "Kim thinks she might have been hiding the fact she had a boyfriend because she knew we wouldn't—I wouldn't—approve. But I can't imagine why." She sighed. "The police have tried to be helpful, but they keep telling us the Illinois Police were the ones who handled the—the crime scene. I think that's what they call it."

I nodded.

"But whenever we ask to speak with them, they—"

"Frankly…," Kim broke in, "We think we're getting a run-around."

"Why?"

"No one returns our phone calls. Or when they do, well, they start talking about the sniper. Whether we know someone who wanted to harm Daria. Which we've answered a zillion times."

"One of the State Police detectives has called me a few times. He's—"

"I don't mean the Illinois cops." Kim's expression hardened. I wondered who she meant and was about to ask when she went on. "But that doesn't matter. It's not what we came for."

"Are you sure she didn't say anything else…at the end?" A note of pleading crept into Irene's voice. "Anything at all?"

"Nothing I haven't told you." I stood up. "Could I offer you some tea?" When in doubt, play hostess. They didn't object, so I started toward the kitchen, glad for the opportunity to break the rhythm. "I'll just be a minute."

I filled the kettle and turned on the flame, wondering how much of Irene's story to believe. The Flynns were three adult women. No matter how close they were, there had to be some friction. And what Irene said about not approving of a boyfriend was odd. Had there been boyfriends in the past of whom she *had* disapproved? It did raise the question whether Daria might have been hiding her boyfriend, at least from her mother. I got out tea bags and mugs, then started back to the living room, nearly colliding with Kim.

"Oh—sorry," I said. "Um, would you like iced tea or hot? I can make either."

"Mother usually drinks hot," Kim answered.

"What about you?"

"What I'd really like is a—oh, never mind."

"I have some scotch," I offered.

"No, I'm driving. But let me help you with the tea." She ran a hand through her hair. "If you don't mind."

"Sure."

"I'll just be a minute, Mother," she called over her shoulder.

Irene nodded and turned her gaze to a framed poster on the wall. Her back was erect, but her eyes were unfocused. I didn't think she was admiring my artwork.

"Is she going to be okay?" I asked Kim.

She followed me back into the kitchen. "Oh, don't let her fool you. She's strong. Ironsides, Daria and I used to call her."

"A stroke can be pretty devastating." I thought about Marv, one of my father's closest friends, who had suffered a stroke last October and passed away after Thanksgiving. Add to that the unbearable grief of losing a child. It wasn't an enviable situation.

"I'm not going to tell you it hasn't been tough. We've had a shitty year. Health problems. Money problems. Now this. But we'll make it." Kim gazed around the room.

How do you recover from the death of a daughter? Or a sister? A knot of tension tightened my stomach. Where was Rachel? As I took out spoons, I spotted the note propped up in its usual spot.

Babysitting at Julia's. Back by dinner. R.

The knot in my stomach loosened. I turned around. Kim was watching me. I realized she must have been saying something. "I'm sorry. What was that?"

"I said, what do you really think?"

"About the sniper?"

"No. About Daria's boyfriend."

I frowned. I'd told them what I knew. "What do you mean?"

"It's just—just that Daria never said anything to me about a man."

I pulled out a tray.

"Then again, she doesn't—didn't always tell me everything. It's possible she was seeing someone. Maybe he worked at the hotel. Or was a customer—excuse me—a patron." She made a sound in the back of her throat. "Isn't that what upscale restaurants call them?"

I got out milk, sugar, and lemon and put them on the tray. Where was she going with this?

"Look." She perched on the counter opposite the stove and rubbed her hands up and down her thighs. "I didn't want to put you in an awkward position with Mother in the room. But—well—since it's just us two, did she say *anything*? Give you a name? A profession?"

The kettle started to whistle. I poured hot water into the mugs. "You mean, did she confess she was having an affair with a married man and was flying off to the Caribbean?"

She flipped up her hands as if to say, "Whatever...."

"It was nothing like that," I said firmly. "She didn't say anything at all."

Kim nodded, almost imperceptibly. "What about the guy who lent her his cell? Did he hear anything about this boyfriend?"

"I wouldn't know. He left before it happened."

"You don't know where he was from?"

I put the kettle back on the stove. "No. He was going on vacation. Fishing, I think."

"You don't know where?"

"I don't even know what kind of car he had."

"You told the police all that, right?"

"Of course." I put the mugs on the tray. "In fact, the police are asking anyone who might know him to call in. You probably saw it on TV."

"Right."

I turned around. "You don't have much confidence in the cops, do you?"

She hesitated, then fingered a lock of hair and tucked it behind her ears. "You know the pledge of allegiance? Where they say liberty and justice for all? Well, when it comes to the police up in my neck of the woods, those things go to the highest bidder."

I waited for her to go on, but she didn't, and I didn't push it. I've had my own run-ins with cops over the years, and while I might even agree with her, I couldn't see how a discussion about the limitations of law enforcement would help. The police were doing everything they could to find the shooter.

I took the tray into the living room.

"She was a good girl," Irene said, picking up the thread of conversation as if we'd never left. "And she did seem happy recently. I suppose it could have been because of a man."

I handed her a mug.

She stared into it. "But why did he abandon her? How can he not come forward? How can he let us suffer?" She pinched the bridge of her nose with her free hand. Something violent seemed to be fighting for dominance, and for an instant, anger won. "Whoever he is, I hope he rots in hell." Then she set the mug down, her anger ebbing as quickly as it had come. She covered her eyes. Kim put an awkward arm around her.

I waited, then said quietly, "Irene, whether you and Kim trust them or not, the police have more information than I do. You need to be asking them these questions. Why don't I give you Detective Milanovich's number?"

I dug out his card from my bag, wrote down the name and number on another piece of paper, and handed it to her. She gazed at it silently for a moment, then raised her eyes to mine. "Well, if you remember something—anything at all, you'll let us know?"

I nodded.

"You might remember, you know, especially when you're going to sleep. Happens to me. I'll be just dozing off when I think of something. Have to get up and write it down. Otherwise, I lose it."

Irene snapped open her purse and dropped the paper inside. Kim helped her mother get up, adjusted the cane, and together they slowly headed out. Irene paused at the front door and laid her hand on my arm. "People always let you down, you know. But you've been very kind."

I nodded politely, unsure whether she'd handed me an insult or a compliment. They went down the front steps, trailing the scent of lavender behind them.

Chapter Eight

Seeing Lake Geneva for the first time was disappointing. My father claimed he'd taken me there as a child, but I have no memory of it. So when I drove up to scout it for the shoot, I was expecting something grand: a vista of sand and water surrounded by thick foliage perhaps, or an expanse of turquoise dotted with snowy white sails.

Unfortunately, the reality didn't measure up. Lake Geneva's beach, at least the public portion, was meager, the parkland behind it sparse, the view uninspiring. To be fair, a good chunk of the public land had been grudgingly coughed up by landowners over the years. The land that's still private, I was told, gives onto pristine woodlands. In fact, a portion of lakefront called Black Point is supposed to be beautiful. But as I drove through downtown, an unimpressive collection of shops trying too hard to be charming, I felt vaguely ripped off.

Another disappointment was the location of the Lodge. Unlike the Geneva Inn, the hotel on the water's edge, the Lodge was several miles inland off Route 50, a nondescript two-lane highway that could have been anywhere in the country. Most of the other hotels, inns, and cottages were inland, too, or at the other end of the lake in Fontana or Williams Bay. I had the impression that this once overwhelmingly residential community had never quite adjusted to its commercial status.

I cut over to Route 50 and turned onto a long, winding drive that took me up to the Lodge. An eighteen-hole golf course lay on one side of the road, and a party of golfers strode toward the tee. In bright red, yellow, and blue shirts, they looked like the flag of a small country, A quarter mile farther up was a large building with stone facings, meticulous landscaping, and a wide circular driveway. I parked in a back lot beside Mac's van. He and his crew had been here since dawn, getting one of Mac's sun-rising-over-the-prairie shots.

I headed past the bronze statue of the man with a child on his shoulders and pushed through the revolving door. The interior had a rustic, woodsy feel, with pebbled walls, nubby upholstery, muted lighting, and carpeting in shades of green and brown. I almost expected to see woodland creatures scurrying down the halls. They'd even carried the natural splendor theme into the ladies' room, where water cascaded down a wall.

I went up the stairs to the second floor, where I heard Mac's voice coming from the ballroom. After navigating around lights and equipment piled on a tarp in the hall, I leaned against the door frame. In the Playboy days, the "Penthouse," as it was called, had been the resort's main nightclub, but in the seventies they'd renamed it the "Showroom" so as not to be confused with the magazine's arch competitor. Reincarnated yet again as the "Evergreen Ballroom," it boasted flocked wallpaper, earth-toned carpeting, and chandeliers with tiny shaded lamps.

I walked in, imagining how the room might have looked thirty-five years ago. Well-dressed couples seated around dozens of small tables. Subdued lighting. The air charged with a subtle electricity. A hushed crowd. A blue-white spotlight slicing through a haze of smoke, picking up a tuxedo-clad Sinatra or Tony Bennett. A platoon of young girls in those absurd Bunny costumes, happily catering to the fantasies of men, blissfully unaware that Gloria Steinem, herself a Bunny, would soon change the way the world thought of them.

I wished there was some way to include that part of the resort's history—the evolution from glittery adult playground to a place where fathers carried kids around on their shoulders. It wouldn't be hard. Snippets of Count Basie on the track, maybe a gauzy filter over the lens. If we kept to a long shot, any actor in a tuxedo would do for a "performer." It wasn't totally out of the question—a few years ago I'd convinced the Water District to let me stage a historical reenactment on video. The only problem was that compared to the bland, humorless owners of the Lodge, the officials at the Water District were wildly progressive.

I watched Mac rehearse a dolly shot down the length of the ballroom. He'd brought a crew of three, but two of the resort's maintenance men were helping out as gofers. They didn't speak much English, but they were getting into the spirit of things, moving furniture and equipment around with cheery smiles and hand gestures. This was probably as close as they'd ever get to show biz.

Once the shot and cutaways were in the can, Mac started to wrap. "Not much here to shoot, Ellie."

"There will be soon enough. The gala we're going to be taping is in here."

"I'll need extra crew."

"And a tux."

"Me?" In all the years I've known Mac I've never even seen him wear a tie, although he insists he wore one to his wedding. "I'm just the hired help."

"You ever notice what the waiters wear in a joint like this?"

He took the camera off sticks. "Of all the gin joints in all the towns in all the world, I gotta wear a tux in this one?"

"It's in the budget."

He muttered as he packed up the camera. Something along the lines of "can't believe it…in this day and age."

"Here's looking at you, kid." I sailed out of the room.

⌒⌒⌒

Before going home, Mac and I stopped at the bar in the lobby, a large space with a view of the pool and lots of comfortable chairs, sofas, and love seats. Years ago the area had been part of the pool, one of those glamorous indoor-outdoor combinations with a bar at the shallow end and ornamental bathing beauties on the side. The post-Hefner owners, though, had reclaimed the space for more conservative—but probably more lucrative—activities.

I sipped a Chardonnay. "You check out the bunny hill yet?" This was a manmade ski hill at the back of the property, not to be confused with other Bunny appurtenances.

"This morning." Mac picked up his beer. "You know what would be really cool?"

"What?"

"To rig up one of their gondolas for a traveling shot up the hill. You think you could arrange it?"

Arranging things is what a producer does. I pictured a slow tracking shot up the hill from the camera's POV. "It's a great idea. Except for the obvious."

"What's that?"

"It's June. There's no snow. Unless Hank can do something in post."

"Change the shot from summer to winter?" Mac shook his head. "He might be able to put a few patches of snow in the foreground. But the whole scene? You've still got leaves, grass, flowers...." He took a swig of beer. "Tricky."

"Well, let's think about it. Speaking of tricks, I've been playing around with an idea." I leaned forward. "We have what—over a dozen locations in the show? I mean, between the airstrip, the spa, the bunny hill, the condos, this place is a world unto itself."

"Right."

"So that's what we do. Create a world. Make the video a 3D map." I cupped my hands. "We start off with an abstract shape. A continent...a country. Who knows? But it's really the Lodge."

"The Land of Lodge?" Mac put in.

I ignored him. "Then, each time we zero in on a location, we do an effect that takes us into the scene. And then another to get us out."

"How about a yellow brick road?"

I didn't respond.

"It could work," Mac admitted. "As long as it doesn't look cluttered."

"We'll be restrained." I motioned with my hands. "Elegant but rustic."

"Get kind of a yin yang thing going?"

"Either that or bring in the Munchkins."

Mac shot me a look.

I peered out at the swimming pool, admiring the planters of annuals and how nicely the colors contrasted with the blue water, when I felt someone's gaze on my back. I turned around. Two cocktail waitresses in faux tuxedos were working the room. One was blond, the other brunette. The blonde had been serving us, but it was the brunette, waiting for her order at the side of the bar, who was watching me. When the blonde came back to the bar, they talked. A brief nod passed between them.

It was still early, and the only other customers in the bar were a group of Japanese tourists swilling pop and a well-dressed woman with a disappointed expression, as though she'd ended up in the wrong resort. The brunette picked up her tray, skirted the Asians, and headed toward us.

She was petite and pretty, with waifish looks that might not age so gracefully. Her youth—she couldn't have been more than twenty-five—helped mitigate the fact that her eyeliner was too thick, her rouge too red, and her red nails too long. "Another round?" she asked cheerfully.

Mac and I exchanged looks. "Sure," he answered.

"Draft and a Chardonnay, right?" She had a heavy Southern twang.

Mac nodded.

"I'll be right back. I'm Pari, by the way."

I looked up. "Pari?"

"That's right. Pari Noskin Taichert?" she said, her inflection turning it into a question, but she went off before we could come up with the answer. "It's unusual. I know," she allowed when she returned with our drinks.

"What?" Mac asked.

"My name." She smiled at him, but not before stealing a glance at me.

"Is that so?" Mac returned the smile.

"Right as rain. The Taicherts come from New Jersey and New York. But the Noskins, now, they pretty much run everything in Pine Hollow."

"Pine Hollow?" Mac asked.

"Kentucky," she said proudly. "The mountains. My family settled the hollow a long time ago."

Deciding that Mac's flirtations were none of my business, I peered outside again. The brightly clad golfers I'd seen earlier were standing around a table, the afternoon breeze fanning their shirttails. Something about one of them reminded me of David, and I felt a pang. Maybe I should invite him to come out. It had been a long time.

"Miss—can I—"

I swiveled around. "I'm sorry. What?"

Pari slipped her tray under one arm. "You the ones doin' all that filming around here, ain't you?"

"Guilty."

"Well, now, if that's not as exciting as a bug in a tater patch, I don't know what is!"

Another one who wanted to touch the glamour. I sighed inwardly. "It's not a Hollywood movie. Just a video about the resort. Like a very long commercial."

She shrugged. "It don't matter. I never seen no TV or movies being made." She gave me a look that was almost sly. "You need someone to do something—what do they call those folks you see in crowds and on the streets?"

"Extras."

"Extras. Yeah. Well, you need one, you just let me know." She patted her hair.

"Thanks, but I think we're all set."

I hoped the finality in my voice signaled the end of it, but she stayed where she was.

"Thanks," I repeated. Now please get lost.

She moved the tray in front of her like a shield. I was about to say something more direct when she tilted her head. "You know, I seen *you* on TV."

"I don't think so."

"Yeah, I did. You were on the news, weren't you? At the rest stop with Daria Flynn."

My stomach clenched. I could deny it. I didn't want to talk— or think—about that day. "You have sharp eyes," I mumbled.

She smiled, as if I'd handed her a compliment. "Well, butter my butt and call me a biscuit. I wasn't sure, you know. I did think to myself—"

"You know, Pari, if it's all the same to you, I don't want—"

"Well, now, here's the thing...."

Mac got to his feet and started walking away.

"Where are you going?" I asked.

"I think I see someone I know. I'll be right back."

"Coward."

He didn't answer. His departure didn't seem to faze Pari. Once he was gone, she moved closer.

"Now, miss, what I was wondering was whether you *knowed* her or not. I mean before she got killed." She lowered her voice. "They didn't say on TV, you know."

"Miss—I mean, Pari." I waved a hand, trying one last time to dismiss her. "Let's not go there. I really don't want to talk about it."

She ignored me. "'Cause, ya see," she said slowly, "if you did know Daria, then maybe you knew she come in here a few times recently."

My hand stopped in midair. "Daria Flynn—came here?"

Pari nodded.

"I thought she worked at the Geneva Inn."

"She come in here afterward. More 'n once."

I thought about the mysterious boyfriend who had abandoned her on the highway. "Alone?"

"Well, I guess that's what's so interesting, isn't it?" Pari's eyes narrowed fractionally, but I saw a gleam of triumph in them.

"I've only been here a few months, you know? But my mama, well, she always told me to use your head for something besides a hat rack. So I pay attention, you know?"

"Is that so?" She had my attention now, and she knew it.

"Mind you, the first time I saw them together, I didn't know."

"Who?"

"It was about a month ago." Her voice dropped to a whisper. "Maybe a little less. She come in kinda late. Around eleven. I was on break. She come into the ladies' room first. Set herself down in front of the mirror. Put on a fresh lipstick, combed her hair just so. The way you do when you're gonna meet someone you like, you know?"

I knew. What I didn't know was why Pari was telling me about it.

"Then she set down at the bar, right next to him."

"Who? Who did she sit down next to?"

She took a breath, then blew out the name, as if it was just too much for her to hold on to anymore. "Luke."

"Luke?"

"Luke Sutton."

"Who is Luke Sutton?"

Pari eyed me as if I was the most ignorant woman she'd ever met. "Only one of the richest men around here. Family's got one of those big places on the lake, you know?"

"No. I don't."

Pari looked around. "He comes in here sometimes. Him and his brother. He's okay. The brother, that is. A good tipper. But maybe I shouldn't be saying nothin', you know?" She looked away.

I rubbed my forehead with my hand. Pari Noskin Taichert and her mountain manners were starting to grate. "Why not?"

"I need this job."

"You're not saying you could get fired for telling me who Daria Flynn was drinking with?"

She hesitated. "Let me put it this way. What would you think if you saw someone cozying up to someone else in the bar, sittin' real close, smilin' from here to yesterday and back, and then you don't hear nothin' more about it after she turns up dead?"

"The police followed up on it, didn't they?"

"There ain't been no one comin' around asking questions." She hesitated. "On my shift, at least."

"Not even after you told them?"

She looked at the floor.

"You did tell them, didn't you?"

She shifted her tray to her hip. "It waren't no secret, you know. Plenty other people saw them together. It waren't just one time, neither."

"You didn't tell them."

An edge came into her voice. "Look, I can't go to the police. I just thought maybe, if you was friends, you might want to know."

Why was Pari confiding in me instead of the police? What did she expect me to do?

"He flies a plane," she said quietly. "Uses the airstrip in back here to land and take off. But I haven't seen him around since—since...." She shrugged.

"Pari, were you and Daria friends?"

She shook her head. "She put on airs, you know?" She picked up my wineglass, empty now, and Mac's drink. "She had no use for me."

I recalled my first impression of Daria on the cell, demanding to know why she'd been abandoned. I suppose someone might have labeled her arrogant, although I'd thought she was just upset. Still, that didn't change the fact that this barmaid had an important piece of information about her. "Pari, you have to go to the police."

But Pari was already on her way back to the bar and out of earshot. I didn't stop her. It was possible the police already knew about Daria's meeting with Luke Sutton. Pari did say other people besides her had seen them, and while I'm no cop, following up on something like this seemed pretty basic. Perhaps the police had already talked to this Sutton man.

If that were the case, though, why hadn't Kim or Irene Flynn said anything about it? When they came to my house, they'd been pumping *me* for information about the mysterious boyfriend. They claimed to have no idea about any man in Daria's life.

I thought about it. It wasn't my responsibility to tell the police. I barely knew Daria Flynn, and I didn't know Luke Sutton at all. And I didn't have any reason—or desire—to get involved in the investigation. I had quite enough on my plate. I stood up, dropped two tens on the table, and started for the exit.

Mac joined me at the door.

"That was a nice vanishing act."

"I told you—I saw someone I knew."

"Your long-lost uncle?" Mac has perfected the ability to slip through walls at the first sign of trouble. I wouldn't put it past him to disappear just so he wouldn't have to plead knowledge about my activities.

"Better." He yanked a thumb behind him.

I looked over my shoulder. The lounge area was filling up now, but I didn't recognize anyone.

"Remember Mister Mustard? Owns the museum in Mount Horeb?"

"How could I forget? How many hundred mustard jars did we shoot?"

"About a truckload."

"He's here?"

Mac nodded.

I looked over my shoulder again. This time I spotted him: a pleasant-looking man in glasses next to an attractive woman with long red hair. He lifted a hand and waved.

"What were we shooting when we met him? Vienna hot dogs?"

Mac snorted. "You've been doing this way too long. It was the Food Marketing Institute."

"I remember now." I waved back.

Mac put his hand on my back and guided me out. "What did the barmaid have to say?"

"Something about a rich guy fooling around with the girl who was killed at the rest stop."

"What rich guy?"

"Sutton. Luke Sutton."

Mac shrugged.

"Family lives in one of those mansions on the lake," I said. "Flies his own plane. You know the type. Probably never worked a day in his life."

Mac squeezed his lips together, the way he does when he's annoyed. I winced. When would I learn to keep my mouth shut? For all his down-to-earth, middle-class ways, Mac had once been a charter member of the same club.

Chapter Nine

There's something about the quality of summer light that pulls me back to my childhood. Driving back from Lake Geneva, the setting sun shimmering like molten gold, I dimly remembered evening skies full of light, warm breezes drifting through the window. Lying in bed under nothing more than a smooth cotton sheet, those being the days before air conditioning, I would watch the slanting rays of the sun inch across the wall. I'd hear my parents talking softly, relaxing now that I was safely in bed. Sometimes their voices mingled with a muted Big Band tune; sometimes with the chirr of crickets. I'd fall into a sound, secure slumber, unaware of the fragility of life.

Maybe that's why I tensed when I passed the rest stop where Daria Flynn had been shot. Two weeks after the tragedy, scrubbed clean of all traces, the oasis was just another outpost on the highway. But the memory of what happened there would be fixed in my mind forever. I flipped on the radio, hoping for Springsteen or Jagger to distract me. I must have pushed the wrong button, though, because instead of classic rock, a chorus of powerful female voices, accompanied by a full orchestra, belted out, "He had it comin'…he had it comin'…."

Rachel and I had seen *Chicago* three times, rented the DVD twice, and bought the CD. We especially liked the number I heard now, "Cell Block Tango," in which female prisoners tell how and why they murdered their men. As I listened to their stories, I thought about Daria Flynn. The female killers on the CD were impulsive; they'd struck out of passion, betrayal, revenge.

Now there were rumors of late-night trysts between Daria and one of the richest men in Lake Geneva. Rumors that Daria's family apparently didn't know about. Daria had been arguing with her boyfriend just before she was killed. Was there a relationship? Had Daria been the victim of the same hot-blooded rage the women sang about? Or was her murder the act of a cold-blooded sniper?

I accelerated past the rest stop. I had a name to go with the boyfriend. The police probably had more. So why hadn't they mentioned him to Daria's mother and sister? I frowned. We've all heard of townsfolk who protect, even embrace, their "favorite sons," despite the fact everyone knows they're troublemakers. They might be scoundrels, the thinking goes, but they're "our" scoundrels, and we'll deal with them. Sometimes you can feel the affection—even pride—for their bad boys.

In cases like that, the task of meting out justice while still keeping the peace falls to the police. But even the best cops aren't immune to pressure, and all the wealth concentrated in Lake Geneva had to be tantamount to a steamroller. Lieutenant Milanovich seemed decent enough, but he was from Illinois. Lake Geneva was in Wisconsin. Different cops, different jurisdictions. It would be easy for reports to be lost, interviews glossed over. Certain facts might never cross Milanovich's desk.

I veered onto the Edens. I should stop speculating. What I'd heard wasn't evidence. It was gossip from a barmaid about whom I knew very little. What was her stake in this? Did she harbor a grudge against Daria? Or was it Luke Sutton? Maybe she'd come on to him, and he hadn't responded. Or maybe they'd had a fling, and she was jealous when he'd moved on. The women in "Cell Block Tango" had killed for less. Or maybe it was his wealth she resented. She'd mentioned it several times. Maybe she just wanted to make life tough for a rich guy. Or maybe she was trying to do the right thing. She had information; she wanted it to get out.

I snapped off the music. Whatever her motivation, it wasn't my problem. My only responsibility in Lake Geneva was to produce a video for the Lodge. The police were working the case. Besides, everything pointed to some psycho serial killer with a thing for young women.

Still, as I barreled down the highway, an image of Daria's mother kept drifting into my mind. Her spine impossibly straight, her voice soft but insistent. "What did my daughter say at the end?" she was asking. "If you remember anything else…. Please. We have to know."

⌐◠◠⌐

I stopped off at Costco for steaks before going home. I'd throw them on the grill and make a salad for dinner. Rachel was into a low-carb diet, though at five-four and a hundred fifteen pounds, she didn't need to be. Given that the teenage body is wholly consumed by either food or hormones, however, I was grateful she wasn't a fanatic. I might convince her to go to Dairy Queen for dessert.

But there was no sign of Rachel when I walked in. The newspaper was spread out over the kitchen table, and a half-eaten tuna sandwich lay on a plate. I glanced at the paper: classifieds for used cars. I dropped the meat on the counter and went back outside. The sun had dipped below the horizon, and it was cool enough to water the flowers. I uncoiled the hose, turned it on, and pointed the sprinkler on the flower bed. The grass was starting to look overgrown and toothy; I hoped Fouad would be back soon. I collected the mail and trudged up the driveway, scanning the bills and junk mail. Didn't anyone write real letters anymore? I was almost at the end of the driveway when a shrill, ear-splitting blast sounded just inches behind me.

Reflex kicked in. I leaped to the side and dropped to the ground. The mail fell from my hands, scattering on the grass. I looked up just in time to see a burst of black metal sweep past not six inches from my foot. It lurched to a stop at the end of the driveway, exactly where I'd stood.

I slowly stood up. It was my ex-husband's car. My heart hammered in my chest, and my skin felt cold. I felt almost giddy, veering between relief and rage. As I ran up to the car, I saw two figures in the front seat. Neither made any attempt to look at me.

I realized why when I came abreast of the car. Rachel was in the driver's seat, shoulders hunched, her hands gripping the wheel. Barry was in the passenger seat, his hand covering his eyes. Rachel stared straight ahead, pointedly ignoring me, even when I pounded on the window.

Barry dropped his hand and lowered the window. "Hi," he said casually.

I wondered if he'd be as casual if he'd been the one to brush up against a ton of moving steel. "What—what the hell do you think you're doing?"

Rachel wouldn't meet my eyes, but Barry leaned back against the leather-covered seat. "What does it look like?" He smiled lazily.

"Are you crazy? Barry, you can't do this! She doesn't have her learner's permit!"

My ex-husband is a dead ringer for Kevin Costner, and despite years of acrimony, I still react when I see him. I planted my hands on my hips, annoyed at myself for noticing his blue eyes that had just the right arrangement of laugh lines, his mostly brown hair that refused to recede though he was well past fifty, the body that still looked buff in cutoffs and T-shirt. His grin widened. He had me, and he knew it. "She's got great hand-eye coordination."

"Especially when she's running over her mother."

Rachel slouched, then twisted around. "This is the first time something ever happened, Mom. I've been doing really well. Ask Dad. I need to get my learner's. Please?"

I knew they were ganging up on me—whenever Rachel wants something and figures I won't cave in, she automatically recruits her father, who's usually all too happy to oblige, particularly if it means overruling me. But getting a driver's license is one of those rites of passage that's more traumatic for the parent—usually the mother—than the child. I couldn't block images of Rachel speeding down the highway at seventy miles an hour, the brakes suddenly failing, the crash and splinter of metal on metal, her young body tossed to the side of the road. I shuddered.

"Mutthher…."

Both Rachel and Barry were watching me, Rachel impatiently, Barry with a hint of amusement, as if he knew what was going through my mind and was enjoying my predicament.

I was reminded of the time when Rachel was a baby and Barry was babysitting. I'd been on a shoot all day, and when I got home, Rachel was in front of the TV in her little swing, her eyes glued to the screen. I followed her gaze, expecting to see Mr. Rogers making some dignified pronouncement or Oscar grousing about life in the trash. Instead the TV was tuned to a kung fu movie, the actors violently jabbing, chopping, and aiming well-timed kicks into each other's groins. Barry was on the edge of his seat, cheering whenever one of them got in a particularly vicious move.

"What are you doing?" I yelled. Rachel promptly started to cry. "We agreed. No violence." I scooped her up from the swing and turned off the tube, which prompted a fresh stream of tears.

"Oh, for Christ's sake, Ellie." Barry got up and snapped the TV back on. "Check out those moves. How choreographed they are. How smooth. This shit's better than ballet!" He pointed to Rachel. "And look! She loves it!"

The punch line was that she did. As soon as I swung her back toward the television, she quieted.

Now, I sighed and opened the car door. "We had a deal, young lady."

"We did?"

"You were going to go on the Internet and find out what you need to give the DMV to get your learner's."

She made a brushing aside gesture with her hand. "I already know. I need—"

"But I don't. And I need to see a list."

She got out of the car, shooting me one of those disdainful scowls teenage girls use primarily on their mothers. She favored her father with a dazzling smile. "Bye, Dad. Thanks."

Barry waved and slid into the driver's seat. As he backed out of the driveway, still grinning, I tried not to think about the fact she'd inherited half her genetic code from him. Otherwise, I might have to shoot myself. Or her.

Back in the kitchen, Rachel opened the refrigerator door and grabbed a can of pop. "Oh, by the way," she said as she flipped open the tab, "I got a job."

I got out salt and pepper. "No kidding! That's great! Where?"

"It's a babysitting job."

"Who for?" I unwrapped the meat and tossed the plastic wrap in the trash.

"Julia Hauldren."

I froze.

"You know. The Julia who's going out with Dad."

I forced myself not to react. After a moment, I said slowly, "She wants to hire you?"

"Yeah. Kind of like a girl Friday. You know, take care of her kids while she's at the store or doing errands. Go to the playground. The beach. That kind of thing."

"How much time does she want from you?"

"She said two or three hours a day." Rachel flashed me a grin. "Pretty cool, huh?"

I sprinkled salt on the steaks. "Fifteen hours a week is a huge commitment, Rachel. Are you sure you're up to it?"

"Of course I am. So can I do it? I told her I could start tomorrow."

Something about the setup made me uneasy. Including the feeling I'd been set up. "Let me think about it."

Rachel erupted into anger. "What's to think about? You've been pressuring me to get a job. Now I got one, and you have to 'think about it'? Mom, that's not fair." She turned on her heel and, in her most self-righteous tone, added, "Daddy warned me that's how you'd react."

I kept my mouth shut, determined to stay in control.

"Why not?" she challenged me. "Why can't I do it? There's nothing around here to do. You're not here. No one is. Not even David. Anymore."

"Enough." I slammed the salt back on the counter. "You can't talk to me that way. Go to your room."

She stomped out of the kitchen and up the stairs. I fired up the grill by myself.

Chapter Ten

I dropped two dollars on the counter at the White Hen a few mornings later. "An iced tea and a glazed doughnut."

It was only nine, but the air was already thick and heavy. I needed the cold drink. I needed the doughnut, too, and I watched greedily as the woman behind the counter speared it with tongs, wrapped it in waxed paper, and handed it over. I wolfed down half of it in the store. A smooth, comforting sweetness coated the inside of my mouth. The woman behind the counter smiled as if we'd just shared a secret pleasure.

A rack of newspapers stood outside, and I scanned the headlines as I walked out. Medicare reductions, a Congressional logjam, Mideast problems. Nothing about the sniper. Or Daria Flynn's death. In fact, the State Police were being remarkably tight-lipped, refusing to talk about the weapon used or what they'd recovered from the scene.

At first their silence triggered a flurry of media analysis, second-guessing, and editorials bemoaning the tragic and unpredictable nature of violence. But a week had now passed with no new incidents, and a week is a century in media parlance. It was summer, the beaches were open, and the press had moved on. If a few people—the victims' families, for example, or the lead cop on the case—were still mired in the tragedies, if their moods were tempered by unsettled feelings in the pit of their stomach; well, that was unfortunate. The rest of us were free to delete the incident from our memories and enjoy the revelries of the season.

I threw away the rest of the doughnut and got back in the car. Merging onto the expressway, I watched waves of heat rise from the asphalt. The Volvo didn't kick out much cool air, and the backs of my thighs stuck to the seat. I gulped my iced tea.

When I pulled into the Lodge's parking lot an hour later, Mac's van was already there. I made sure I had sunscreen and water, got out of the car, and left the windows open.

In addition to the hotel, the Lodge had its own condominium complex. About fifty semidetached townhouses occupied the west side of the road. Mac and the crew were setting up to shoot B-roll of the exteriors when I arrived.

"How's it going?" I asked.

Mac nodded. "Good. But it's supposed to storm later. Don't know how much we'll actually get in the can."

I looked up, shading my eyes. The glare from the sun was unrelenting, but a band of dark clouds had gathered in the west. "Let's push to shoot the airstrip and the bunny hill—otherwise, we'll be behind schedule."

Mac gazed at the crew, two burly young men who were setting up the camera on a wheeled dolly. "We'll do our best."

I watched them rehearse a tracking shot of the condos. The facades of the buildings were white with black shutters and doors, producing a monochromatic sameness that you often see in housing developments. Still, according to the realty manager, who came outside to watch the shoot, sales were brisk. And most of the owners lived less than 500 miles from the Lodge.

"Why do people vacation so close to their homes?" I asked.

"Lots of reasons," she explained. "No crowded planes to Florida. Or problems on the highways. And when you think about it, we have pretty much everything any other resort has. In spite of the weather." She described the indoor pools, spa, tennis courts, and running track, then went on to quote statistics that claimed Americans rarely ventured farther than 700 miles for a vacation. "But even if that weren't the case," she chirped, "wintering is very much a tradition in these parts."

"What do you mean?"

"Well, you know that Lake Delavan used to be the winter circus capital of the country."

Delavan is a Wisconsin resort area with its own lake about ten miles from Lake Geneva. It's similar in size and trappings, but not quite as upscale.

"Circus? As in Barnum and Bailey?"

She smiled. "The same. That's where they got their start. At one time, in fact, over twenty-six traveling circuses used to camp there over the winter. Of course, this was a hundred and fifty years ago."

"Winter in Wisconsin? With all the snow? Why not Florida or someplace warm?"

She smiled. "They claimed a four-season climate was necessary for the well-being of the horses. Delavan was famous for its lush pastures and pure water. It was a good place to stable the animals."

"I had no idea. The only thing I know about Delavan is Lake Lawn Lodge." The resort is a less elegant version of the Lodge but still one of the better-known places.

"Most Chicagoans don't. But time was you'd see hundreds of clowns and circus performers and animal trainers. Some of them even came into Geneva. Course, it all came to an end by 1900."

"Why?"

"The railroad came through, and most of the circuses folded. The others eventually did move to warmer climates." She shrugged. "But there's a circus cemetery in Delavan. And they've got a statue of a giraffe in the middle of the town square."

Compared to Chicago, the clusters of small towns outside Chicago don't cast a huge shadow, but they do have their place in history. How did the people of Delavan feel about being overrun by clowns, I wondered. Did they resent the intrusion into their well-ordered Wisconsin lives? Or did the presence of the circus foster a tolerance for eccentricity—a sort of reverse civic pride?

As Mac and the crew recorded a second take, I decided it might be interesting to compare the descendants of Delavan families who'd lived with the circuses to the Lake Geneva locals who'd tolerated the Playboy Club. It could make an interesting sidebar. Or maybe not. Many of Lake Geneva's residents were hard-nosed businessmen. If revenues from the Playboy Club and other resorts helped fill the town's coffers and kept taxes down, why complain? Still, it was worth considering.

By the time we'd finished filming the condos, an angry gray cloud cover had overspread the sky. The air was unusually still.

"Think we have time for the airstrip?" I asked.

"If we hustle," Mac answered. I went with him to get the van so we could stow the equipment if it rained. We drove to the back of the resort.

The airstrip was originally built by the Playboy Club to fly Hollywood entertainers in and out for shows. It consisted of one narrow runway, but its concrete base had long ago buckled and tall weeds pushed through the cracks. A sign on a white frame building beside it said AIRPORT, and a small hangar stood a few yards away. Trees flanked the buildings, and a stand of evergreens loomed on one side of the landing strip.

Directly across from the airstrip was a makeshift assortment of pink and white flowers that looked like they'd been transplanted from a nursery. An assortment of equipment lay nearby, including three huge riding lawnmowers that were almost the size of tractors. It was probably some kind of staging area for landscapers.

"So what do you want to do here?" Mac asked.

Nothing, I thought. In fact, at the moment, I would have preferred to be drinking at the bar in the Lodge. I don't like flying. It's not just a case of butterflies during takeoffs and landings. It's more like a herd of water buffalos trampling through my stomach. It doesn't help to tell me about the science and physics of flight. I don't have the slightest interest in thrust and propulsion and lift. I know the truth: it's duct tape and rubber bands that keep planes aloft. And don't tell me I have unresolved issues about control. I know that, too. The problem is that the year I spent in therapy was undone by the two-hour film *Castaway*. I will fly if I have to, but I usually prime myself with wine or tranquilizers. Or both.

"So what do you want to do?" Mac repeated.

"I don't know."

Mac started across the tarmac, aiming his exposure meter up. "Well, we need to figure it out. We're losing light."

I looked up. The clouds had gathered together and lowered. "What about a traveling shot down the runway? We could put the camera in the car and—"

Mac shook his head. "We don't have a car mount. The shot would be too jumpy."

I took a look at the patchy grass, the buckled pavement, the loose chunks of concrete on the runway. He was right. "Maybe we should wrap for today and rent one tomorrow."

"It's your budget."

"Do you have any other ideas?"

He scrutinized the runway, then looked back at the hangar. "Maybe." He started to trot back to the van.

"What? Tell me."

"Hold on."

Mac knows more about depth of field, lighting, and camera movement than anyone I know, and he usually comes up with a creative approach to even the most mundane shot. I ran a hand through my hair, relieved he had an idea. As my hand brushed my ear, I felt something fall off. "Damn."

Mac stopped halfway across the tarmac. "What's wrong?"

"My earring. I think it fell off."

Mac gave me a blank look, as if anything to do with jewelry was beyond his comprehension. I fingered my ear. I don't wear pierced earrings—I'd tried them as a teenager, but developed nasty lumps of scar tissue and let the holes close up. Today I'd been wearing a pair of gold clips set with delicate blue amethysts.

They were a birthday present from David. "You go ahead. I have to find it."

He nodded and went toward the hangar. I studied the ground. A patch of weeds poked through the concrete under my feet. The earring was probably hidden somewhere in them. As I bent over for a closer look, a low whine from one of the lawnmowers started up behind me.

I got down on my hands and knees and searched through the weeds. No earring. I started to make circles with my hands. Still nothing. The whining sound grew louder, but I didn't pay attention. I couldn't lose the earring. Not only would David think I was careless, but he might see it as a symbol of our deteriorating relationship. I kept hunting.

Suddenly two things happened at once. The whine became a deafening roar, and out of the corner of my eye, I saw Mac gesturing wildly. He was pointing up to the sky.

I twisted around and looked up. A plane had dipped down through the overcast and was descending fast over the runway. And I was directly in its path.

Chapter Eleven

The next minute was probably the longest of my life, but even now, I only remember fragments. The roar of the engine vibrating through my skin. A powerful surge of air slamming into my ears and throat. A flash of white hurtling toward me. The sickening realization that I was about to be ripped apart on impact.

My breath tore from my throat. I was gripped by a fierce panic. I heard Mac screaming at me to run, but my limbs wouldn't move. Then, everything went into slow motion. The plane, barely a hundred feet off the ground, swooped down like a bird of prey. My hands grew slick. Strange, haphazard thoughts ricocheted through my head. I admired the plane's graceful descent. I wondered what Rachel was doing. I knew I'd never find my earring. I decided that my fear of airplanes wasn't so irrational.

The shriek of the engine finally pulled me out of my stupor. The plane was almost directly above me, its roar so loud I thought it might split the ground. The vibrations sent tremors through me, rattling bones I never knew I had. My muscles locked, but I *had* to move. I dropped to a crouch in the weed patch, threw my arms back, and hurled myself off the runway.

I fell backward but caught myself with my hands. The plane touched down not more than thirty feet from where I'd been. I gulped down air. Mac and the crew ran toward me, firing anxious questions. "Are you okay?" "Do you need some help?" "Should we call an ambulance?"

I shook my head. "I'm all right." I took some breaths to steady myself.

The plane taxied down the runway. Now that it had landed, I could see it was a two-seater with a blue stripe running down a white body. Two figures hunched in the cockpit. As it slowed, individual blades of metal slowly resolved out of the grayish blur of the propeller. When the blades stopped, the pilot jumped out and ran toward us. He was wearing black athletic shoes, faded jeans, and a white golf shirt. A thick silver belt buckle flashed at his waist. His arms were freckled, and he was fair-skinned— probably the kind who turned lobster red in the sun.

Mac and the crew stepped aside to let him through.

"Who are you and what the hell were you doing?" The pilot had been wearing shades, but as he approached me, he took them off and slipped them on top of his head. He wasn't tall, and looked perhaps in his late forties, with a lean face, curly salt and pepper hair, and an equally curly beard. His eyes were so blue a summer sky might be jealous. I might have described him as nice-looking if those eyes hadn't been spitting fire.

I got to my feet slowly, checking to make sure nothing was broken or sprained or bleeding. "My name is Ellie Foreman," I said. "I'm producing a video for the Lodge."

He hesitated a moment, looking puzzled. Then his eyes narrowed and his mouth tightened. "You have a permit for that?"

"A—a what? Are you crazy? You nearly kill me and you want to know if I have a permit? Who the hell are you?"

He held out his hand. "Airport regulations say any commercial activity on airport property requires a permit. Let's see it."

I glared at him, quavering with suppressed fury. Meanwhile, the other man in the cockpit approached but stood a foot or so behind us. He looked about the same age as the pilot. He didn't seem eager to participate in the conversation. It was clear he was deferring to his buddy.

I ignored the pilot's hand, still extended in the air. "I thought this airstrip was deserted."

"You thought wrong," he barked. "This is the only working airstrip in Lake Geneva, and it's used on a regular basis."

"I—I didn't know."

He nodded. "That's obvious. What did you say your name was?"

"Ellie Foreman."

His eyes flickered over me. "Well, Ellie Foreman, next time you might want to figure out the lay of the land before you commandeer an airstrip."

"And you might want to respect the rules of video production," I shot back. "Like not interfering when the camera's rolling."

His expression didn't change. I felt my cheeks get hot. It was a lame comeback, and I was sure he knew it. Mac hadn't begun to set up the camera. "Video, huh?" He threw me a hard look. "You're one of those TV newspeople who hang around dredging up smut."

The muscles at the back of my neck tightened. Who was this man? "I have nothing to do with television news. I shoot corporate films. The Lodge is my client, and no one ever indicated this airstrip was in use. By the way, if I hadn't just been almost mowed down by your runaway plane, I might be a little more cooperative," I said icily. "So if you'll excuse me...."

I started back toward Mac's van. I hadn't reclaimed the upper hand, but a grand exit does wonders for one's wounded pride. At least I hadn't let him relegate me to the same level as "those TV newspeople." Although that's exactly what I used to be.

"New owners." The pilot snorted to his companion. "No one has a clue what's going on."

I stopped and turned around. He pinched the bridge of his nose. He was still clearly annoyed, but some of the rancor had faded.

The other man put his hand on the pilot's arm. "Something obviously fell through the cracks. I'll take care of it, Luke. Just thank God everyone's okay. How 'bout we all call it a day? Unless you want to file a report," he called over to me.

But I didn't answer. I was staring hard at the pilot. "Luke?" I tensed. "You're Luke?"

He gave me a curt nod.

"Luke Sutton?"

He didn't answer. Nobody moved. The air pressed down on me. I detected the faint smell of sulfur.

"That's right." He scowled.

A drop of rain splattered on the tarmac. Then another. And then, right on cue, a fork of lightning cracked the sky, followed by a crash of thunder. All at once a sheet of rain, seemingly materializing out of nowhere, lashed the ground. As if by some unspoken accord, everyone sprang into action. Mac and the crew raced toward the van. Luke Sutton stomped over to a Toyota Camry behind the hangar.

Needles of rain stung my face. Luke Sutton was the man Pari had seen with Daria Flynn at the Lodge. Part of me wanted to follow him and ask if Pari Taichert had it right. Had he been going out with Daria Flynn? Did he know anything about her murder? But I couldn't. Instead, I watched silently as he got into the passenger seat of the Toyota.

I ran over to Mac's van, feeling wet and disheveled and unsettled. I hoped Mac had a towel in the back. But Sutton's flying buddy remained on the tarmac, standing in the rain. What was he waiting for? Reluctantly, I retraced my steps, trying to ignore my clothes, which were now glued to me like a second skin.

"Is there another problem?" I asked.

The man crossed his arms. "You never said whether you wanted to file a complaint."

"A complaint?"

"You have the right."

I considered it. If the airstrip was indeed used on a regular basis, we shouldn't have been anywhere near it. On the other hand, no one at the Lodge had said it was in use, and we had no reason to think there would be any traffic. At the very least, there had been a colossal miscommunication. But no one was hurt. I would survive. And if we wanted to spend the money, we could always come back with a car mount. I didn't need to waste time on paperwork. Still, I wasn't inclined to let anyone off the hook. Especially anyone named Luke Sutton. Once I had the chance to collect my thoughts, I might figure out how to leverage the situation.

"Let me think about it."

Sutton's companion nodded. He was slim, with straight dark hair receding from his forehead, and widely spaced dark eyes. Like Sutton, he was dressed casually. I wondered if he was the other Sutton brother. The good tipper. The nice one. "Are you Luke Sutton's brother?"

To my surprise, he shook his head. Hunching his shoulders against the rain, he held out his hand. "Sorry to meet you under such awkward circumstances. I'm Jimmy Saclarides, Lake Geneva chief of police."

Chapter Twelve

The cameraman drove the van back to Chicago, but Mac and I decided to wait out the storm. Mac got into my Volvo, and we drove into Lake Geneva to dry off and grab a late lunch.

"You sure you're okay, Ellie?" Mac asked.

"I lost an earring my boyfriend gave me, I made an enemy at the airstrip, and we didn't get any footage. Other than that, I'm great. How about you?"

"Hungry," Mac said.

I circled the three or four blocks of downtown Lake Geneva. "So what do you feel like? There's supposed to be a Greek restaurant somewhere around here."

"In Lake Geneva?"

I nodded. "Unless it's just a restaurant that happens to be owned by Greeks."

"Which would be every restaurant in Chicago."

"But we're not in Chicago. Look for a place like Greek Islands."

We turned onto Main Street, and I cruised slowly down the block.

"I don't believe it." Mac straightened up.

"What?"

"We just passed something called Mount Olympus."

"Bingo."

Mount Olympus had none of the affectations of Greek Town restaurants: no stucco, faux Doric columns, blue décor. And no trellised grapevines, fake or otherwise. The restaurant was sandwiched into a narrow space between a jewelry store and an art gallery. It had a plain black door. The only indication it was a restaurant was the lettering on a plate glass window through which you could see a large hunk of lamb revolving on a spit.

Inside, we were hit by a tangy mix of garlic, lemon, and roasted meat. The smell was so tantalizing I overlooked the shabby room, chipped counter, and neon Budweiser sign on the wall.

A man seated at the first of about twelve tables was nursing a clear liquid in a shot glass. He didn't look up when we passed, though a bell tinkled when we entered. We sat at a table behind him. Only three other tables were occupied. A swinging door was cut into the wall behind the counter, and I heard a clatter of dishes on the other side. A moment later, Kim Flynn pushed through the door, balancing a tray of food.

She wore a long apron tied around her waist. The top of a pink T-shirt peeked out underneath. Her legs were bare; she must have been wearing shorts. Her hair was tied back in a ponytail and covered with a hairnet. She threaded her way past our table.

"Hello, Kim."

Her eyes widened when she saw me. She set the plates down two tables away and then worked her way back. "Foreman, right? Ellie Foreman?"

I nodded and motioned to Mac. "This is Mac Kendall. We work together."

As soon as Kim mentioned my name, a frown spread across Mac's face. He must have realized I had an ulterior motive for coming here. He doesn't like it when I do that.

"Mac, this is Kim Flynn…. Her sister was Daria Flynn, the woman who died at the rest stop."

Mac's frown deepened. Then he remembered his manners. "I'm sorry about your sister."

Kim dipped her head in acknowledgment, then looked at me. "Well, this is a surprise." She glanced out the window. "Especially with the weather."

"We were shooting at the Lodge but got rained out. I remembered your mother mentioning the restaurant. Are you still serving lunch?"

She hesitated, as if she wasn't convinced that's why I was there, but then her business sense kicked in. "Of course. Let me bring you some menus."

As we waited, Mac nudged me under the table with his foot. His voice was barely above a whisper. "You said you were putting it behind you."

"I was. But then…." I told him about Kim's visit to my house with her mother. I stressed how needy they'd seemed. How desperate. And that I'd said I'd let them know if I discovered anything.

Mac folded his arms. He wasn't buying it.

Kim brought the menus. "Sorry to be so slow. We're a little shorthanded. One of my guys—well, he just up and left. How did you know this was our place?"

"We guessed. Your mother did say it was a Greek restaurant."

"You were lucky. There's two of them in town, you know."

"There are two Greek restaurants here?"

She nodded. "The other one is Saclarides.'"

"Saclarides? As in Jimmy Saclarides? The chief of police?"

An odd expression crept across her face. "How did you know?"

Mac, who'd been growing increasingly agitated, stood up. "Can you point me to the facilities?"

Kim gestured to the back.

"Order me a gyros, okay, Ellie? And a Coke."

"Sure." Mac disappeared. "And I'll have a Greek salad." I looked up at Kim. "And a Diet Coke."

She scribbled our orders on a pad.

"Luke Sutton."

She started. "Excuse me?"

"That's how I met Jimmy Saclarides."

Her eyebrows shot up. "I'll be right back with your drinks."

She disappeared through the swinging door. When she came back with the pop, she was more composed, but I knew she was waiting for an explanation. I took a quick sip of my drink. "Luke Sutton nearly ran me down in his plane today. Jimmy Saclarides was with him."

She looked startled. "You're kidding. Are you okay?"

"I'm fine. But that isn't the reason I'm here. Meeting him reminded me of something I heard at the Lodge, and I wanted to ask if you knew about it."

She stuffed the pad into her apron pocket.

"We were having a drink there a few days ago, and there was this waitress, Pari something...."

"I know Pari."

I forgot. Subtract the tourists, and this was a small town. "She said your sister and Luke met there for drinks. More than once."

"Luke Sutton and Daria?"

When I nodded, she looked at the ceiling, then the floor. Then she looked back at me. "You're sure?"

Again I nodded. "I was thinking, well, I wondered if the police knew. And if they did, what they were doing about it. It's not like the Suttons aren't well known. You know what I mean?"

She nodded, a distracted, absentminded gesture. What was she thinking?

"And then, when it turned out Jimmy Saclarides was riding shotgun in the plane with Sutton...." I looked out the window. The rain was starting to let up. "Well, I guess I'm beginning to see your point."

"My point? About what?"

"About the police up here. Selective justice."

She ran her tongue around her lips. Her expression changed again, confusion giving way to an almost steely look. She waved a dismissive hand. "Oh, just—just forget what I said before. I was pissed off. Everyone knows Luke and Jimmy are friends. They have been for a long time."

"That's exactly my point."

"Yeah, but Jimmy Saclarides…well, his family and ours are close. Our mothers are best friends. He and I grew up together. We even went out in high school."

"You and Jimmy Saclarides?"

"We used to call him Super Chief. And not for the train."

"Well, this close family friend has a buddy who just might be the man who abandoned your sister at the rest stop."

A door in back squeaked. Mac was on his way back.

"That's just—I can't believe that. When were they supposed to have—have been together?"

"According to Pari, it was late. Ten, eleven at night."

"But when? A month ago? Six months? A year?"

"Not long before she died."

Mac came back and pulled out his chair. The scrape of the legs against the tile floor grated. Kim blinked, as if the sound had refocused her attention. A tiny vertical line creased her forehead. "Well. I guess I'll have to ask Jimmy about it." She looked over, as if seeing me for the first time. "Hey, thanks for coming in to tell me. I appreciate it." She forced a smile, then started back to the kitchen. "Your food's probably ready."

I watched her go. That wasn't the reaction I'd expected. Suspicion, alarm, even rage. But not blasé detachment. I glanced at the old man at the next table. He hadn't given any indication he knew we were there. But he was a fixture. He belonged. Not like me, an outsider who seemed to be discovering what everyone already knew and didn't much care about.

—◦—◦—◦—

That night I went online and Googled the name "Sutton." After wading through pages of websites about the London borough, hotel chains, and even a publishing company, I clicked onto a website that traced the history of trains.

In the early days, rail cars were equipped with a metal bar and ring on each end called a "link and pin." The cars were manually attached by workers who braced themselves between the cars and dropped a metal pin into place at the exact moment the holes in the bars lined up. This was a delicate and dangerous operation. The slightest mistake in timing meant a man could be crushed, and it wasn't uncommon to see railroad workers missing a finger, an arm, or even a leg.

The first patent for an automatic coupler was granted in 1873 to a store clerk in Atlanta. An improvement to the device was patented twenty-four years later by Andrew Beard, a former Alabama slave, who himself had lost a leg in a coupling accident. By the turn of the century, the government mandated the addition of automatic couplers to every rail car in the country.

Enter Luke Sutton's great-grandfather, Charles. A farmer from the same part of Alabama as Beard, Sutton claimed to have purchased the rights to the coupler from Beard. He started Sutton Rail Services, which, over the next fifty years, grew into a huge concern. By the 1930s, the company was manufacturing over half of all the automatic couplers in the world; in fact, it narrowly escaped antitrust action under FDR. When Sutton died right after World War Two, his son, Charles Junior, took over.

Curiously, no one knows what happened to Andrew Beard, the slave who sold his invention to the Suttons. There is no record of his life—or death. But ten years later when Charles II died unexpectedly in an automobile accident, his son Charles III took the reins of the company. He had been only twenty-two at the time and was still running the company today. His son Chip, Charles IV, was executive vice-president.

Was "Chip" a nickname for Luke? Maybe his full name was Charles Luke Sutton. Or was Chip the other Sutton brother? If I could find an organization chart, I could answer that question. Except that a privately held company isn't subject to the same disclosure requirements as a publicly owned one, and there's no obligation to list the company officers. I went back to Google and entered the name Charles Sutton. Happily, I ran across an article from *Forbes* profiling Sutton Services.

Charles Ashcroft Sutton III was the CEO. His son, Charles Ashcroft Sutton IV, executive vice-president. Ashcroft was his grandfather's middle name, his great-grandfather's, too. The CFO was Henry Banker; Jeffrey Hopkins, first vice-president. The article went on to name several other officers, none of whom were female, and none of whom I recognized. The name Luke Sutton was nowhere in the article.

I typed in "Chip Sutton." A few sites popped up. From one of them, I learned that he was married to Jennifer Brinks from Detroit, an heiress in her own right. They lived in Winnetka, the next village over from me. She sat on the board of several North Shore charities. Then I entered the name Luke Sutton. I got nothing.

I twirled a strand of hair around my finger. The Sutton family was fabulously wealthy, rich enough for their sons to have planes for toys. But only "Chip" followed his father into the family business. Why didn't Luke? What did he do for a living—if he, in fact, did anything besides meet Daria Flynn for drinks at the Lodge?

And what about Jimmy Saclarides, Lake Geneva's chief of police? If he and Luke Sutton were best friends, I could understand the guy wanting to protect his friend. But how far did that protection stretch?

Chapter Thirteen

"Do you know how to spell 'arrogant'?"

Susan and I hiked down the bike path the next morning.

"He even demanded to see a permit, for god's sake!" I grumbled. "Like he was the schoolyard bully and I was supposed to hand over my lunch."

Yesterday's storm, fierce but brief, left underbrush strewn on the ground. But it was still hot and humid, one of those summer days that bears down and smothers you with its weight.

Susan skirted the underbrush. It was a metaphor for her life. A tall, willowy redhead who turns the word "elegant" into a transitive verb, she never seems to make a misstep. She has a solid marriage, two well-behaved kids, and a part-time job that she loves. And unlike me, she's always ready for her close-up. While I had thrown on cutoffs, dirty sneakers, and an oversized T, Susan wore khaki shorts and an ivory shirt that set off her creamy complexion. The sun caught sparks in her hair.

"A permit? Does he own the airstrip?" she asked.

"Just a Cessna or two. But you know who his flying buddy was?"

"Who?"

"The chief of police of Lake Geneva."

Her brows drew together. "So?" Susan's husband is active in village politics. She's used to hobnobbing with VIPs.

"Susan, a waitress at the Lodge told me he and Daria Flynn had drinks together there. More than once. Then Daria was abandoned at the rest stop by her boyfriend. Just before she was killed."

"And the significance of that is…?"

"Well, if the chief of police is your best friend, you can get away with a lot."

Susan threw out her hand, like the Supremes used to when they performed "Stop in the Name of Love." "Slow down, there." I stopped.

"Just because two people have drinks together doesn't mean they're in a relationship. And it certainly doesn't mean the man had anything to do with her murder." She looked at me. "Unless there's something you're not telling me."

"But just suppose he *was* Daria's lover. She's young, beautiful, and ambitious. He's rich and powerful, and his best friend is the chief of police. You know how those things work."

"Ellie, you know better than to string together a lot of hypotheticals."

"If you'd had the same kind of run-in with him as I did, you might, too. But here's the kicker."

Susan smiled triumphantly. "There is something else."

"Maybe. When I told Daria's sister about seeing them together, she seemed—well, after some initial surprise, altogether unconcerned. But just a week or so ago, she was complaining the police weren't doing enough to find the killer."

"Wait a minute. You told Daria's sister that she'd been seeing this—this Sutton?"

I explained how we'd gone to the restaurant during the storm. As we rounded a bend, the bike path sloped up. It wasn't a hill, but it did require me to put my effort into walking rather than talking.

Susan took advantage of my silence. "Tell me something, Ellie. Why would you (A) believe a cocktail waitress, whom you never met before, and who might or might not be telling the truth? And (B) start to spread rumors…hurtful ones, by the sound of them?"

I tried to reply, but she cut me off.

"But (C) and this is the most important part, why are you still involved in this? It has nothing—absolutely nothing—to do with your life. You swore up and down a few months ago you wouldn't go near anything that even smelled dangerous."

"I only went to the restaurant for one reason," I said defensively. I told her about Irene and Kim Flynn's visit to my house. "Her mother, who's just recovering from a stroke, by the way, kept asking me about Daria's last words. As if that somehow held the key to her death. She begged me to get back to them if I thought of anything else. That's not getting involved. It's just compassion. Any mother would do the same."

Susan nodded. "But why you? Didn't you tell me two different police forces are working the case?"

I looked at her sideways. "That's right."

"Don't you think that between them they're covering all the possibilities?"

"I wouldn't know."

"That's my point. Maybe they already know about the drinks at the Lodge. Maybe there's a perfectly logical explanation. Just because you don't know it, doesn't mean it isn't there."

I shrugged. "It's—it's just that Luke Sutton was so damn sure of himself. So cocky. Like he was protected by his wealth. And nothing he could possibly do or say would ever be challenged."

Susan tilted her head. "Ahh…now we get to the root cause. He trampled on your ego. And you want payback."

"No." I made one more attempt to defend myself. "I just can't abide people with moral certainty."

"What do you mean?"

"I'm talking about people who reduce everything all down to a simple formula, the underlying assumption of which is that they're right and just and powerful and nobody else is."

"Which is something you'd never think of doing."

"I try not to," I said weakly.

"You do try." She flashed me a smile. "That's what I love about you."

As we reached the other side of the slope, Susan stepped up her pace. I kept up easily. A friend's smile can work wonders.

"The thing is you're probably right. When I reported it to Kim, she said Sutton and the police chief had been friends for a long time, and—get this—this police chief and her family are friends, too. She didn't seem to think any of it was important."

I shook my head. "Small towns."

"Sorry?"

"Eliminate the tourists, and Lake Geneva is basically a small town. Everyone knows everyone else, and everyone's history is tied up with their neighbors'." I pictured the old man at the restaurant. "It breeds an acceptance that outsiders can't penetrate." I sighed. "I suppose it really was a sniper attack."

"If it looks like a fish, and smells like a fish...." Susan changed the subject. "Hey, did you hear about the new wonder drug they're testing? I can't remember the name, but it's supposed to tan you, help you lose weight, and increase your libido all at the same time."

"Wow. Bring it on!"

"The problem is they've decided to release it as three different drugs," she said ruefully.

I grunted. "Well now, isn't that the American way? Squeeze out every penny of profit you can."

She laughed. "By the way, Doug and I are throwing a barbecue on July fourth. Will you and Rachel come? David, too."

"I haven't talked to him recently."

"Well, then, call him. You guys need to spend more time together."

I didn't answer.

"Ellie, six months is a long time to keep a relationship at bay. You can't play this out much longer."

"I'm not playing. And now there's his uncle Willie to consider." He'd moved in with David while he was being treated for kidney disease.

"So, invite him out, too. And your father. They're about the same age, aren't they?"

I wavered. Inviting David out was a huge risk. Although I missed the sharing and the intimacy, I'd been hurt. I was afraid. "I'll think about it."

Susan peered at me. "Don't think too long."

"I'm not sure about Rachel, though."

"Oh?"

"Speaking of arrogant, my daughter seems to have landed a job with Ms. North Shore."

"Who are you talking about now?"

"Julia Hauldren," I said, my voice tight.

"Julia? Arrogant? Where'd you get that idea?"

"Come on, Susan. Just look at her—perfectly done hair. And nails. And makeup. Even her tan. She obviously has a high opinion of herself."

"Sounds like you were describing me."

I stopped, startled. "You? Oh, no. You're different."

"How do you know she isn't, too?"

"She's going out with Barry." I started walking again. "She's got to be pretty superficial to put up with him."

"Funny about that," Susan replied. "One of my best friends was married to him, and I don't think *she's* superficial."

"Okay." I smiled ruefully. "He does give good face."

"Excuse me?"

"He's good looking, he takes care of himself, and he's a lawyer. I can see why he'd be considered a catch." A flock of sparrows suddenly lifted off a bush and scattered into the sky. "It's only when you live with him that you realize that's all there is."

Susan grunted. "I still don't see the problem here."

"It seems Julia wants Rachel to babysit a few hours a day. She's paying good money, too."

"Given that Rachel is only fifteen and can't get hired in most places, this is a bad thing?"

"You sound like you're defending her. Julia, that is."

"Do you know her?"

"I don't need to. I know the type."

"Uh-huh. So this is all conjecture. First impressions on your part."

"I'm usually right."

"You're sure about that?"

Why is it a raised eyebrow from Susan can make me doubt everything I learned since kindergarten?

—◦—◦—◦—

That evening Rachel and I went to dinner at a cafeteria-style salad bar that seemed to stretch from here to California, which was probably where the chain started. I loaded my plate with every green, red, and yellow vegetable ever propagated; added a layer of croutons; drenched all of it in a thick, creamy dressing; and tried to convince myself I was eating light.

Sliding our trays up to the cash register, I glanced over at Rachel's. She'd been more moderate with her salad, but she'd speared a large chunk of pizza bread, and I knew she'd probably want frozen yogurt for dessert. I made a rough estimate of what I owed and was digging my wallet out of my bag when something else caught my eye. At first I couldn't figure out what it was, then it dawned on me. It wasn't what was on Rachel's tray, it was what was clutching the tray. Rachel's fingers. Her nails were bright pink. Almost fuchsia.

Rachel had never used nail polish. As far as I knew, she was still biting her nails well below her fingertips, which made a coat of polish look like a brightly colored pea. Now, though, her nails were a vision: glossy, buffed, no cuticles in sight. She even had perfect little half-moons at the base.

I reached for a roll and stole a glance at my own nails. I don't do polish. The few times I tried, it chipped within minutes and I ended up scraping it off with my teeth. In fact, except for the brush in the shower, and the occasional file, I don't pay much attention to my nails. Where had Rachel learned?

I paid the cashier and headed for a table. The interior designer had made sure the place didn't look institutional: blond wood furniture, upholstered cushions, and lots of ferns. Twenty years ago, it would have been a bar. We unloaded our trays and sat down.

"Nice manicure," I said casually.

Rachel put her fork down and stretched out her fingers the way women do when they want to show off their hands. "You like it?"

"Very impressive." I stuffed a chunk of tomato in my mouth. "What inspired you?"

Suddenly Rachel's manner changed. She shrugged too quickly and wouldn't meet my eyes. "I—I just felt like it."

"Did Katie help you?"

She shook her head and slumped in her seat. I buttered my roll, wondering why she seemed so uneasy. Then, in a flash of understanding, it came to me. She'd been babysitting all day. "Julia Hauldren did it."

If it were possible for someone to slide so far under the table they'd disappear completely, that someone would have been Rachel.

I put down the knife, unprepared for the stab of jealousy that sliced through me. Why didn't Rachel come to me? True, I don't have much interest—or knowledge—about fake nails and manicures, but wasn't that one of those things a mother and daughter were supposed to do together? Not that my mother and I ever did. I couldn't even recall any frivolous shopping expeditions. She was always too busy. I'd resolved to be different with Rachel, to make sure we spent time doing lighthearted, fun things. What happened? Was I just too busy—like my mother? Or had my role been usurped?

I'd have to puzzle it out later. Rachel looked miserable, and it wasn't her fault. To be honest, it wasn't Julia's either. I might even be making too much of it. I dug down deep for a cheery smile. "It looks fabulous. And very professional."

Rachel brightened. "You really think so?"

I nodded. "Could you teach me how to do that?"

She straightened up and flashed me a smile. "Cool. Let's stop at the drugstore on the way home."

Chapter Fourteen

The third sniper attack happened July fourth.

David and his uncle, Willie, had come out that morning—after some trepidation, I got up my nerve and issued the invitation, which David promptly accepted. Dad joined us, and we spent the first part of the day at our village's Fourth of July celebration, the highlight of which is a slow-moving bicycle parade. A huge red fire truck, klaxon blaring, precedes an army of bikes, all of them festooned with ribbons, feathers, flowers, and whatever else kids have found to decorate them with. The procession slowly advances through town, where it meets up with another throng of kids and bikes from the other end of the village. In a clever pincer move, the two groups converge on the park for relay races, burgers, and pop. It's definitely small town, even corny, but I love it.

In the afternoon we trooped over to Susan's. Everyone was fascinated by Willie, especially Rachel, who, after her initial shyness, bombarded him with questions about life in Germany. Her curiosity made me realize how sheltered her life was. With the exception of Fouad, she hadn't come in contact with many people who weren't white, American, or middle-class.

It had been almost three months since David and I had seen each other. Taller than me by half a foot, he looked fit, healthy, and now that summer was here, nicely tanned. His angular face was balanced by deep blue eyes that had seen their share of sadness, but with his tan, his thick white hair seemed to glow. He looked happy to see me, but I found myself being too polite, treading carefully as I would with a guest.

The best part of the day was watching my father and Willie. They immediately settled themselves under the umbrella on Susan's patio, and within minutes, a cloud of smoke from my father's Havanas rose above their heads. It could have been an Impressionist painting: two elderly gentleman—my father, small and wiry, his bald head reflecting the sun as he bobbed in and out of the shade; Willie, tall, even formal in sports shirt and slacks. Both men were determined to overcome the language barrier, and between their Yiddish and Willie's pidgin English, they seemed to be succeeding. Willie periodically ran his hand through his thick white hair—now I knew which side of the family David's came from—and I saw lots of gestures.

The two men had a lot to talk about. Both were German Jews who'd gone through the war and bore the scars to prove it. My father had been drafted, while Willie was on the run from the Nazis. They shared something else as well. My father had been in love with Lisle, Willie's sister. David's mother. They'd had an affair before the war, but it ended when Lisle fell in love with David's father.

It was nearly eleven by the time we got home from the fireworks. Willie pled exhaustion, and I made up a bed for him on the family room couch. Afterward I tiptoed into the kitchen thinking I'd open a bottle of wine. As I rummaged in the drawer for the corkscrew, I saw the blinking red light of the answering machine. I wasn't expecting any calls. Rachel and Dad were with me; Barry was probably with Julia. I went to the machine. Three messages had come in. I punched Play.

"Hello. This is Mike Corbett from the *Trib*. We'd like a comment from you about the sniper attack for the morning edition. If you could give me a call—we're extending our deadline." Three phone numbers followed: the office, his home, and his cell.

Which sniper attack? Both had occurred weeks, even months, ago; why would a reporter be calling me for a comment now? I advanced to the next message. It was another reporter, a woman full of sound and fury. I didn't catch her name, but her question was clear. "Miss Foreman, did you happen to see the man described by the witness in Chicago at the Lake Forest oasis?" She, too, left three phone numbers.

What man? Where? There was one more message on my machine. I played it. "Miss Foreman, Detective Milanovich." His soft, honeyed voice was unmistakable. "Would you mind calling me as soon as you can?" He reeled off one number.

I checked the clock. It was too late for the news, and turning on the radio in the kitchen would disturb Willie. I rubbed the back of my neck. Then I hurried up to my office.

A minute later, I was reading the story on a local TV station's website. Without the prattle of reporters and anchors, the silence was eerie, and the website's powerful graphics made it more disturbing. A third shooting had occurred at the O'Hare oasis near Schiller Park, a rest stop off Interstate 294. The story was chillingly familiar. A green pickup with a camper shell had pulled into the oasis, circled the perimeter, then slowed less than fifty yards from the restaurant. A young single mother was coming out of the restaurant, her two children trailing behind her. The woman was shot twice, once through the chest and once in the throat. She died instantly. The pickup accelerated and raced out of the oasis.

I covered my eyes.

"What is it, Ellie?"

I hadn't heard David come in. I twisted around and pointed to the screen. He came over and read, then put his hand on my shoulder. "What does this mean?" he asked softly.

I took a breath. "I didn't tell you before, because I didn't get a chance, and well, I didn't think…I mean, who would have…."

"What's going on?"

I explained what happened to Daria Flynn. To his credit, David listened without interrupting. I was grateful. I didn't need any comments about putting myself in harm's way. "Apparently, there's been another attack."

"So I gather." He shook his head. "What an unnecessary loss. And on a holiday."

I nodded. David certainly knew about loss.

"So why are people calling you about it?"

"I'm not sure."

I figured it out when I read on. Buried deep in the fourth graf of the story was a female witness' claim that she'd seen the shooter. She was exiting the restaurant at about the same time as the victim, and had seen a flash of someone in the bed of the pickup just before the camper shell's window closed. The article described a white man wearing a tank top with something—a necklace or lanyard perhaps—around his neck. The witness had the impression of hair swept off his face with a headband, scarf, or bandana. And that the man had a beard. She also was able to get a few numbers of the license plate. The State Police had issued a number to call for anyone with more information.

"That's why," I said aloud.

David squinted at the monitor.

I gave him a minute to read it. "They want to know if I saw anyone fitting that description at the oasis where Daria was killed."

"And did you?" he asked gently.

I faced him, a mix of emotions roiling my stomach. "No."

⁓⁓⁓

Milanovich picked up on the first ring. The number had to be his cell.

I identified myself. "I heard about the shooting. I'm so sorry."

"Not as sorry as I am, Miss Foreman," he said wearily.

"Her kids—how old are they? I mean, what will they—"

"Let's not go there right now." His voice was tight.

I glanced over at David, who moved a pile of folders and eased himself down on the daybed.

"You see the news?"

"On the Internet."

"Then you know a witness saw someone in the back of the pickup."

"I just read that."

"It may have nothing to do with the Flynn girl. And the witness was at least fifty yards away from the vehicle. So the details are sketchy."

"The article on the website said long hair, tank top, bandana. And a beard."

"What do you know?" he said dryly. "They got it right this time."

I mentally replayed the events at the Lake Forest rest stop, trying to call back the details. I remembered the man with the cell phone, the elderly man and woman—

"Hey."

Milanovich picked up on it. "What?"

"A couple of teenagers came into the restaurant. They were wearing tank tops."

"What colors?"

"I don't—"

"Colors stay with you, Miss Foreman. Just relax. It'll come."

I took a slow breath and squeezed my eyes shut. "One of them was red, I think. Another was white. Or gray."

"Red? Are you sure?"

"I think so." Had the witness spotted something red on the shooter? "But I don't think any of them had a beard."

He ignored that. "How long after you saw them was the victim shot?"

"It couldn't have been more than two minutes."

"Did any of them come out while you and the victim were talking?"

I knew he was trying to work out whether one of them might have had enough time to exit the restaurant, make a run for the pickup, and swing back up the ramp firing a high-powered rifle. But I'd had a clear view of the door during our chat. No one had gone in or come out. I told him.

He grunted dismissively. "So…you see anyone else at the rest stop? Anyone at all? With or without a beard?"

I mentally replayed the rest of the tape. "No one." Then a thought occurred to me. "What about the pickup? Was it the same one as the other two?"

He didn't answer for a minute. Then, "It's already leaked to the media, so I'll tell you. It looks like this one matches a pickup that was stolen from the Ace Hardware parking lot in Glenview last winter."

A chill ran through me. The store was ten minutes from my house. "Oh, God. Does that mean the sniper—"

"It means nothing. Ace Hardware's a popular place. Lotta workmen stop in for supplies. The shooter had his pick."

"But this one is so close…."

"Not to Schaumburg, which was where the other one was stolen."

"Hold on. You said last winter?"

"I did."

"So this could be the same pickup that was used in the first shooting back in April."

"Miss Foreman—"

"But not in the second."

He cleared his throat. "So you never saw anyone fitting that description at the Lake Forest oasis?"

He hadn't answered. "No," I repeated.

"What about the driver? Anything come to you since we last talked?"

I thought back. The sun visor had been pulled down. I'd seen nothing.

"No." I chanced another question. "Detective, do you think all three attacks are linked?"

"I don't think anything, Ms. Foreman. I collect evidence."

"I get the feeling you think the same truck was used in the first and the third shooting, but not in Daria Flynn's."

"There are similarities," he conceded. "But there are differences, too." Which, by his abrupt silence, he wasn't about to tell me.

"I'm sorry I can't be more helpful, Detective. Is there anything I can do?"

"Just call if something else comes to you."

"I will." I looked over at David. He was trying hard to control his impatience. I should get off the phone.

I turned back to the computer. "Detective, are you—well—I suppose...no. It doesn't matter anymore. Forget it."

"Forget what, Ms. Foreman?"

I didn't know whether to say something. Tonight's events probably made it a moot point. But hadn't Milanovich just said to tell him if I remembered anything else? I gripped the phone. "I learned something up at Lake Geneva. I'm sure it has nothing to do with the case, and you may already know...."

"What is it?" he said tiredly. I wondered how many more calls he would be making this night.

"Well, I was talking to a waitress at the Lodge—that's where I'm shooting the video."

"Yes."

"Well, apparently, one of the sons of a wealthy family up there met Daria Flynn for drinks at the Lodge right before her death." I hesitated. "And given that she and her boyfriend had a fight, a boyfriend who still isn't—"

"Who was this man, Ms. Foreman?"

"You don't know?"

"I don't have time for games," he said impatiently.

"I'm just asking whether you already know about this—this situation."

He cleared his throat. "The name, Miss Foreman."

I took a breath. "Luke. Luke Sutton."

"Sutton?" He didn't say anything for a moment. Then, "I'll look into it."

"Okay. But like I said, I don't think—"

"Thank you for the information, Ms. Foreman. Have a good night." He disconnected.

I held the phone for a minute, then put it back on the base. A moment later, a pair of hands massaged my neck. "All done now?"

I stretched, then reached back and covered David's hand with mine. "For tonight."

"What are your plans? For the rest of the night, that is?"

I twisted around. "Don't think I have any. Why? You have an idea?"

He smiled, bent down, and kissed me. I registered the familiarity of his lips, the lingering smell of his cologne—a new musky scent. When had he switched from Aramis? I barely had time to turn off the computer before he pulled me out of the chair and steered me toward the bedroom.

Chapter Fifteen

I rubbed grit out of my eyes the next morning, wondering why it seems to show up only in summer. Something to do with sweat, I guessed. Or humidity. Today's weather augured both. It was only eight, but the sun was blindingly harsh, and a southerly wind gusted in hot, angry air. I flipped on the air conditioning.

I hadn't slept much, and when I did, unsettling dreams tumbled through my brain. There had been a lot of red in one, followed by a hiss of air that at first I thought was a tire deflating. Then the hiss turned into Daria Flynn's last breath, and I watched her collapse in slow motion. I came awake all at once.

When I got downstairs, Rachel was already gone, and the note, explaining she was at Julia's, was the same one she'd written the other day, except that she'd scratched out "Wednesday" and written in "Friday." Underneath her scrawl was David's careful penmanship: "Out for a run." The splash of running water from the bathroom told me Willie was showering.

I turned on the TV in the family room. The latest sniper attack was all over the news. After a rehash of the events, illustrated with tape, the anchorman pondered whether the third Chicago shooting would affect summer travel. There was file footage of the DC and Ohio sniper attacks a few years ago. "Is this the beginning of a new wave?" the anchor posed in his wrap-up. "Should you change your vacation plans?"

I went back into the kitchen, filled the coffeepot with water, and opened the cabinet where I keep coffee and filters.

"Damn."

I barely had enough for two cups. Sighing, I threw on a pair of sandals, snatched my purse, and ran out to the car.

In the grocery store, I grabbed a cart without thinking and steered it to the coffee aisle. We were planning to meet Dad for brunch later, so I didn't need much more than a can of French Roast. After dropping the coffee in my cart, though, I started to wander through the aisles. I wasn't really conscious where I was headed. Something was closing in. Something I didn't want to confront. Was it the sniper attack?

I ended up opposite the caviar in the gourmet food aisle. At least a dozen small jars, both red and black, lined the shelf. I reached up, took one, and checked the price. Twenty-eight dollars. Were they kidding? I started to put it back. Then I stopped. I wanted the caviar. I deserved it. I looked carefully up and down the aisle. I wouldn't necessarily have to pay for it; no one would know. I opened my bag.

All at once, a familiar itchy sensation crawled over me, and awareness kicked in. Years ago I used to shoplift. I like to think I was sick during that period of my life, and in a way, I was. My marriage was collapsing, my mother was dying, and I felt inadequate as a mother to Rachel. Stealing was the only way I knew to make myself feel better. The high, the rush of taking something and getting away with it, was exhilarating. After a while, I began to crave it. I tried to convince myself it wasn't so bad; I never took anything expensive. Just candy, pens, the occasional bracelet.

The problem was it was a crime. And it became an even bigger problem when I was caught. One day a department store sales clerk saw me stealing a blouse. She called security; security called the cops. Barry eventually came to the rescue, and I joined a twelve step program. I learned—or so I thought—to control my impulses. I got divorced. I buried my mother. Gradually the compulsion subsided. So why was it back today?

I gripped the cart with a clenched fist. The caviar was in my other hand, grinning at me, daring me to palm it. I squeezed my eyes shut. As I did, an image of David flew into my mind. Not just David. David and me in bed. Last night. And with it came a memory.

Decades ago, before I was married, I went to southern Illinois to shoot part of a documentary for Channel Eleven, the public television in Chicago. I drove down the night before, planning to meet the crew in the morning. That evening I stopped into the hotel bar—a disco, really—where a two-man band played a medley of Loggins and Messina. They weren't bad, and after three whiskey sours, they were even better. In the dim light, the lead singer looked just enough like Kenny Loggins that I started to imagine things. He apparently did, too, because, a few hours after the last set, we ended up in his bed.

The next morning, in addition to a hangover, I was nursing a powerful case of bedder's remorse. In daylight, the singer didn't look a thing like Kenny Loggins. He looked like the stranger he was. And while I certainly wasn't a prude, I felt waves of shame sweep over me. I fled back to my room and showered for about an hour. Eventually I forgave myself, but I vowed never again to sleep with a man I didn't love.

And I didn't. Until last night.

I thought I wanted to. I'd invited David out to visit. I'd even made room for his uncle. I tried to summon up the heat I used to feel, and for a short time, I pretended it was there. When he fondled my breasts, I arched up to meet him. And when his hands found my hips and rocked into me, the tension built.

But then, without warning, the feeling disappeared. I didn't want to make love. The problem was we were already so far into it, I didn't know how to stop. I sank back against the bed, my muscles suddenly lethargic. His hands felt rough. His weight suffocating. I went through with it anyway. I tried not to dwell on it, and I wondered how much longer he would take. Eventually he finished, but it was perfunctory.

Afterward David lay on his side, his expression shuttling between uncertainty and sorrow. I steeled myself for the inevitable confrontation, but it never came. At one point he lifted his eyebrows fractionally, but when I didn't say anything, he sighed quietly, almost imperceptibly, and rolled away from me. I got up and took a shower.

Now, in the store, my hand clutched the cart's handlebar so tightly my knuckles went white. If I let go, even for a second, the caviar would end up in my bag. I was afraid to look at the caviar. I was afraid to look away. My legs felt like they'd been nailed to the floor.

"Ellie...how are you?"

The voice was as sharp as a siren. I whipped around. A woman wheeled her cart up to me. I knew her. We worked out together.

"Cindy. Hi. I—I'm good," I said haltingly. "How are you?"

She grabbed her shoulder-length hair and flipped it to one side. "You know. Same old same old." She paused. "I haven't seen you at Bodyworks recently."

Her voice came at me from a distance. Did she know how close I was to the edge? I swallowed. "I've been—working on—on a new show. You know. Up at the crack of dawn."

She flashed me a smile. "I know how that is. I just finished my shift."

I seemed to remember she was a nurse. She hesitated for a moment, glanced over at the caviar, then at me. I held my breath. She knew. She must. I waited for the accusation. Instead, she gave her cart a little push. "Well, nice running into you. See you in class."

I nodded. At least I think I did. She wheeled her cart to the end of the aisle and disappeared. I put the caviar back on the shelf and, before I could think about it, shoved my cart forward. When I reached the front of the store, I raced to the express lane, threw the coffee on the belt, and thanked God for putting Cindy in my path.

Chapter Sixteen

I was still shaky when I got home. I'd have to talk to David. Soon. For now, though, I was grateful I hadn't done anything foolish. I got out of the car, grabbed the coffee, and started inside.

The squeak of a noisy suspension made me turn around. A red pickup with rust stains on its body rounded the corner and rolled up the driveway. As Fouad slid out of the car, I glanced at my shaggy lawn. "I've missed you," I said.

"Hello, Ellie." He went to the back of the pickup and unloaded the lawnmower, hedge clippers, and pruning shears.

"Where have you been?"

He carried the tools over to the flower bed without answering. I watched him pinch dead petunias.

"Fouad? What's wrong?"

It was early, the heat of the day still ahead, but beads of sweat had already popped out on his forehead. He pulled out a handkerchief and wiped his brow. Then he shook his head, his expression so mournful that for the first time since I'd known him, I thought he might break down. "It is Ahmed."

Despite the heat, a chill spread over me. "He—he—did he go to Iraq?"

Fouad dabbed at his forehead with the handkerchief. "I do not know."

"What do you mean?"

"About a week ago we woke up, and he was gone. We do not know where he is."

That didn't sound like the responsible student I'd heard so much about. "What happened?"

Fouad didn't answer. Then he sighed. "There was an argument. He and Hayat—no, that's not fair. All of us argued."

"About Iraq?"

"His girlfriend. Iraq. His future. It ended badly. When we woke up the next morning, he was gone. Clothes. Passport. Everything." Fouad covered his eyes with his hand. I could tell he was struggling to hold himself together.

"What about Natalie? Does she know anything?" Ahmed's sister was two years younger. Fouad used to tell me how close they were.

"He did not confide in her. Or so she claims."

"Oh, Fouad. I'm so sorry."

He shook his head again and patted his eyes with the handkerchief. Then he balled it up and jammed it into his pocket. "When I came to this country, I didn't think about the consequences of raising children. I worried about their safety. Their comfort. Their happiness. But I did not think that I was raising half-breeds—"

"That's a harsh label," I interrupted. Had that come from Ahmed?

"It is the truth. They are not fully American, nor are they Syrian—or, in our case, Iraqi. We've stripped away their heritage and given them McDonald's and the mall in its place. Is it any wonder they do not know who they are?"

"But Ahmed and Natalie have achieved so much. Johns Hopkins. Duke. I know how proud you are of them."

"They speak English with no accent. They wear the right clothes. They buy the right toys. But you do not see the dark side. At the first sign of trouble, they are labeled. Attacked. Or even worse, ignored. The struggle, it is subtle—and insidious. How can I blame them for floundering?"

"Don't you think you might be too hard on yourself? And Ahmed? He's intelligent. And talented. He'll find his way, maybe sooner than you think. And no matter how he's feeling right now, he knows in his heart the enormous sacrifices you've made."

"No." He looked at me, his dark eyes sad. "I think I have failed, Ellie."

A lump rose in my throat. I pushed it down. I wished I'd had a quote from the Koran. Fouad usually found solace in it. "What can I do?"

He closed his eyes. "I do not know."

"Have you called the police? Filed a missing persons report?"

His eyes opened, a bitter edge sweeping across them. "They are not convinced he's missing."

"That's crazy. Why not?"

"They made a few calls. He was working at the Senior Center clinic, you know...."

I didn't, but I nodded.

"They say he is twenty-one. Has a mind of his own. He will turn up, they say. I should not worry. But...." His eyes narrowed. "If his name was not Ahmed, I am sure they would be trying harder."

"What about his girlfriend? Did you call her?"

Fouad clamped his jaw tight. "We do not know where she lives. She has been—well, as you know, Hayat has not—we called Johns Hopkins to try to find out her parents' names. Perhaps a phone number. But they would not release any information. Privacy issues, they say."

"What did you say when you called?"

He took a few steps back toward the flower bed, looking confused. "The truth, of course."

I frowned, imagining Fouad or Hayat with their thick accents trying to explain to a bureaucrat that their son was missing. "What's her name? Ahmed's girlfriend?"

"Rana. Al Qasim. She calls herself Ronnie, I believe."

I folded my arms. Our eyes locked.

Fouad tipped his head to the side. "What is it, Ellie?" He peered at me across the flower bed.

It was my turn to shake my head but, apparently, it didn't mask my expression.

"I know that look on your face. You have something in mind."

⌐⌐⌐

I dropped David and Willie at the airport without talking to David. I didn't know how to begin. Should I tell him that the notion of life as fundamentally joyful was as elusive to me as a lifeboat in a stormy sea? That I didn't believe I deserved love? Or intimacy? We were practiced at the art of evasion, anyway. If it was never said, it wouldn't need to be countered, defended, or retracted. So I said nothing, and smiled a little too brightly when I kissed him good-bye.

Back home that afternoon, the heat seemed to flatten everything, muting colors and muffling noise. Even the dust motes seemed lethargic. I washed dishes, wishing Rachel was home. We could pack up and go to the pool. Or the beach. If she wasn't already there with Julia.

I trudged upstairs to my office and booted up the computer. While I waited, I looked out at the honey locust tree on my front lawn. Usually its fronds shimmer in the sun, glazing the room with sparks of light. But there was no breeze today, and its leaves drooped listlessly. I swiveled around, noting the litter of files on the daybed, the picture of David on a shelf, the delicate ceramic shoe Susan gave me a few years ago.

Rachel would be gone in a few years. The house would be too big. And even more silent. Maybe I should sell and buy something smaller. Move back into the city. Isn't that what most empty nesters do? But what if you were alone? Was there a special housing development for people who'd failed at relationships?

I turned back to the computer and checked the news. A rash of new stories had proliferated overnight, everything from so-called forensics experts speculating how the three sniper attacks were related, to conspiracy buffs sure they were politically motivated, to religious nuts predicting the end of the world. In a carefully worded statement, a State Police spokesperson neither confirmed nor denied any links between the attacks, saying only that they were "examining the evidence and looking for leads." He went on to caution the public not to change their travel plans or to panic.

Which, of course, was precisely what the media were trying to get everyone to do. I read quotes from people regretting that family reunions had been canceled, or that weddings were now up in the air. A suburban mayor held a press conference to encourage residents to stay put this summer "safe and sound" in their backyards. There was even one of those interactive polls. "Vote yes, if you're going to change your vacation plans. See results instantly!"

The operative theme was fear. Sensationalism. And the sense of urgency was palpable. The media played up the similarities between the three attacks, starting with the fact that the victims were young women, they'd all been shot at a highway oasis by someone in a green pickup, and all with some kind of high-powered rifle. Whether they were all the work of one gunman didn't seem to matter. I got up and paced around the room. The problem was that sensationalism wouldn't do anything to lighten Irene Flynn's grief. Or that of the children who'd lost their mothers.

⌐⌐⌐

A few minutes later I clicked onto the Johns Hopkins website. Five minutes after searching the site, I dialed a number. A female voice answered confidently. "Student Affairs."

Was that deliberate? An inside joke?

"Hello." I'd tried something similar to this a year or so ago, and it worked. I took a breath and plunged in. "My name is Ellie Foreman, and I have kind of a strange situation here."

"Uh—oh—I'm not sure I understand." She had that distinctive Baltimore—or was it Baldmer—accent, the one with rounded "o's" and the occasional "hon" tacked on to the end of a sentence, but only if you were a favored personage.

"I live in Chicago, but I seem to have found a wallet that belongs to one of your students. There's some money in it, and a couple of credit cards, and a student ID."

"Yes?" This woman sounded clueless. Was that a plus or an obstacle?

"I'd like to return the wallet, but given that it's summer, I'm sure most of the students are gone. And since I found it in Chicago, I'm thinking the owner might be out here. But there's no address or phone number in the wallet. Which is why I'm hoping you can help me."

"You know, this really isn't the right department—"

"The student's name is Rana Al Qasim. Here…let me spell it for you."

"Hold on," the voice said. "I'm not sure—"

Keep talking, Ellie. "It seems to me, at least, that she—or he…" I added hastily, "…would want to know it's been found. It wasn't a lot of money. About a hundred dollars. But I guess, for a student, it could be. A lot, I mean. I'd hate her—or him—to think it's been stolen."

There was silence on the other end of the line. Then I heard a sigh. "What did you say your name was?"

Progress! I repeated my name. "As I said, I'm in Chicago, and if Rana lives here, or she—or he—is visiting here, and lost their wallet, they're probably very upset."

"Look, what I'm going to do is transfer—"

I barreled on. "You just can't be too careful these days, with all this identity theft, you know? Rana is probably going crazy. I'd hate for them to have to call the credit bureaus and Social Security. My wallet was stolen last year, and I spent months sorting it out. If there was just some way you could give me a phone number…."

"I can't do that."

"Of course you can't. I understand." I hesitated a beat. "But what if I give you *my* number and you called Rana's family—and then they can get in touch with *me*. I'm not going anywhere. Of course, that's a roundabout way to do things, but it's better than going through a lot of red tape, don't you think? I mean, we're just talking about a wallet here."

"I don't know."

I waited, then sighed theatrically. "I suppose I could always send it to you in the mail. But if Rana is here in Chicago…you know…visiting or something…well, that just seems like a waste of time. And effort. Are you sure you can't just call them and have them call me?"

"Hold on a minute."

I drummed my fingers on my desk. The recorded music in the background was infuriatingly cheerful. She was gone so long I started to despair. Finally, she clicked back on.

"Miss Foreman?"

"Yes?"

"Rana Al Qasim lives in Phoenix, Arizona."

Phoenix?

"Her parents' number is 602-842-9387."

"Thank you so much. You're terrific."

I heard her take a breath. "Listen, do me a favor, hon."

Hon? "Anything."

"You didn't get her number from this department."

"Of course not."

"And next time, you might want to work on your story. Parts of it were a little lame."

Chapter Seventeen

A thousand points of light. Once the rallying cry of a Republican administration, it was an apt description of the gala at the Lodge. A team of party planners had transformed the ballroom on the second floor into a forest that included trees, grassy paths, and, in one corner, a babbling brook with replicas of frolicking woodland creatures. Sewn through the tree branches were tiny Italian lights that twinkled in the air currents. Dozens of small tables were covered with silk cloths and topped with centerpieces that were garlands of green. Pastel blossoms were woven through them, and lit tapers flickered nearby. A harpist in a cream-colored gown strummed quietly at one end of the room, while a trio of musicians warmed up at the other. Republican or not, the effect was stunning. I expected Rosalind or Puck to bound out of the woods any second.

A crowd of nearly two hundred well-heeled people filled the room. The women, formally dressed and weighed down by jewelry that had probably been brought out of storage, glittered as gaily as the Italian lights, but the men, in tuxedos that differed only in their choice of cummerbund, all bore a resemblance to Alistair Cooke. There was probably enough wealth concentrated in that room to pay off the national debt. Even the waiters reeked of substance.

I wandered through the crowd, the scents of designer perfumes breaking over me. I was feeling rather elegant myself; I'd broken down and bought a new pantsuit—a two-piece outfit made from silky, ivory material. Its fitted bodice actually made me look like I had a shape. Rachel had—rather expertly, I thought—pulled my hair up into a sophisticated twist, leaving tendrils curling down my cheeks. She'd done my nails as well. Since we would be shooting late, the Lodge had comped us rooms, and when I put on my makeup earlier, I decided I still cleaned up pretty well.

Now, I looked around searching for Mac and the crew. The décor, while lush, would wreak havoc with the lighting. Shadows from the artificial trees would be problems, and the Italian lights might wash out completely. We would be using a Frezzi attached to the camera for close-ups, but we'd have to be careful if we shot wide. It was too costly to light the entire ballroom, so we planned to make do by riding the gain and opening the iris. But it was a risky proposition. Too much of either would make the shots fuzzy or overexposed.

I found Mac with the harpist, shooting a close-up of her fingers plucking the strings. Despite his distaste for formalwear, he looked handsome in his tux; he cleaned up pretty well, too.

After discussing the lighting, we decided to try an establishing shot anyway. Hank could play with it in post, and if it didn't work, we would cover the scene with B-roll. Mac would shoot as many close-ups as he could, after which we'd throw up some lights in the hall for interviews.

As Mac and the crew drifted away, a waiter passed with a tray of drinks. I took a glass of wine, then stepped back to let a generously proportioned woman take hers. As the waiter handed her a cocktail napkin, I studied her outfit: a mint green gown with matching feathered boa. I sipped my wine. I thought feathered boas had been put out of their misery forty years ago.

The woman took a long pull on her drink, then waved to someone I couldn't see. She made a quarter turn and waved to someone else. Then, with unmistakable disdain, she muttered under her breath, "Wouldn't lift a goddamn finger for any one of them if they were drowning in the lake."

I tried to swallow a giggle, but something resembling a bleat came out of my mouth. The woman whipped around. Her face was unnaturally red, and her hair contained an excess of henna, but her features were even and attractive. You could tell she'd been a beauty in her youth. A Kathy Bates type, now in her sixties.

Her gaze swept over me. I couldn't tell if she was worried about what she said or couldn't care less. She hiked her shoulders and draped the boa more snugly around her. "Nice outfit," she said. "You get it just for this?"

I felt my eyebrows arch. "How did you know?"

She smiled knowingly. "I know everyone up here. But I've never seen you."

An elderly man brushed by her. "How are you, Henry?" She clasped his arm, forcing him to stop.

He pasted on a smile. "Willetta."

"It's been entirely too long since I've seen you," she gushed. His smile wavered. Her face took on a mournful cast. "How are you bearing up?"

The man mumbled something I couldn't hear, then politely disengaged his arm. As he disappeared into the crowd, she shook her head. "Hasn't been the same since his wife died. It's a wonder he can get himself dressed in the morning. And to think he built Briarly Manufacturing from the ground up." She turned back to me.

"Who are you?" I asked.

"You first. That's how it works."

"Ellie Foreman. I'm a video producer from Chicago. I'm shooting a documentary about the Lodge."

"Show business?" An eager expression came over her face.

"Not really. Corporate videos."

She seemed not to have heard. She drained her wine, deposited it on the tray of a passing waiter, and reached for another. "As a matter of fact, I used to be in show business."

"Is that so," I said without much enthusiasm. Everyone's a performer.

"I don't talk about it much. Especially around here." She rolled her eyes. "But you—well...." She might just as well have said, *You're an outsider—you don't count.* "I come from the Carlucci family."

I blinked.

"You've heard of them, of course."

The Barrymores, the Fondas, the Baldwins. But the Carluccis? "I'm afraid not."

"Well, my dear, you should have. They were the star acrobats of the Big Top circus."

"Circus performers?"

She flicked the tail of her boa. "My grandfather came over from Italy at the invitation of Lester Cruickshank," she said proudly. "He owned Big Top and saw Grandpa perform in Europe. My father and uncles took over when he retired. I grew up there."

"You lived with the circus?"

"Yes, but I was more interested in the horses and elephants than the tightrope. I wanted to be the girl who rode bareback."

I remembered what the realtor at the Lodge said about Delavan being the winter circus capital of the country. "Did you live in Delavan?"

She nodded. "I did indeed. Met George—my late husband—over here one Christmas. It was love at first sight." She snapped her fingers. "That was it for the circus." She appraised me with grudging respect. "So you're from Chicago?"

"The North Shore." I paused. "Boy, you sure give those jokes about running away and joining the circus new meaning."

"I can do you one better. Did you know they once buried an elephant in Lake Delavan?"

My mouth opened. She grinned. "I'm Willetta Carlucci Emerson. What did you say your name was?"

"Ellie Foreman."

"Now why does that name sound familiar?" She took a canapé from a passing waiter. The waiter handed her a napkin. She chewed the appetizer. "Haven't I seen you somewhere? On TV?"

I didn't answer.

"In the papers?"

I shrugged.

She brightened. "You're the woman who was with the poor Flynn girl! On TV!"

I nodded glumly.

"You were standing next to her when she died."

"It wasn't a great day."

"I understand. My house was robbed once. I wasn't home, but I couldn't sleep for weeks afterward. You feel so—so vulnerable." She nodded theatrically. "Now, tell me something. Do they think all the shootings are related?" She shivered. "Because if they are, well—"

"They're not saying." This wasn't the place to analyze the minutiae of the sniper attacks. "Did you know Daria?"

"Everyone knows everyone up here." As if to prove the point, she waved to a woman a few feet away. "A very sweet girl, I understand. Ambitious, too."

"Ambitious?"

"She was a chef, or some such, at the Geneva Inn. Quite good. I've eaten there more than once. Never had a bad meal. She could have gone anywhere." She sniffed. "Makes you wonder why she stuck around."

"Why did she?"

"Family, I imagine." Willetta shook her head. "Such a tragedy. Are the police any closer to finding the guy?"

"They have a description of a possible suspect."

"I see." She went back to scanning the crowd. "Well, let's not chat about such depressing subjects, shall we?" Seconds later, she seized the arm of a passing man.

The man stopped. When he recognized who had corralled him, he gave her a big smile. She patted her hair coquettishly.

I could see why. Although he had to be in his seventies, he was remarkably well preserved. Not much hair, except for a fringe around the back, but a well-shaped head, bright blue eyes, strong chin.

"Chuck, where have you been keeping yourself? I haven't seen you in days." She turned to me. "This is my neighbor. We share a dock. Chuck, this is Ellie."

"A pleasure." He flashed a smile and extended his hand. We shook. He turned back to Willetta. "I found a new book about my man. Been reading it all week."

At my puzzled look, Willetta explained. "Now that he's retired, Chuck spends all his time reading about Thomas Jefferson."

"Now Willetta..." he cut in. "That's not fair. I still work. A little." He winked at me.

Willetta giggled and stroked her boa. "Chuck happens to be the foremost authority on Thomas Jefferson around here."

I perked up. Someone who was interested in something besides making and spending money, or talking about others who did.

"You know who he was, of course?" he asked.

I wasn't sure if he was serious, although given what they're teaching in school these days, he could have been. "Third president. Scientist. Inventor. Intellectual. Wrote the Declaration of Independence. Owned slaves but had a long-term relationship with one of them. Died on July fourth, fifty years after the Declaration." I stopped, having exhausted everything I knew about the man.

He nodded approval. "It's reassuring that someone still has a patina of knowledge about great figures of history."

I fidgeted, aware he was both complimenting and insulting me.

"You mentioned the sciences," he went on. "But did you know the man pioneered aspects of archeology, paleontology, and botany that still are considered important today?"

"No, I didn't."

"Or that he was, in effect, the first American commissioner of patents?"

I shook my head.

"Or that Mr. Jefferson, as he was wont to be called, spoke five languages and was the president of the American Philosophical Society?"

"Sounds like a Type-A."

"Actually," he laughed, "Jefferson was fairly…laid back, I think is the term you use. So much so that he left no treatise, no document summarizing his take on life. Or his political philosophy. All we're left with are educated guesses about his values."

"What about the Declaration of Independence? That's a pretty clear statement."

"A beautiful document, but written for specific times and circumstances. Weaving together contributions by several people."

"Wait a minute. Are you saying the Declaration was a work by committee?"

"Exactly. Jefferson was drafted into the process at the last minute. Not because he'd been vocal on the issues. In fact, he was known as the quiet member of Congress. It's questionable whether he believed in equality at all. But he was a good writer and they needed one."

"Behind every politician is a good speech writer," I cracked.

He peered at me. "Are you a lover of history?"

"I think it gives us perspective on the present."

"And what do you do? In the present?"

A waiter passed behind Willetta with only one glass of champagne on his tray. Chuck and another man reached for it at the same time. Chuck grabbed it first and took a long sip. The other man shot Chuck a withering look, then backed away. Chuck gave him his back. "Now what is it you do?"

I put my empty glass on the tray, feeling suddenly cold. "I—I'm a video producer," I said cautiously.

"Ahh. And what are you doing here?"

I told him about the video. He nodded a few times and seemed interested. It was as if the incident with the other man had never happened.

A thought occurred to me. "Would either of you be willing to talk about your history in Lake Geneva on camera? I'd love to hear more about the circus and its influence on the area." I turned to Chuck. "I take it you've lived here a long time, too?"

"Every summer since I was born."

"And always reading," Willetta chimed in.

"Not much else to do, if you're not a boater."

"You don't like the lake?"

"Not any...." He paused. "You can't stay on the water all the time. So I read." He shrugged. "Helps beat the heat."

"I thought the lake keeps things cool. Like in Chicago."

"There's a difference between Lake Michigan and our little pond. There are days when you think you've stumbled into Death Valley."

"Remember the summer of fifty-seven, Chuck?" Willetta brushed her hand across his arm. "Even the ice didn't help."

"Ice?" I looked from Willetta to Chuck.

"At the beginning of each summer," Chuck explained, "people would drag large blocks of ice into their basements. They'd set fans up and let the cool air circulate through the house."

"The ice man always came around Memorial Day," Willetta added.

"Where did the ice come from?"

"The lake."

"Lake Geneva?"

Chuck nodded. "The lake freezes solid every winter. Before it thawed, men would chop up large chunks of it and store them in an ice house until summer. By the end of August, of course, most of it was melted." He smiled genially. "At one time ice was a huge business. Lake Geneva ice was transported as far south as Chicago."

"I had no idea how much history there is up here. Would it—could I—would it be possible to see an ice house? Maybe there's a way to include it in the video."

"We have an ice house," Chuck began, "but it's been converted into a tool shed."

"I'd love to see it."

He looked me over, then balanced his drink in one hand and fished out a card from his pocket. "Well, I'm in and out a lot, but why don't you call my assistant and we'll see if we can set something up."

"I'll do that." I smiled. "Thanks."

He nodded, then turned away to greet someone else.

"What an interesting man," I said to Willetta.

"The best neighbor I've ever had."

It was only when I held up the card to read his full name that I gasped.

Chapter Eighteen

"What's wrong?" Willetta wrapped her hands around her wineglass.

"Chuck..." I spat out. "He's Charles Sutton."

"Charles Sutton the Third."

I looked at his retreating back.

"What's wrong, woman?" Willetta repeated. "You look like you've just seen a ghost."

I made some quick calculations. Chuck was in his seventies. Luke Sutton looked somewhere in his forties. Which meant Chuck was Luke Sutton's father. I tried to recover. "It's just—well, I've heard the name."

"Not surprising, given who they are." She eyed me carefully. "Or were. Before the tragedy, of course."

"What tragedy?"

"And now, with his wife, Gloria...." She looked at me meaningfully.

Mrs. Charles Sutton. Luke Sutton's mother. "Which one is she?"

Willetta waved a hand. "Oh, Gloria's not here. She doesn't— she keeps to herself. Rarely leaves the house." Willetta peered at me. "You didn't know?"

I shook my head.

"But you're from the North Shore. Chuck and Gloria live in Lake Forest during the winter."

"That's all well and good, but I don't know what you're talking about."

"I tell you what. You come on over to my place sometime. I have all sorts of pictures and stories about the way Lake Geneva used to be. And what happened around here. You can even bring your camera if you want. I live next door to the Suttons, by the way. I'm in the book."

"Thanks."

She winked at me, then pulled her boa more snugly across her broad shoulders and swished away.

I watched her go, grateful she was so willing to share information. I couldn't help but be curious about the Suttons. And surprised. Charles Sutton was, except for the champagne incident, charming. Not at all the evil robber baron I'd imagined. And while his son, Luke, was a different matter, my curiosity about the family and the tragedy they'd suffered was piqued.

I turned around, a trickle of sweat inching down between my shoulderblades. The press of people, the wine, the close air were making me uncomfortably warm. I caught a glimpse of glasses on a tray and zeroed in on them. When I got there, I discovered Pari Noskin Taichert, clad in a tuxedo, passing drinks with a practiced smile. Of course. The Lodge would be using all their staff to work the gala. Happily, there was one glass left on the tray.

"Hello, Pari."

She looked over, but when she recognized me, her hostess smile disappeared.

"I said, 'Hello, Pari.'"

She continued to ignore me.

I sidestepped around to her face. "Excuse me, but—"

"Just leave me alone." She handed the last glass to a man whose forehead was bathed in sweat.

I'm not sure if it was the tone of her voice or the fact I was hot and cranky and fed up with trying to be charming to people who didn't care about me, but I snapped. Impulsively, I grabbed the empty tray from her hands and hugged it to my chest.

Pari went rigid.

"Gimme that back. You can't do that. I'll lose my job for sure."

She reached for the tray, but I held on to it. "Not until you tell me why you're so angry."

"You're crazy, lady." There was a desperate quality to her voice. "Give me that back!" I knew if she made a grab for it, and I didn't relinquish it, we could end up making a scene. Which would not be helpful—for either of us. She seemed to know it, too, and stood uncertainly. A man waved an empty glass toward me. I held out the tray. He deposited it with a frown, as if he knew something was wrong but didn't know quite what.

Pari made another attempt to snatch the tray from me, but I grabbed the empty glass and swooped the tray out of reach. "Talk and you get it back."

She shot me another dark look and scanned the crowd. Then in a voice so low I could barely hear her, she said, "Why'd you go to the police? I ast you not to."

"Come on. You knew I would."

"Yeah, well, Chief Saclarides was all over me like the skin on an onion. And now everybody thinks I'm a snitch. No one'll talk to me. I probably won't last another three days here."

"Pari, it was the right thing to do."

"Easy for you to say."

"Calm down. In the final analysis, it wasn't even very important."

A woman in a tight black sheath cut me off and set down an almost full glass of red wine on the tray. I guess she didn't like the vintage. Before moving on, she looked down her nose at me as if to deplore the quality of the hired help.

"Since the last shooting, the police are going in a completely different direction. They even have a lead on a suspect."

Pari glared at me, obviously unimpressed with my analysis. "That don't help me much."

I understood what she was saying. In her mind, I'd undermined her at her job. Made her an "untrustworthy." Even though she was the one who first volunteered the gossip.

"Pari. If something happens—if you lose your job—I want you to call me. I'll help you out. Let me get you my card. They're out in the hall." I loosened my hold on the tray.

She blocked my path. "I don't need charity from you. What I need is for you to go away and leave me be." With that she snatched the tray out of my hands. The movement was so abrupt that the glass of red wine on the tray went flying, hit the floor, and shattered. Splattering the front of my outfit.

A moment of shocked silence followed. Pari scowled defiantly, as if daring me to make a scene. Then, clutching the tray in front of her, she turned on her heel and was gone.

I caught my breath and looked down. Big splotches of red and pink were spreading across my new silk pantsuit. It was so saturated in some spots that the wet penetrated down to my skin. To make matters worse, people's gazes were drawn to the spectacle, and I was the object of unwelcome attention. They probably thought I was too drunk to hold my liquor.

Trying to be as inconspicuous as a woman in an ivory-colored wine-stained outfit could be. I pushed my way through the crowd. I wondered if I even cared. I didn't know most of these people, and with the exception of Willetta Emerson, I wasn't sure I liked the ones I did. But I was out the cost of a new outfit, and I did care about that. I sighed. The way my luck was going, the next person I'd run into would be Luke Sutton.

↝↜↝

If being a little psychic is like being a little pregnant, I should have been able to bend a spoon. It wasn't Luke Sutton standing in the hall, but rather, the next best—or worst—thing, depending on your perspective. Jimmy Saclarides, Lake Geneva's chief of police and the man who'd been riding shotgun in Luke Sutton's plane, was lounging against the railing.

He nodded in recognition. "Evening, Miss Foreman."

I'd been hurrying to the ladies' room, but, in truth, there wasn't much I could do about the wine stains. The material was silk; I couldn't soak it in cold water. If there was any chance of reclaiming my outfit, I'd have to depend on the kindness of dry cleaners. I made a right turn and veered toward Jimmy. "You have a habit of turning up when I least expect it."

"That's exactly what the guy said when I caught him ripping off the bank." He smiled affably.

The amusement in his eyes surprised me.

He looked toward Mac, who had set up at the end of the hall. A couple had just finished their sound bites and were strolling back into the ballroom. "Working tonight?"

"Just trying to get some 'color.'"

He swirled the amber liquid in his glass. Bourbon, I wondered. Or scotch. "Color? Like Jimmy Piersall?"

"Excuse me?"

"Piersall, the baseball player. My namesake. After his playing days were over, he was the color man on the Sox broadcasts." He laughed. "God knows they needed something."

"I wouldn't know. I'm a Cubs fan."

"It figures." He smiled again. Then his attention focused on my outfit. "Those red—or are they pink—designs are, er, interesting. You get 'em done just for tonight?"

I felt my cheeks get hot.

"You want to talk about it?"

Something in the way he said it made me think he wasn't talking about my outfit. This was one of those good news–bad news situations. The good news was that someone in Lake Geneva actually seemed pleased to see me. The bad news was it was one of the people about whom I had the most misgivings. Jimmy Saclarides had apparently given Pari a hard time about talking to me. And though he didn't seem to be very aggressive about it, theoretically he was working the case with Milanovich. He *was* the chief of police. For all I knew, he could have been furious Pari talked to me rather than going directly to him.

Did that mean he didn't know about any meetings between Daria and Luke Sutton? Unlikely. If Luke and Jimmy were as close as I thought, it was possible—even probable—he would have known about their connection from the start. So why had it fallen on my shoulders to reveal it? Was Jimmy covering for his friend's affair? And if so, why?

I crossed my arms. Despite the absence of evidence tying Luke to Daria, despite his title, despite his apparent kindliness, I didn't trust Jimmy Saclarides. "Where's your friend tonight?"

He took a casual sip of his drink. Too casual. "Luke never comes to things like this. At least since he's been back."

He didn't have to ask who I was talking about. "What do you mean 'back'?"

"He's been living out West. Just moved back a year ago."

He looked past me, his gaze caught on something or someone behind me. "But his brother—now that's a different story."

I spun around. A man was coming toward us. His steps were measured, as if he was trying to hide how much he'd been drinking. An average build, he looked to be in his fifties. Curly gray hair dipped below his ears. He had a broad forehead, and his eyes were the same deep Sutton blue I'd seen before. I would have labeled him good-looking were it not for the fact that those eyes were barely more than slits.

"Jimmy." He punched the police chief playfully in the shoulder. "You sly devil. Always cornering the best-looking woman in the room."

Jimmy stepped back, which caused the man's fist to hang in midair. "How are you, Chip? Where's Jen?"

"Back in Winnetka, as usual." Bending over, he swept his hand through the air in a mock bow. It narrowly missed Jimmy's glass. When he realized how close he'd come, he straightened up. "Once again, disaster narrowly averted." He grinned ruefully. "I'm Chip Sutton. And who would you be?"

Jimmy piped up. "This is—this is the woman who's producing the video about the Lodge."

Chip appraised me. "Beauty…and talent, too?"

He was laying it on thick. But then, he'd been drinking. "You must be Charles Sutton's son."

For an instant, his eyes lost focus. "The inimitable Charles Sutton. Scholar, businessman, captain of industry. And father, par excellence. Yes. I am his son."

I ignored his sarcasm. "I just met him."

He swayed slightly and covered it by grabbing Jimmy's arm. He let go a moment later. "I'm not surprised. My father's always one step ahead of everyone else. But I hope you'll give me a chance. I might not be first out of the gate, but I have staying power." He cracked a smile. Or what I'm sure he thought was one. I fidgeted uneasily. Then he squinted, his gaze focusing on my bodice. "What happened to you, my dear?"

In his state I was surprised he saw it. "An—an accident."

"You must be terribly uncomfortable. Can't you change into something else?"

"If I had anything to change into, I would."

"I'm sorry. I wish there was something I could do." He shrugged, then let his gaze rise to my face. "What was your name, again?"

"Ellie Foreman."

He cocked his head. "That sounds familiar. Have we met?"

"I don't think so."

Jimmy cut in. "Chip, this is the woman I was telling you about." He fixed Chip with a knowing look.

Chip looked bewildered.

"The one from Chicago, who reported seeing Luke and Daria Flynn together."

My stomach twisted.

It took time for Chip to register what Jimmy was saying, but when he did, a flush broke out on his neck, and his eyes turned as hard as metal. "You?" He took a step back.

"Chip." Jimmy grabbed his arm. "Not now."

Chip brushed him off, his drunken bonhomie gone. "So you're the one I've been hearing about."

I steeled myself.

"The one who likes to frame other people for murder."

I stood there, speechless.

"Or maybe you're the type who just likes to invade other people's privacy."

Jimmy stepped forward, physically shielding me. "Chip, give it a rest."

Chip didn't move, but his eyes snapped with anger. "Why, Saclarides? We're the victims here. Not her." He faced me. "We— my family—we're easy targets for the likes of you. You just can't resist, can you? What are you getting out of it? A book? A movie deal? Going on all the talk shows?"

Jimmy's voice went tight. "This is your last warning, Chip. Go home and sleep it off."

Chip glared at Jimmy. "Why? So you can make nice to this—this piece of work? Three sniper attacks, and they still won't leave us alone. Who is she, anyway? She can't even keep her clothes clean."

"Go, Chip. Now."

After wavering for a long moment, Chip turned and lurched toward the stairs. He was muttering under his breath.

I watched him go, wondering how—or if—he was going to make it home, then realized somewhat churlishly it didn't matter. Chip wasn't my problem. Unlike Jimmy, who had evidently shared considerable information with Chip. Wrapping myself in a cold anger, I turned back.

"You knew."

"Of course I did."

"You didn't tell me."

"Didn't need to."

"How did you find out?"

He shrugged. "It's gossip. Old gossip at that. Doesn't have anything to do with the case."

"It was Milanovich, wasn't it?"

"A murder investigation is police business. And it's gonna stay that way."

"Then why are you telling the Suttons what's going on?"

He leveled a hard look at me. "I'm doing what I need to do. You'll have to accept that." He paused. "But I am sorry for the way Chip came after you. That wasn't right."

"I can tell how sorry you are."

He rubbed a finger across his face just above his lips. "Ellie, when I ran into you, I was really hoping we wouldn't—wouldn't have to deal with any of this. At least for tonight."

I had the sense he was telling the truth. Still, I shook my head. He might not have lied, but he had been less than candid. It was clear where his priorities lay. Then again, had I really expected anything else?

"Listen. People up here value their privacy. That's one of the reasons they live here. They get upset when someone asks too many questions."

"Well, the way I see it, the best way to stop questions is to answer them fully the first time." I paused. "Assuming they have nothing to hide."

He didn't answer.

Chapter Nineteen

Mac left early the next morning, but I stuck around, indulging myself with a day at the spa, compliments of the Lodge. They'd heard about the incident with my outfit, and this was their way of offering an apology. After a massage, manicure, pedicure, and facial, I decided maybe the shoot wasn't so bad after all. I packed up around three, unsure whether I was a beauty queen in training or a turkey trussed and dressed and ready to roast.

Instead of taking Route 50 to I-94, I drove through downtown Lake Geneva. It was a hot gray day, and it felt like a storm was moving in. I grabbed a frappuccino at a Starbucks and was just getting into my car when the door to the drug store across the street opened. Luke Sutton came out carrying a small plastic bag. Glancing up at the overcast sky, he went around to the back of the store and disappeared.

I sipped my drink, then got out of the car. A pay phone was just outside the coffee shop. I walked up and checked the phone book.

A few minutes later I turned into a semicircular gravel driveway off South Lake Shore Road. A procession of lakefront estates, each one larger and more luxurious than the next, flanked the street. F. Scott Fitzgerald was right. The rich are different. It's not just their sense of entitlement, or their casual plundering of resources. I think it's a sense of "apartness"—that they are not bound by the same rules as the rest of us. They seem to exist in a parallel universe, partaking of ours only when it suits them.

I parked in front of a stately Tudor with steeply pitched gables, a half-timbered exterior, and tall, diamond-paned windows. I walked to the front door and started to press Willetta Emerson's doorbell. Then I reconsidered and walked back down her drive and about 100 yards down the road. Charles Sutton's estate sat precisely in the center of a circular driveway, well recessed from the road, but plainly visible. It was a red-brick structure, with four white columns supporting a large portico. Behind the portico on top of the house sat a wide octagonal-shaped base. Above that was a white dome.

I don't know much about architecture, but the house had a classical, familiar look. Small windows peeked out just below the dome, and I thought I saw a skylight as well. I'd seen this house before. But where? When I got it, I sucked in a breath. Charles Sutton had built a replica of Monticello, Thomas Jefferson's home.

I peered up the driveway. Two small statues flanked the front entrance. From a distance, I thought they were replicas of those little black jockeys in red jackets you used to see on lawns before they became unacceptable, but as I squinted, I realized I was wrong. The statue on the left was a cowboy, with a ten-gallon hat, chaps, lasso, and two six-guns. On the right was an Indian in feathered headdress, buckskin clothes, and warpaint. No pseudo-Southern gentility here. Someone had a Midwestern sense of humor.

I retraced my steps to Willetta Emerson's home and rang the doorbell. Seconds later someone waved to me from a window, and a moment after that Willetta answered the door. Dressed in a brightly printed caftan, she made a stark contrast to the gray day.

"Hiya, cutie. You didn't waste any time, did you?"

"It's not a bad time, is it?"

"Of course not. I'm glad for the company. Too quiet around here since George passed on." A trace of sadness came over her, but it resolved quickly. "Come on in."

Like the gown she wore at the gala, the predominant color in Willetta Emerson's home was green. The furniture, mostly white wicker, was upholstered in material splashed with green ferns and leaves. Matching wallpaper festooned the walls. The effect was more Miami Beach than Lake Geneva, which, combined with the staid Tudor architecture, made some kind of statement. I wasn't sure what.

She led me into her kitchen, a large room with a slate floor, forest green cabinets, and a butcher block table. Motioning me to sit down, she took the kettle to the sink. "I'll make some tea." She turned on the faucet, then checked a clock on the wall. It was almost four. "Aw, hell, it's five o'clock somewhere."

She switched off the water, opened a cabinet, and pulled out a full bottle of bourbon and two shot glasses. She poured two fingers into each glass and brought them to the table. "Here." She passed one to me.

I took a sip. The liquor burned my throat. Willetta downed hers in one gulp and smacked her lips. "So, Miss Ellie Foreman, what would you like to know?"

I leaned back. I couldn't remember the last time someone had actually invited me to ask questions. I plunged in. "Well, for starters, I just took a look at the Sutton estate. It looks like a replica of Monticello. Was that intentional?"

Willetta laughed. "You ever been there?"

"Charlottesville? No, but I've seen pictures. The dome, especially."

She nodded. "Yeah, the hallowed dome. Chuck says it was pretty unusual for the architecture of the time. When he remodeled the place, he said he couldn't think of a better design. From the dome right down to the ice house."

I sipped my bourbon. Talk about hero worship. Chuck Sutton could have done anything he wanted to his mansion, yet he chose to emulate Thomas Jefferson. Right down to the house he lived in.

"Where is it—the ice house?"

"In the back. You should check it out."

"I couldn't. I don't want to trespass."

She waved her hand. "You know how it is. Everyone has a ton of security, and no one turns the damn things on. You're not planning to rip them off, are you?"

I didn't reply.

She grinned. "Just teasing. They converted the ice house into a tool shed a long time ago, but it looks pretty much the same. Except they removed the iron grate in front. And added a new floor. It used to extend twenty feet underground." She refilled my glass. "Like a well. The ice man would fill it up every spring."

"Who were the ice men?"

She held up a finger, stood up, and went into the living room, where she pulled a scrapbook from a drawer. Coming back, she thumbed through it and set it down on the table. The scrapbook was open to a photo of a man wearing overalls in the driver's seat of a wagon. A team of horses was hitched to the wagon.

"My father took this a long time ago. It's one of the ice men. They were mostly farm and railroad workers."

"They moonlighted?"

"Not really. Back in the old days, the Wisconsin Central was supposed to go through Walworth County clear up to Lake Superior, so a lot of Germans, Scandinavians, and Irish came over to work on it. In fact, there's an area just out of town used to be called the Irish Woods. But the railroad fell through, and the immigrants scattered. Some farmed, some moved to the cities, some became ice men."

"Do you have an ice house?"

"George tore it down when we bought this place. He built a swimming pool instead. Would you like to see it?"

"Sure."

We went out to a sprawling backyard that included a rectangular pool, a cabana with a striped awning, and a bricked-in patio. At the far end of the yard was the dock, and beyond that the lake. The water was throwing off tiny bursts of light. A stand of evergreens stretched across one side of the yard, forming a natural barrier between Willetta and the Suttons, but I caught a glimpse the Suttons' backyard.

The back of the house, the side that faced Lake Geneva, was just as imposing as the front. Columns flanked the door here as well, but instead of a portico, a sizable deck extended outward, and the octagonal base beneath the dome was more apparent. The broad, sloping lawn was heavily wooded. Flower beds had been dug at the edge of the evergreens, and a rainbow of blossoms danced in the breeze.

About thirty yards away, just under the shade of a huge oak tree, was a rounded structure made of stone and wood. It looked to be about ten feet high.

Willetta gestured. "That's the ice house."

"It looks like an igloo."

"It does at that." She smiled. "The man who used to deliver their ice became their caretaker, you know."

"Oh?"

"But Herbert left after the—the drowning."

I turned around. Willetta was staring at the dock. "The drowning?"

"It was horrible," she said.

"What was?"

She sighed. "The Suttons have the two sons. Chip's the oldest, then there's Luke."

"Right."

"Well, there was a younger sister. Anne. She was a few years younger than Luke." She paused. "She drowned when she was sixteen."

I winced.

"She was a beautiful girl. Apple of her parents' eye. They always wanted a girl, after the boys."

"What happened?"

She motioned me back to the house. "Come on in. I have the newspaper articles."

We went back into the kitchen, and Willetta paged through the scrapbook. When she found what she wanted, she spread it open and laid it on the table. I peered over. An article from the *Tribune* was taped to the page. The portion under the tape was darker than the rest of the article, which was faded and yellow and looked like it might dissolve at any moment. It wasn't long, only a few paragraphs.

Daughter of Wealthy Industrialist Drowns in Lake

*Lake Geneva, June 19. Anne Fitzgerald Sutton, the
only daughter of Chicago railroad magnate Charles
Sutton III, was found dead at their summer estate
in Lake Geneva, Wisconsin, the night of June 19.
According to sources, her death was the result of
drowning. The 16-year-old heiress had attempted to
board the family dinghy after dark but fell off the
dock and became entangled in the lines. Her body was
found by the estate's caretaker. Police are investigating.*

*Willetta Emerson, a neighbor in the resort town
with whom the Suttons share the dock, expressed shock
at the young girl's death. "This is a tragedy of the
worst order. We are stunned."*

*Miss Sutton, who was home for the summer,
attended Miss Calloway's, an exclusive boarding
school in Connecticut. She planned to make her debut
next year and travel abroad after graduation. She
was the great-granddaughter of Charles Sutton, who
was credited with inventing the automatic coupler on
rail cars. She leaves not only her parents, Gloria and
Charles Sutton III, but two older brothers, Charles IV
and Lucas. The family is in seclusion.*

I slowly closed the scrapbook and shivered. The Sutton girl
had been sixteen when she died. Rachel was fifteen.

Willetta was watching me. "The family was never the same."

I remembered how, at the gala, Willetta said that Gloria
Sutton was reclusive. Was this why? A family torn apart; a
mother paralyzed with grief and guilt—guilt, because no matter
what the circumstances, a tragedy like that would plague any
parent. "Why didn't anyone untangle the ropes?" "Why was she
by herself?" "If only I had been there...." I shivered again. A
mother withdraws from the world, leaving her sons to fend for
themselves emotionally. Maybe that accounted for their behavior.

Except…. "Their father seems to have moved on. He socializes. Smiles. He's almost friendly."

"That's true."

I bit my lip. I hadn't realized I'd said it out loud.

"I wondered about that, too." Willetta had a curious look on her face.

"What?"

She picked up the bourbon and, without looking at me, poured more for both of us. "Well, you see, part of the story never made it into that article. It came out later."

"What part is that?"

She sat down and tossed back the bourbon. Her eyes grew wet and wide, then returned to normal. "People around here wanted to keep it quiet. For the sake of the family. And who they are."

I waited.

"The truth is, it was pretty clear she was raped. Maybe she tried to resist—who knows—but she was overpowered. Then she was murdered. Strangled, then drowned." Willetta twirled her glass on the table. "Her body was naked when they found her. The police never found who did it. They said it was some kind of vagrant. An intruder. You know, like the Percy girl."

I felt a chill. Valerie Percy, one of Senator Charles Percy's twin daughters, was brutally murdered in 1966 in their Kenilworth home. Someone allegedly broke into the house in the middle of the night and pummeled the girl to death with a ball-peen hammer. In that case, there was an intense investigation, but the murderer was never found.

I reached for the bourbon. "When did—when did Anne die?"

"The summer of seventy-four. June."

Almost ten years after the Percy murder.

"Were there any witnesses? Any evidence?"

"No one saw anything. But it wouldn't have been hard for someone to tie up at the dock, come on up, and do whatever it was they wanted. Especially in the summer, when there's so many people on the water." She motioned toward the window. "It was after that we put in all the burglar alarms and electric fences and things."

"Willetta, the article makes it sound like an accident. How could a murder like that have been covered up? I mean, the police, the press—I would have thought—"

"It wasn't covered up. That was just the first article. Look here." She opened the scrapbook again to another article about a week later. The headline, from the *Tribune,* read, SUTTON GIRL FOUND MURDERED. And another, from the *Daily News,* LITTLE EVIDENCE IN MURDER OF ANNE SUTTON. And yet another from the *Sun-Times*: MORE QUESTIONS THAN ANSWERS...THE REAL STORY BEHIND THE SUTTON TRAGEDY....

I didn't remember the coverage. But that was the summer Nixon resigned. I was young and political and wholly consumed by Watergate, Nixon's refusal to hand over the tapes, and the impeachment hearings.

"It was different back then," Willetta went on. "At least around here. People weren't so interested in cashing in on other people's troubles. Not that there weren't a lot of questions, mind you. In fact, just a few years ago one of those investigative reporters—isn't that what you call them—came out from Chicago and was snooping around, asking all sorts of questions."

I leaned back in my chair. That could explain why Luke Sutton and his brother were so quick to paint me as one of the "enemy."

"Nobody wanted the circus that surrounded the Percy murder," Willetta went on. "And the chief of police didn't want to sully the town any more than it had been."

"Not Jimmy."

"Oh no. Henry Babcock was the chief of police back then. Jimmy was just a kid—well, a teenager. The theory was it was someone who came in off the lake, maybe looking to rob the house or something. When he saw Annie—well, she was always a friendly little thing—hell, she probably offered to help the creep. Maybe promised him a meal or something to drink. Then, one thing led to another, and, well, for the most part, they kept the details quiet. But it wasn't a cover-up. Just respecting their feelings. The Suttons are a prestigious family, and people figured they were entitled to grieve in private."

"They never came up with any suspects?" I asked.

Willetta cocked her head. "Well, there was one."

"Who?"

She reached for her glass. "The Suttons' caretaker."

"The one who found her body?"

Willetta nodded. "I never knew exactly what happened. We went abroad that summer. In fact, we left soon after Annie died. By the time George and I got back—it was about a month later—Herbert had disappeared, and rumors were flying."

"Rumors that he killed Annie?"

"That he raped her, killed her, maybe knew the person who did. It was all very murky and speculative." She sniffed. "I tried not to listen, of course, George and I being so close to Gloria and Chuck."

"Of course."

"At any rate, nothing ever came of it."

"He wasn't charged?"

"No." A slightly puzzled look came over her. "He wasn't. Everything died down after that."

"You mean after he left town?"

She nodded.

"And never came back?"

"Not that I know of."

"Where'd he go?"

"I have no idea." She shrugged, then looked at me. "Sometimes it's best not to pry, you know?"

"So the caretaker finds Annie's body, no one can come up with any suspects, then he suddenly disappears off the face of the earth." I flipped through the scrapbook. "You don't have any articles about that part of it."

"I told you. We were in Europe. By the time we got home, it was pretty much over." She broke off, the remnants of deep sadness on her face. Then, as though ashamed I'd caught her in a vulnerable state, she poured herself another shot.

I looked through the kitchen window. The view gave onto the stand of evergreens and, beyond that, the Suttons' backyard.

Willetta followed my gaze. "Sometimes I see Gloria walking around the yard. But she never leaves the grounds. Got a nurse-type person with her all the time. They call her a housekeeper." She shrugged. "But her job is to keep Gloria—quiet. You know what I mean?"

I nodded.

"Nothing was the same afterward," she sighed. "Luke left right afterward. Didn't come back until last year. Chip was the only one who stuck around."

"Seems like he moved on, too. I mean, he got married. Went into the family business."

"Uh-huh." Willetta's face was impenetrable.

For some reason I remembered Pari Noskin Taichert saying Chip was a good tipper. Was that his quid pro quo? A way to buy silence about his boozing? I stood up and put my hand on Willetta's shoulder. "Thanks, Willetta. I appreciate everything you've told me." I took a last sip of bourbon.

She waved away my thanks. "Hey, how about that interview?"

"How about next week?"

"Grand." She stood up, too. "We—we won't be talking about Annie, will we?"

"No, of course not. I want to hear about the circus."

"And how I met my wonderful George?"

"And how you met your wonderful George."

Her face brightened.

Chapter Twenty

Before getting into the car, I made my way down to the dock. Sailboats tacked back and forth on the lake. A group of kids roared past on jet skis. Some had girls in the back, their arms wrapped around the drivers. The Hells Angels of the nautical set.

I thought back to Willetta's comment about security. After what happened to Anne Sutton, I would have thought Monticello would be locked up tighter than Fort Knox. Except, as we've learned, it's hard to sustain a "red alert" for thirty days, let alone thirty years. Not that the ravages of the tragedy hadn't marked the Suttons: the wife was a hermit, one son was a drunk, and the other one had only just come back to the family fold.

The sun finally broke through the clouds and sat low in the western sky. A breeze stirred the trees, and the tangy scent of pine sap drifted over me. It was time to leave. As I headed back to the car, I peeked at the Suttons' property one last time.

I froze. Someone—a man—was walking around the ice house. No. Not walking. Tiptoeing. He was hunched over, wearing a long-sleeved plaid shirt and olive drab pants. He moved stealthily, as though he wanted to remain hidden. Although his back was to me, I had the impression of a tall man. He disappeared around the back of the ice house.

I stood still, my senses on alert. Then I relaxed. It was probably the gardener or the caretaker or whatever they called them up here. But why was he sneaking around? Or was he? Unsettled by Willetta's story, I could be imagining things. But then where were his gardening tools? When Fouad works, he spreads everything out across the lawn, and he wears pants with lots of pockets so his hand tools are within reach. The man I saw didn't have any equipment, although, to be fair, he could have just finished stowing it in the tool shed.

I shrugged. It was an odd way for a gardener to behave. But then, everyone up in Lake Geneva was a little odd.

It was dusk, and the smoky aroma of meat from my neighbor's grill filled the air. An accident on I-94 had snarled traffic just past the toll booth, and the drive took over two hours. I finally turned onto my block, tired, cross, and anxious to wash up. But as I pulled into the garage, the wooden ladder that extends down from the attic stood directly in my path. Someone had lowered it from the ceiling but neglected to put it back up. I slammed on the brakes an inch shy of impact. Who was rummaging through my attic? This wasn't the kind of day for unexpected events or visitors.

I slid out of the car, went to the ladder, and peered into the attic. It was dark and quiet. I walked around to the front of the house. No one there either. I came back, took out my key, and quietly let myself into the kitchen.

No one was inside, but they had been. Dishes littered the counter and spilled into the sink. A jar of chocolate sauce sat on the table with splotches of brown congealing on its surface. A half-gallon of vanilla ice cream, mostly melted now, lay on the other counter. Next to it was the better half of a grilled cheese sandwich. The smell of grease hung in the air, and the frying pan on the stove was coated with a layer of crust.

I let out my breath, went to the refrigerator, and poured a large glass of water. As I took a sip, a series of squeals chorused through the window. I looked out to see a towheaded little boy furiously pedaling Rachel's old tricycle, the one we'd stored in the attic. Rachel and a towheaded little girl raced behind him.

I took my water outside. The kids were shouting, the girl demanding that her brother give her a turn. The boy refused and pedaled faster. And Rachel was hollering just as loud as they were. When they reached the end of the block, the boy turned the tricycle around, but Rachel blocked him and lifted him off. The little girl threw herself on the seat. As they made their way, the little boy tried to outrun his sister, who shrieked in delight at his pursuit. Rachel tried to keep up, but her face grew bright red, and her chest rose and fell.

"Not so easy, is it?" I said as they came abreast of me.

Rachel pretended to shrug, as if agreeing with me would imply some kind of psychic defeat.

"How old are they?"

"Charlie's six. Melanie's four."

"I guess that makes you the Perle Mesta of the preschool set."

"Who?"

"Never mind."

She looked at me. "Mother, you are so dorky sometimes."

"I thought you were spending the day at Dad's."

"Daddy and Julia went shopping. We decided to play here for a change. Julia said it was okay."

I harrumphed. If the disaster in the kitchen was any indication of what went on at her house, I wasn't surprised.

"Which reminds me. Can I have fifty dollars?"

"Excuse me?"

She yanked a thumb toward Charlie. "He broke my CD player. He thought it was a Frisbee."

"What about all the money you're making?"

"Come on, Mom. It's in the mother-daughter handbook. Page seventy-two. Daughters are allowed to get their allowance plus whatever money they make on their own."

"You must have the revised version. Mine says young ladies need to learn the value of money, which happens only by earning and saving for what they want."

Rachel scrunched up her face and walked away.

When I finally managed to go online, I did another search on the Sutton family, looking for anything I could find on the daughter. A few articles mentioned the sons but no daughter. I Googled again, plugging in the date of her death, and the words "Anne Fitzgerald Sutton." This time, I got a few hits: the same article from the *Tribune* I'd seen in Willetta's scrapbook, and an even shorter one from *The New York Times.*

I wondered if the investigative reporter whom Willetta said showed up in Lake Geneva ever wrote his article. If he did, it wasn't on Google. I tried another news database, but came up empty. If someone was trying to discourage press coverage about the murder, they'd done a good job. I was about to give up but decided to search the Wisconsin papers, just in case Willetta had it wrong, and the reporter hailed from Milwaukee or Madison, not Chicago. I clicked onto the *Milwaukee Journal Sentinel* and entered Anne's name.

There it was! I clicked on a headline that said, 25 YEARS LATER, STILL NO ANSWERS. The article was a roundup looking back at historical events a quarter-century ago. Several unsolved crimes around the state were reexamined, including a bank robbery in Madison in which two security guards were gunned down, the kidnapping of a ten-year-old boy, and Anne Sutton's murder. I started to read. It wasn't a long article, and the part devoted to Anne Sutton was only one paragraph. Still, I had to suppress my shock at the last sentence.

> *At one point suspicion centered on the estate's care-taker, which was heightened when he fled Lake Geneva after the crime. Today, though, police admit there was never any solid evidence linking Herbert Flynn to the Sutton girl's murder, a fact which his wife Irene and her two daughters have repeatedly declared.*

Chapter Twenty-one

I printed out the article feeling foolish, the way you do when you realize everybody else knows something that you don't. Why hadn't anyone told me Herbert Flynn was the caretaker who found Anne Sutton's body? Why didn't I know Daria Flynn's father had worked for the Suttons? True, it had been thirty years ago, ancient history in most people's lives. True, there was no reason to link Daria Flynn's death to Anne Sutton's. True, revisiting the event would resurrect painful memories for many people. Even so, there had been a relationship between the Suttons and the Flynns, a relationship that had apparently spanned several decades, but no one had seen fit to mention it.

Why did people think Herbert Flynn committed the murder, I wondered. Was there something shady in his past? Was he a shifty, untrustworthy type? Sometimes the mere perception of guilt, especially when someone is dislikable, can trigger a rush to judgment. And who had first made those accusations? Had one of the Suttons seen something that made them think Herbert killed Anne? It was odd; he'd been the one who found her body. He should have been considered a hero. Instead, he'd fled town in disgrace.

I reread the article, wondering if anyone at the *Journal Sentinel* might have more information, when the phone rang.

Rachel answered and began an animated conversation. I figured it was one of her friends, so I was surprised when she called upstairs a minute later. "Mom…it's David."

I stared at the cordless, then picked up the phone.

"Hi."

"Hi, Ellie."

"So long, David," Rachel said cheerfully. I heard the click as she hung up.

There was silence.

I cleared my throat. "How are you?"

"Ellie, we have to talk."

My skin felt itchy. "I know."

"I don't like being in—in this no-man's-land. I feel like I'm stumbling through fog."

This wasn't a new conversation. We both knew our relationship was flawed. What I didn't know—and David probably didn't either—was whether we could salvage it. Can relationships really be repaired or is that just Dr. Phil's hype? As I thought about it, I almost missed what David was saying.

"…little, my mother used to tell me the story—"

"I'm sorry. What was that?"

He paused, then sighed. "I was saying when I was a little boy, my mother told me the story of the nail. You probably know it. A long time ago, a merchant made a lot of money at a fair and started home on his horse."

I steeled myself. "And?"

"According to the story, he stopped at a town and the stable boy said his horse needed a nail in his shoe. The man ignored the boy's warning—he was in a hurry. At the next stop, he was told the horse needed a new shoe. The merchant still didn't pay attention, and the horse began to limp, then stumbled, then fell down and broke its leg."

"For want of a nail…."

"What was that?"

"Nothing."

David went on, "We've crippled the horse, Ellie, haven't we?"

I pictured him in his townhouse in Philadelphia holding the cordless. Was he staring out at the cherry trees in his backyard?

Was he wearing shorts or sweats? A T-shirt or a button-down?
"Yes." It came out as a whisper.

Silence hung between us. Finally, I said, "So, what do you
want to do?"

"I think we should put the horse out of its misery."

More silence.

"Then I guess there's not much more to say."

"I guess not."

"Ellie…."

"David…."

"Never mind."

I hung up and buried my face in my hands. I heard noise
from a sitcom on the tube downstairs. The laugh track was
punctuated by an occasional chuckle from Rachel. I heard her
shuffling from the family room into the kitchen. The slap of
the refrigerator door. The snap and hiss of a can opening. It was
over. No trumpets. No announcement. Just canned laughter and
the snap of a pop-top.

I heard Rachel climbing the steps. A moment later, she
appeared at the door to my office, the can of pop in her hand.
"So what's going on with David?"

I opened my mouth. Nothing came out.

She took a long sip. "You broke up, didn't you?"

I nodded slowly.

Rachel stared at me. Then she said, "I wish I were at Julia's.
I like it better there."

Chapter Twenty-two

My father was the one I called the next morning.

I'd spent a sleepless night filled with terrors. It was my fault David and I were finished. Even my daughter didn't want to be around me. I was incapable of sustaining intimacy with any man. A failure in the relationship sweepstakes. As the sky lightened, I felt the need to connect with someone who loved me unconditionally. There was only one person.

I met Dad at Bagel World, a kosher deli in Skokie. I don't keep kosher, and neither does my father, although he claims his parents did. But I remember a conversation with my grandmother: I must have been about ten, and my opa had already passed on. Oma and I were putting dishes away. I knew we were supposed to store the meat dishes separately from the dairy, but Oma said not to bother.

When I asked why, she confessed she wasn't really *kashrut* anymore. It was the dishwasher, she explained. "It makes things too easy. First you're sneaking in *parve* dishes with meat, then *parve* with milk. Pretty soon, you're mixing milk with meat. There's no point after that." She shrugged. I remember I thought she was overly rigid. Surely God didn't send you to hell for a little mixing. She shook her head. "You're either kosher, or you're not," she said. Then, with the same dry sense of humor that my father inherited, she added, "Now pass the bacon."

Dad was already in a booth. His arms were so skinny they protruded from his sleeves like a kid in a shirt too big for him.

His face brightened when he saw me. I threw my arms around him. He seemed surprised but pleased by my display of affection. "I should get a welcome like that from every woman I meet."

I sat down opposite him. "I've missed you."

"That's what they all say. Must be my princely good looks." He slid his hand over mine and gave it a squeeze. "*Nu?*"

"I—I'm okay."

His eyebrows shot up. "What's wrong?"

Why is it that people assume something terrible has happened unless you're brimming with joy? Or was it just my father? I glanced over at the next table, where a group of young orthodox Jews, with full beards, black hats, and *payos* dangling down their cheeks, were talking passionately, their faces serious and intense.

Maybe it was cultural.

"Let's order." We went to the counter, where a man with a flowing mustache and a stern expression took our order and gave us a number. As we waited for drinks, I started to tell Dad about my dealings with the Suttons.

He put two iced teas on his tray. "Suttons—the railroad family?" He carried the tray back to our booth.

I followed him. "You know them?"

"What dealings do you have with them?" Dad often answers questions with a question. It's the lawyer in him.

I added sweetener to my tea. I didn't want him to worry. Or to pry. Which was about as useful as a three-dollar bill. He does both. "You remember the woman who was shot at the rest stop?"

His eyes narrowed.

I cut him off before he started. "Don't worry. I'm not in any kind of trouble. But the woman who was killed—Daria Flynn—had been seeing one of the Sutton sons. There are two, you know. I've met them." I paused. "And their father."

I launched into a description of Luke and Chip. I left out the part about the near miss with Luke's plane, but I didn't spare anything about the sons. When I got to their father, though, my tone changed. "He was pleasant. Even charming. And apparently, one of the foremost authorities on Thomas Jefferson."

Dad threw me a dubious look.

"You don't believe me."

"This is Charles Sutton you're talking about?"

I nodded.

He laced his hands together and leaned forward. "You know that saying 'shirtsleeves to shirtsleeves in three generations'?"

"Sure. But the Suttons are well into their fourth, and they're still as rich as Croesus."

He waved his hand dismissively. "I'm talking about cycles of behavior. Personalities."

I frowned. Where was he going with this?

"I'm sure the first Charles Sutton was a charmer, too," he said. "Would have to have been to get that patent."

"You know about the automatic coupler?"

"Everyone does. It's practically folklore. Charles Sutton sweet-talked a former slave into selling him the patent. Then *he* went out and made a fortune on it, while the slave disappeared off the face of the earth."

"Disappeared? Are you implying something?"

Dad spread his hands, affecting an injured look. "Me? Who knows what happened a hundred years ago? I'm just glad Sutton didn't talk the poor shlub into selling him the Hope diamond."

The man behind the counter yelled out our number. I went to get our sandwiches: tuna on a bagel for me, smoked fish and cream cheese for Dad. As I brought them back to the table, Dad said, "You understand what I'm telling you?"

I sat down. "Not really."

"Ellie, these are people who will do anything to get what they want. They don't let anyone stand in their way. Certainly not a former slave. In fact, these people remind me of David's—"

"I get it." I took a bite of my sandwich. The last thing I wanted was to bring David into the conversation.

My father picked up a fork. "Did you know that Charles Sutton made a run for the Senate?"

I stopped chewing. "This Charles Sutton?"

My father nodded, speared his pickle, and sliced it into wedges. "You'd see him at all sorts of functions. Glad-handing, schmoozing, building friends and allies. Then all of a sudden, he drops out. *He* practically disappears, in fact."

My brain started to race. "When was this?"

"I think it was in the early seventies. Chuck Percy was still Senator. I remember the cracks about two Chucks in the Senate. You know that riddle about how much wood can a woodchuck—"

"I remember." I was curious about the timing. "Why did he drop out?"

Dad chewed his pickle thoughtfully. "Why the questions? I thought you weren't mixed up with them."

"I'm not. But—"

"But nothing. I know when I'm being pumped. Especially when the pumper is my daughter. What's going on? *Emmes.*"

I sighed. *"Emmes"* means no fooling around. "I just saw some old newspaper articles about them."

"Yeah?"

Halfway through my explanation, Dad cut me off. "I'd forgotten about that. The daughter drowned. It was a tragedy. That's why he dropped out of politics."

"It wasn't just a drowning, Dad."

"What are you talking about?"

"She was murdered." I explained what I'd learned from Willetta Emerson.

"Now you mention it, I do remember something about that. Or was that the Percy girl?"

"It was both of them."

"You're right." He picked up his bagel. "How ironic. Didn't get the guys in either case, did they?"

"No."

He took a bite of his sandwich. "Didn't they have a suspect in one of them?"

My father and his memory. I nodded. "There was some suspicion that the Suttons' caretaker did it, but they never found any evidence. And he left Lake Geneva afterward."

Dad picked up his iced tea, took a sip, and looked down his glass at me. I knew what he was thinking.

I debated whether to tell him whose father the caretaker turned out to be. I decided not to. He'd fret and arch his eyebrows and warn me to back off. "Dad, I'm not involved in anything. Don't worry."

"Good." He set down his glass. "Then I don't have to give you the speech."

"No. You don't." I patted his hand. "But it is curious. Chuck Sutton seems okay, even to have moved on since his daughter's death, but his wife hasn't."

"Your children are supposed to outlive you. Not the other way around."

I thought about Luke and Chip and Anne Sutton. They were close in age. Did they play hide and seek together in the icehouse? Climb trees in that beautiful backyard? Tell secrets and laugh and fight? I never knew what it was like to have siblings. There was just Mother and Dad and me. "Sometimes I wish I'd had a brother or a sister, you know?"

Dad pushed his plate away. He moved his glass two inches to the right. Then he sat very still. "What do you mean?"

"Just that sometimes I wish I weren't an only child."

My father didn't move. "You know what a rough time your mother had with you," he said quietly. "The doctors told her she shouldn't risk it again."

"I know." I took a sip of tea. "But don't you ever wish you'd had another child?"

My father gazed at me for a long, uncomfortable moment. Something was off. "Dad, what's wrong?"

"What else did your mother tell you?"

"About what?" Two could play the question game.

Another silence.

"Dad?"

His eyes flicked over me, but I sensed he wasn't really seeing me. Then he sighed. "She never wanted you to know. Honestly, I don't know why. It wouldn't have made any difference. But I promised to respect her wishes."

A buzz skimmed my nerves. I put my hands in my lap. "What didn't she want me to know?"

He swallowed. "You had an older brother. He was born with severe deformities. He only lived a day."

His words lingered in the air: unreal, almost fantastic. "A brother." I said slowly. "Did he have a name?"

"Joseph."

"Joseph," I whispered. I had a brother named Joseph.

"Your mother nearly died giving birth to him. And as it turned out, there was a reason. He—he was never meant to come into the world."

"And I never knew."

"She didn't want you to." My father pressed his lips together. "Your mother—she blamed herself. She thought there was something wrong with her. She couldn't form children, or bear them, or something. And though she loved you to distraction, she still carried that sorrow to her grave."

I looked down at my hands, still folded in my lap. There had always been a distance between my mother and me. I didn't know why, but I was aware that she was never fully happy. Or satisfied. She'd worn her unhappiness like a gossamer wrap; never admitting it, never complaining. I'd always assumed it was my fault. That somehow I'd fallen short. Done something to displease her. When the cancer came, and I was an adult, it was too late to heal the breach. Even at the end, when I held her hand, and there was nothing more to lose, we never talked about it.

"I never agreed with her, Ellie," my father said. "It was wrong. We should have told you."

I nodded. I was grateful—I think—that Dad finally acknowledged it. We didn't say anything more about it, but he hugged me close when I dropped him off. I drove home thinking about family secrets and their unintended consequences. My mother had gone through life feeling less of a woman because of Joseph. Even my birth wasn't enough. The distance, the coolness—it wasn't my fault. I was just a tacit reminder of her failure.

Thoughts and feelings I'd never entertained before sifted through me. In one way, a burden had been lifted from my shoulders. I hadn't done anything. Still, the echo of my mother's sadness resounded. I'd had an older brother. It had only been for a day, but he existed. I wished I could have seen a picture of him, fingered a lock of his hair. But there were no mementoes—I would have found them when I went through my mother's things. Did they have a funeral service and sit *shiva*? Or did they just say *kaddish*? I didn't know Jewish law concerning the death of an infant. I wish I did. Maybe I could honor him in some small way.

Chapter Twenty-three

A few days later, Mac and I went back with the crew to the air-strip to shoot pickups. We'd rented a car mount to film a traveling shot down the runway. Before we set up, Mac dropped me off at the Lodge's offices to check in. They apologized again for our earlier difficulty and said they'd discussed it with the police. They admitted they didn't have anyone monitoring the airstrip but couldn't guarantee when there might be an occasional take-off or landing. They were working on the problem, though.

I met the crew at the hangar. It was late afternoon and the air-strip looked deserted. I spotted the Cessna and two other planes inside, but no one—and, more significantly, no planes—inter-rupted our shoot. Aside from a bump or two due to the runway's patchy surface, I was pleased with the shots. Hank probably could smooth out the bumps in post, even speed up the motion so it looked like a plane taking off.

I was watching Mac and the crew break down the camera, thinking how we'd edit the sequence, when it came to me. "Of course!" I exclaimed. "Why didn't I think of that before?"

"Excuse me?" Mac looked up.

"You know what we need?"

"What?"

"An aerial."

Mac frowned. "An aerial?"

"For the opening of the show. Think about it. We're introduc-ing the Land of Lodge. What better way to do it than with an aerial of the compound? We start wide: We see Lake Geneva, the lake, the roads, the town. Then we slowly zoom in—or maybe cut to a series of shots, each one closer and closer—until we dissolve to a ground shot."

"You mean like those shots of the earth from space, and then you move closer and closer and you finally zoom in on the man walking down Main Street?"

I cocked my head. "Well, maybe not that grandiose, but yeah."

Mac considered it. "It could work."

I beamed, grateful for Mac's approval, however understated.

He looked around. His gaze stopped at the hangar. "You know anyone with a plane?"

"Um…actually, I thought maybe you might be able to scare one up through your uncle."

"I told you. We haven't spoken in years."

"It was just a thought." I paused. "Maybe the Lodge can recommend someone."

"I have another—"

The sudden whine of an engine cut through the air. I jumped at the sound, but it wasn't a plane. A green pickup was heading down the access road. It veered onto the tarmac and swerved to a stop. Luke Sutton slid out and headed over to the hangar.

Mac turned around. "What's that they say about prayers being answered?"

I stared at the truck.

"You're not still pissed about the other day, are you?"

"He drives a green pickup."

"And I drive a blue Expedition."

"The shooter in all three sniper attacks drove a green pickup."

"Ellie," Mac said with a trace of scorn, "get over it. There are hundreds—no thousands—of green pickups in the world."

Luke let himself in a small door on the side of the hangar building. Mac started walking toward the hangar.

"You wouldn't dare," I called after him.

Mac turned around. "You want the shot?"

"Not if I have to—to suck up to him."

Mac stopped and gave me a shrug. "You're the producer."

The overhead hangar door rolled up. The interior went from gloomy to bright, bathed in the afternoon sun. Mac went back to the camera. The Cessna started to roll out of the hangar, with Luke Sutton in the cockpit. He was wearing sunglasses. Then the plane stopped, and the cockpit door swung open. He jumped down and walked over. Mac put the camera gently on the ground. He and Sutton exchanged nods. I stood behind Mac.

"What can we do for you?" Mac asked.

With his sunglasses on, I couldn't tell if Sutton was looking at Mac or at me. "It occurred to me I probably should check before I go up this time. I don't want any problems when I land." He gestured toward me. "I'm sure you don't, either. Are you still going to be here in, say, two hours?"

Mac pointed to the camera on the ground. "We're pretty much all wrapped up here. Right, Ellie?" He turned around. "Unless you want to do that other thing."

My throat closed up. I wanted to kick him. I wouldn't ask Luke Sutton for help. Not when he'd nearly run me over in his plane and never apologized. Not when I had questions about his relationship to Daria Flynn.

Mac waited for what seemed to be an eternity, then shrugged. "I guess we're on our way. But hey. Thanks for checking."

Luke gave us—Mac?—me?—another nod and started back to the Cessna. Mac folded his arms. Another eternity passed. Luke was about to hoist himself back up in the cockpit when I reconsidered. Maybe I was being shortsighted. If he did help us out, there might be a way to ask him—subtly—about his meetings with Daria Flynn. Get his take on the other shootings. His relationship with Jimmy Saclarides.

"Hold on a minute," I called.

Luke stopped.

"We—Mac and I—would like to ask you a question."

He turned around.

I looked over at Mac. He was watching me with interest. I took a step forward. "We'd—I'd really like to get an aerial shot of the Lodge. From the air. For the video. Would you—I mean—do you think you'd be willing to help us out?"

Luke stood there, not saying anything.

"We could pay you," I added. "Not a lot. But enough to cover your fuel."

The lowering sun glinted behind him, throwing his face into shadow but shooting a corona of rays around him. "I might."

"Really? That's great."

"But I can only take up one of you." He yanked a thumb back toward the Cessna. "There are only two seats."

"That's okay," I said quickly. "Mac's the cameraman. I won't be going."

Luke came back over. Something about him: the tilt of his head, his stance, the way he slid his hands in his jeans pockets, made me think he was pleased. "When did you want to do this?"

"Anytime it's convenient. Over the next few days."

Mac cut in. "Actually, Ellie, shouldn't you scout the shot ahead of time?"

A ripple of panic shot through me. I spun around. "That won't be necessary," I said worriedly. "I trust you."

"But you're the producer. You call the shots."

What was he doing? He knew how I felt about planes. "Mac, like I said, I trust you to get the shot."

"It's me you don't trust," Luke said.

I whipped around. "No. That's not it. I mean—not really." Did he know about my fear of flying? How could he?

He planted his hands on his hips. "I'm going up. You could check out the shot right now."

I ran a hand through my hair. "I—I don't think so. It's late."

Despite the shadows, I thought I saw a smile on his face. "Are you afraid?"

"Of—of course not," I blustered.

Mac made a small snorting sound but covered it with a cough. What was going on? Was there some kind of private old boys' network that made guys like these stick together?

Sutton waited.

"We're finished here, Ellie," Mac said. "You coming or not?"

Suddenly I remembered. I couldn't go up in the plane. I'd driven out with Mac, and my car was at his studio in Chicago. I motioned toward Mac. "I can't. I—they're my ride. I have no way to get back."

"You can take the van," Mac offered. "I'll drive back with the crew."

I skewered him with a hard look.

He pasted on a bland expression.

Luke watched.

No more excuses. I had to decide.

⌒⌒⌒

As soon as I was strapped into the Cessna, I knew I'd made a mistake. I was voluntarily going up in an airplane, something I'd never do by choice. Even worse, I'd put my life in the hands of someone I barely knew. And trusted even less. What was I thinking? How could I have been so stupid?

The interior of the Cessna didn't help. The cockpit was more cramped than a car. My head grazed the ceiling, and I had to keep my knees bent. A bewildering jumble of dials and gauges, each of them probably measuring something critical for our survival, were built into a wood-paneled console in front. The leather seats swiveled and were surprisingly comfortable, but they were nothing like a commercial airliner's. A contraption that looked like half a steering wheel was wedged in front of both seats. Why was there one in front of me? Was I supposed to do something?

Sutton strapped himself in and started the engine. The roar was so deafening my body started to vibrate. I leaned toward him. "You know, maybe this wasn't such a great idea."

He studied the dials in the cockpit.

"Listen, Luke…."

He did something with the throttle that kicked the engine up another notch. The Cessna started forward and taxied to the end of the runway. I put my hands over my ears.

He reached behind the seats and pulled out two pairs of headphones. "Here. Put these on." He handed one pair to me and slipped the other over his ears.

"Now," he yelled. He pulled back on the wheel. The engine grew even louder.

I put them on, and we accelerated. As the plane gathered speed, the familiar panic started to build. The hangar flew by in a blur of white. The trees at the edge of the runway loomed ahead. We were going to crash into them! I squeezed my eyes shut and recited the Sh'ma. At least I would die quickly. Then the plane lifted, and I felt it buck. There was a powerful surge, and we angled sharply up.

When I dared to open my eyes, we had cleared the trees by at least fifty feet and were climbing fast. I glanced over at Luke. His features relaxed. He checked the dials again, then looked over at me. He did something with the wheel and the plane leveled out. He pushed his sunglasses on top of his head.

"Take a look." His voice came through the headphones, tinny and nasal.

I peeked out. The ground was rushing away from us, but the higher we went, the more I could see. Below us was the Lodge: the hotel, the condos, the pool, the spa building, even the bunny hill. To our right a palette of earth colors—fields and crops—stretched to the horizon. To our left lay Lake Geneva, whitecaps sparkling in the late afternoon sun.

"Is this what you're looking for?"

"It's perfect."

"Good." He pulled on the wheel. The nose shot up again. I gripped my seat. He saw it. "You're afraid to fly, aren't you?"

I bit my lip. How did he know? I nodded.

His face softened. He did something with the wheel. The plane started to bank. "Don't worry. I've been doing this a long time. I want to get back just as much as you."

We rose even higher. Long shadows crept across the ground. A blush stained the western sky. Despite the roar of the engine, I imagined a deep silence on the ground.

"Nice, huh?" For the first time since I'd known him, he smiled. Such a sunny, wide-open smile, I had to smile back.

"It is."

"Why do you think I'm involved in Daria Flynn's murder?"

His frankness caught me off-guard. I ran a finger underneath the strap of my seat belt. "If you're not, why haven't you said so?"

"Because everyone knows I'm not."

"Everyone who counts."

He squinted.

"Including the chief of police, who happens to be your best friend."

"I thought so." His voice through the headphones turned grim.

"Thought what?"

"You think because Charles Sutton is my father and Jimmy Saclarides is my buddy, I can get away with anything."

"Like I said, if you haven't done anything wrong, why not say so?"

"You've heard about an individual's right to privacy?"

I shook my head. "Everybody up here falls back on that. But don't you think you should have waived it in this situation? I mean, your reputation was at stake."

"My reputation's been trashed for years," he said tiredly. "I don't care about that."

"What do you care about?"

"My mother. She doesn't need any more publicity."

He stared straight ahead. I wasn't sure how to respond. After a moment, he motioned out the window. "Now look."

We were much higher now. Below us stretched a ribbon of highway. Cars crept in both directions, resembling those miniature models little boys collect. Dollhouse buildings with postage-stamp lawns sat beside them. Every so often, a highway cloverleaf twined around the road. We weren't that far up, but I felt strangely exhilarated, almost as if I'd run a marathon. I made it. I was flying!

"You know where we are?"

"That's 94. The toll road."

He nodded. "The Lake Forest oasis is directly below us." He started to bank the plane again. But as the plane rolled diagonally, there was a bump. Fear spiked through me.

"That was just an air pocket," he said through the headphones. "In summer, the heat rises, and when it hits cooler air, you feel a bump or two. Nothing to worry about."

I nodded. I wanted to say thank you but something held me back. He glanced at the dials on the cockpit. One of them was called an altimeter, I suddenly remembered. It measured how level you were. Eventually the lines on the altimeter went horizontal.

"I did see Daria Flynn," Luke said. "A couple of times."

I looked over.

"But it was all business."

He had this habit of suddenly sprinkling critical bits of information into the conversation.

"She wanted to start her own catering business, and she wanted to cater my airline."

"Your airline?"

"It's a new business venture."

"Like United and American?"

"No. A no-frills kind."

He was starting an airline? "Why? I mean, how? Where? When did you start?"

He smiled. "You missed 'who.'"

"Sorry. I just meant...well, I didn't expect—"

"Because I don't *need* to work for a living?"

I felt my cheeks flush. "Well, to be honest, yes. Partly. Why didn't you go into the railroad business?"

He hesitated for a moment. "I've been flying all my life." I wondered about the pause. "I was about ten when my uncle took me up in his Piper for the first time. I never knew you could feel so—so full of possibilities. There's something liberating about being in the air. That feeling never went away. Even in the army, I couldn't wait to go up."

"You were in the army?"

"Something wrong with that, too?"

I smiled. The way he answered a question with another reminded me of my father. "Rich men's sons usually got out of the draft. Or went into the Guard."

"There was no draft. I enlisted."

I looked over, surprised. Luke Sutton was flouting all my preconceptions. "Why?"

"I needed to get away and…well…." He paused. "Who the fuck knows?" It came out hard, and for a moment, the anger was back. "They trained me on high-powered rifles. We had to hit targets from five hundred yards." I had the sense he was trying to work something out. Get it right. "But then they let me fly. It helped pull me out of it."

"Out of what?"

He looked over, startled, as if he'd revealed something he hadn't intended. "Nothing." He stared straight ahead, quiet for a moment. Then, "Nice country, isn't it?"

I looked through the windshield. The sun was on our left. Large patches of farmland swam all the way to the horizon, where they were sliced off by a sharp delineation between land and sky.

"If we kept going north, we'd hit the lake country." He gestured through the window. "We have a fishing cabin up there. That's where I was when Daria Flynn was killed."

I cocked my head.

"But you don't have to believe me. You can check with the guy who manages the airstrip outside Star Lake. It's in Vilas County. In northern Wisconsin. His name's Norman Desmond."

Was that the truth? Slip enough cash into the right hands, and people will say anything you want. And Luke Sutton had enough cash. Still, he knew I could follow up.

"What did you tell Daria Flynn? About the catering?"

"I told her I'd think about it, but honestly, the only catering I can afford is jet fuel. I didn't see how I could do it."

"You told her that?"

"I never got the chance."

"So why doesn't anyone else know this?"

"Who says no one knows?"

I sat back. Once again, I'd been put in my place. I was an outsider. No. If he really believed that, I wouldn't be up in the Cessna with him. "So you flew planes in the army, and now you're starting an airline. What did you do between?"

"You ask a lot of questions, you know that?" But there was no rancor, and his voice was soft. "I lived in Montana."

"Doing what?"

"I worked on a ranch for a while. Then I bought it."

"Oh."

"I can give you names there, too, in case you want to check it out." But there was a smile on his face.

"That won't be necessary," I said primly.

A moment later, he turned the wheel, and we started to bank. I clutched the edge of my seat.

"All under control," he said. "Look. I gave you answers. Now it's your turn. Why do you think I was involved with Daria Flynn's murder?"

I gazed at him, looking for any clue that he was still angry. All I saw was curiosity. I took a breath. "Daria was abandoned by her boyfriend at the rest stop. But no one, including her family, seems to know who her boyfriend was. Then, when one of the waitresses at the Lodge told me she'd seen you and Daria together, I just...well...."

"Assumed I was her boyfriend?"

"I wasn't sure. But then, when I saw you with Jimmy Saclarides and found out he was the chief of police, and then I found out Herbert Flynn used to work for you, I—"

"Herbert." His mouth tightened, and he went silent.

"I'm sorry. Did I say something wrong?" I asked through the headphones.

He didn't answer, but something about the way he'd said "Herbert" told me to back off.

The drone of the engine seemed to grow louder. Apparently, his mood could change like quicksilver. Had I blown it? Strange. Now the situation had reversed itself. I wanted him to believe me. I cast around for something to say. I remembered what he'd said about his mother.

"My mother passed away about eight years ago."

He didn't answer right away. Then, "Mine might as well have."

"How can you say that?" It came out more sharply than I'd intended.

"When I was a kid, she was always singing. Playing games with us. Making us peanut butter sandwiches. But now...." He broke off, as though he didn't want to be reminded that life had once been happy and cheerful and full of promise. "What happened to yours?" he asked after a while.

"Pancreatic cancer. It was quick, but we had the chance to say good-bye."

He kept his eyes on the dials. "That can't have been easy."

"It wasn't." I paused. "I—I'm sorry about your sister," I added.

He nodded back.

Below us evening spread across the ground like a blanket. Purple shadows covered everything, but at our altitude, we could still see the sun. A small rosy disk, it fell slowly toward the horizon, shooting off glints that frosted the hills with fire.

"I'm sorry, too," he said.

I looked over, puzzled. "For what?"

"The way my brother treated you. At the Lodge."

"Who told—oh, Jimmy. Of course."

"Chip has"—he hesitated—"issues."

The incident at the Lodge seemed like a long time ago. Up here I felt insulated. Out of time and place, but safe. As though I could say anything. Was that the attraction for Luke? A free-fly zone, where honesty and candor reigned? Maybe that's why

I said what I did next. I hadn't told anyone, not even Susan. I looked out my window. I could just see the moon in the eastern sky, crystalline silver and blue and perfectly round.

"I just found out I had a brother. An older brother. He only lived a day. I never knew him."

"You just found this out?"

"My father told me the other day. It's hard to believe they kept it from me all these years."

"Maybe they were protecting their privacy. Maybe they didn't want to inflict it on you. It was their hurt. Their pain."

"My mother took it hard," I admitted. "Like I said, I never knew him, but it's made a difference."

"How?"

"As an only child, sometimes I felt like I was marooned on an island by myself. Now I know there was someone else on that island. He didn't stick around very long, but I wasn't alone, after all. Do you know what I'm saying?" I shook my head. "Sorry. I'm probably not making any sense."

"More than you know."

We didn't say anything for a moment.

"We're almost back now, aren't we?"

"Yes." He almost seemed wistful. Then he grinned. "Now, be honest. Flying's not so bad, is it?"

I smiled back. "It isn't."

"You just need more experience. Which you're going to get right now." He looked over. "Bring us down, Ellie."

"What?"

"Here." He took my hand, placed it on the control wheel, and covered it with his own. "Ease it forward. Nice and slow." I felt him press against my hand. "That's it. Don't be afraid. Just feel it."

The plane shifted under our hands. We started to drop, but it was a gentle descent. Not at all the nightmarish image I had of planes falling out of the sky. As the plane responded to my hand, I felt a new, almost inexplicable feeling. Power. And control. Amazed, I glanced over at Luke, about to tell him I think I finally got it. But when our eyes met, his expression had changed. The smile was still there, but something else was just behind it. Something fiery and passionate and wanting, something that took my breath away. His hand was still pressing down on mine. I felt the fire jump to my skin.

Chapter Twenty-four

When we landed, I climbed out of the plane, and Luke rolled it back into the hangar. After locking the hangar door, he followed me over to Mac's van. It was dark, but a spotlight on the outside wall lit the planes of his face. "I enjoyed that, Ellie."

"I did, too." My arms hung at my sides. I didn't know what to do with my hands.

"Next time you go up, maybe you won't be as scared."

I nodded. His eyes held mine, as if he wanted to say something more but couldn't. Or wouldn't. The breeze picked up, carrying his scent. I breathed it in. I wanted him to touch me; I was afraid that he would touch me.

I forced myself to step back. This was crazy. It was just my hormones. Or the fact that David and I were through. He stepped closer and brushed the side of my cheek with his fingertips. A few strands of hair had come loose. He tucked them behind my ear.

I trembled. "My hair must be a mess."

"You're beautiful." He raised a finger to his lips.

I reached up and wound my fingers through his beard. A gentle tangle of gray and brown, it was surprisingly soft. He leaned over and kissed me on the cheek. "Good-bye, Ellie." Then he turned, walked away, and climbed into his pickup.

I fumbled around for the keys to Mac's van, finally locating them under the seat. I stabbed at the ignition several times before the key slid in. I couldn't remember ever feeling so clumsy. Or needy. Or elated.

⌒⌒⌒

It was well after dark by the time I got home. Rachel had grilled burgers for dinner, but I wasn't hungry. I figured I could manage dessert, though, so we drove over to Dairy Queen. Soft ice cream should be one of the world's seven wonders. First, you get to watch it ooze out of the machines, cascading and twisting into thick, lazy swirls. Then you get to flick your tongue around a mound of cold, sweet creaminess. Finally you draw it into your mouth, savoring the fact that it's solid enough not to melt, but not hard enough to choke you. Three awe-inspiring sensations in one food item.

Rachel chattered on about a lifeguard at the pool who'd asked for her phone number. I tried to pry out how old he was, whether he drove, or was still in high school, but after a few nonanswers, the kind that fifteen-year-olds have perfected, I realized she either didn't know or wasn't about to tell me. My third degree could wait until he came to the house. If he did.

Back home, I changed into an old T-shirt that doubles as a summer nightgown and tried not to think about Luke Sutton. I turned on the TV news in my bedroom and got into bed. It had been a week since the third sniper attack, and media coverage had fallen off. Tonight, though, the station I was watching proclaimed a major development.

According to their investigative reporter, the State Police had discovered a shell casing at the O'Hare oasis crime scene. "It was a .223," the reporter announced, "which, after careful study and comparison, was found to have come from a semiautomatic weapon like this one, a Bushmaster 223." The story cut to a shot of a high-powered rifle, which looked like any other gun to me until the reporter added, "Often referred to as the civilian version of the military M16, the Bushmaster is a favorite of former military personnel or those who want the feel of a military weapon." The reporter went on to say the Bushmaster had been the weapon of choice for snipers in other states and could hit a target as far as 500 yards away. It was also remarkably easy to learn how to use.

The story cut back to the reporter on camera. "But—while police sources say bullet fragments from the April sniper attack are consistent with this type of gun, they aren't saying that about the Lake Forest incident."

I sat up.

"In fact, our sources tell us that bullet fragments used in the Lake Forest sniper attack probably came from a .308 caliber bullet. Those bullets are typically used in bolt-action rifles like this Remington." Another weapon flashed onto the screen. It looked different from the first one, but I couldn't really tell how.

"The significance of this is that with two different rifles and two different caliber bullets, we may be dealing with two different shooters."

I leaned forward.

The broadcast cut to a back and forth between the anchorman and the reporter.

"So the shooter at the O'Hare oasis, the one with the beard and bandana, might not have acted alone?" asked the anchorman.

"Not exactly, Marty. What I'm saying—and what police have to be looking at—is the possibility of a copycat."

"At the Lake Forest oasis?" the anchorman asked.

"Right," the reporter answered. "And there's another anomaly as well."

Anomaly? Someone else I knew used that word.

"Only one shot was fired at the Lake Forest oasis, but witnesses at each of the other two rest stops heard several shots. As many as five or six."

"This is a big development, Bob. Two snipers instead of one. What are the police saying?"

"They're not confirming or denying anything. In fact, they have not returned my—our calls."

The anchorman continued, "Now, let's clear one thing up. Whether we're dealing with a copycat or not, police still believe that two people were involved in each of the three sniper attacks. A driver and a shooter."

"That's correct, Marty. Which means we may be dealing with four people now, instead of two."

"Is there any reason to think the discovery of the shell casing at the O'Hare oasis will answer that question?"

"Unfortunately, no."

"I see." The anchorman nodded sagely, although if his fuzzy questions were any indication, I doubted that he got it. "Well, thanks for your exclusive report, Bob. I know you'll keep us posted on all the developments." The two men traded smiles.

I zapped the tube with the remote. Despite a thick anchorman, this *was* a major development. Up until now, the idea that Daria's death was caused by someone she knew was just speculation and gossip. But now, there seemed to be some evidence supporting that theory. Sure, it could have been a sick weirdo intent on making a name for himself. But what if it wasn't?

I crept downstairs, trying not to disturb Rachel, who'd gone to sleep early. The reporter would never reveal his source, but I suspected I knew who it was. How many people would use the word "anomaly" in the same context? Detective Milanovich had to be frustrated by his lack of progress—a carefully planted leak might cause the dam to break.

But that wasn't what why I went into kitchen and poured myself a large glass of wine. Luke Sutton said he'd been at his fishing cabin when Daria Flynn was killed. And that their meetings had been strictly business. But now that I knew some of the history of the two families, I wasn't sure whether to believe him. What's more, I couldn't ignore three other facts: Luke drove a green pickup, he had a beard, and he knew how to use a high-powered rifle.

Chapter Twenty-five

I rose sluggish and heavy the next day and brewed a strong pot of coffee. I'd spent the night in a restless haze, thrashing from one side to the other. My mood matched the weather, a grim overcast with humidity so thick I felt like I was swimming through air. I'd promised Mac I'd scout locations in Lake Geneva for B-roll, but I was already thinking up ways to procrastinate. I looked over at Rachel, who had made an early appearance. "Hey, sweetie, I'm going up to Lake Geneva to do some sightseeing. You want to come along? We can stop at the outlet mall on the way."

She looked up from the back of the cereal box she was reading and arched her brows. They merged together just like my mother's used to. "When would we be back?"

"I'd say around three."

She thought, then shook her head. "Julia wants me by noon."

A twinge of jealousy shot through me, but I forced a smile. "Sure. Hey, you must have a bunch of money by now. Want me to take it to the bank for you?"

"No, thanks. I'm saving up for an iPod. If I pay for it, Dad said he'll give me a hundred dollars' worth of downloads."

I kept the smile pasted on. "Must be nice."

I trudged upstairs and threw on my clothes. But my mind wasn't on cover footage. I went into my office and booted up the computer. Ten minutes and a few phone calls later, I was talking to Norman Desmond, who owned a bait and tackle shop in Star Lake and managed the airstrip on the side.

"Desmond here...." His voice was deep but oddly musical.

"Mr. Desmond, my name is Ellie Foreman. You don't know me, but I think you know a friend of mine."

"And who might that be?" His inflection in just five words spanned at least an octave.

"Luke Sutton."

There was a pause. "Well, now, miss—what did you say your name was?"

"Foreman."

"Well, Miss Foreman, I might. Then again, I might not."

An equivocator. Just what I needed.

"That's odd, because he mentioned you by name."

"Lotta folks know me up here. Got the only bait and tackle shop around. Look, I'm kinda busy right now. Is there something I can do for you?"

"You manage the airstrip, too, don't you?"

"That's right." He chuckled. "Not that we get all that much traffic."

I found myself mimicking his singsongy speech patterns. "Well, I wonder whether you could confirm something for me." He didn't answer. "Do you recall if Luke flew up to Star Lake on Thursday, the third week of June?" I scrambled for a calendar. "That would have been the nineteenth. He said he thought so, but I figured you'd know, since you manage the place."

I heard a swishing noise, then his voice, somewhat muffled. "No, no. You want to go after some muskies, best to start with some weighted suicks. Try some of those Reef Hawgs over there." Another swishing sound, and he was back.

"What'd you say you did, Miss Foreman?"

"I didn't."

He paused. "You a reporter?"

"No," I said. "I'm not a reporter."

"Well, that narrows things down. You're a friend of Luke's?"

"That's right." Did I sound as uncertain as I felt?

"Well, you see, now, Miss Foreman, I got a problem. I just don't feel right tattling on someone's whereabouts to a perfect stranger. 'Cause as nice as you sound, we don't know each other from Adam, I don't know why or what you're gonna do with the information."

"But I'll be glad to—"

"And frankly, Miss Foreman, folks up here don't like people knowing their business. So, until I know you a little better, or Luke tells me it's okay to talk to you, I'm gonna have to pass. I hope you understand." His rich tones resonated through the telephone.

"Mr. Desmond, I'm just trying to pinpoint—"

"Hey, why don't you come on up and try some real fishing? Be happy to set you up with the right lures."

"If I did, would you tell me about Luke?"

"No, but I'll tell you how to catch a boatload of muskies."

⌒⌒⌒

Two hours later, I hugged the shore of Lake Geneva heading toward Black Point mansion. The most exclusive part of the resort town, Black Point is a woodsy, secluded area that stretches over a hundred acres and contains over seventy species of evergreens, according to the city's website. The mansion itself has more than twenty rooms and is considered one of the best examples of the "great summer houses." Its most unique feature is a tower that rises four stories off the ground and can be spotted from other points around the lake. I only caught a glimpse of it, though; I hadn't called ahead, and the gates to the property were shut tight. There had been some controversy about it recently, I'd read. Visitors were probably scarce.

I made some notes and then swung back into town. I took a look at the Golden Oaks mansion, which had been built by a doctor whom some called the father of Lake Geneva. It was now a bed-and-breakfast. Then I checked my map and drove past Maple Lawn, one of the oldest estates in the area; the old Wrigley estate called Green Gables; and mansions that once belonged to Montgomery Ward, John M. Smyth, and Richard Sears. Someone had told me members of the Outfit vacationed here during the summer, too, but somehow I didn't think their homes would be on the map.

All that wealth made me hungry, so just after two I parked behind the Mount Olympus restaurant. Although it was cloudy, it was still high season, and Main Street was thronged with summer people. Inside, nearly all of the tables were occupied. Kim bustled back and forth, as did a tall, gangly teenage girl with stringy blond hair. Summer help. The old man who'd been sipping ouzo the first time I came in was there, too.

I grabbed a spot at the counter, figuring I'd have to wait, but the teenager promptly fished out a pad from the pocket of her apron and came over. I ordered a Greek salad with anchovies and a Diet Coke. She dutifully wrote it down and then disappeared through the swinging door.

While I waited, I thought about a trip Barry and I had taken to California when Rachel was a baby. We'd gone to Monterey and stopped in at the aquarium on Cannery Row. The second floor housed a huge circular tank of anchovies. Anchovies are tiny fish, but what they lack in size they make up in speed, spinning around the tank so fast it's impossible to track one fish. What we saw was a dizzying blur of silver, punctuated by an occasional burst of light when sunlight or the flash of a camera hit the tank. But the most fantastic part occurred when they changed direction. Hundreds, or maybe thousands, of the tiny creatures suddenly stopped, turned around, and whirled the other way. Simultaneously. I remember feeling dumbfounded as I watched. What prompted them to switch directions? Some kind of cosmic group consciousness? Or was it the random act of one anchovy—incapable, for whatever reason, of going with the flow—that triggered a chain reaction?

I was still ruminating when my lunch arrived. I eyed the anchovy on my plate. Was he the troublemaker? If so, he'd paid dearly for it.

"She get it right?" a voice said behind me.

I twisted around. Kim Flynn was wearing a long apron over a T-shirt and jeans, and her hair was tied back in a ponytail. With her hair off her face, she looked younger and more vulnerable than before, and very much like her late sister. She yanked a thumb in the direction of the teenager who'd taken my order. "She's new. Gotta make sure she's doing it right."

"Hello, Kim." I set my fork down. The girl was now serving a table in the back. "She did just fine."

"Good." Kim nodded and went behind the counter. "So what brings you back here? Besides our great food?" She busied herself refilling a salt shaker. Her expression was neutral. It occurred to me I'd never seen her smile.

"I was scouting some locations for the video. Some of the old estates. They're magnificent."

She didn't say anything.

"Hard to believe people could afford to build such huge homes."

She shrugged.

A great conversationalist Kim wasn't. I wondered how to broach the subject that was on my mind. "Kim, did you happen to see the news last night?"

"No." She folded the flap on the box of salt. "Actually, I'm kind of busy right now. Can this wait for a few minutes?"

"Oh, sure. Sorry. I'm glad you're so busy."

She nodded, a nod that was hard to read. "We need to be. Got a lot of bills to pay. But things should slow down soon."

I ate my salad at a leisurely pace, and thirty minutes later, the activity inside the restaurant did slow. Only two tables of customers remained. Even the man sipping ouzo was gone. Kim cleared the dirty dishes and motioned to the teenager to sponge down the tables. Wiping her hands on her apron, she rejoined me at the counter.

"So what's going on?"

I pushed my plate away. "There was a story on a Chicago news station." I went into the fact the police were analyzing shell casings and bullet fragments from all three sniper attacks. "Turns out the bullets used in the first and the third attack were probably .223s."

She gave me a puzzled frown.

"They're used in high-powered assault rifles, like an M16. But the interesting thing is that they don't think that was the weapon used in Daria's death."

"Oh?" I got the feeling she was trying to figure out what was so significant about that.

"Bottom line, they found fragments that indicate the bullet was a .308." When she frowned again, I added, "Which means a different rifle was used to kill Daria. One that wasn't used to kill the other women. And a different rifle could mean a different shooter. Which means it could be a copycat."

She picked up the box of salt she'd been using to fill the salt shakers.

"But it also opens up the possibility it was someone she knew."

She held the box of salt to her chest. "I'll believe it when they get the guy." She looked around, her gaze settling on the teenage waitress. "Is that why you're here?"

Kim didn't think much of police investigations, I recalled. "No, like I said, I was scouting locations for cover footage. I might do an interview with Willetta Emerson. I understand her family were circus people at one time."

She seemed unimpressed.

"I'd also like to find someone who knows something about the ice men."

"The ice men?" She put down the box. This time, she seemed surprised. "What do you know about them?"

"Not much. Except that it was a pretty good business at one time. At least until refrigerators became common."

"That's true."

An awkward pause ensued. I wasn't winning any points in the conversation derby. "By the way, I heard about Anne Sutton."

She eyed me curiously. "You're seeing all our dirty laundry, aren't you?"

I ignored the crack. "Did you know her?"

"Everybody did."

"Do you remember when she died?"

"Of course," she snapped. "It changed—it changed everything."

"In what way?"

For an instant she looked startled, as if she hadn't meant to say it out loud. A stray lock of hair came loose across her face. "It was—well—one of those things you don't forget."

"Like where you were when you heard Kennedy was shot."

"I was just a baby then." She pushed the lock of hair back under her hairnet. "Well, if that's all, I've got to—"

I decided I might as well just come out with it. "Kim, I found out your father worked for the Suttons."

She hesitated for a long moment. Then, "Of course he did."

That wasn't the reaction I'd expected.

She shook her head as though I was the most ignorant person on the planet. "My father was the Suttons' caretaker for years. He's the one who found Anne Sutton's body."

I ran a hand through my hair. I thought I'd discovered a significant relationship between the Suttons and the Flynns. But Kim made it seem trivial.

"How did he happen to work for them?"

She eyed the salt, as if the answer was written on the back of the box. "My grandfather Flynn was the ice man in these parts. My father followed him into the business."

"Your father was an ice man?"

She nodded. "It didn't last. Eventually, the business collapsed, and the Suttons hired Dad to take care of their estate." She paused. "He was lucky to get a job."

"How long did your father work for the Suttons?"

The same lock of hair fell in front of her face. She tossed it back. "He was there before I was born. I guess about twenty years. Until Anne died. He—he went away after that."

"It must have been hard," I said quietly.

"What are you talking about?"

"To live with all that suspicion."

Her face turned steely. "What do you know about that?"

I shrugged.

Kim sniffed. "Willetta Emerson. That woman will say anything to anyone."

"I understand the pressure that must have put on you."

"Why do you always say that?"

"Say what?"

"That you understand. You sound like Clinton, you know? You can 'feel our pain.'"

I was taken aback. "I'm sorry. I just wanted to—"

"You're just trying to get as much information as you can." She glared. "What I can't figure out is why."

"That's not fair, Kim. Your mother asked me to get back to her if I remembered anything. That's all. I have no ulterior motive." Which had been the case. Until the other day.

She shot me a dubious look. "You want to know what it was like? Okay, I'll tell you." She planted her hands on her hips. "It's been a real bundle of laughs living around here. First off, everyone else had a father. I had—Mother. Other mothers stayed home and took care of their kids. My mother had to work, and so did we. We were here after school every day. No Girl Scouts. No cheerleading. No driving around. We had to do our shifts. But that wasn't the worst part."

She took a breath. "Do you know what's it like to be excluded… ignored…pitied? I couldn't go to school without other girls whispering. Couldn't go to the store without people talking behind their hands. Look, there go the poor little Flynn girls." She scoffed. "And why? Because some rich man with a lot of power decided to persecute my father. He had nothing to do with Anne Sutton's murder. But no one believed him."

"Why not?"

"You have no idea who you're dealing with up here, do you? No one crosses Charles Sutton. Or anyone in his family." She exhaled scornfully. "Yeah. I guess you could call it pressure."

"If it's that bad, why do you stay around? Why not just pick up and move?"

"Where am I gonna go? My mother won't leave. Her family's been here forever. And I don't have enough money to set up a new household. Besides, now, since she's been so sick...." She gazed around the restaurant. "I'm trapped. I have no options." Her rage etched deep lines on her face. "That's what the Suttons did to me."

"But Daria left...or was planning to."

"Daria always did what she wanted. She was very good at taking care of herself. She never would have—"

"Kim, stop this. Right now," an angry voice cracked.

Kim spun around. Irene Flynn had come through the swinging door. She must have been standing there for a while, but I was so involved in talking to Kim, I hadn't registered her presence.

"Mrs. Flynn. I had no idea you were here."

It had only been a few weeks since she'd visited my house, but Irene had changed. Her face was pinched, and the lines carved across her forehead seemed deeper. Her spine was still impossibly straight, but she still looked weary and fragile, not nearly strong enough to handle a shift in the kitchen. But then, the will to persevere can overcome all sorts of deficiencies, and Irene certainly had the will. She leaned against the wall. "Kim, you have more important things to do than whine."

I rose to Kim's defense. "It's my fault, Mrs. Flynn. I was just telling her what I heard on the news last night, and then we just started to—"

"Is—is it something about Daria?" Irene asked.

Kim shook her head. "She was asking about Dad. And Anne Sutton."

A series of emotions paged across Irene's face. A frown, then concern, then something deeper. Almost fear. "Who told you about that?"

"Willetta Emerson." Kim spat it out.

"Figures." Irene flicked her hand dismissively.

"I found some articles also," I added.

She looked at me with empty eyes and a tight-lipped smile that only the most naïve person would consider mirthful. "Anne

Sutton has nothing to do with Daria. If you have news about my daughter, that's one thing. But don't come here gossiping about events from thirty years ago."

"Well, Irene, as a matter of fact, I do have some news about Daria."

"What's that?" She looked slightly irritated. I had the feeling I was keeping her from something important.

"You remember the rumors about meetings between Daria and Luke Sutton?" She tensed. "Well, it seems as if Daria wanted Luke to hire her."

"What?" Kim looked incredulous.

I told her what Luke had said on the plane. When I had finished, Kim ran a hand through her hair, her fingers tangling in the hairnet. Given her bitterness toward the Suttons, she probably thought her sister was consorting with the enemy.

"How do you know that?"

"Luke."

She looked confused. "You talked to Luke?"

"Yesterday."

"Where? How?"

"At the airstrip. We were shooting pickups, and—and he was there." I didn't go into details.

Kim's gaze locked on me. The corners of her mouth twitched, but as with her mother, it wasn't a smile. I shifted. Both Flynn women were making me nervous. And when I'm nervous, I talk too much. "Like I said, he's—he's starting a new airline. No frills. It seemed reasonable, you know. With Daria wanting to be a caterer and all."

Kim's stare deepened. I felt like an insect pinned under a microscope.

"And now you don't think he and Daria were having an affair?"

"It doesn't seem as likely as before." I was babbling now. Filling the air with noise. I needed to change the subject. "Did I tell you I saw the Suttons' ice house the other day?"

If anything, Kim's expression hardened. "You seem to be traveling in all the right circles."

I forced myself not to react. "I was hoping to include something about the ice business in the video. You know, this is what Lake Geneva used to look like a century ago. That kind of thing." I stopped. I was repeating myself.

Now both Kim and her mother were staring at me.

"It would have been wonderful to get a shot with ice inside, you know? For the video. But it probably won't happen. I understand they use it as a tool shed now."

Neither woman said anything.

"At least that's what I guessed when I saw their gardener."

Kim stood very still. "Their gardener?"

"A tall man with a plaid shirt. He was just finishing up for the day. At least that's what it looked like." Kim's attitude was taking its toll. I was spouting effluents. Anything to get her off my back.

There was a moment of awkward silence.

Then, "Well, now, Miss Foreman," Irene Flynn said tartly, "I think it's time to stop focusing on Daria." She drew herself up. "I know I asked you to get back to me if you remembered anything Daria said. But I had no idea you would stir things up like this. We need to move on. So, it's over. No more of this." She slipped her hands behind her waist and untied her apron. "Kim, I need some air. I'm going for a walk."

"Give me five minutes, Mother. I'll go with you."

"No." Irene waved a hand. "You have the restaurant to run. I'll be fine."

Kim looked worried.

"I'll take the cane." Irene pushed through the swinging door. A moment later, I heard the angry clatter of pots.

Kim eyed me. "I'd better go."

I hoped she didn't see my relief.

Chapter Twenty-six

I threw down a ten-dollar bill and went out to my car. It had taken all my energy to deal with the Flynns. The experience reminded me of the police interrogation the time I was caught shoplifting. I'd done the same thing then, too: jabbered away, confessing to everything, just to make it stop. I'd make a lousy career criminal. Still, I was grateful Irene's focus on her daughter's death appeared to be waning. Maybe she *was* trying to move on. I should probably cut her—and Kim—some slack.

Back in my car, I adjusted the rearview mirror, checked my seat position, and ran my hand down the strap of my seat belt. I was finished for the day, but I didn't want to go home. Kim's venom toward the Suttons had unnerved me. Not just because she thought the Suttons were powerful and devious and would do anything to have their own way. I wanted to believe Luke was different. But I couldn't. I didn't know. The one attempt I'd made to find out—confirming whether he'd been at the family's fishing cabin when he claimed to be—hadn't been very successful.

And yet, ever since the plane ride, I'd been parsing every word of our conversation. Had he meant something significant when he said he enjoyed himself? What was he really saying when he apologized for his brother? Or when he kissed me on the cheek? I was aware that my feelings for him had developed fast. Maybe too fast. But I couldn't do much to stop them. Correction. I didn't want to.

I sighed and started the engine. It was time to go home. I was backing out of the lot when I saw Irene Flynn emerge from the rear of the restaurant. She tentatively made her way to the gray Saturn, wearing the same troubled expression I'd seen inside. She'd said she was going for a walk; her cane must have been in the car. I waited for her to open the passenger door and get it. Instead she went around to the driver's side.

When she climbed into the driver's seat, I grew alarmed. She was still recovering from a stroke. She shouldn't be driving. When she started the engine, I tensed. She was taking a huge risk. What if she had an accident? Even my father, who is still relatively healthy, surrendered his license a few years ago, admitting that his reflexes weren't what they once were. Irene was younger than Dad, but her health was more precarious.

She keyed the engine, threw the car in reverse, and swung out of the lot. The car lurched forward and she turned onto Main Street heading west at a fast clip. Why was she in such a hurry? Was she still upset about our conversation? There *had* been a palpable shift in her mood when I brought up Anne Sutton and Herbert. But he'd been dead for thirty years. Why would discussing him make her so irritable?

I checked the time. It was still early, and I didn't have any place I needed to be. I debated whether to follow Irene, at least for a few miles. It was out of my way—but I'd feel better if I knew she was okay. She was only about a block ahead. I pulled out behind her.

⁓⁓⁓

In thinking over the events of that afternoon, I still find it hard to believe Irene didn't know I was following her. I had no clue how to tail someone, and she'd seen my car. The only conclusion I can draw is that she was so focused on her destination she was oblivious to the journey. We drove west on Route 50 past a string of farms, tract houses, and farm implements dealers. The sky was still gray, a humid, sweat-soaking gray. I rolled the window down and heavy air rushed in, smelling like a mix of manure, honeysuckle, and the slightly astringent odor of asphalt.

Ten minutes later, we cruised past a golf course attached to Lake Lawn Lodge. Landmarks started to appear closer together, and I realized we were on the outskirts of Delavan. Irene turned off the highway and then turned again. I stayed a few car lengths behind. We clattered over railroad tracks, and after another turn, she started down a street whose name was a number—Sixth.

We were on a residential block, not very well heeled by the look of it. Some of the houses looked seedy and run-down. One had boarded-up windows, another a yard of packed dirt marked by a rusty tricycle and a flat tire. Irene seemed to know where she was going. Two thirds of the way down the block, she stopped at a one-story house with aluminum siding. The windows were covered with yellowed shades. A rickety porch led to a door with a thick mesh screen.

I waited at the other end of the block. The street was quiet. No children playing outside. No one walking a dog. Time seemed to have passed over this stretch of civilization. Time and attention. But something had drawn Irene here.

She slid out of the car and made her way to the porch, leaning heavily on her cane. When she reached the front door, she shifted the cane to her other hand and pressed the buzzer. A minute later, she rang again and switched the cane back. When nothing happened after a third ring, she pulled the screen door open. Sneaking a look in both directions, she pushed on the front door. A wedge of black space appeared; the door was unlocked. She went inside.

I chewed my lip, unsure what to do. I decided to wait five more minutes, then cruise slowly by the house. If I saw nothing unusual, I'd head home. I leaned back against the headrest to wait.

Two minutes later, the front door flew open, and Irene Flynn stumbled out with the cane, her free hand clasped over her mouth. She staggered off the porch. The screen door banged loudly. She lurched across the yard. With a strength I wouldn't have thought possible, she flung open the car door. Before getting in, she gulped down a few ragged breaths. She glanced back at the house over her shoulder, then buried her face in her hands.

Finally, she threw herself into the Saturn, started the engine, and pulled away so fast the tires squealed.

A chill crawled up my spine. I looked back at the house. The door was still ajar. Whatever Irene had just seen or done had filled her with dread. I didn't know what to do. Should I try to catch up with the Saturn, intercept Irene, and make sure she was okay? Or should I take a look myself?

I wasn't foolish enough to go into a strange house alone. Especially if whatever was inside was as frightening as Irene thought it was. But something inside wasn't right. Maybe I should go to one of the neighbors. No. How would I explain what I was doing here? But I couldn't leave. What if someone was hurt?

In the end, I compromised. Irene would be back at the restaurant at some point. I could find her later. But I'd probably never come back to this house again. I decided to walk up to the front door. I wouldn't step inside, and if I didn't see anything, I'd leave. But if I did see something—well—I'd deal with it.

I climbed out of the car. I crossed the yard, looking to see if the neighbors were watching. I didn't notice anyone, not even a flutter of a curtain or shade. I stepped up onto the porch. The floorboards squeaked. I rapped on the screen door.

"Hello?" I called out. "Anyone home?"

No response.

"Hello?" I repeated.

Nothing.

I took a breath. The front door was open, revealing a yawning mass of black. I wouldn't step across the threshold, but if I opened the screen door, I could lean my head in. I grabbed the handle and pulled.

The smell overpowered me right away. I've smelled rotting meat before. This was similar, but sweeter and more powerful. I pinched my nostrils. My pulse pounded in my ears.

The entranceway narrowed to a shadowy hall leading to a room at the back of the house. The edge of a table and a couple of chairs showed through. A kitchen. Light spilled from the room, illuminating something sprawled just outside in the hall. I squinted. As my eyes adjusted, my stomach roiled.

It was a man's body. His face, or what had been his face, was bloated, and his features swam on a bluish sea of skin. Dark stains saturated his clothes, smearing the floor beside him. I staggered back onto the porch. The screen door banged shut. I covered my mouth with my hand. I didn't know who he was, but I'd seen him before. He'd been wearing the same plaid shirt and olive drab pants.

Chapter Twenty-seven

My hands were still shaking even after I called the police. It took a few minutes to figure out which police department should respond, but once they determined I was in Delavan, a dispatcher told me to stay where I was. I clutched the steering wheel and squeezed my eyes shut, trying to erase the images of the body. I've seen dead bodies before—my mother died in my arms—but I'd never seen one like this.

Eventually, a white patrol car pulled up, and an officer got out. After confirming I was the person who had made the call, he pulled plastic gloves over his hands and went inside the house. He came back out a moment later and jogged to his cruiser. Ten minutes later, more squad cars and an unmarked arrived. A young detective questioned me. From his bleached hair and grunge style, I guessed he considered himself the Brad Pitt of southern Wisconsin. I told him everything, including the fact that Irene Flynn was the person who had led me here. Brad told me to wait in my car.

Thirty minutes later a blue and white squad car with the Lake Geneva Police insignia screeched to a stop in front of the house. A uniformed officer jumped out of the driver's side; Jimmy Saclarides got out of the other. He came over to the Volvo with Brad. I rolled down the window.

"Are you okay?"

I looked at him, back at Brad, and burst into tears.

⌐〜〜⌐

Darkness was rapidly encroaching when the Walworth County Sheriff's van pulled up. Inside were two men who, after conferring with the officers on the front lawn, grabbed a large backpack, a Polaroid camera, and a video camera, and headed into the house.

Jimmy detached himself from the knot of officers. He'd given me time to pull myself together, even given me tissues from a box inside his cruiser. Now he walked around to the passenger side of the Volvo, opened the door, and climbed in.

"So what were you doing here, Ellie?"

I confessed, somewhat guiltily, that I'd been following Irene.

"Why?"

I told him about my visit to the restaurant and her reaction to our conversation. Jimmy's eyebrows knit together. "She told you to butt out?"

I nodded. "I'd been telling Kim about the second sniper attack and the fact that the bullet fragments didn't match the others. Then we started talking about Herbert Flynn and Anne Sutton, and her demeanor changed."

"You were talking about Herbert?"

"I just found out he was the caretaker for the Suttons when Anne was killed."

Jimmy looked past me. He didn't say anything for a moment. "A bad business, that."

"It sounded horrible. So unfair."

"It was a long time ago." He refocused. "What do you mean, Irene's demeanor changed?"

"She grew—agitated. She took off her apron and told Kim she was going for a walk. Then she jumped in the car and took off." I rubbed my hands on my jeans legs. "I was worried. I thought she might not be well enough to drive. Especially since she took off so fast. I thought I should make sure she was okay."

Jimmy looked as if he understood. In fact, his equanimity made me think I wasn't telling him anything new.

"Why is it you don't seem surprised?"

He gazed at the house.

"Jimmy, I realize I'm not from around here. And I know there's a lot of history—between you and the Flynns and the Suttons—that I'm not a part of. But Irene Flynn did ask me to get back to her if I heard anything about her daughter's death. That's what I was doing.

"Now she's changed her mind. That's fine. I don't want to be in the middle of something I'm not supposed to be. But given what I found inside that house, it's clear that something is very wrong." I nodded toward the house. "And I'm involved whether I want to be or not. The man in there doesn't look like he died from natural causes."

Jimmy didn't say anything.

"Was he murdered?"

He didn't answer for a moment. Then, he nodded, almost grudgingly. "It looks as if we have a homicide."

"Who is he? What happened to him?"

He turned around. "Ellie, did you ever think there might be a good reason why we don't broadcast our problems?" Jimmy's voice was sharp. "That it has something to do with not stirring up old memories? Painful ones that never healed?"

"It's a little late for that, don't you think?"

"Why? Because you've heard rumors of relationships, news stories about copycat murders, and you put two and two together and come up with—I don't know—six?"

"You forgot strange men lurking around the ice house at the Suttons."

Jimmy frowned. "What are you talking about?"

"I didn't see the face of the man who was hanging around the tool shed at the Suttons the other day. But I did see his clothes."

Jimmy's faced darkened.

"The man was wearing a plaid shirt and olive drab pants. Just like the man in that house."

⌒⌒⌒

Jimmy got out of my car and fished out his cell phone. When the call went through, he stepped away, preventing me from overhearing the conversation. I guessed it was someone back at the police station and that it had to do with locating Irene Flynn.

Meanwhile, the detective who looked like Brad Pitt came out of the house carrying a plastic sandwich bag. Inside the bag was a small object about the size of a deck of cards. But his deceptively casual shamble didn't mask his excitement, and he went over to an older man in a police uniform and white shirt who had just arrived and looked like he might be his boss. Jimmy joined them.

"I think we have an ID on the victim," Brad said confidently.

The older man scratched his nose with his index finger. "What'cha got?"

"It's a bank book, sir. A passbook from a bank in Chicago."

"And?"

"The name on the account is Herbert Flynn."

Chapter Twenty-eight

It was after ten by the time they let me go home, but a cloud cover blanketed the night sky, holding in the day's heat. The evidence technicians had finished, and the coroner was preparing to move the body. I'd been questioned so thoroughly by Jimmy and the Delavan cops I was convinced the only thing they didn't know was the name of my best friend in kindergarten.

I drove home, trying to make sense of what I'd heard. Herbert Flynn—Irene Flynn's husband, Daria's Flynn's father—had been gone for thirty years. "Herbert's gone…" Irene told me. I'd assumed that meant he was dead. But Herbert Flynn was the man walking around the ice house at the Suttons'. Which meant he was very much alive. Or had been, until a couple of days ago.

Which also meant that Irene Flynn knew he was alive and had commandeered the Saturn to visit him. Why? Was it something I said at the restaurant? If so, what? And why was Herbert back in her life? Or had they been in contact the entire thirty years he'd been "gone"? I couldn't imagine anyone living in that ramshackle house for three decades—and the bank book from Chicago indicated he didn't—but if he had been elsewhere, where had he been and when did he come back? Why wasn't he living at home? And why, after everything that happened, was he lurking around the Suttons' ice house?

The stripes dividing the highway lanes zipped by in a blur, unnaturally bright from the throw of my headlights. The timing was almost too precious. Daria Flynn was killed at a rest stop in

June. A month later, her father, who'd presumably been gone for thirty years after being suspected of killing Anne Sutton, returned and was killed. Was there a connection? When I'd mentioned it to Jimmy, his frown deepened, but all he said was, "Yes. It is interesting." Even I knew that was cop talk for "we're all over it."

Chapter Twenty-nine

I woke up the next morning to a steady rain. I threw on a pair of shorts and a T-shirt, made coffee, and prowled restlessly around the house. I'd planned to go over to Mac's to edit, but I called and told Hank to go ahead without me. His rough cut would be better without my *shpulkes*.

I wandered back into the kitchen and took out the vacuum. Cleaning the house usually centers me—I subscribe to the "ordered house–ordered mind" theory of housekeeping. I started to dust and vacuum the family room, but it was a halfhearted effort. Before long I gave up and watched the rain pool unevenly on the street, forming series of puddles that eventually over-flowed into each other to form larger ones. The rain drumming on the roof was a solemn accompaniment to my thoughts.

I wasn't a party to the history between the Flynns and the Suttons, but I had found Herbert Flynn's body, and I'd met pretty much everyone in both families. All of which gave me an awkward but genuine connection to them. I doubted I'd learn much more from the Flynns, however. They were probably besieged with police anyway.

But there was another possibility. I grabbed my bag and headed out to the car. I'd already dealt with the Hatfields. It was time to try the McCoys.

When I pulled up to Monticello, I saw several cars including a police cruiser and a van parked in the Suttons' circular driveway. Maybe this wasn't such a great idea. When I spotted Luke's pickup, though, a pleasant shiver ran through me. I trotted up to the front door, dodging the rain, trying to convince myself he wasn't the reason I was here. I was about to lift the brass knocker when I noticed a buzzer on the side of the door. A series of musical notes chimed when I pressed it. Footsteps approached right away. Maybe they were Luke's.

They weren't. A matronly woman wearing thick glasses, a blue shirtwaist dress, and white gym shoes opened the door. "Yes?"

I drew in a breath. "Mrs. Sutton? I'm sorry to disturb you, but I was wondering if I could speak to Luke."

"Who are you?" she asked crisply.

"My name is Ellie Foreman. I'm—"

"Sit there." She pointed to what looked like a pair of silk upholstered deck chairs on either side of a long walnut console. "I'll see if Mr. Sutton can see you. I'm Mrs. Baines."

Of course. The housekeeper. I sat in one of the chairs. Mrs. Baines climbed a set of stairs that, from my vantage point, seemed to ascend directly to the dome on top of the house, though there had to be a landing and second story tucked behind them. Even though it was raining, light poured in from the windows. The marble floor, in alternating squares of black and white, was art deco, but the portraits on the walls, formally posed people whom I didn't recognize, gave out a John Sargent turn-of-the-century feel. The console was so ornate and glossy I felt insignificant in the low-slung deck chair beside it. Which probably was the intention.

A short time later, a door closed somewhere upstairs, and a man came down the steps.

"What do you want?" I gazed into a pair of angry eyes. Chip Sutton was wearing pressed jeans and a crisp button-down oxford shirt, but there was stubble on his chin, and his eyes were bloodshot. He gripped the edge of the banister.

"I—I'd like to speak to Luke."

"What about?"

"It's—it's confidential."

"You're kidding, right?" He kept a tight grip on the banister. "I don't think my brother wants to talk about anything with you. Especially anything confidential."

"Why don't you let him decide?" Perversely, his hostility buoyed me.

"You think you can just show up, demand to see my brother, who you practically accused of murder, and expect to be welcomed with open arms?" His finger stabbed the air in my direction. "Who the hell do you think you are?"

This was the worst of all possible outcomes. I drew myself up, affecting a calm I didn't feel. "Look, Chip, I don't want to cause a scene, but—"

"Chip, dear, who's there?" A female voice cut me off.

Chip looked over his shoulder. Then he looked back at me. The female voice called again. "What's going on, son?"

A wraithlike woman descended the stairs behind him. She was wearing a white silk robe. Her hair was so blond the light seemed to bounce off it, but there were deep lines on her face. I put her somewhere in her seventies. She looked like she'd been in the process of putting on makeup but had been interrupted. One eye had eyeliner and mascara, but the other was naked.

When she saw me, she stopped on the bottom stair. "Annie?" she asked tentatively. "Is that you?" Her voice was soft, almost breathless. A cloud of perfume surrounded her. Chanel.

I looked at Chip. A strange expression had come over him: pain, sadness, and something else I couldn't identify. He clasped the woman's hand.

"No, Mom. It's not Anne. Annie's gone."

She turned to me with a deep frown. "Anne's gone?" She gazed at me, as if my face held the answer to her question. Then a beatific smile came over her. "Of course. She's at school." She nodded, the kind of nod that expects an affirmative response.

Chip shot me a warning look.

"Mrs. Sutton. My name is Ellie Foreman."

She gave me a blank look. Then a small smile. "Have we met?"

I smiled back. "No. I'm here—well—I was hoping I could see Luke."

Her smile widened into a grin. "Luke, is it? I should have known. All the girls want to see Luke." She turned to Chip. "Don't they, sweetheart?"

She glanced back at Chip, who stood behind her, his arms stiffly folded.

"Now, Chip," Gloria went on. "Don't be cranky. Your turn's coming."

Chip's Adam's apple bobbed up and down. He was controlling himself. But just barely.

I cleared my throat. "Mrs. Sutton, could I see Luke now?"

She faced me again, as if for the first time. "Of course. Let me find him for you." She came down the last step and started across the marble floor, the scent of Chanel trailing her. As soon as she was out of earshot, Chip muttered, "Get out of here. Before I get the police."

Gloria disappeared through a door on the first level. I stood my ground. "Not until I talk to Luke."

Chip squeezed his eyes shut for an instant. When he opened them again, the anger was still there, but something else was there, too. Futility and sorrow, both wrapped up in an oddly desperate quality. For a quick second, he looked almost human. "You have no idea what you've done."

I wondered what he was talking about. It didn't take long to find out. Gloria came back into the hall, striding purposefully in my direction. I craned my neck, hoping that Luke was behind her, but she was alone. Her forehead was now lined, and the lower part of her jaw flickered.

"I'm sorry, but Luke isn't available right now," she said coolly, her cordiality gone.

"He's—he's not?"

"He's not seeing anyone. But I'll tell him that you called."

"Mrs. Sutton, are you sure? I don't—"

Chip stepped in front of his mother. "You heard my mother. Now get out."

I looked at Gloria, then at Chip. Gloria stood in the hall, not moving. Her eyes lost focus and she went limp, like she might collapse at any time. Chip grabbed his mother's arm and steered her toward the stairs. She offered no resistance. "Mrs. Baines? Where are you? Mother's robe is dirty. You need to change it."

I watched Chip half push, half drag his mother up the stairs. I hadn't seen a speck of dirt. At the top of the landing, he turned around. His parting words sliced through me like a knife. "Are you satisfied?"

Chapter Thirty

I let myself out of the Suttons' home and started back down the driveway. Rain lashed my skin and clothes, but I didn't notice. It was clear Mrs. Sutton was more than a recluse; something was seriously amiss. I wondered whether she was getting any help, aside from a housekeeper who whisked her away at the first sign of distress.

I headed to my car. Luke's mother was nuts, his brother pathetic, and his father was obsessed with a man who'd been dead two hundred years. Despite their cushion of wealth, this was not the profile of a steady, secure family. I could hear my father. "Stay away from these people," he would say, shaking his head. "They have *tsuris.*"

"Ellie! Ellie Foreman!"

I spun around. Willetta Emerson was waving to me from the far end of the Suttons' driveway. Huddling under a red umbrella, she made a stark contrast to the gray, rainy day.

"What are you doing here?" she asked.

I went over and shook my head. My clothes were plastered to my skin, my sandals squeaked, and I was shivering.

"I was trying to talk to Luke Sutton."

"You were, now?" She looked me up and down, a nimble feat considering her eyebrows were as high as the sky. Water dripped down between my shoulderblades.

"It's about Herbert Flynn, isn't it?" She didn't wait for an answer. "This is just—well, it's such a tragedy." She twirled the stem of her umbrella. "What's your connection to him?"

"I was there when they found his body."

Her mouth opened. Then, she put her arm around my shoulder and started walking me up the path. "Well, now, you just come on inside with me."

I ducked under her umbrella and let her take the lead. As we got to her front door, she glanced back toward the Suttons' driveway. "That's Jimmy Saclarides' car in front of yours. They've been here all morning. Look."

I hadn't realized the gold Toyota Camry parked ahead of my Volvo was Jimmy's. The only time I'd seen him behind the wheel was in a cruiser. Was he closeted in the house with Luke? Was he the one who told Gloria that Luke couldn't see me?

"No, over there." Willetta motioned.

She pointed beyond the Toyota to the Suttons' backyard. I looked over. The door to the ice house was open, and yellow crime scene tape was stretched around it. A pile of boards and planks were heaped on the lawn near the entrance. "What's going on?"

She flashed me a significant look and steered me inside. We went into the kitchen, where I sat in the same chair. Willetta went into a small room off the kitchen and returned with a towel. While I dried off, she took the kettle to the sink and started to fill it. Then she turned off the faucet. "No. This calls for something stronger."

Opening one of the cabinets, she pulled out a new bottle of bourbon and tore off the paper seal. She settled herself in her chair and poured a shot for both of us. She picked hers up and swilled it down. Her eyes grew watery. She pushed my shot toward me. I shook my head.

"I was checking the downspouts outside this morning. One of 'em broke off, and with all this rain, I wanted to make sure it wasn't flooding the window well. It was, and I was thinking I'd have to call the handyman when a couple of police cruisers and Jimmy's car pulled up to Chuck's." She stopped. "I haven't seen that many policemen since…well…." She reached for the bourbon and refilled her glass. "Well, knowing how skittish Gloria is with strangers and all…."

I took a sip. "Skittish" was putting it mildly.

"Well, I decided to do the neighborly thing and go on over. Gloria might need some help. Women's help, you know?" She shot me a sidelong glance, as if she was testing out her theory on me. I kept my face neutral. "So I did. And…." She nodded at me. "She did."

"Mrs. Baines couldn't provide it?"

"She's—well—she's just the housekeeper. She needed someone to hold her hand." Willetta shrugged again. "So I went into the study. That's where everyone was holed up. And well, it seems as if the police found a bank book that belonged to Herbert Flynn."

"I was there when they found it."

"Child, we do have a lot to talk about." She gazed at me with something close to admiration. "Then you know Herbert barely had enough to rub two sticks together."

I shook my head. "No one said how much was in it."

"Well, I can tell you it wasn't much. The police called and went right down to the bank—it was in Chicago." She looked at her glass. "I always wondered where Herbert went to. Anyway, that's when they found out he had a safe-deposit box, too."

"A safe-deposit box?"

"They got some kind of special order to open it up, and when they did, they found a key."

"A key?"

"Turned out to be a key to the lock on the ice house. Course it was old and rusty, and it didn't work—Chuck had replaced the lock."

"Then how did they know it unlocked the ice house?"

"They didn't. They guessed. Jimmy said someone had seen Herbert around the ice house recently."

I raised my hand. "Guilty."

"Well, you're all over the place, aren't you? How do you find the time to make your video?"

I ignored the dig. "I saw him the day I was here talking to you. I thought he was the Suttons' gardener."

Her eyebrows arched again.

"Wait a second, Willetta. Are you saying the police linked that key to the ice house just because I saw him there? That sounds like a pretty flimsy connection."

"No. There was a note, too."

"A note? In the safe-deposit box?"

"No. In the Delavan house. Herbert wrote it."

"What did it say?"

She threw up her hands. "Now, that's the thing. I don't know. When they brought it up, Gloria—well—she got upset, and I had to take her upstairs and bring her a cup of tea." A frustrated look came over her. "But whatever he wrote, it was enough for them to come over here first thing, break the lock, and start tearing up the floor of the ice house."

The pile of boards on the lawn.

"But here's the thing. They found something inside the ice house."

I felt goosebumps on my arm. "Inside?"

"And that's where it gets interesting." Willetta cleared her throat. "I told you I was making Gloria a cup of tea, right?"

I nodded.

"So I brought it upstairs, and then I told her I had to go use the facilities, you know? I ran downstairs as quick as I could and listened from the other side of the study door."

"And?"

She took a long, slow sip of her bourbon. It was all I could do not to grab her glass and throw it on the floor. "They found a bundle of Annie's clothes hidden under a loose floorboard."

"Annie Sutton?"

She nodded. "Shorts, a T-shirt, bra, and panties." She paused. "Turned out to be the clothes she was wearing the night she was killed."

I blew out a breath and took a sip of bourbon. "How'd they get in the ice house?"

"I guess that's what they're trying to figure out. Anyway, they were all folded up nice and neat. Imagine. After all that time." She shook her head. "They took 'em away, of course. To do some tests."

"What kind of tests?"

"I'm not real sure. I think it was something with initials."

"DNA?"

"That's it."

I took another sip of bourbon.

Willetta rolled her empty glass in a little circle on the table. "But you know what boggles the mind?"

"What?" My voice cracked from the liquor.

"All these years, everyone thought Herbert was dead. But there he was, living less than a hundred miles away." She rubbed the back of her hand across her mouth. "And to think his wife was supporting him all that time. Just goes to show, you never know what other people are up to."

"Irene was supporting him?"

"Apparently she was sending money from the restaurant to him. Explains why the place was always on the brink."

"Jimmy told you all this?"

"Not me, sweetheart. It was Chuck he was telling."

Ah, the privileges of wealth. A direct line into police matters. "So Irene knew he wasn't dead?"

"I guess so."

"But she told everyone he was."

Willetta nodded.

"Why'd she lie?"

"Good question, isn't it? Maybe he was sick and got better. Maybe he couldn't keep a job. Maybe she wanted the girls to think he was dead." She tossed back her shot. "But really, who knows? That family—well, they're peculiar. Always have been."

"When did Herbert come back?"

"Don't know that either. According to Jimmy, Irene claimed he just showed up at her door in the middle of the night, not long before Daria was killed. Out of the blue. Gave her and the girls the fright of their lives, Jimmy said."

"So all three of them knew he was back?"

"Sure sounds like it."

"Do the police have a theory why he was murdered?"

"The only thing Jimmy said was that the sheriff's department has been canvassing Herbert's neighborhood, and someone saw a man visit Herbert. But it was at night when it was dark, and they couldn't give a description."

I pondered it. "Do you think his murder has anything to do with the clothes they found in the ice house? Or Annie's murder?"

"Well, now, those are all good questions, aren't they? You can bet someone's gonna find the answers before long." She picked up her glass, looked at me, then put the glass down. "You said you came over to talk to Luke, right?"

"That's right."

"Why?"

"Uh, well, I—I wanted to ask him some questions. We—we met a while back, and I just needed—well, I wanted to see him."

She looked as if she understood what I wasn't saying. "Well, sweetie, if I were you, I might rethink it. Whatever reason you came for."

"Why?"

"Because of what they found along with Annie's clothes."

I felt a chill. "What was that?"

"Chip identified it, and Luke didn't deny it."

"What?" I could have strangled the woman. "What did they find?"

"It was a shirt that belonged to Luke. A baseball shirt he wore when he was a teenager."

"So?"

She sighed. "There were brown stains on it, Ellie. Brown stains they think are blood."

Chapter Thirty-one

A nameless, formless dread chased me through the night, and I woke up the next morning without the layer of protection that keeps demons at bay. I pulled on shorts and a T-shirt and poured most of a strong pot of coffee down my throat, listening to the TV people commemorating Richard Nixon's resignation. It was a big anniversary, and silver-haired pundits were remembering that August in Washington: the drama of the impeachment hearings, the sense that events were hurtling toward critical mass, the release and crippling exhaustion when he finally resigned. One commentator recalled how DC was a ghost town that weekend—no one could bear to stay in the city. I remember Gerald Ford telling the country that our long national nightmare was over. I also remember believing him.

Now, I looked out at a perfect summer morning. The only reminder of the past two days was a soft breeze that stirred the leaves of the locust tree and made them glitter. I wouldn't need to water the flowers, but the grass needed to be cut. I thought about borrowing my neighbor's lawn mower and soothing myself with the balm of the mundane.

First, though, I dug out my address book and looked up a number.

A woman's voice picked up when I dialed. "Georgia Davis."

"Georgia, hi. This is Ellie Foreman."

"Ellie. How are you?"

"Hanging in. How about you? How's life now that you're not on the force?" Georgia Davis and I had both been involved in a murder investigation last winter. She was a police officer at the time. Now she was a private detective.

"I seem to be making a living."

"You like it?"

"I like being my own boss. How's Rachel?"

I filled her in. Georgia and Rachel met when Georgia was still a cop. In fact, she'd known Rachel before she knew me. Rachel had been hanging around with the wrong kids and had gotten herself in trouble. Georgia had been so decent about the whole thing I'd almost revised my thinking about cops.

"Sounds like everything's going well."

"It's not me," I protested. "When Rachel knows what she wants, she goes after it all by herself. And God forbid anyone gets in her way."

"Like mother, like daughter."

I laughed.

"So what can I do for you?"

"I have a question about DNA tests. How long does it take to get a reading on what's there or what isn't?"

"Why?"

"Um, well, I don't know if I—"

"Too much information?"

"Kind of."

"Should I be worried?"

"No. I'm not in any kind of trouble. This time."

"Not yet, you mean."

"Georgia...."

"Sorry. Hmm. DNA, huh? Okay. Like everything else, it depends. What the material is, what you're looking for, whether it's a heater case. You know?"

"Isn't there some kind of ballpark figure?"

"Let's put it this way. If you go through the system, like most police do, it would probably be about six weeks or so."

"That long? I thought—"

"Typing blood is easy. So is screening blood and urine for drugs. DNA is a different animal."

"Can't you do it faster?"

"Like I said, if it's a heater case, sometimes you can get it down a little. But it has to do with growing stuff in test tubes. It's the kind of thing that can't be rushed."

"So, for six weeks, everything is in limbo while the tests are being done?"

"That's a blink of an eye for some people."

"Well, tell me this. If something has been underground for say thirty years, and they just unearthed it, would they be able to test it for DNA?"

"They can try, but whether they get anything is hard to say. There are basically two kinds of DNA tests, but both of them require a certain sample size. More important, those samples can't be contaminated or degraded. Which might be the case if the material was out in the elements a long time. Temperature changes, moisture, the length of time it's been in the ground can wreak havoc with the stuff and make the sample unusable." She paused. "And I gotta tell you, thirty years is a long time."

I groaned.

"How was the material stored?"

"It was wedged under a floorboard in a tool shed."

"Was it protected?"

"You mean, was it enclosed in a plastic bag or something like that?"

"How about a hermetically sealed box?"

"It's that sensitive?"

"Uh-huh. And that doesn't take into account whether it was handled properly at the scene."

"So what you're basically telling me is that it doesn't look good."

"Ellie, I have no idea what the situation is. And I'm no expert on DNA. I'm just telling you what I know."

"I understand."

"Anything else on your mind?" she asked after a pause.

"Would most cops know that?"

"What do you mean?"

"Would most cops know as much as you about DNA?"

"Ellie, I hardly know anything."

"You know more than me."

"Well...I suppose they would. At least around here. Anything else?" she asked.

"That's it."

"Okay. Take care of yourself. And Rachel."

⌒⌒⌒

I was just coming home after dropping Rachel at Julia's, thinking I might go for a run on the bicycle path, when I saw a red Dodge Ram parked in the driveway. Fouad, in white painter's pants and a striped T-shirt, was bent over the bed of the truck. I beeped the horn. He straightened up and waved. I pulled up behind him.

"Fouad!"

As he walked over to greet me, I noticed the spring in his step. "I am glad to see you, Ellie. Thank you."

"For what?"

"The phone number."

"What? Oh." I'd almost forgotten about my call to Johns Hopkins. I'd left the number on Fouad's machine.

"What happened? Did you find Ahmed?"

He smiled enigmatically. "In a way."

"You're going to have to be less mysterious."

"Let me put it this way. I know where he is."

"Not the Mideast."

He shook his head. "He's in the Midwest. Minnesota. A cabin in a little town in the northern part of the state. He is with Rani."

"How did you find out?"

"When I called Rani's parents, it turned out they were as upset as we were. Rani had run away as well—and left no word where she was going. Hayat and I were frantic. We did not eat.

Or sleep. Or work. That is why I was not here." He motioned with his hand.

"Don't even think about it," I said.

He nodded. "During all this time, Natalie was there. She did not say much, but she was watching us."

Natalie, two years younger than her brother, was waitressing for the summer at one of the restaurants in the Glen, a section of Glenview that had been recently developed.

"Then one night, Rani's father called. Her mother had some sort of attack. From the stress. They took her to the hospital."

"Oh, no."

"She will recover, but everyone was upset."

"Of course they were." The summer I was twenty I hitch-hiked across country in an attempt to "find myself." I had a blast, coming home only when I ran out of money. I had no idea how worried my parents were until, years later, I imagined Rachel doing the same thing.

"Natalie was dismayed when we told her about Rani's mother. She came home early from work, locked herself in her room, and stayed there all night. The next morning she confessed that she knew where they were. I think she just couldn't watch us suffer anymore."

"Ahmed told her?"

Fouad nodded. "They are close."

Things change. I remembered Fouad's rueful stories about how much they fought when they were younger. At the time, he couldn't understand; he rarely fought with his siblings. But he was raised in a different culture, a different world. "What in heaven's name are they doing in Minnesota?"

Fouad started to say something, then apparently thought better of it. He shrugged.

"Oh." I swallowed. I couldn't help wondering what I'd do if I discovered Rachel was holed up in a cabin someplace with her boyfriend. Somehow, I didn't think I would be as stoic.

"Natalie told us they were in a cabin near a lake. I called the proprietor. A lovely woman. She told me not to worry. She would keep an eye on them. Then we called Rani's parents."

"So you haven't talked to Ahmed in person?"

"He called the next day. He says he has much thinking to do. But we should not worry. He will finish his schooling in Baltimore. And then we will all sit down together and discuss his future."

"You have to be so relieved. Thank God for Natalie."

"The Lord takes daughters from among the angels." He put a hand on my shoulder. "You, too, Ellie."

"Who? Rachel?"

He laughed. "No. You."

"Me?"

"If we had not contacted Rani's parents, we would not have known about her mother. That was—how do you say it—the turning point."

"I'm sure Natalie would have told you eventually."

Fouad didn't look convinced. "He swore her to secrecy."

"He will forgive her."

"He already has." Fouad flipped up his palms and spread his arms. "Praise be to Allah. It is a beautiful day, and life is good."

I didn't reply.

Fouad dropped his arms. "What is wrong, Ellie?"

I didn't answer right away. I didn't want to intrude on his joy. Then I remembered what a good friend he was. Friends share their joys and sorrows. "I have a problem. I don't know what to think or who to trust."

He took my arm. "Come. We will talk." He guided me to the pickup, where we sat on the tailgate while I went through the chain of events: Daria Flynn's death, her mother's visit to my house, the rumors about Luke and Daria, the third sniper attack, Annie Sutton's murder and Herbert Flynn's part in it, the plane ride with Luke, Herbert Flynn's death, his mysterious note, the clothes from the ice house. Fouad listened without interrupting.

"The kicker was they found a baseball shirt with the girl's clothes. It belonged to Luke. They're saying it has bloodstains on it."

Fouad got up, turned around, and took out the lawn mower from the bed of the truck. Bending over, he unscrewed the gasoline cap and checked the level. "Which casts suspicion on him."

"The caretaker, Herbert, had been suspected of her murder. In fact, it got so bad he left town after it happened. But now that he's dead, and they found her clothes and Luke's shirt, well…."

"Ellie, do you have feelings for this man? This Luke?"

I looked at the ground.

"What about your friend David?"

"David and I—well, it's over. We just didn't want to admit it."

Fouad scratched his cheek. "So you have met a new man, and you are afraid he might have been involved in his sister's death."

"The facts seem to line up."

Fouad replaced the gasoline cap on the lawn mower. "Do they? You do not know why this Herbert was at the ice house the other day. Or why he was killed. Or how the baseball shirt came to be with the girl's clothes."

"Herbert used to be the caretaker of the Suttons' estate. He was the one who found her body. Soon after that, he became a suspect in the crime. But no one ever found any evidence. After he left town, they said her death was caused by an intruder or a vagrant." I told him about the Percy daughter's murder. "So there was some kind of precedent, so to speak. At one point, there was even speculation it could have been the same guy. Killing again after ten years. It didn't amount to anything, though."

"Go on."

"Thirty years later, Herbert, who everyone pretty much thought was dead, turns up back in Lake Geneva. He writes a note to someone, and shortly afterward is murdered. For real, this time. When the police look into it, lo and behold, they find Annie's clothes in the ice house. And Luke's shirt. With the bloodstains."

Fouad pushed the mower to the edge of the grass. "Whose blood is it?"

"Don't know yet."

"Do you really think this Luke—the man you might have feelings for—might have killed his sister?"

I followed him over to the lawn. "I don't want to, but...."

"If that's true, why would he—or anyone—hide her clothes—and his shirt—in an ice house all this time? Why not burn them or throw them away?"

"I don't know. Maybe he panicked and left them in there figuring he'd get them later, but then for some reason didn't. Or maybe he thought no one would find them—there used to be a hole that extended down twenty feet, like a well, before they built a floor over it." I paused. "Except they were found wedged under a loose floorboard. They couldn't have been thrown down the hole." I frowned. "Oh well, that doesn't matter. The important thing is that they were found."

"So, this brother, or whoever it was, killed his sister thirty years ago. And then killed the caretaker...this Herbert, too?"

"I don't know why Herbert was killed. I do know I saw him lurking around the ice house recently, the same ice house where the clothes were found." I went on. "And they found a key to the ice house in his safe-deposit box."

"Which proves, without any doubt, there is a connection."

I looked at my sneakers. "Well, when you put it that way, I—I'm not sure."

Fouad nodded. "It is wise not to judge unless you are wearing judges' robes."

"Is that from the Koran?"

He shook his head. "It is something Hayat and I are trying to remember." He looked at me with an expression I could only interpret as "If the shoe fits...."

I felt chastened. "There's something else," I said a little tentatively. "But maybe I shouldn't bring it up."

Fouad held out his hand, palm up. "I did not mean to intimidate you, Ellie. I love our talks, whether they are about our children or your—your experiences."

I laughed. "All right. It's about the death of Herbert's daughter, Daria."

"The girl who was killed by the sniper?"

"That's what's so puzzling. Everyone, including the police, thought it was the same sniper who shot the other two women. You know, random attacks on young women. But now, there's some evidence that that it wasn't part of the same pattern. The rifle used in Daria's shooting wasn't the same one that was used in the other two. Which means it might not be the same shooter."

"How does that tie into the Suttons? Or the Flynns?"

I hesitated. "Let's put it this way. There seems to be a web of 'coincidences' that connect the Flynn family and the Sutton family to a string of murders that began with Anne's in 1974. And I'm not sure I believe in coincidence. What is it they say?"

"I believe Albert Einstein once said, 'God does not play dice with the universe.'"

I gazed at Fouad. The depth of his knowledge always surprises me.

"Ellie, do you really honestly think this Luke is involved in two—no—possibly three murders?"

"I don't want to believe it. But he did leave Lake Geneva right after his sister died, and he stayed away for a long time."

"That doesn't mean he committed murder."

"I realize that. That's why I want to see him. I need to talk to him. Even if he didn't do anything, it's clear something is very wrong with that family. I need to know what."

Fouad frowned. "If this man killed his sister, then killed the man who reminded him of it, he's lied about it for thirty years. What makes you think he'll tell you the truth now?"

I folded my arms. "Fouad, whose side are you on?"

Smiling enigmatically, he pulled the cord on the lawn mower. The machine roared to life. "Yours," he shouted. "Once you decide what it is."

Chapter Thirty-two

I should have known it would be all over Lake Geneva the next day. I didn't have any reason to be there, but I invented an excuse and drove up. I stopped into the Lodge first, ostensibly to make sure we hadn't missed any important scenes. I dropped in to the spa, then the pool area, then the kitchen. Some of the Lodge's employees were longtime residents, and wherever I went, the Sutton family was the topic of conversation.

Most of it wasn't flattering. As people realized that the Sutton girl's murder had surfaced again and that her brother Luke could be involved, all the simmering resentment of the working class toward the rich worked up to a full boil. Everyone had a pet theory, or variation of one, but most hypothesized that Luke had probably tried to molest his sister, and when she resisted, possibly with some kind of knife or other sharp object, killed her. And then fled rather than own up to it. As far as Herbert Flynn was concerned, most thought he witnessed the event, saw Luke stash his sister's clothes and his bloody shirt in the ice house, and threatened to expose him. But the Suttons somehow managed to turn the tables on Herbert and forced him to flee. And then, for whatever reason, when Herbert came back after his daughter was killed and actually contacted the Suttons, well....

People seemed to be reluctant to make the final leap, but it wasn't clear whether that was because they didn't believe the Suttons were capable of multiple murders, or because no one wanted to be the first to accuse them. Given what apparently went on behind closed doors at Monticello, however, some people were starting to wonder if Daria Flynn's death somehow figured into the mess, too. After all, Luke and Daria *had* been seen together at the Lodge.

This was the biggest news to hit this closed community in decades, and I listened carefully. The Suttons and the Flynns were in seclusion, which meant the restaurant was closed. Not that I had much to say to either Kim or her mother. Irene had decided not to hold a funeral service for Herbert. I wasn't surprised. After letting out that he was dead all these years, she might have found it awkward to bury him again.

After leaving the Lodge, I drove aimlessly down Main Street, listening to Cathy Richardson, the best thing to happen to the Chicago music since blues, sing about the "Road to Bliss." I thought about trying to see Luke, but my reception at Monticello had been so icy I wasn't prepared to risk it again. The odds of Luke answering the door himself were slim anyway, and I assumed the family would refuse to let me see him. As far as I knew, Luke hadn't been formally arrested, but I gathered he was virtually a prisoner in his parents' home.

Cathy belted out a song about how "sometimes it's not the notes you sing, but the spaces you leave in between." I turned off Main and swung past City Hall, the tan and white building that also houses the police department.

There were a lot of spaces between Luke Sutton's past and his present. There had to be a way to fill them. A block past the police station, I had an idea.

～～～

"What makes you think he wants to see you?"

Jimmy Saclarides took off his reading glasses and wiped them on his sleeve. I was sitting across from him in his second-floor office at police headquarters.

"I'm not sure he does, but I want to see him, and you're about the only person who could arrange it."

I didn't have any illusions Jimmy would help me out. Given that I'd been the one to spread rumors about Luke and Daria

Flynn, given that I'd basically accused him of being in the Suttons' back pocket, and given that I'd been the one to call about Herbert Flynn's body, I'd caused him plenty of problems. And yet, I remembered the flicker of pleasure we'd shared at the gala. Under different circumstances, we might have been friends. And if anyone had any influence over Luke, it had to be Jimmy. It was worth a try.

He slipped the glasses into his shirt pocket. "Luke has a lot on his mind right now."

"I'm aware of that."

"What would you say if I asked why you feel such a need to see him?"

"I—I'd tell you it was personal."

He gazed steadily at me.

"Is he under arrest?"

He shook his head. "But under the circumstances, he's consented to stay here—in Lake Geneva—until the investigation is complete."

"The DNA tests."

He didn't answer but shuffled some papers, then thumped them on his desk. He was sliding into the role of bureaucrat.

"Please, Jimmy. I need to see him. Just for a few minutes. I—I want him to know he has a friend."

"A friend, huh?" I could tell he was weighing it. He knew me as an adversary; he had no reason to help me. Unless Luke had said something to him about me. Made it known he liked me, or at least didn't consider me an enemy. But even if he had, I wasn't sure if Jimmy was wearing his cop hat or his best friend hat. I steeled myself for his answer.

Surprisingly, his expression softened. "Well, I guess Luke could use a friend right about now."

An hour later I found myself on a twenty-two-foot Boston whaler motoring across Lake Geneva. The media was staking out the Sutton house from Lake Shore Road, and Jimmy decided it would be less disruptive to arrive by water. He had "borrowed" the whaler from the Lake Geneva Marine Police, who, technically, were independent of the city cops, but I guess if you're the chief of police, you can commandeer whatever vehicle you need.

Small whitecaps puckered the surface, and the lake was choppy, but the boat cut through the water like a blade. As we approached the estate, I realized I hadn't seen this view of Monticello before. From a distance, the dome glowed in the sun, and the grounds looked deceptively beatific. We coasted up to a Y-shaped dock that edged both Willetta Emerson's and the Suttons' backyards. A dinghy tied to a post bobbled in our wake.

"This used to be people's front yard, once upon a time." Jimmy maneuvered the whaler broadside. Tiny waves lapped the side of the boat.

"Excuse me?"

"The mail used to be delivered by boat. Still is during the summer. Supplies and provisions, too."

He jumped out and threw a tie over a post. I stepped gingerly onto the dock. Some of the wooden planks squeaked when I put weight on them, and the whole thing needed a coat of paint. Given what had occurred here, though, I could see why the Suttons weren't inclined to maintain it.

"It'll be better if you wait here," Jimmy said when we reached the end of the dock.

I nodded and stayed where I was. When five minutes had passed, I started to pace along the evergreens that provided the barrier between the Suttons' and Willetta's property. I wondered if I was making a mistake. Not that I thought it was dangerous to see Luke, but it might be foolish. For years when I was married to Barry, I looked the other way when I saw a side of him I didn't like. It was only when that side of him dominated the others, and life became an impossible nightmare, that I realized how deeply in denial I'd been. Was I doing the same thing now?

I was heading back toward the dock when the door to the veranda slid open and someone came out. Average height, wearing jeans, his shirttail hanging over them. It was Luke, and he was alone. My heart started to pound. He stopped on the deck, shielded his eyes to take a bearing, and came toward me. He walked with a heavy, slow tread, and his shoulders were more hunched than I remembered.

I waited until he reached the trees. "Hello, Luke."

"Hello, Ellie."

I took a closer look. His eyes were red, his skin blotchy, and his beard needed trimming. More worrisome, though, was his expression. Where I'd once seen anger, another time a boyish smile, now I saw defeat. He looked sideways at me, as if he expected me to come down on him.

"I'm so sorry." It came out impulsively.

He nodded.

"How can I help?"

"You can't. The wheels of justice and all that."

"There must be something I could do."

"You did. You came to see me." He mustered a smile.

My stomach flipped. I smiled back. For an instant we were back up in the plane.

The instant passed. "People—well, there's a lot of speculation about—well, you and Annie and Herbert Flynn. Is there anything you can tell me? Anything at all?"

"The lawyers have ordered me not to say a word to anyone."

So much pain was etched on his face it was all I could do not to open my arms to him. Instead I shoved my hands in my pockets. We started walking toward the road.

"What—when do you think it will be resolved?"

"I don't know."

"They're doing DNA tests on all the clothes, right?"

"How do you know that?"

"Everybody knows, Luke."

He nodded curtly. "Sure. Can't keep a secret in this town."

I didn't argue. "Did Jimmy say how long it would take?"

He shook his head.

"A friend of mine, a former police officer, says it can take as long as six weeks. What are you going to do in the meantime?"

"I don't know."

"But you can't just—I mean, I wouldn't be able to sit by and let some result of a test determine whether I'd spend the rest of my life—"

"I'm not you."

I turned away, but he grabbed my shoulders and spun me around. "I don't mean it like that. It's just—would it make a difference if I said I didn't do it?"

"If I believed you."

He looked at me for a long moment. Then he dropped his hands. "Walk with me."

We started toward the road again but angled away from the media stakeout.

"It's not just your sister. People are starting to mention Daria Flynn."

"I didn't kill anyone."

"Then who did?"

He stopped walking. "Maybe this wasn't such a good idea."

"Seeing me? Please. Don't say that."

He turned around. "I wanted to. I've been thinking about you ever since—but you ask so many questions." He blinked.

"Okay." I raised a finger to my lips. "No more questions."

We started walking again.

"Well, just one more."

He stiffened.

"Did your sister have dark hair?"

He turned to me with a bewildered expression. "Why?"

"Your mother called me Anne when I was here before."

"You were here?" His gaze turned calculating.

I flipped up my hands in a gesture of frustration. "They didn't tell you?" He shook his head. I explained about my encounter with Chip and his mother.

He frowned and, after a pause, said, "Yes."

"Yes, she had dark hair, or yes, no one told you?"

"Both."

Another silence.

"Ellie, why did you come here?"

I heard a universe of emotion in the way he spoke my name. "I had to."

He just looked at me. We were behind the road about a hundred yards from the house. Thick shrubbery separated the road from the Suttons' lawn.

"It's just that, well, now that they found your—the baseball shirt—I'm having a hard time with that part of it."

He kept his mouth shut.

"This is the first anyone's heard of bloodstains. I thought she drowned. But now, with the shirt and the bloodstains, it seems as if there might have been a weapon of some kind. You know, a knife. Or another sharp object. Or God forbid, a gun. I was just thinking, if that weapon could somehow be found or accounted for, it might—"

Luke stopped. I stopped, too. He looked at me with an odd expression.

"What?"

Then he slowly shook his head. "It's nothing."

"You're lying."

He shook his head again, almost as if to clear his head. "Stop, Ellie. Just stop. It's out of my hands. And yours."

A ripple of frustration pulsed through me. How could he crumple like that? Give up so easily? But then, there were probably battalions of lawyers back at the house. He had to do what they said.

"Okay," I said after a pause. "But I—I want to ask you one more question."

A smile played around his mouth. "You don't think you've used up your quota?"

"This is personal. The plane ride," I said softly. "Was it—was it as—magical as I thought?"

"What do you think?"

"I—I thought so. But now, I'm not sure."

His smile vanished. "Well, then, I guess that makes you just like everyone else."

"No." Suddenly, I wanted to stamp my feet. Energize him. Make him jettison this pessimism, the passive acceptance of defeat. Even if it meant directing his anger at me. "You don't understand. In a way, I feel—responsible."

Surprise flooded his face. "For what?"

"I told people about you and Daria. I called in the report of Herbert's body."

But if it was anger I was trying to kindle, I failed. "You did what you had to. In the final analysis, it won't make any difference." His gaze swept over me. "I'll be honest. I didn't like you at first. I thought I had good reason. But now…." He swallowed. "It would probably be best if you went away."

"I can't." I looked at the ground. "It felt so easy. Right. I've never felt that way before. As if—"

"It was supposed to be?"

I looked up. "Yes."

"I know."

His arm brushed mine, and his breath grazed my cheek. He framed my cheeks with his hands, pulled me close, and kissed me. His lips were soft. He leaned closer and wrapped his arms around me. I moved toward him and slipped my arms around him. My fingers brushed the back of his hair. When we broke apart, we were both breathless.

"Why you?" he whispered. "Why now?"

I didn't have an answer.

Chapter Thirty-three

By the time Jimmy and I got back to shore, it was well past lunch, and I was hungry. Either Jimmy was, too, or he wanted to pump me about my visit with Luke, because he said, "You want to grab some food?"

"Sure."

We turned on Broad, then drove down a short alley that opened into a parking lot. At the edge of the lot back on Broad was a cheerful white brick building with blue shutters and door. A sign on the door said Welcome to Saclarides.

We parked and got out of the car, but as we were walking up to the door, Jimmy's cell chirped. He fished it out of his pocket.

"Yes….When?...Are they sure?… Okay, do what you have to and get back to me. No, I'll handle it." He flipped up the phone and looked at me. "I have to make a call."

"No problem."

Jimmy walked into the restaurant, punching in a number on his cell. I stayed outside and pulled out my cell to call home. Rachel was at Julia's, and the machine picked up. I pressed in the code for my messages. Two hang-ups. Then a familiar voice.

"Hi, Ellie. It's David. We haven't talked in a while. Please call."

I disconnected and shoved the cell back in my bag.

When I entered his family's restaurant, two round, older, dark-haired women were cooing over Jimmy so enthusiastically he was blushing. You'd think he'd just come back from the front.

He introduced me. "My mother, Helen, and my aunt Ava." They beamed at me and led us to their number one booth, as they called it. There was no spit of lamb in the front window, and blue tablecloths covered the tables. Small vases with artificial flowers sat on top. This was a more upscale version of Mount Olympus. Still, the same lemony garlic scent I'd smelled at the Flynns' hung in the air and made my mouth water.

As we sat down, Aunt Ava began a rapid-fire discourse in what I assumed was Greek. Jimmy answered back. The woman folded her hands and smiled. "*Kalos.*"

"What was that about?" I asked after she'd left.

"Ava says she knows what you want to eat."

"She does?" I'd been wondering why she hadn't given us menus.

"It's her little ritual. She tells everyone what they want to eat so that when she brings out whatever it is she's cooked, they'll think she made it especially for them."

"I'm sure it'll be delicious. Whatever it is."

"It usually is."

He went to the bar at the back of the room while I burrowed into my chair, the cushion of which was surprisingly soft. Jimmy examined several bottles of wine in a wine rack. He chose one, then grabbed an opener and two glasses, and brought them back to the table. Opening the bottle, he filled one glass with white wine and handed it to me.

"What about you?"

He shook his head. "Still on the clock. But you go ahead. You'll like it. It's the closest thing you'll get to a Greek Chardonnay."

"How do you know I like Chardonnay?"

He shrugged. "Isn't that what you were drinking at the gala?"

He was observant. Good thing in a cop. I took a sip. "It's good." Then, "You're going to eat, too, aren't you?"

"And risk the wrath of the mother goddesses if I don't?"

Was Jimmy married? I didn't recall him saying anything about a wife or family. As he sat down, the door to the restaurant opened, and Kim Flynn stepped in.

I tried to suppress my shock.

She glanced around and saw me, then Jimmy. She frowned. "Special occasion, Jimmy?"

He didn't miss a beat. "Thanks for coming by so soon, Kim."

My nerves jangled. It was Kim he'd called on his cell.

"You got me at a good time," she said coolly. "The restaurant being closed and all."

He gestured. "Please join us for a drink. Lunch, too, if you want." He called to his mother in Greek. She answered, but this time her smile faded.

"Kim, my mother and aunt extend heartfelt condolences," Jimmy said, pouring her a glass of wine. "And of course, you have mine as well."

She nodded and took the glass.

"How's your mother?"

"You mean since you ran us through the mill?"

"That's not fair."

"You're right, Jimmy. You were just doing your job." She recited it like it was rote. "So, what's going on?" Kim asked. "Why did you want to see me?"

He looked at me, then at Kim. He kept his mouth shut.

I took the hint. "Why don't I just go to the ladies' room?" I stood up.

"Thanks, Ellie." Jimmy looked relieved. "I'm sorry. I didn't know when we drove over—"

"Hey. Don't make her disappear on my account," Kim broke in. "I don't have anything to hide. The whole fucking town knows our business anyway." She glanced up at me. "Plus, she's dying to know what you want."

I stood there, a little nonplussed by Kim's token, but accurate, observation.

Jimmy shrugged and waved me back into my chair. I sat down. Kim folded her hands on the table.

"Kim, did you have a guy working for you a month or so ago?"

She nodded. "He washed dishes. Picked up supplies. But he only lasted a few weeks. Why?"

Jimmy ignored her question. "Why didn't he last longer?"

"He wasn't reliable. He'd come in late, sometimes as much as two hours. He would leave for long periods of time. Once in a while, he wouldn't come back."

"What was his name?"

"Let's see." She looked off, like she was thinking. "Billy, I think. Billy Watkins."

Jimmy nodded.

"Why?"

"The Walworth County Sheriff's office busted a meth lab out near East Troy. In a barn. When they went in, they found a body inside. It'd been there awhile. Two or three weeks, they figure."

I winced.

"His ID said he was William Watkins."

Kim's eyebrows shot up. "You know, I had a feeling about him."

"How come?"

"He was pretty vague about his background. I figured he might have done some time. But I wanted to give the guy a chance. Did he have a record?"

"About a mile long. Mostly possession. Intent to sell."

"How did he die?" she asked.

"He was shot. With his own rifle. They found it in the woods a hundred yards from the barn."

Jimmy watched Kim's reaction. It wasn't much. She took a sip of her wine. "Pretty gruesome." She put her glass down. "How did you figure out he worked for us?"

"He had a pay stub from Mount Olympus in his things. When did you let him go?"

"It's been a while. Before Daria died, I know that."

"You remember the day?"

"Not offhand," she said. "But I can check. Why all the questions?"

"Just trying to tie up loose ends. You were his last employer."

She looked him in the eye. "Jimmy, we've known each other too long for that kind of bullshit. You call me, ask me to meet you here, and start pumping me. What's going on? Do you think there a connection to Daria? Or my father?"

"Do you?"

"How would I know? I do think it's a hell of a coincidence." She took a sip of wine. "But you're the police. What do you think?"

"I think it's a hell of a coincidence, too. Especially when you factor in the rifle."

"The one they found in the woods?" I asked.

"Yup. They're checking it for prints now."

A sick feeling crept over me. "It was a Remington Bolt Action 308, wasn't it?"

Jimmy nodded.

Chapter Thirty-four

The same gun that was used to kill Daria.

I turned to Jimmy. "Does that mean Watkins is the sniper? The shooter who went after Daria?"

"Not at all. There are hundreds, if not thousands, of those rifles around," Jimmy said. "Like I said, I just think it's a hell of a coincidence. Right, Kim?"

"I don't think he ever met Daria," Kim said, not missing a beat. "She wasn't around the restaurant much. But then, come to think of it, neither was he." She looked at Jimmy. "Have you told my mother?"

He shook his head. "I just found out."

"So what happens now?" she asked.

Jimmy didn't say anything.

"What are you going to do?"

"Actually, Kim, I'm not going to do anything."

"What do you mean?" I asked.

He hesitated before answering. "I'm going to recuse myself from all the investigations. The sheriff's office is taking over."

Kim looked shocked. "Why?"

"Because—because Luke is my friend. Staying on would be a conflict of interest."

"Luke?" Kim said. "What does that—"

I cut in. "Are you saying there's a connection between Daria's case and what happened to Herbert Flynn? And this—Billy Watkins?" I asked.

"I don't know."

It wasn't a no. But it wasn't a yes. "I'm confused," I said.

"Join the club," Kim said.

I tried to recap. "Daria is murdered, maybe by a sniper, maybe not. Herbert Flynn is murdered. Luke's being questioned about his sister's murder. And Herbert worked for Luke's father when the sister died."

Kim laced her hands together. Jimmy looked solemn. I could understand why he removed himself from the case. The mere recitation of the events seemed to connect them, to give some legitimacy to their linkage. But even if they weren't connected, it would be impossible for him to be objective. He'd been an integral part of both families' lives.

"Will removing yourself free you up to do things on an 'unofficial' basis?" I asked.

"No. I'm out of it," he said firmly. But the look on his face made me think he was as apprehensive about the outcome as I.

His mother came out of the kitchen carrying a large tray. She brought over two plates loaded with moussaka, dolmades, and slices of roasted lamb. On separate plates were hearty portions of Greek salad, toasted bread, and a whipped pink dish that I think was caviar dip. I scooped up a forkful of moussaka and shoved it in my mouth. Hot, tangy, and creamy at the same time. I took another bite. Then another. Despite the situation, or maybe because of it, I was ravenous. I looked over at Jimmy's plate. He hadn't touched his meal.

"Eat."

He gave me a small smile. "You sound like my mother."

"We read the same handbook."

He picked up his fork and dug in. For a moment, the only sound was the clink of forks and knives. Kim watched.

"You should try some," I said to her.

She shook her head.

After making a considerable dent in the food, I wiped my napkin across my mouth. I felt calmer, more in control. Jimmy seemed more relaxed, too.

"Is there anything we can do for Luke?" I said. "What if we tried to establish an alibi for him for the night his sister died?"

Kim turned to me. "Why would *you* want to do anything for Luke Sutton?"

I didn't answer.

"The DNA tests will be a big piece of that," Jimmy replied, ignoring Kim. "If they exonerate him and he has an alibi that can be confirmed, he might be okay."

"But that's at least six weeks from now."

"Talk about coincidence," Kim cut in.

Jimmy looked over. "What, Kim?"

"I think it's mighty coincidental you decided to remove yourself from the investigation. Your timing couldn't have been more perfect."

"What are you getting at, Kim?" he said.

"What I'm getting at is that the Suttons get people to do their bidding whenever they choose. My father was alive a few days ago. Now he's not. You should be on this like a laser beam. Instead, you're backing off because 'Luke Sutton is your friend.' *That's* what I call a coincidence."

A muscle in Jimmy's jaw flickered, but his reply was calm and deliberate. "Kim, it's actually in your interest to have me off the case. *Because* of my association with Luke. The sheriff's department won't have any conflict."

I interrupted, hoping to forestall an argument. "Kim, why did your father come back after such a long time?"

She looked over, paused for a minute, then said, "Mother had the stroke. She was on the edge for a while. He—he just showed up."

"It had to be a shock seeing him, after thinking he'd been dead all those years."

"It was." The slightly dazed look on her face seemed genuine.

"What did your mother tell you when he disappeared?"

"She said he was going to Milwaukee or Chicago to find work. But then when he never came back, she said he got sick. Had a heart attack or something. And couldn't get in touch with us." She fingered her glass abstractedly, as if she just realized how inadequate her mother's explanation had been. But then, children tend to accept the inexplicable from an adult. Especially a parent.

"Except now it turns out she was in touch with him all along."

Her contemplative mood shattered. "What does that matter?" she snapped. "The point is he's dead. And everyone, including our brave chief of police, wants to give the family who forced him out of town to begin with a pass. Don't you see? It's happening all over again," she fumed. "And how is Luke going to produce an alibi after thirty years anyway? You think he's going to remember where he was and what he was doing on a particular night? Even if he could, who would believe him?"

"You never know," I said, forcing myself to remain calm. "I can remember thirty years ago. It was the summer Nixon resigned. I was glued to the TV. Remember, too, we're talking about the night his sister was killed. I'll bet he can recall exactly what he was doing."

Jimmy's brow furrowed, as though he was trying to call back the years. He glanced at Kim. "Wasn't that the summer Luke managed the airstrip?"

"The airstrip at the Lodge?" I asked.

He nodded. "When the Playboy Club owned it, we all worked there over the summers. Luke managed the airstrip. Made sure the performers got in okay, got them into a limo, and took them up to the hotel. I worked with the grounds crew. You worked there, too, didn't you, Kim?"

She gave us a curt nod.

"Well," I said, "what if we can prove he was working the night his sister died? Can we check the logs or something?"

For a moment, Jimmy sat up straighter, looking interested in spite of himself. Then he slumped. "There won't be any records." He shook his head. "The place has been through two or three owners since then."

"Are you sure?"

"There won't be anything. If there ever was. I couldn't be involved in finding it anyway."

"But I can."

"Why are you so interested in helping Luke Sutton?" Kim cut in.

I looked over. Her expression was angry and probing, but something else was there, too. Something almost predatory. I chose my words carefully. "Because I don't think he did it," I said after a pause.

Her eyes narrowed, and I could tell she didn't believe me. But there was no way I was going to share my feelings about Luke with her. I turned back to Jimmy. "What about witnesses?"

He shrugged. "I would imagine it depends who they are."

"There's you," I said.

"Forget me. Conflict of interest is written all over my face."

"What about Kim?"

"You're kidding, right?" she scoffed.

"Ellie," Jimmy said, "finding someone who saw Luke on a particular night at a specific time thirty years ago—it's like trying to find a needle in a haystack. Impossible." He scowled. "And I shouldn't be having this conversation. I've already said too much."

"Hold on, Jimmy. Just for a minute. Suppose that—for some crazy reason—we could find someone. Wouldn't that help Luke?"

"I don't know. Maybe."

"But it wouldn't hurt."

"No. It wouldn't hurt."

I looked at Kim. She was staring straight ahead.

Chapter Thirty-five

I went over to Mac's the next morning. Hank had created some dazzling eye candy in the form a three-dimensional cube with transparent sides. Each side of the cube contained a shot from one of the locations we'd filmed at the Lodge. As the cube twisted and rotated across the screen, a freeze-frame from each location came full screen and then shrank back to its side of the cube. The effect was similar to one of those screen savers on your computer, but better. The pacing between transitions was deliberate but not sluggish, and each freeze-frame was a Cartier-Bresson moment.

My cell trilled while we were running through it.

"Ms. Foreman?" I recognized the honeyed voice right away.

"Detective Milanovich. How are you?"

"Excellent, as a matter of fact."

I'd never heard him so cheerful.

"We think we may have found the pickup that was used in one—or more—of the sniper attacks. It was abandoned in the forest preserve. Off Dundee Road. Not far from you. I was hoping you'd have some time to take a look at it."

I doodled uneasily on a yellow legal pad. This was a good thing, wasn't it? Whatever they found—particularly if it led to the driver or the shooter—would put an end to all the speculation and conjecture. And lead them away from Luke. "Of course."

"Good." Milanovich reeled off an address in the Glen. "We're borrowing the North Shore Task Force facility. When can you get here?"

An hour later I was in the part of Glenview that was once part of the Naval Air Base but had been sold to developers. I'd produced a video for the Glen for one of those developers. I drove down Patriot Boulevard and turned in to a parking lot in front of the new fire station. Hiking around to the back, I came upon a huge building that occupied most of an otherwise vacant field. The entrance was open so I walked in. It looked like an old airplane hangar with high ceilings and a concrete floor. Two white trucks with NORTAF stenciled on their sides were parked against a wall. The green pickup was parked behind them.

Milanovich was hovering near the pickup. He was wearing the same navy shirt and chinos as the first time I'd seen him. The truck had been raised on a frame rack and was hanging a few feet off the floor. Two men, who by their uniforms and bright purple gloves were probably evidence technicians, were working over the vehicle. One was dusting the surfaces with a thick gray paste; the other leaned into the bed of the pickup with what looked like a hand-held vacuum cleaner.

The detective greeted me with a rare smile. "Nice to see you again, Ms. Foreman."

I nodded and started to walk around the pickup. "It's okay for me to do this, right?"

"That's why you're here."

The pickup was dirty, the camper shell had been removed, and the license plate was gone. I made a large circle and came back to Milanovich. "I don't know."

He looked disappointed.

"I only saw it for a few seconds. It looks like the same one, but I can't swear to it." I shrugged. "I'm sorry."

He made some notes on a clipboard. "That's all right."

The tech who'd been searching the back of the pickup came up behind us. He was holding a small plastic bag. "Hey, Walt. You might want to take a look at this."

Milanovich twisted around. Inside the bag was a small brass cylinder, less than an inch in length. Milanovich eyed it carefully, then arched his brows so high I thought they might stretch past the top of his head. "Well, now that's a whole different kettle of fish."

I peered at the bag, trying to figure out what the brass cylinder was.

Milanovich took pity on me. "It's a shell casing, Ms. Foreman. The protective covering that wraps around a bullet."

I blinked.

"If it matches the fragments we already have, I'd say we're in good shape."

"I got more good news," the other tech piped up from the bed of the pickup.

Milanovich whipped around.

"I just lifted a great pair of prints."

Milanovich looked positively joyful.

⌐⌐⌐

"It's a problem," Susan said as we walked the bike path that afternoon. A spring-like breeze tossed a cool wash of air around us. "How can you possibly believe this man?"

"I don't think he did it." I skirted a heavily leafed bush bowed over by its own weight.

"Right." She sniffed. "Neither did Ted Bundy. Or Gacy. Or Andrew Cunanan."

"Susan, that's not fair. There's absolutely no evidence linking him to any of the rest stop murders."

"I don't have to be fair when it concerns my best friend. This is a man who refuses to talk about his sister's murder, but yet his shirt shows up with her clothes. This is a man who claims to have been at his fishing cabin when the girl was killed at the rest stop, but you haven't the faintest idea whether that's true. Tell me, where did he say he was when the other man—Herbert Flynn—was killed?"

"I've been meaning to find out."

"You do that. And by the way, if I recall, a month ago you were wondering whether he *was* involved in the rest stop murder."

"I was wrong."

"You thought he was an arrogant, spoiled, rich boy then. Were you wrong about that, too?"

I winced. "Yes."

"Ellie, why don't you go down to Cook County Jail and fall in love with a prisoner? It would be a lot safer."

"Susan! Stop."

She stopped and faced me. "I'm sorry. But did you ever think that possibly—just possibly—all of this is part of a rebound effect?"

I felt myself get tight. "What are you getting at?"

"What I mean is that—is this attraction a reaction to your problems with David?"

"David?"

"The two of you never really gave it a chance. You let yourselves be buffeted by events. Neither of you slowed down long enough to evaluate things. It's not all passion and butterflies, you know."

"I'm aware of that," I snapped.

"Are you?" She peered over. "Sometimes I wonder."

I picked up a stone and palmed it. Being criticized by a daughter, an ex-husband, even a father is one thing, but when it's coming from your best friend, it's quite another. "David and I aren't together anymore," I said slowly. "And whether I'm on the rebound or not isn't the issue. The fact is that I don't think Luke Sutton killed anyone. At the same time, I do concede there is a lot he's not talking about. But that's because his lawyer advised him not to."

"Great," Susan said. "Not only are you hot for his body, but you're willing to look the other way at the gaps—I mean canyons—in his story."

"Susan, why are you being so—so judgmental?"

She picked a leaf off a bush as we passed. "Listen to me, Ellie. What if the shoe were on the other foot? What if I broke up with Doug and got involved with someone who might be connected—hell, might even be a suspect—in not one, but possibly two—no, three—murders, if you count the caretaker." She paused. "You'd be all over me in a heartbeat. What do I have to say? I'm worried about you." She started down the path again. "And I'm not the only one."

"What does that mean?"

She turned around and bit her lip. Then, "I swore I wouldn't tell you."

"Tell me what?"

"Your father called me."

"Dad? What about?"

"You haven't talked to him in over a week. He doesn't know what you're up to. Or why you haven't called. He thinks you're angry at him."

I thought about it. Dad had called a couple of times since we had lunch. I hadn't called him back. "Did he say why?"

"No." She peered at me again in her expectant but knowing way. When I didn't answer, she said, "Are you angry?"

I ran my fingers over the stone in my hand. "I don't know. Maybe I am. Subconsciously."

"Why?"

"Because…." This time I stopped. "I just found out I had a brother."

Susan slowed. I told her about Joseph. Three horizontal lines appeared on her forehead when I had finished. Finally she said, "So you're punishing him for not telling you about a brother who lived only a day or so, years before you were born?"

"I—I didn't think I was. But I'm entitled to be upset, aren't I?"

"Upset, maybe. Sad, certainly. Angry? I don't know. This all happened before you were born. It didn't affect you. It was something your parents had to deal with. Which they ultimately did, by having you."

"Still, it would have been nice if they'd shared it with me."

"Would it have made a difference?"

"It might have explained a lot about my mother—and my relationship with her. I always wondered why she was so—so remote. And my father—well, he basically admitted they should have told me."

"Your mother had her reasons," Susan said. "And while you might not approve of them, why hold them against your father?"

A wave of guilt started to bubble up from my gut. Susan was right. That's what I'd been doing. "I—I'll call him."

Susan nodded, and we picked up our pace.

"But you see? Lousy communication isn't limited to the Suttons," I said. "Lots of families have secrets."

"But not every family is connected to three murders."

"Listen to me. To believe Luke killed his sister, you have to believe he was capable of raping her, and then, for whatever reason, killing her or letting her drown. He's just not that kind of man. No one knows what happened to Herbert Flynn. And as far as Daria Flynn's murder is concerned, well, that's just malicious gossip." I paused. "Except now it turns out a former employee at the Flynns' restaurant is dead."

"Another body?"

I explained about Billy Watkins.

"My god, Ellie. There are dark doings in that town. Four murders, bloody shirts, rifles, meth labs….You know I love you, but this time, you might have gone too far."

"Just a minute. Bear with me. We've already established that the communication in the Sutton family is miserable. That no one talks to anyone. What if Luke's being pressured to keep his mouth shut?"

"By whom? Why?"

"I don't know. Someone in the shadows?"

"Now we're moving into conspiracy theories." Susan rolled her eyes. "What is it you really want from me?"

"An open mind, for starters."

"Now who's being snippy?"

I stopped and spread my hands. "I'm sorry. I guess I am on edge. And I do know you're only looking out for my interests. Thank you for caring."

She ran a hand down my arm. "I'm sorry, too. I can get carried away." She smiled. "Okay?"

"Okay." I smiled back. We started walking again. "But I would like to do some research."

"What for?"

"Turns out Luke managed the airstrip at the Playboy Club the summer of seventy-four. If we can prove he was working at the time his sister died, it might exonerate him."

"Why don't you just ask him?" Then she corrected herself. "Oh, right. He's not talking." She pursed her lips. "Why can't his lawyers find an alibi for him? Why do you have to do it?"

"I don't have to. I want to. It's not a big deal. I'll just put out a few feelers. Try to find someone who worked or was hanging around there that summer."

Susan didn't say anything.

"You think it's a lousy idea."

"You know I do." We marched to the end of the path. The sun, released from the shade of the trees, cast a hard glare on us. Then she sighed. "I probably shouldn't tell you this."

"Tell me what?"

She turned around. "I'm going to regret it, I'm sure. But I know someone who worked up at the Playboy Club. She was a bunny."

"A bunny? That's perfect!"

"I don't know when she worked there—it might not have been the same time you're looking at. But she might know someone who was there in seventy-four."

"Who is it? I'll call her."

She eyed me curiously. "You already know her."

"Susan...."

"I want you to know I don't approve of any of this."

"I hear you. Now, who are you talking about?"

A tiny smile appeared on her lips. "Julia Hauldren."

Chapter Thirty-six

This was turning out to be a day of making amends. As soon as I got home, I called my father. "I'm sorry, Dad."

"For what?"

"I blamed you for not telling me about Joseph. I was wrong."

"We should have told you."

"Mother had her reasons. I just wish—well—it doesn't matter anymore."

"You always thought she didn't love you."

"How did you know?"

"I'm not totally oblivious, sweetheart. I could see how much you wanted her approval. And how your sweet little face crumpled when you didn't get it." He paused. "But she loved you, Ellie. More than life itself. She just couldn't express it."

My eyes felt hot. I wasn't sure I could speak. "Thank you, Daddy," I finally managed.

We were quiet. Then he cleared his throat. "Now, what's this I hear about you and the Sutton family? I thought I told you—"

Susan. "Er...nothing, Dad."

"When you say that, I worry more."

"It's just—I think someone is being falsely accused of a crime."

"Someone who happens to have the name Luke Sutton?"

How much had Susan told him? I debated whether to ask, then decided not to. I didn't need his disapproval, too. "Dad, I'm not in any danger. And I don't intend to be."

"Not the physical kind."

"What are you getting at?"

"The Sutton family are bad news. Always have been."

"Why? Just because their daughter died and the mother couldn't handle it?"

Dad was quiet a moment. "Ellie, Charles Sutton is not a man to be trifled with. He's powerful. And cunning."

"How do you know?"

"The rumor is he tripled the family's assets by his acquisitions and investments."

"That's bad?"

"Not necessarily. But he always seems to get what he wants."

"He's mostly retired now."

Dad blew out a breath. "You think that means he's relinquished control? Sweetheart, I know you and David are having problems, but—"

"It's more than that, Dad. We're not seeing each other anymore."

There was silence. "I'm sorry."

"So am I."

Dad had always been fond of David. Part of it was the fact that he'd once been in love with David's mother, but now something occurred to me. Was David, in some way, a surrogate for the son my father never had? I closed my eyes. "Sometimes you just have to cut your losses and get out," I said quietly. "At least, that's what someone who I know and love tells me."

"You know you've had an impact when your children quote you," he grumbled good-naturedly. "You just don't know if it's good or bad. But listen, sweetheart, about the Suttons—"

"If I didn't have you, Dad, I'd be lost," I cut in. I couldn't hear any more. Luke wasn't like his father, or the rest of his family. Was he? "I love you. I'll call you tomorrow."

⌐⌐⌐⌐

The next thing I did was swallow my pride and drive over to Julia Hauldren's. She lived a few blocks away in a small brick colonial that wasn't much bigger than mine. In the front yard were a tricycle, a bike with training wheels, and a kiddie swimming pool, filled. A few twigs floated on the water's surface.

Rachel looked shocked when she opened the door. "Mom. What's wrong?"

"Nothing, honey." I gave her my most reassuring smile. "I just wanted to see how you were doing."

She didn't look convinced.

"Can I come in?"

She stepped back, and I walked into Julia's living room. It looked like a tornado had touched down. The TV blared, and small plastic tubs of paint littered the floor. Newspapers had been thrown down haphazardly, and sheets of construction paper smudged with every imaginable shade of paint lay on top. In the center of the floor, like the eye of the hurricane, were Julia's daughter and son stretched out on the floor, calmly painting. The little girl had red smears on her arm; the boy had suspicious colors in his hair. Rachel might be the Pied Piper of the preschool set, but her housekeeping skills were more like Pig Pen's.

"Does Julia know you make this much of a mess?"

Rachel hung her head. "I clean up before she gets home."

"You do?" I have to read her the riot act before she'll deign to pick up anything at home. "When will she be home?"

Rachel glanced at a wall clock in the kitchen. "Actually, she should be back in a few minutes." She came out and scurried around, picking up newspapers and sheets of construction paper, some of which were still wet.

While she straightened up, I looked around. Julia's house was less than a mile from mine, and judging from the mismatched furniture, which on the North Shore we call "eclectic," not shabby, she was on a similar budget. She had more of a knack for decorating than me, though. I spotted a faux-cloisonné enamel bowl that probably came from Tuesday Morning and an Oriental runner in the hall that I thought I remembered from Costco. Rachel stopped cleaning long enough to call over her shoulder, "Mom, I don't need a ride home, you know. I rode my bike."

"I know."

She turned around and stared at me. "So why are you here?"

"Actually, I wanted to talk to Julia."

"About what?" she asked suspiciously.

"It's not about you," I said. "Or your father."

Rachel squinted as if she didn't believe me. I shrugged. She opened her mouth but was cut off by the slam of a screen door. A voice called out from the kitchen. "Hey, guys, I'm home. Anyone here?"

"Hi, Julia," Rachel answered. "We're in here."

Footsteps clacked across a narrow hallway, and Julia appeared at the entrance to the living room. When she saw me, she stopped. She was wearing cutoffs, a pink T-shirt, and sandals. Her blond hair was pinned up in a twist. "Ellie. Is something wrong?"

"Everything's fine." I tried out a smile.

She didn't return it. "Oh. You're here to pick up Rachel." She turned to Rachel. "I thought you rode your bike."

"Actually, Julia, I came to talk to you. If that's okay."

The frown deepened, but she was polite. "Of course."

I shot a sidelong glance at Rachel, who, despite her efforts at cleaning up, was listening to us with three ears.

Julia nodded. "Rachel," she said sweetly. "Honey, would you mind throwing the kids into the tub while I talk to your mother?"

"They're not dirty. We went swimming."

Julia just looked at her. Rachel shot a sullen look at me, then Julia. "Come on guys," she sighed. "You heard the drill sergeant."

Julia and I exchanged smiles as they trooped up the stairs. Then Julia turned to me. "How about a glass of wine?"

I checked my watch. Barely four. I nodded.

"Follow me." She led the way back into the kitchen. Two bags of groceries sat on a butcher block table. She got out two glasses, opened the fridge, took out a half-gallon jug of wine, and poured generous amounts into both.

"Thanks," I said as she handed one to me.

She took a sip of hers and then started to unpack the grocery bags. "Hope you don't mind." She pulled out a box of Cheerios, lettuce, and a box of Wheat Thins, and started to put them away. Then she brought the box of Wheat Thins over to the table and ripped the plastic liner. "I love these." She dipped in and brought out a handful. "Less than ten calories apiece. Much better than chips." She pushed the box toward me. "So, what's going on? Is something wrong?"

Shaking my head, I grabbed some crackers. "Everything's fine. And I want to thank you for giving Rachel something to do this summer. It's been a godsend for her."

"For me, too. I don't know what I would have done without her. During the school year, there's time to regroup before three o'clock, you know? But in summer, with two kids underfoot all the time, it can be a long day."

"Why don't you send them to camp?"

"Can't afford it."

I stuffed three crackers in my mouth, embarrassed. "I'm sorry."

Julia turned around. "No problem." She hesitated. "Their father—well—he's not that dependable with his support payments."

"I know that tune," I said between bites. Then I realized who I was talking to. "Oh, shit. I—I'm really putting my foot in today."

"Don't worry about it." She started to giggle. "They're all the same, aren't they? Men, I mean."

"Well." I finished chewing and allowed myself a shy grin. "Well, not all of them."

"Name two who aren't. Excluding ex-husbands."

I picked up my glass. "Not on a bet."

She folded the now empty paper bags and put them in a closet. The sounds of running water drifted down from upstairs. I heard Rachel say, "Alley oop. In you go."

Julia refilled our wineglasses and sat down. "Okay. What gives? I know this isn't a social visit."

I straightened up. "Okay. Here it is. You were once a Playboy bunny up at Lake Geneva, I understand."

A look of surprise came over her. "Who told you?"

"Why? Is it a secret?"

"Not at all, but it's not something I go around broadcasting." She waved a hand. "At least in this neighborhood."

"It was Susan Siler," I confessed.

She nodded. "Nice lady. Your friend. Yes, I did tell her about it. I worked up there for three seasons. Made a lot of money. Put myself through college with it."

"Really?"

"With more left over."

"Wow."

"I made close to fifty grand over the course of the summer. And that was twenty years ago."

I whistled softly. "That's serious money."

"The tips were incredible, especially if they gave you a good schedule." She sipped her wine. "People don't realize that. The Playboy bunnies I knew were—are—some of the shrewdest, smartest, most ambitious women I've ever met."

"Wasn't Gloria Steinem one?"

She nodded. "We have these Bunny reunions every couple of years, and it's amazing to hear what everyone's doing now. Lawyers, doctors, horse owners, nurses, real estate entrepreneurs...all because they used their Bunny income as a steppingstone. In fact"—she looked around, a little sadly, I thought—"I'm about the only one who got married and did nothing." She leaned back. "But you didn't come here for a history of Bunnydom. What do you want to know?"

"Did you work there in the seventies? Seventy-four, to be exact?"

She hesitated and then shook her head. "People tell me I look younger than I am. But I'm not that old. I was there near the end. In the eighties. Why?"

"I'm trying to find someone who might have been there the summer that Luke Sutton managed the airstrip."

"Luke Sutton? *The* Luke Sutton?"

"Did you know him?"

"I didn't know any of the Suttons. Everybody's heard about them, though. The sister died, the brother's a drunk, mother's kind of crazy? He was supposed to be the only sane one. He got out."

Susan and my father had said pretty much the same thing. An edgy feeling crawled over me.

"Is that the same Luke Sutton who's been in the news recently?"

I nodded.

Her eyebrows lifted, but she didn't say anything. She reached for the wine bottle and poured us each another glass. The sounds of shrieks, laughter, and splashing floated down the stairs. "I hope she took out towels," Julia said.

I looked around. "I can't believe how neat she is here. She doesn't lift a finger at home."

"She's getting paid for it." Julia shrugged. "Makes a difference."

I nodded. She was right, of course.

We were silent for a moment. Then she jumped up and hurried over to the counter. "Hold on. I know someone who may have worked up there in seventy-four. I met her at a Bunny reunion." She pulled open a drawer and dug out a personal phone book. Flipping through the pages, she screwed up her face. "Damn. I thought I had it."

"That's okay."

"No. I can get it. I just have to make a couple of calls."

"You wouldn't mind?"

She smiled. "No problem."

I brightened. "I really appreciate it."

She nodded. We lapsed into another silence, but neither of us seemed to be in a hurry. I still had most of a glass of wine, and so did Julia. I suspected she had just as many questions as I, and I wondered whether either of us was brave enough to ask them. Oh hell. Someone had to start. "So, how are you and Barry doing?"

She looked as if she'd been expecting it. "Fine. He's been nice to me."

"No reason not to be. You're a nice person."

"Thanks." She smiled. "And thanks for sharing your daughter with me. I know that had to be hard."

"It was."

She nodded. Another short silence, then we both started talking at once.

"Did you really—"

"How long have you been divorced?"

She answered first. "About two years now."

"It's been longer for me." I sipped my wine. "But, of course, you already know that." I put the glass down. "Shit, you probably know all the gory details, too."

"Barry's mentioned it once or twice," she admitted. "But I take it all with a grain of salt."

I looked up. "You do?"

"He's a man, isn't he?"

"Yes, he definitely is."

"No more need be said." She giggled.

I grinned. "All right, then."

She laughed and raised her glass. "Men. Can't live with them, can't live without them."

I raised mine, and we clinked. "But we're trying."

We laughed so hard that Rachel yelled from upstairs, "What's so funny?"

That set us off even more. I gestured to the ceiling and then flattened my palm in a questioning gesture. Julia answered between giggles, "Nothing, sweetie. Your mother and I are just talking."

It only took a few seconds for Rachel to scramble down the stairs and bounce into the kitchen. "What about?"

"Noth—nothing." By now I was laughing so hard I had trouble getting the words out.

Rachel planted her hands on her hips. "Oh God, you're getting drunk together. I'm telling Dad."

That prompted another round of guffaws. I doubled over and pressed a hand on my stomach, which had started to spasm. "You didn't leave the kids in the tub, did you?" I finally spit out.

"Of course not." Rachel gave us an evil look and stomped out.

"She's something else," Julia finally said.

"Yes…she…is." I gasped for breath, trying to control my laughter. Eventually, the spasms subsided. I took a breath, picked up my wine, and finished it off. "So, what went wrong with your marriage, if you don't mind me asking?"

Julia tipped her head to the side. "You really want to know?"

When I nodded, she paused, then picked up her glass and swirled the wine. I heard a tiny plop. "It was the mackerel loaf."

"Excuse me?"

"The mackerel loaf," she said solemnly.

I frowned. "Julia, what the hell are you talking about?"

"Okay." She drained the rest of the wine and set down her glass. "I had this great salmon loaf recipe. It's been in my family for ages. Handed down for four generations."

"Salmon? I thought you just—"

She cut me off with a raised finger. "It was—it *is* fabulous. You make it with a white sauce and mayonnaise and olives. Maybe pimento. Gives it both a sweet and sour flavor. I mean, this thing was delicious. You serve it for brunch or dinner, and everyone oohs and ahhs."

"Yeah?"

"Well, one day my husband told me to make it, except he didn't want me to make it with salmon. He wanted me to make it with…" She paused again and wrinkled her nose. "…mackerel."

"Mackerel?"

"Mackerel."

It was my turn to pause. "I'm not sure I know what mackerel tastes like."

"I'm sure you don't." She sniffed. "If you did, you would never buy the stuff."

"That bad?"

When she nodded, I poured the last of the wine into our glasses. "Where do you get mackerel?"

"It comes in a can," she said.

"It does? I thought you could only buy it fresh." When she shook her head, I asked, "What does it look like?"

"It's gray."

"Gray," I repeated.

"Iron gray."

"Where do you buy it? At an army-navy surplus store?"

"Just about."

I drank more wine. "Okay. What did you do when he said he wanted the mackerel?"

"I tried to talk him out of it, but he insisted. The salmon didn't cut it. He had to have the damn mackerel. The salmon was from my side of the family, he said, and my side of the family has no taste in anything, including food. But mackerel, now that was something special. He went on and on. In fact, he gave me so much shit about it I eventually threw up my hands and made the damn mackerel loaf."

"You did?" I marveled.

"I did."

"How was it?"

"It tasted awful. Even the kids thought it was gross. They poked at it but wouldn't touch it."

"What about your husband?"

"He ate it."

"The whole thing?"

"I don't know about the leftovers."

"Why not?"

"I filed for divorce the next day and moved out."

Chapter Thirty-seven

Julia Hauldren was as good as her word. An hour later she called with the number of Sharon Singer, a former bunny who worked at the Lake Geneva Playboy Resort during the seventies. I thanked her and vowed not to let my prejudices get in the way of a possible friendship again.

Sharon and I made a date for coffee the next morning. But after we hung up, I stared at my computer monitor. There had to be something else I could do. Someone else I could talk to about Luke or the Suttons or what went on that summer. I pulled out a sheet of paper and a pencil and started to list everyone I could think of who had a relationship with the Suttons. When I got to Chip, I tapped the pencil on my desk.

Five minutes later, with the help of Google and the crisscross phone directory, I had what I was looking for. I got in the car and swung east on Willow Road.

Tucked away on some private streets in Winnetka are huge homes that you can get to only if you know they're there. I turned down White Oak Lane and slowly made my way down a one-lane road more like a driveway than a street. I stopped at a stately red brick Georgian home with a gravel-lined drive in front and a backyard that looked like a miniature forest preserve. Just visible in a clearing on the side was a tennis court surrounded by a tall chain-link fence. I couldn't see the players, but I heard the plop and twang of a serious rally.

I got out of the car and rang the doorbell. The chimes echoed noisily inside, and a moment later, the plop and twang ceased. A moment after that, the door was opened by a tall, slim woman with short black hair held off her face by a sweatband. She was wearing a powder blue tennis dress, and the sheen of sweat on her face said she was one of the players.

I took a breath, hoping Jennifer Brinks Sutton, Chip's wife, was nothing like her husband. "Mrs. Sutton, I'm sorry to intrude, but I'd like to talk to you. My name is Ellie Foreman, and I'm a friend of Luke's."

For a moment she didn't reply, just stared at me with dark, piercing eyes that made me think she saw straight through me. Then, a female voice called out behind her. "Everything okay, Jenny?"

She turned away from me and answered, "Everything's fine." She turned back and looked me up and down, her gaze taking in my jeans, T-shirt, and sweaty palms. "So what can I do for you, friend of Luke's?" she said with a curious but not unkind expression.

I sagged in relief. "I was hoping you might talk to me about the night Anne Sutton died. I know you weren't married to Chip then, but maybe he—or someone else in the family—said something afterward that would help Luke establish an alibi for that night."

She eyed me again, and I sensed she was deciding whether or not to talk to me. Finally, she opened the door wide. "Come in."

She led me down a wide hall with a marble floor. On the left was a formal living room with a thick carpet and wall sconces that looked like mini-chandeliers. It was filled with delicate Louis XVI furniture, and a whiff of furniture polish drifted out as we passed. On the right was a wide, winding staircase that made the one Clark Gable carried Scarlett up look shabby. We ended up at the back of the house in a wood-paneled great room with twelve-foot ceilings. Another woman, also in tennis gear, sprawled on a long couch.

"I hope I didn't ruin your game, Mrs. Sutton," I said.

"We were almost done anyway," she said. "And please. Call me Jen." She gestured to the other woman. She was slim also, but petite and blond. "This is my friend, Julie Nothstine."

We exchanged nods, and Jen went behind a bar in the corner. "Please, sit down. Would you like a drink?"

"Thanks." I sat down in an oversized navy blue armchair, watching as she filled three glasses with ice and poured Diet Coke into each. She handed one to me and one to her friend, then sat down on the couch a little too close to her. Julie threw her arm on the back of the sofa. Jen relaxed against her arm, sipped her drink, and shot me a defiant smile. I sensed she was daring me to judge her.

I returned what I hoped was a disarming smile. "Are you keeping up with events in Lake Geneva?" I began cautiously.

She rearranged herself, curling her legs underneath her. "I've been reading about it in the paper. God, what a mess *that's* turning out to be. Glad I'm not there."

Why was she relying on the newspaper, I wondered. Shouldn't Chip be calling her, giving her a blow-by-blow?

She watched me, a little smile tugging at the corners of her mouth. "You're wondering why I'm reading about it in the paper instead of talking to my husband."

I looked at her, startled. "You read my mind."

She hesitated, then tipped her glass to me. "To Chip Sutton." She took a sip.

Julie followed suit. They traded smiles.

"What's so funny?" I asked.

Jen hesitated. Then, "You know that line from *Fiddler on the Roof?* The one about the czar?"

"May God bless and keep the czar...far away from us?"

"That's the one," she said. "Well, that's the way I feel about Chip."

I wasn't sure what to say.

"And by the way, I haven't been totally honest about something. I do know who you are. Chip called a few weeks ago and asked me to check you out. He doesn't like you very much."

"I had that feeling."

"Which predisposed me to like you right away. Then, after I did some checking, I decided I liked you even more. You made the WISH video, right?"

I'd produced a video for WISH—Women for Interim Subsidized Housing—last winter. "How did you know?"

"Word gets around. I sit on several boards. Infant Welfare, Northwestern Settlement. I have an interest in children's issues. Chip says it's my misplaced motherhood. We never had any."

"I'm sorry."

"Actually, now I'm glad. I wouldn't want them to see how much I despise their father," she said scornfully. "Believe me, I'm just thankful he stays up in Lake Geneva." She placed her hand on Julie's knee.

I sipped my drink.

She eyed me. "You're wondering why we bother to stay together at all, aren't you?"

"The thought did cross my mind."

"It's simple." She leaned back, her hands flopping in her lap. "Together, we're worth more than a small country. It makes for a mutually satisfying strategic alliance. Strange bedfellows and all that."

I put my drink down. I wasn't interested in any of her bedfellows, strange or not. "Jen, I really came to ask you about Luke."

"Right." She sighed. "Poor Luke. I don't know how he managed to survive in that nest of vipers. If only I'd met him first...." She looked wistful for an instant, then flashed Julie a smile and snuggled in next to her. "I didn't get to know him till he got back from Montana. A good person. But such a lost soul." She looked over. "He's quite a catch, you know."

I felt my cheeks get hot.

"Mmm...I thought so." She laughed. "But don't worry. Your secret is safe with me. I'm harmless."

And I'm Grace Slick. I had the feeling Jen Sutton could turn into a barracuda at will. I looked around. The kitchen extended off the great room. A pizza box lay on the counter. Magazines and today's newspaper were spread out on the coffee table in front of me. Two half-filled coffee mugs lay on top.

She followed my gaze. "Sorry for the clutter. It's just such a relief to live like a normal person."

"Pardon me?"

"When Chip's here, it's always a struggle." At my frown, she went on. "He's—well, let's just say, he's a tad obsessive-compulsive."

Julie snorted. I looked at Jen.

"He's got a control jones you wouldn't believe. Everything has to be in order. And I mean perfect order. No coffee grounds in the sink. Toilet paper torn off at the perforations. Once he went into a tirade about the shelf paper lining the cabinets. It was crooked. And his clothes." She rolled her eyes. "His shirts have to line up in his drawer just so. Jesus, he even inspects the damn linen closet. Not that he's ever made a bed in his life, but the maids have to fold the sheets and pillowcases to his precise specifications. If they don't, he fires them." She shook her head.

"My pantsuit," I murmured.

"Excuse me?"

I remembered how concerned Chip had been by the wine stain on my outfit at the gala. I'd thought he was just being rude, but apparently, there was more to it. "I had a run-in with him along those lines." I gazed around.

She waved a hand. "I live a normal life when he's not here."

I nodded politely. "So you didn't know Luke thirty years ago?"

"Thirty years ago I was spending summers on Mackinac Island. I didn't know the Suttons existed. And while I regret that isn't still the case, I can tell you unequivocally that Luke Sutton is the last person I'd suspect of hurting—much less kill-ing—anyone."

I was stacking plates in the dishwasher that night when it hit me. Despite Jen Sutton's explanation, I'd been pondering how she could stay married to Chip. I wasn't sure whether to pity her, be irritated, or admire her behavior. I could never live with a man like Chip. Inspecting the linen closet, drawers, even sinks. Making sure everything was perfectly aligned. I barely even fold the clothes out of the dryer. Fortune or not, I'd have been gone the first year.

Suddenly, I gasped, nearly dropping the plate I'd been holding. The clothes. Anne Sutton's clothes. When the police found them in the ice house, they'd been neatly folded.

Chapter Thirty-eight

I called Jimmy early the next morning. He wasn't in his office, and I didn't want to leave a message on his voice mail, so I hung up. I drove downtown and parked a block away from the East Bank Club in River North. A combination health club, restaurant, and gathering place, it was one of the first of its kind twenty years ago. It was also one of the few that has maintained its cachet.

I waited on a padded marble bench in the lobby. Across from me was the pro shop, which featured leather jackets and a polka dot party dress in its window. It was only midmorning, but plenty of people streamed in and out. Didn't anybody work? I tried not to feel intimated by the parade of women with sports bags slung over their shoulders. Some had long frizzy hair, others the short, wet sculpted look, but all of them were incredibly fit. Even the pregnant women looked better than I did, although at $3,500 a year for dues, they should.

A chic-looking woman in casual sweats skipped down a flight of stairs and made her way over to me. Her blond hair hung straight to her shoulders, and her makeup was carefully applied. I doubted she was there to work out.

"Are you Ellie?"

I stood up. "You must be Sharon."

We shook hands. She was so fit and her face so unlined it was impossible to determine her age. She led me back up the stairs, and we went into the grill, a cheerful restaurant with an art deco floor and impressionist prints on the walls. Within seconds, we both had coffee, and she had ordered omelets with sourdough toast.

"I didn't expect breakfast," I said. "Thanks."

"Any friend of Julia's is a friend of mine." She laced her fingers and stretched out her arms as if she'd just gotten out of bed. "Julia said you had questions about the Playboy Resort."

I nodded. "You were a bunny in Lake Geneva during the seventies, right?"

"Five years."

"Were you there in seventy-four?"

"I sure was." She looked off as if remembering. "That was the summer I almost applied to be a Bunny mother. Changed my mind, though."

"A what?"

"It's kind of a Girl Scout leader for bunnies. The den mother."

"I didn't realize you had—"

"You wouldn't believe how strictly we were supervised. The company was very protective of the Bunny image. For good reason. They taught us everything."

"What do you mean, everything?"

"Oh, my. Let's see. They taught us how to serve, how to taste wine—we wore these little silver wine-tasting cups around our neck. How to make people feel at ease, make sure they were having a good time." She straightened up at my smirk. "Hey, let's make one thing clear. There was absolutely no hanky-panky going on with bunnies. If you stepped out of line in *any* way, you were out."

"Really?"

"You better believe it."

"So the Bunny mother was your chastity belt?"

"In a way. She was generally a former bunny herself, so she knew the score. She'd try to point you in the right direction, but God help you if you got caught fraternizing. They were so strict we couldn't even be seen with a man on the premises unless we had written permission. And that included your father. Even then, you always had to be with another female. If you weren't, even the Bunny mother couldn't save you."

"Sounds like a prison."

"Maybe to you." She smiled. "But I don't regret a single minute. Where else does an eighteen-year-old make fifty grand a year without being on your back?" She shrugged. "Let's face it. I'm no great brain, and I don't have much talent. I knew from the get-go my looks were my ticket to success."

"That sounds harsh."

"Not when you're pulling down a hundred and fifty or two hundred dollars a night," she said. "It was a great gig. All we had to do was smile, be perky, and follow the rules. Everything else was thought out and prepared in advance. Hell, even our costumes matched the décor."

"Really?" I was interested in spite of myself.

She leaned forward. "The VIP Room was done up in silver and blue, with lots of smoky mirrors on the walls. We would dress in these royal blue velvet costumes with silver trim. The fabric was the same velvet they used in the booths. All the serving dishes were silver, too. Including our wine-tasting cups."

"So you actually tasted the wine?"

"Of course." She nodded. "That's how I learned all that stuff."

I felt a newfound appreciation for the Playboy organization. "Are you sad that it's over?"

"Sure. Maybe a little."

"I guess women's lib pretty much put an end to it."

She frowned. "Oh, I don't think so."

I looked over. "No?"

"It probably didn't help, but the real blow was the murder of Dorothy Stratton."

Dorothy Stratton. A long-ago memory surfaced. A Playboy bunny and aspiring actress. Brutally murdered by her estranged husband. At the time it was a sordid affair, full of gossip and innuendo. She'd been having an affair with film director Peter

Bogdanovich. I seem to recall rumors of others, too. Even Hugh Hefner.

"There was so much bad publicity about it that things kind of fell apart," Sharon explained. "Particularly for Hef. He took it really hard."

"Was he having an affair with her?"

"Who knows? Maybe it was just a father-daughter thing. I don't know. But he lost interest in everything for a while, and then, well, nothing was the same. The resort went downhill. It closed a year or so later." Her face took on a determined smile. "But that's not the period you're interested in, is it?"

"You're right. I'm wondering about the summer that Luke Sutton ran the airstrip."

A gleam came into her eyes. "Luke Sutton, huh? How come you're interested in him?"

I didn't feel like explaining. "Did you know him?"

She giggled. "Everyone knew Luke."

Our omelets came. Sharon sprinkled salt and pepper on hers and took a small bite. "He was a hottie."

I tore off a piece of toast and stuffed it in my mouth. "He was?"

"Oh yes. Lots of the girls would sneak down to 'visit' him at the hangar on their break. Of course, if they got caught, they were screwed." She took another bite of her omelet. "Didn't seem to stop some of 'em. Although, now that I'm thinking about it, they weren't that concerned about bunnies socializing with the staff. Customers and performers were the no-no's." She started telling me about a popular singer who performed at the resort but couldn't keep his hands off the girls. "One of my friends was caught in his room. She was fired the next day."

"Umm." I chewed another piece of toast. "So, what about Luke?"

"Oh, yeah. Sorry." She got a faraway look in her eyes. "Well, actually, from what I remember, Luke kept pretty much to himself."

"He did?" I don't know why that made me feel better—it was thirty years ago—but it did.

"No, wait a minute. How could I forget?"

My spirits sank. "Forget what?"

"There was this townie."

"Townie?" I picked up my fork and dug into my omelet.

She nodded. "She worked as a maid over the summer. The poor girl was head over heels in love with Luke. Followed him all over like a puppy dog."

I froze, my fork halfway to my mouth.

Sharon didn't seem to notice and shook her head. "She was relentless."

"Wha—what happened?"

Sharon shot me a meaningful look. "What do you think happened? I mean, what do you suppose a man's going to do when a girl keeps throwing herself at him?"

"She threw herself at Luke? This townie?"

"It was pitiful."

"Do you—by any chance—remember her name?"

She chewed thoughtfully. "Let's see. No. She had dark hair. It was long. She wasn't bad looking. Actually, I do remember when they finally got it on. You'd think she'd just won the lottery."

My stomach turned over. "They—they got it on?"

"Well, that's what she told everyone. You know that thing women do when they think they've got something going. They start talking about what they're gonna do with the guy. Use the word 'we' a lot. That kind of thing."

I kept my mouth shut. My appetite vanished.

Sharon kept eating. Then she brightened. "I remember her name now. It was Kim."

Chapter Thirty-nine

I drove back to the North Shore feeling like I'd been duped. Once again, I was the last person to know something that had occurred up in Lake Geneva. And even though it had happened thirty years ago, it felt personal. Why didn't I know? Why hadn't anyone told me?

I rolled down the window. To be fair, there was no reason for anyone to tell me about an affair that happened thirty years ago. It was none of my business. Whatever had occurred between Luke and Kim was in the past. Kim's hatred of the Suttons had undoubtedly destroyed whatever feelings she once had. It was probably just a summer fling. They were both teenagers, probably in heat and eager to experiment with sex. For all I knew, Kim might even be embarrassed about it now. I certainly had regrets about some of my past exploits.

Except, according to Sharon, she'd flaunted it around the Playboy Resort. Made sure everyone knew they were an "item." Was that just the posturing of an insecure girl? Or was it something else? And what happened to break them up? I wondered if it had anything to do with Annie's death, and the suspicion about Herbert's role in it. Was the pressure just too much, the Capulets and the Montagues come to blows?

I looked out through the windshield. A dirty gray overcast had lowered, punched through with darker storm clouds. I'd intended to go over to Mac's to edit, but I knew I wouldn't make it. A storm was about to break, and I knew where I wanted to be when it did.

⌐—⌐—⌐—

I parked on the street in front of the police station in Lake Geneva. Inside, I climbed to the second floor and went down the hall. The chief of police's door opened to a reception area with a desk, a couch, and several chairs around a low table, but no one was behind the reception desk, and the door to Jimmy's office was closed.

Through the door I heard him on the phone, and while his end of the conversation was muffled, his voice sounded tense. I sat in one of the chairs, picked up a three-month-old copy of *Police* magazine, and thumbed through it restlessly.

Jimmy had to be under tremendous stress. Although he'd removed himself from the investigations, he had to be mentally picking at the pieces, trying to make sense of them. His position made him privy to critical information, whether he chose to do anything with it or not. I wondered how that information affected the way he felt about people he'd known all his life.

I remembered how he'd questioned Kim at the restaurant the other day. His tone seemed cooler than usual. I hadn't seen him with Luke since they'd found Annie's clothes and Luke's shirt, but his attitude toward him had to be in turmoil, too. How are you supposed to feel when your best friend could be a murder suspect? And what about Chip? How would Jimmy react when I told him what Jen Sutton said?

I'd just read the same sentence three times—something about SWAT team training—when footsteps thudded down the hall. A moment later, a man walked into the reception area. About average height and weight, he was wearing horn-rimmed glasses, and his buzz cut needed a trim. I stared at him. Something about him was familiar. He stared at me, too, and tipped his head to the side.

We both got it at the same time.

"You're the guy with the cell phone!"

"Jesus, you were there, too!"

"The police have been looking for you."

"I know." He nodded. "I just came back to civilization." He took a few steps and held out his hand. "Steve Davis."

I stood up. "I'm Ellie Foreman."

He motioned with his hand. "Are you with the police?"

"Just an interested bystander. Where have you been?"

"I've been fishing for the past three weeks in Wisconsin."

"Fishing. That's right. 'Hope you catch some big ones.'"

"Actually I did."

I let it go.

"There weren't any phones, TV, or papers. I stopped into a Denny's for some breakfast on the way home, and when I picked up a paper, I read about the shooting. My God, it must have happened a minute or two after I left."

"Exactly right."

"I realized right away I must be the one they were talking about, and since I was heading back in this direction, I figured I should come in."

A public-spirited citizen. I was impressed.

"Did they—do they know who her boyfriend was?" he asked.

If he only knew. "No one's come forward." I eyed him. "That's why your cell phone is so important." I looked at Jimmy's door. It was still closed, and I could still hear him on the phone. "Steve—you don't mind if I call you Steve?"

He shook his head.

"Would you mind—could I take a look at your phone? I won't make any calls. I just want to take a look."

"You want to see if the calls she made are on my call log?"

"Well, as a matter of fact…."

"I didn't check. I thought maybe the police ought to do that." He shot me a questioning look. "They might have a special way of doing it to get fingerprints or evidence, or something."

Just my luck, an armchair detective. Probably learned it on *Law and Order*. I rubbed my thumb and index finger together. "Um, you know, Steve," I said sweetly, "if they needed to identify whose prints were on it, you'd be absolutely right. But in this case, everyone knows Daria used your phone. Her prints will turn up all over it. Nothing will happen if we just take a quick peek."

He didn't reply for a moment. Then he hunched his shoulders. "Well, I guess it's okay."

It was all I could do not to grab it after he fished it out of his pocket. Silver and black, it looked like every other cell phone I'd ever seen. I turned it on, and once it warmed up, I pushed Menu, then Call Log, then Dialed Calls . I started scrolling and breathed a prayer. Calls normally stay in the phone's memory for thirty days, give or take a day. The problem was it had been almost that long since Daria Flynn's murder. It was iffy.

I scrolled past a bunch of calls with area codes 312 and 847. "Do you live on the North Shore?"

"Wilmette."

"What a coincidence. I live off Happ Road."

"I know it well."

I kept scrolling. What was the area code up here? I should know it from all the calls I'd made to the Lodge. Of course—262. I kept scrolling. More 847s, and then a 914. He had friends in Westchester County, NY. That was followed by a 516. Long Island. Then I froze. What if Daria's boyfriend didn't live in Wisconsin? What if he lived in Chicago, or even on the North Shore? A wave of anxiety washed over me. If that was the case, I might have already passed the number. There was no way to tell. Maybe I should let the cops go over it. They could print out the log and identify each number more easily than I.

No. Not yet. I kept going, hoping I wasn't scrolling through the numbers a second time. Two more 847s. It didn't look good.

Bingo! I scrolled past a 262 area code. And after that, another. And then a third! I frowned. Three calls with 262s? Daria had made only one call. I showed Steve the cell. "Do you recognize any of these numbers?"

He took the phone and squinted at the tiny screen. He nodded. My spirits sank.

"The third one. It's the number of the fishing camp I stayed at. But the other two...." He shook his head. "I don't know."

"Are you sure?"

"Positive. Why?"

"There are three calls here with a 262 area code. There should only be two. The one you made, and the one Daria made to her boyfriend."

"Daria was her name?"

"Yes. Daria Flynn." I found a scrap of paper in my bag and wrote down the numbers, but as I jotted them down, again I realized I could be wrong. The first call might have been to her boyfriend's home. But what if he wasn't there? She might well have called his work number, or his cell. That would account for the extra call.

"Which way was she headed, this Daria?"

I looked up. It was odd, given how steeped I was in the case, to think Steve Davis didn't know anything about her. Odder still that he'd asked the one question no one seemed able to answer. "She—I think she was trying to go home." I didn't want to be rude, but I needed to focus on the calls. "The calls, Steve. On your phone. There are three with a 262 area code. You made one. Daria made another. What about the third? Is it possible you forgot you made it? Or was it possible Daria made more than one call?"

"Lemme think. Actually, now that you mention it, she did."

"Did what?"

"I'm pretty sure she made two calls."

That explained it. I dug out my own cell and dialed the first number. It rang three times, then switched over to voice mail. My heart was pounding. I was finally going to find out who the boyfriend was. Please don't let it be—

"Hi, this is Fred Baker." The voice paused. "And that's exactly what I do." He chuckled. "Cakes and petit-fours are my specialty, but I'm game for anything. Leave a message."

I gripped the phone. Could Fred Baker have been Daria's boyfriend? They were clearly in the same business: he was a baker, she a sous-chef. They could have met through their work. He sounded warm. Friendly. Even had a sense of humor. How could he not have come forward? He had to know the police were looking for him.

Unless he had something to hide. Unless coming forward would expose something he couldn't afford to reveal. I shivered. I'd been thinking about leaving a message, but I abandoned the idea and hung up. Then I checked the second number I'd written down and punched it into my cell. Three rings, then it, too, went to voice mail.

This time a female voice came on. A familiar female voice. "This is Mount Olympus restaurant. Serving the best Greek food in Lake Geneva. We're closed right now. Please call back."

My stomach turned over.

"Well?" Davis pointed with his chin toward the phone, but when he saw me, his brows knit together. "What's wrong?"

Daria hadn't called Fred's office. Or his cell. She'd called Mount Olympus. I lowered the phone. "I—I'm not sure."

I scribbled the two 262 numbers on another scrap of paper. "You need to show these to Chief Saclarides." I stuffed my cell in my bag and started for the door.

"Where are you going?" He gestured toward Jimmy's closed door. "I thought you were waiting—"

I hesitated. "Tell Chief Saclarides I need to—"

Suddenly the door to Jimmy's office opened. He stood there in his uniform and white shirt and looked from me to Davis. "Tell me what? What are you doing here, Ellie?"

"I—I. This man needs to talk to you. And so do I. He's the man who lent—"

"I can't. Not now." His face was drawn and pained.

"Why? What's wrong?"

"Luke's gone. He took off in his plane this morning."

Chapter Forty

I braced myself against the glass door. I felt light, unanchored. "What do you mean, Luke's gone? Where?"

"I don't know."

"He flew his plane?"

Jimmy nodded.

"When?"

He looked like he wasn't sure he wanted to tell me. Then he leaned against the door and sighed. "Not long after the sheriff's deputies found the shoe print outside Herbert Flynn's house."

"A shoe print?"

"They lifted it from the lawn. About a foot away from the front porch. They're running tests on it now."

"And you think he ran because he knew the shoe print was his?"

"It doesn't look good." His face was grim.

I hoisted my bag up on my shoulder. "Jimmy, I know this isn't a good time, but you need to talk to him." I gestured to Davis. "He was the one who let Daria borrow his cell phone."

Astonishment came over Jimmy's face.

Davis introduced himself. "I've been on vacation the past three weeks. No TV or papers. As soon as I realized who she was and how I tied in, I came over." He glanced at me. "And then when I met Ellie here, well, she found the numbers on my call log."

Jimmy leveled me with a look. In other circumstances, it might have turned into a smile, but it didn't get that far.

"I wrote them down." I pointed to the piece of paper in Davis' hand.

Jimmy took the paper and studied the numbers. "I know this number. The second one." He pulled out his cell and punched it in.

I waited for him to make the connection.

"Oh God." It came out quietly, sounding more like a prayer than an exclamation. He clicked off. A distant look came into his eyes.

"Daria made two calls," I said. "One was to someone named Fred Baker. The second was to Kim."

"I know what the first call was about," Davis piped up.

I spun around. "You do? Was he her boyfriend?"

Davis looked puzzled. "Her boyfriend? I—I don't know. I suppose he could have been."

"What does that mean?" Jimmy asked.

"My impression was that he was someone she was working with. At least that's what she said when she asked to borrow the phone."

"She was calling a coworker?" Jimmy squared his shoulders and refocused, all business now. "From the restaurant?"

"More like a partner, I think. There was this party she was catering somewhere in Lake Bluff. He was supplying the pastries and cakes and they were going to deliver them to the house. Her car broke down and she didn't have the money to get it repaired, so there was—there was this arrangement. She got dropped off at the oasis, and he was going to meet her. I got the impression they were heading toward Lake Bluff."

Jimmy started to nod. "She was stranded on Route 50 a few months ago. One of my deputies on patrol picked her up." He turned to Davis. "Did she say who dropped her off?"

"No, just that she was being picked up. But then she got upset, so I figured he wasn't coming."

"So the fight was with this—this Fred," Jimmy said. "In her catering business. Who might have been her boyfriend. But they made up afterward, right?"

I wasn't sure whether Jimmy really believed that or whether he wanted it to be true. I turned to Davis. "When did she make the second call?"

He looked confused. "Right after she hung up on the first. She started to give me back the phone, but then she asked if she could make one more call."

"Why don't I remember that?"

"You'd gone inside."

"Of course." I went in to get a drink. By the time I came out, Daria must have been talking to Kim. I'd missed the end of her first call and the beginning of the second. "I didn't realize that. I assumed she was on the same call."

Jimmy didn't say anything.

I bit my lip. "Oh God, Jimmy. The person I heard her apologizing to wasn't her boyfriend. It was Kim. She'd been fighting with her sister."

Jimmy cut in. "So when she asked whoever it was to come soon...."

"It was Kim. Kim was coming to pick her up."

Chapter Forty-one

Jimmy called in a deputy to take Steven Davis' statement. Before he arrived, Jimmy asked Davis for his phone. Davis handed it over goodnaturedly. "The wife's been bugging me to get one of those fancy ones with a camera anyway."

Jimmy sent another deputy over to the Flynns' home to stake out the place.

"You're not going to arrest her?" I asked.

"For what? Having a fight with her sister?"

"She was supposed to pick up her sister. She never did. She lied about it. And in the interim, Daria was killed."

"Ellie, it's still speculation. And I don't have time to work it through right now." He gathered his wallet and keys from his desk and stuffed them in his pocket.

"Where are you going?"

He checked his watch, opened a drawer behind his desk, and pulled out a map.

"You're going to look for Luke."

He didn't answer.

"I'm going with you."

"No." He shook his head. "This is police business."

"You're lying."

He looked over. "What are you talking about?"

"You said you were removing yourself from the investigations. But you're going to try and find him anyway." When he didn't answer, I added, "You want to get to him before anyone else."

He threw me a look but didn't deny it.

"Jimmy, I have to go with you. I need to see Luke. And I have things to tell you. About Chip."

"Chip?"

"I talked to his wife."

"Jen?"

I nodded.

He hesitated, but then shook his head. "It'll have to wait until I get back."

"It can't. I—I think I might know what happened to Annie."

Jimmy stared at me. "How could you?"

I stood my ground. "Please, Jimmy. We have to talk."

"I've got to go."

"Okay," I shrugged. "If that's the way you're going to be, I'll just follow you in my Volvo."

His eyes narrowed. "You wouldn't do that."

"Try me."

He walked to the door, shaking his head. I followed two steps behind. He stopped and turned around. "Christ. Just get in the car."

"It's more than speculation," I explained on the way to the airstrip. We were in Jimmy's gold Camry. "It fits together. I should have known when she came to my house."

"Kim came to your house?"

I nodded. "Not long after Daria died. Irene was with her." I explained how they'd come, ostensibly to ask me about Daria's last words. "But then Kim came into the kitchen and pumped me about Daria's 'boyfriend.'"

"What did she ask you?"

"She wanted to know if Daria said anything about him to me. Whether I'd seen him. If I knew what he looked like. What he did." I took a breath. "I thought she was genuinely trying to identify him. But now, I see it was all a sham." I glanced out the window. "Then there were the times I talked to her in the restaurant. Told her what I'd learned from Willetta, from you, even Luke. She was clever. Always two steps ahead of me." I looked over. "I didn't see it, Jimmy. I fucked up."

"You couldn't have known."

I shook my head. "Jimmy, I was the one who perpetrated the myth of a boyfriend picking her up. Me. I led you and the police astray. And then spreading the rumors about Luke and Daria." I squeezed my eyes shut. "And all the time, it was Kim. Jesus, what did I do?"

"Anyone could have made the same assumption, Ellie. You didn't know Daria made two calls. And I have to warn you. There's still no proof Kim was involved in Daria's murder."

"Not yet."

"What's the motive, Ellie? Why would she kill her sister? And why go through all the maneuvering to make it look like a sniper attack? They lived together. If Kim wanted to kill Daria, there are much easier ways than staging a shooting at a rest stop."

"If you're so unsure, why'd you send a deputy to stake out her house?"

"Because—because I think it's a good idea to keep tabs on her. We're going to have another talk when I get back."

We turned onto the access road to the Lodge and drove around back to the airstrip. Jimmy had called ahead, and one of the staffers at the Lodge raised the door to the hangar. Although I'd peered in several times before, I hadn't actually been inside. I followed Jimmy into a cavernous room with a cement floor and skirted a jumble of ropes, tarps, and other equipment. I stopped in front of a white plane with a blue stripe running down its side.

"The Cessna!" I exclaimed. "It's here." I looked around, half expecting to see Luke emerge from the cockpit, slipping his sunglasses off and greeting me with a smile.

Jimmy walked around the plane, rubbing the back of his neck with his hand. "But the other one isn't."

"The other one?"

"Luke has two planes, both of them Cessnas. One of them is equipped with pontoons."

I blinked. Two planes. Of course. There had been more than one plane parked here. "So that means—"

"He's planning to land on water."

I hesitated. Then, "I think I know where he is."

"I do, too."

⌒⌒⌒

The drive to Star Lake took over five hours. A steady rain dogged us for the first two hours, sharp tiny bullets that exploded on contact with the windshield. Jimmy tried one last time to persuade me to go home, but when I refused, he threw up his hands. "Suit yourself."

I called Rachel at home and told her I was going to northern Wisconsin. She said she'd spend the night at Barry's.

As we headed north, the steady thud on the roof of the Toyota faded to an occasional plink. The scenery changed, too, forests of evergreens and deciduous trees now pushing in from both sides of the road. The insulation of a thick cushion of green was oddly comforting, and we started to talk.

I told him what I'd learned from Jen Sutton.

"So Chip is obsessive about being neat," Jimmy summed up. "And Annie's clothes were neatly folded." He shook his head. "I don't know. It's thin."

"Oh, come on. How many sexual predators take the time to fold their victim's clothes afterward?"

"It's bizarre, I'll grant you, but—"

"But it could be."

"If you're right, why was it Luke who bolted? And what about his baseball shirt?"

"I don't know. Maybe Chip was wearing it for some reason."

"And what about the bloodstains?"

"What about them?" I peered over at Jimmy.

He shook his head. "You know I can't talk about that with you."

"Maybe not. But I can. I don't think it was Luke."

"If you're right, why didn't Luke tell me a long time ago?"

"How could he, Jimmy? You're the chief of police."

He didn't look convinced.

"How do you turn in your own brother for murdering your sister?"

"Luke knows the difference between right and wrong," he said stubbornly.

"Jimmy, think of the pressure he was under. Chuck Sutton is a master at twisting people's arms. Guilt. Threats. Bribes. Whatever it takes. What makes you think he wouldn't do the same thing to his own family?"

"So he convinces his sons to keep quiet and pins the blame on Herbert Flynn," Jimmy said.

"And when that doesn't work, he comes up with the intruder theory."

Jimmy was quiet. Trees and bushes zipped past in a blur of green.

"It'll be interesting to see if the DNA tests back up my theory."

He didn't say anything.

I eyed him. "In fact, the results should answer a lot of questions."

He still didn't say anything.

"Right?"

He rubbed a finger across his nose. "Right."

I studied his face and folded my arms.

He looked over. "What?"

"Tell me something, Jimmy. I'm no expert, but I thought material that's been in a damp environment for a long time with temperature changes and other kinds of corrosion could become so badly contaminated it wouldn't yield any DNA at all."

"Is that so." He gripped the wheel.

"That's so." I kept my eyes on him.

He kept his eyes on the road. "You know, my father is a pretty smart guy for eighty-one," I said after a while. "In fact, I value his advice more and more every day."

"Yeah? What does your father say?"

"Ancient Chinese proverb. Never try to con a con."

His mouth twitched.

"There are no DNA tests, are there?"

He looked over.

"You know the clothes are too badly contaminated to get any results. You're using the threat of tests to flush out the Suttons." When he didn't answer, I added, "Slick move."

"You didn't hear it from me. And I'll deny it if it gets out."

"Don't worry." I readjusted myself in the seat. "So do you think it will work?"

"It seems to have jarred something loose or we wouldn't be here now." He shrugged. "I just hope—well—maybe it's better not to."

"What are you going to do when we get to the cabin?"

"I'm going to lay it out for Luke and convince him to come back."

"Do you think it'll work?"

"I don't know."

"Why do you think he ran?"

"Don't know that either. Maybe because he's guilty. Maybe he just needs to think things through."

"You don't think he killed anyone, do you?"

He didn't answer for a long time. Then, "I've lived here all my life. I thought I knew everyone. Now...." His voice trailed off. I'd never seen him look so sad.

"People always let you down," I said quietly.

"What?"

"Irene Flynn said that when she and Kim came to my house."

"Luke never has."

"You're his friend."

"Or the biggest fool east of the Mississippi."

"It was the note, wasn't it? Herbert Flynn's note started it."

Jimmy didn't answer.

"Herbert Flynn wrote something that implicated Luke."

"You know I can't tell you that."

The fact he didn't deny it was proof enough. What did the note say? Did Herbert see Luke and his sister together? Did he see him rape her? Kill her? Then stash her clothes in the ice house? Or did he see someone else? Someone wearing Luke's shirt? Someone he could have mistaken for Luke?

We drove on in silence. Then, "Jimmy, did you know Kim and Luke had an affair?"

No answer.

"Thirty years ago. The summer Anne Sutton died. When you all worked at the Playboy Club."

The overcast, tinged with shadows, smudged the leaves on the trees with gray.

"You knew."

He cleared his throat. "It was a long time ago." The words came out thickly, as if he was pulling out something that had been stuck for a long time.

I told him what Sharon Singer said about Kim. "I wonder if the rumors about Daria and Luke upset her."

He threw me a sharp look. "Are you saying she was jealous—that she was still carrying a torch for Luke and that's why she killed her sister?"

"I'm just looking at it as an outsider. Luke and Daria are seen together at the Lodge. Kim finds out. A few weeks later, Daria is killed. The timing is—interesting."

"The shooter was a man. In all three cases. Kim couldn't be that—that twisted."

"The second sniper attack was an anomaly. Different bullet fragments. Different rifle. The same kind that the guy who worked at Mount Olympus owned. You can't tell me you haven't been thinking in those terms."

"Of course I have. But I still don't think there's much of a motive. Kim kills Daria because Daria was meeting someone Kim shacked up with thirty years ago? I don't think so. Even if it happened, don't you think I would have picked it up?"

"You've been friends your entire life. Your families are close. Maybe that's what Kim was counting on. Exploiting your relationship, figuring she'd be the last person you'd suspect. You said yourself you're not sure you really know anyone."

He slid a couple of fingers up and down the steering wheel.

A minute later, his cell phone chirped. He pulled it out. "Yeah?" He paused. "Hello? Anyone there?" He snapped it off. "Shit."

"What's wrong?"

"No service."

Chapter Forty-two

The town of Star Lake, between the Eagle River and the upper peninsula of Michigan, is one of a collection of small towns in northern Wisconsin that used to be home to the logging industry. But logging has moved on, and today Vilas County is known mostly as a resort area. The snowmobile was invented in neighboring Sayner, and with miles of trails winding through the area, the town claims to have started the winter sport. In summer, visitors flock to hundreds of nearby lakes, including Star Lake, for which the town was named.

The overcast thinned as we drove north, and strips of blue sky appeared between the clouds. My cell didn't have any service either, so we stopped at a gas station on Route 70 to use a pay phone. I bought a Reese's bar and took it outside. The climate was different up here. Not just cooler; the air was lighter and somehow fresher. I'd heard black flies were a problem in summer, but they must have been seeking more attractive targets, because they didn't bother me.

Jimmy came back to the car, looking solemn. "There's been a development."

I pitched my candy wrapper into a trash can.

"The police found some prints on a green pickup that had been abandoned in the Forest Preserve in Illinois."

"In the bed of the truck?"

He looked surprised.

"I was there when they found them," I explained.

"Well, then, you might be interested to know who they belong to." He hesitated. "Billy Watkins."

The guy who worked at Mount Olympus. And owned a Bolt Action Remington rifle.

"There's more." He looked troubled. "The deputy staking out the Flynn house said Kim took off a couple of hours ago. He followed her as far as Route 39. She's headed north. The sheriff's department is looking for her."

Route 39 was the highway we'd taken coming up to Star Lake.

"Jimmy, does she know about the fishing cabin?"

"A lot of people do. Luke's been coming up here since he was a kid."

⌒⌒⌒

Heading into Star Lake, we drove through winding country roads marked with letters instead of names. The legacy of the lumber industry was ubiquitous, and nearly all the buildings were some variation of wood or log cabin. Jimmy studied his map only once, but he drove like he knew where he was going. Eventually, we turned down a dirt road. It hadn't rained this far north, and the tires kicked up dust. We made a left onto a side road so thickly wooded it was little more than a trail. A hundred yards beyond was a large clearing, and in the middle of the clearing stood a cabin.

I'd been expecting a small, shabby place, the kind of cabin you see in books about Abraham Lincoln. I was wrong. The structure was built with Scandinavian scribed logs, but the "cabin" was as large as my house. Glass windows and sliding doors hugged three sides of the building, and the bottom half was supported by fieldstone. The walk to the front door was lined with peonies and scrub roses, and I thought I saw a solar panel on the roof. Stands of conifers and cedars flanked the property.

I caught a glimpse of a picnic table through a cluster of reeds and bushes and, beyond that, an expanse of water almost as blue as the sky. I got out of the car and started toward the lake.

"Ellie. Don't trespass. Wait here. He knows my car."

But I was already cornering the house. As I reached the back-yard, I tripped on a large rock in the grass and lost my balance. I fell to my knees and threw out my hands to steady myself. As I straightened up, a voice growled, "Don't move."

Without moving my head, I looked up. Luke Sutton stood over me, aiming a shotgun at my chest.

His voice was angry and rough. "Why are you here?"

"I—I came with Jimmy. He's out front."

He eyed me suspiciously. Then he shouted. "Sack—you out there?"

Jimmy's voice came back. "I'm here, Luke."

"Go back home. I don't want to see you." His face hardened. "Either of you."

There was no reply from Jimmy. Luke kept the shotgun trained on me. My heart was pumping wildly.

"I told you. Get out."

I swallowed. "No. We—I—wanted to talk to you."

"What about?"

I looked up. "A lot of things," I said lamely.

"So talk."

I started to gesture toward the gun, but as I did, Jimmy appeared around the back. When he saw Luke, he froze for an instant but recovered quickly. "Luke, that's not going to help." He walked slowly toward his friend.

Luke looked from Jimmy to me and back. "Stop it, Sack. Don't come any closer. I've had enough." He swung the shotgun toward Jimmy.

"I know you have, Luke," Jimmy said quietly. "So have I. That's why I'm here. I want to help."

He seemed to consider it. Then, "Sure."

Jimmy took another step forward. Luke waved the gun. "I told you. Stop. Drop your weapon."

Jimmy stopped. "I didn't bring one, Luke. You can search me."

Luke ran his tongue around his lips.

"Luke, listen. Whatever's going on, we can deal with it. I'm your friend."

Luke swung the shotgun back to me. "What are you doing here?"

"I—I need to know the truth."

"Why? So you can put it in your next video?" he spit out. "Poor little rich boy murders his sister, maybe a few others, too?"

"No," I said softly. "Because I'm—I care about you."

A moment of absolute stillness followed. I heard the coos of birds, the plop of something riffling the water. A cloud that had been covering the sun broke apart, releasing a ray of light that shot into the lake. Luke slowly lowered the gun and laid it on the ground. Straightening up, he went to the picnic table, sat down, and cradled his head on his arms. Jimmy sat next to him. I slid onto the bench on his other side. The afternoon sun danced on the lake. The only thing I heard was the distant chirr of insects.

I wasn't sure how much time passed before Luke pulled himself together. But the sun was arcing toward the west when he raised his head and took a long breath.

"You okay, pal?" Jimmy asked.

"I'm just so fucking tired." He ran a hand over his hair and beard. He looked at Jimmy, then at me, his eyes softening as they passed. Despite everything, my heart skipped a beat.

"Those DNA tests you're doing?" He looked at Jimmy. "You're not going to need them. I can tell you what's on Annie's clothes." He took another breath, as if fueling himself with courage.

"Chip's semen." He paused. "And it's his blood on my baseball shirt."

Jimmy made a show of not reacting. I sat very still.

"He was—abusing her. He'd been doing it for a while. But I didn't know." He looked dazed, disoriented. "Oh shit. I didn't want to know. But all those years—oh God. I knew something was wrong. But Jesus. He was my older brother."

"What happened the night Annie died?" I asked.

It came out slowly. "I was working at the airstrip. Mom and Dad were at the races. They had a new horse at Arlington and wanted to see him run. They were going to spend the night there. They did that a lot. Chip and Annie were home." He bit his lip. "I should never have left."

"Why?" I breathed.

"I knew something was wrong. Chip and Annie were barely speaking. It'd been that way for a while. At the time, I remember thinking—oh God—rationalizing that it was just a fight over things. That maybe Annie was 'borrowing' some of Chip's things like Chip did with me. He'd take my records. Sometimes my clothes."

"The baseball shirt."

He nodded. "I figured Annie was doing that to Chip. And that Chip was pissed off. But then she called me right after supper. At the airstrip. Asked if she could come by. She wanted to talk. I told her sure." He blinked. "She never showed up. I waited, but she never came." He shifted. "But you have to understand. She never said anything. Not one fucking word." He gripped the edge of the table. "I—I might have been able to do something. But I didn't know."

Jimmy cut in. "Annie never asked anyone for help. Don't you remember the summer I tried to teach her to waterski? She wouldn't let me. She always had to figure it out for herself."

"Thanks, but that won't cut it. I was her older brother. I was supposed to be there."

"You were seventeen," I said.

"I should have called. At least found out where she was. Maybe that would have helped. But I figured she blew me off and went out with her friends. You know, found something better to do." A strangled sound came out of his throat.

"What happened then?" Jimmy asked.

"When I got home, Chip wasn't in bed. Neither was Annie. I thought Chip had gone to the Sugar Shack, you know?"

"The Sugar Shack wasn't known for checking IDs back then," Jimmy said to me.

"I figured Annie was sleeping over at a friend's," Luke went on. "I was wiped out so I went to bed. But a couple hours later, I woke up. Someone was beating down the door. Shouting. Yelling. It turned out to be Chip. He was falling down drunk. I mean, Chip had been drinking for a while, but this was over the top even for him. He went into the bathroom and threw up. Eventually, I got him into the shower. Then I asked him where Annie was."

Jimmy winced.

"He wouldn't answer. Then he said he didn't know. I went downstairs to make a pot of coffee. While it was brewing, I decided to call one of her friends to make sure she was there. I was just picking up the phone when Herbert showed up."

"Herbert Flynn."

He nodded. "Scared the shit out of me. Just kind of appeared. I saw his shadow in the outside light."

"He didn't ring the bell?" Jimmy asked.

"Herbert always came around to the kitchen. The cook or the maid would let him in. Anyway, when I opened the door, he looked me up and down. Then he glared. I mean, if looks could kill….I asked him what was going on. I mean, it was probably around three in the morning by then." Luke faltered. "He—he looked furious. But pale. And he was trembling. Actually trembling. He asked me if I knew where Annie was."

Jimmy's head came up.

"When he said, 'Do you know where your sister is,' I got scared. It was three in the morning. Why would Herbert ask me something like that? I told him I thought she was at her girlfriend's house. But that I was just going to call and make sure." He hesitated. "I remember he looked like he didn't believe me."

"Maybe he didn't know what to believe," I said.

"I think—maybe at that time—well, who knows?" Luke shrugged. "Anyway, then I asked why he was asking. He mumbled something, but I didn't know what he meant. I kept asking him. Finally he told me to come with him. I followed

him down to the pier. That's when I saw her. In—in the water."
He started to blink.

We waited.

"She was floating facedown. Her hair was all spread out
around her. And she was naked. Her skin was so white. The
moonlight." His voice cracked. "For a minute, I thought maybe
it was a joke. That she'd roll over, and grin at me. 'Fooled you,
Luke.'" He swallowed. "It didn't happen."

"What did you do?"

"We pulled her out of the water. Herbert tried to give her
mouth to mouth but nothing happened. I tried, too." A sob came
out of his throat. "I—I'm not sure what happened next. I know
I called my father. He told me not to do anything else until he
got there. They must have flown down the highway—they got
home before dawn. Herbert was gone by then."

"He left?" Jimmy asked.

Luke nodded.

"When?"

"I don't remember times. I do remember Chip came downstairs after his shower. He looked like shit. He didn't say much.
He kept rolling his shoulder. I remember that."

"Rolling his shoulder?"

"Like it hurt. When I asked him, he said he must have pulled
a muscle on the boat that afternoon."

"What happened when your father got home?" I asked.

Luke looked toward the lake. "He—it got confusing. He was
on the phone a lot. Mother collapsed. Our doctor came. The
housekeeper—it wasn't Mrs. Baines then—was there, too."

"What about the police?" Jimmy asked. "When did they
get there?"

Luke looked blank. "I—I don't remember exactly. Maybe
the next morning?"

"Your father didn't tell you to call them first thing? Even
before they got home?" I asked.

Luke shook his head. "No. He specifically told me not to do
anything until he got there."

Jimmy and I exchanged a glance.

"I do remember that Father talked to Chip first, then to me."

"What did he say?"

Luke shifted his gaze. "He came into my room. I'd been lying down, not sleeping, of course. It was impossible to sleep. Anyway, he came in and sat down on the bed, and said something to the effect of 'We're a family, son. And we're going to stick together. That's the most important thing. I'll take care of everything.'"

I frowned. "That's all?"

"That's all I remember."

I rubbed my forearm with my other hand. "What did he mean?"

"I didn't know. Not then. But after it became clear the whole thing was going to be pinned on Herbert, and then an 'intruder'... ." He looked at both of us in turn. "I started to figure it out."

Jimmy looked down.

Luke clasped his hands on the picnic table. "We never talked about it again. Mother grew more and more reclusive, and then she just...." His voice trailed off. "I just—well—tried not to think about anything. I smoked a lot of weed. Did some drinking myself. But it weighed. Eventually, I left."

"I knew you changed after that," Jimmy said in a low voice. "I thought it was just Annie."

I interjected. "That's when you enlisted?"

He nodded. "I didn't care where I went or what I did. Even if I lived or died."

"Instead of dying, you became a fighter pilot."

Luke shrugged.

"And then you went to Montana."

"It was a thousand miles away."

"Why did you come back?"

"There comes a time—well, I thought, maybe, I could start over. It had been almost thirty years. I was an adult. I missed the Midwest. And I wanted to start the airline. I couldn't do that out there."

"Didn't you wonder why no one ever told you the truth?"

"No." It came out fast and firm. "I wouldn't let myself. I didn't trust my memory anyway. Until the other day. When you came to the house with Jimmy."

I frowned. "Me?"

"It was what you said when we were walking. About the bloodstains." He looked over. "That there must have been a sharp object involved."

"Well?"

He sighed. "Chip had a fishing knife. A Green River. It was a five-inch filleting knife. He bought it at the bait and tackle shop up here. It was his favorite possession. He always carried it. Even at home."

I sucked in a breath.

"I remembered not seeing it after Annie died. It just—kind of disappeared."

Jimmy folded his arms.

"Once you mentioned the bloodstains, I realized they could have been caused by the knife. So I tried to figure out when I'd last seen it. That's why I came up here."

"To find the knife?" I asked.

He shook his head. "I was pretty sure it was gone. But I did want to check with Norman Desmond, see if he remembered when he sold it to Chip. See if the timing fit."

"I talked to him." I recalled our conversation. He'd told me nothing.

"He mentioned that."

"Well? Did the timing work?"

Luke ran a tongue around his lips. "Perfectly. Norman sold it to Chip about a year before Annie died. Like I said, it disappeared after that. But the night of the murder, when Chip was favoring his shoulder—"

"You think it could have been a knife wound?" I cut in.

"Annie was a fighter. She never gave up. Even when it was just a game."

I got up and started to pace. "So pinning the murder on Herbert Flynn, throwing suspicion on him, that was all a cover-up by your father?"

Luke didn't say anything.

"And when no one could come up with any evidence, your father came up with the Sharon Percy theory."

Luke nodded.

"Which, except for the Flynns, suited everybody's purposes," I said. "Until Herbert Flynn came back."

Jimmy's brows lifted.

"Once we got the note, everything changed. It was like a time warp." Luke looked at Jimmy. "Flynn claimed he finally had the evidence that would exonerate him and prove who really killed Annie. But if we wanted him to stay quiet, we had to pay him an enormous amount of money."

That must have been what Herbert was doing at the ice house. Looking for the clothes to blackmail the Suttons. Maybe he saw Chip stash them in the ice house. "Why did he wait so long?"

"My father can be very persuasive. He has 'resources.'"

"The carrot and the stick," Jimmy said.

"It must have been a hell of a carrot," I said.

"I think it was more like a stick," Luke said. "I'm sure my father explained in very clear terms what might happen to Herbert or the members of his family if he said anything to contradict the 'official' line."

My father's words about Charles Sutton came back to me. *He didn't care who got in his way.*

"So Herbert fled Lake Geneva," Jimmy said.

"And put his family through more anguish," I said.

Luke blinked.

"But then Irene got sick, and Herbert came back."

Jimmy rubbed his hands together, all business now. "All right. I've heard enough. Let's get you out of here."

"Why?" Luke asked.

"You have to come back to Lake Geneva and tell the sheriff's deputies everything you just told us. And I don't want you running into Kim Flynn."

"Kim? Why would Kim be coming here?" Luke spread his hands.

"She took off a few hours ago. My men say she's heading north."

"Why here?"

Jimmy and I exchanged another look. "Because she thinks you're responsible for her problems," I said. "And she might have orchestrated Daria's murder."

"Kim killed her sister?" Luke shot us a dubious look.

I told him about the calls on the borrowed cell. When I'd finished, he shook his head. "I don't believe it. Kim wouldn't kill anyone."

"How do you know?"

He looked at the ground. A flush crept up his neck and ears.

"It's all right. I—I know about you and Kim," I said quietly.

His mouth opened slightly. "How?"

"It doesn't matter."

"It—it was a long time ago." He looked up. "Kim was beautiful, but she was never very—stable. She had these—fantasies." He shrugged. "I didn't buy into them, but when a woman throws herself at you...." His neck and cheeks turned bright red. "Annie's death put an end to it. And then I went away. When I came back last year, Kim came to my apartment. She said she still wanted something between us. There isn't—there never was. I told her that. After that I made a point of staying clear of her."

I felt a stab of both guilt and triumph; guilt for thinking of my relationship with Luke at a time like this, triumph that Kim had no claim on him.

"Luke, does Kim know about this place?" Jimmy asked.

"I never brought her here—"

"But it's been in the family since you were a kid. It's possible she knows where it is?"

"It's possible."

"Okay. Let's get you both back downstate."

"I don't know," Luke balked. "Maybe this isn't such a good idea."

"There isn't any other solution," Jimmy said. "I'm going to call in. See if there's any word." He pulled out his cell, snapped it on, and gazed at the tiny screen. "Dammit. Not again." He looked at me. "Is your phone working?"

I pulled it out and checked. I shook my head.

"If you want to make a call," Luke said, "you have go down to Desmond's bait and tackle shop in town."

"I'll be back in a couple of minutes." Jimmy waved a hand. "Luke, get your things together. We'll all drive back together."

"I have the plane," Luke offered.

"No," we both said in unison.

Chapter Forty-three

The interior of the cabin was as impressive as the exterior. Light spilled from the windows, and there were beamed ceilings and lots of polished wood, all of it a warm, inviting peanut butter brown. Plus all the conveniences you'd expect: dishwasher, microwave, washer-dryer.

I followed Luke upstairs to a cheerful room with a brass bed and braided Indian rugs. The walls were white, with wood moldings, and the window gave onto a beautiful view of the lake.

He pulled out a suitcase from under the bed. "The best muskies in the world live in Star Lake."

"I don't know the first thing about fishing."

"I don't either," he admitted, grinning. "That's not why I come up here."

"This was your sanctuary."

He opened a five-drawer captain's chest, took out some clothes, and tossed them into the suitcase. "That's right."

I looked out at the lake. A man and a boy were rowing past us in a dinghy. The boy dipped his oars in the water, his arms stretched out in front of him. As he pulled through the water, he leaned forward, hunched his shoulders, and splayed his elbows. Then he dipped the oars and repeated the action. The rhythm was mesmerizing.

I felt Luke's hands on my shoulders. "I'm sorry about the way I treated you," he said. "I wouldn't be up here if it wasn't for you. Thank you."

I kept my eyes on the boaters.

"Why didn't you give up on me?"

I turned around slowly. "It was the time in your plane. You were—you knew I was afraid. You were—so caring."

"And now it's your turn?"

I shook my head. "You came back here on your own."

"It's going to get ugly."

"Not if you want the truth to get out."

He shook his head. "Even with the truth. It will be a long time before anyone speaks the Sutton name without disgust."

"I have faith."

"Faith, huh? Is that what I need?" He moved closer. "What are you, Ellie? My savior, my jailor, or my lover?"

"What do you want me to be?"

"Let me show you." He slipped his arms around me and kissed me. I leaned into him.

I heard a rustle, then a few footfalls, like someone sprinting up the steps. A harsh voice cut in. "Well, now, I guess this is one of those scenes, isn't it?"

We broke apart. Luke spun around. I sucked in a breath.

Kim Flynn was standing in the doorway. Her hair was mussed, her cheeks were crimson, and she was breathing hard. And she was aiming a pistol at us.

To his credit, Luke stayed calm. "What kind of scene are you talking about, Kim?"

"Like in the movies, when the wife catches her husband with another woman."

"It must be a movie I've never seen."

"Don't play coy, Luke. It doesn't become you." She gestured toward me with the gun. "You're the one I'm here for."

My stomach clenched.

"How did you know we were here, Kim?" Luke said neutrally, as if she was an unexpected, but not unwelcome, visitor.

"Her daughter." She pointed the gun at me. "I called her house. She told me you were driving to northern Wisconsin."

I felt the blood drain from my face, realizing how close Kim had gotten to Rachel, even just on the phone.

"I didn't realize you knew about this place," Luke said smoothly. I could tell he was trying to draw her out, slow things down while he thought of a way out. I tried to remember what he had done with the shotgun. Was it downstairs? Or out in back? Either way, I realized dismally, it didn't matter. There was no way I could get to it in time.

"I found it a long time ago." She favored him with a smile. "When you were still out West."

"You've been here by yourself?"

"Once or twice." She seemed to fill with pride. "I slept in that bed. I knew it was yours."

I must have moved just slightly, because Kim straightened the arm holding the pistol. It was an automatic, I thought. Like my father's Colt. But smaller. Shit. Where was Jimmy? How long did it take to make a frigging phone call?

"Kim. This isn't the way." Luke reached out his hand. "Let me help."

"Get away from me, Luke."

"But Kim...."

"No, Luke," I cut in. He was doing it wrong. We should humor her. "Kim is right. Your family has treated the Flynn family very badly."

Luke shot me a look. I stared him down. Then I saw it register. He turned back to Kim. "She's right, Kim. I—I guess I never realized it."

I tried to estimate how far I'd have to lunge to bring her down and whether I could do it before she got off a shot. She was over eight feet away. Too far. But what if I could edge closer? If I was within five feet, I might have a chance.

"We knew we'd get our chance. If we could just be patient." She laughed, a tinny, high-pitched chuckle.

I cleared my throat and inched forward. Kim swung her arm my way. "Don't even think about moving," she barked, her voice icy.

I went rigid. My pulse pounded in my ears. Where the fuck was Jimmy?

"We had to wait, but then it happened."

"What?"

She smiled, the same mirthless smile I'd seen on her mother. "DNA."

I wasn't sure I'd heard her right.

"DNA," she repeated. "When DNA tests started to be used, my father knew he had the proof he needed. He knew whose DNA would show up on Annie's clothes. And the baseball shirt. He knew Annie wasn't killed by an outsider. He knew it was either you or Chip. But when he tried to tell your father, your old man told him if he didn't keep quiet, he'd make sure *he* was convicted. And then he tried to pin it on him anyway. My father had to run for his life. But he knew his time would come."

I glanced at Luke, then at Kim. "Your father got it wrong, Kim," I said quietly.

Her eyes narrowed. "What are you talking about?"

"The clothes were in the ice house—unprotected—for thirty years. Whatever DNA might have been there has most likely been contaminated. There's virtually no chance they'll find anything of value at this point."

She leveled the gun on me. Her nostrils flared. "You're lying. You'd say anything right now."

"Ask Jimmy."

"Jimmy's the one that ordered the tests."

"It was a ploy to squeeze out information."

"You're a liar," she repeated. But uncertainty flashed briefly across her face.

Where was Jimmy?

She read my mind. "I don't believe Jimmy's here. You're making that up, too."

"She's telling the truth." Luke held out his hand. "He's making a call. Please, Kim, put the gun down. We'll talk."

She gave a defiant shake of her head. "Back off, Luke."

Keep her talking, Luke, I screamed in my head. It might distract her, and I could take her. But Luke was silent and cautious, keeping his distance as you would with a wounded, feral animal. I had to think of something. "When did you first get the idea to blackmail the Suttons, Kim?"

"It was my father's idea. After Mother got sick, the medical bills nearly put us under. The restaurant was in trouble. We were living on credit. It was just a matter of time before everything collapsed. We needed a miracle. That's when Dad told me what he'd seen that night."

"You and he planned it together after he came back?"

"It was our only option." She glanced at Luke. "We had to even the playing field."

"Did your mother know?"

"Are you crazy?" She made a small, snorting sound. "She had a hard enough job just trying to recuperate."

"What about Daria?"

She didn't answer.

I thought about the timing. Herbert's return. The second sniper attack. Daria Flynn's murder. Suddenly, the last piece fell into place. "Daria knew, didn't she?" I said. "Daria found out about your scheme."

Kim looked up, startled, but then her expression hardened. "She didn't want us to do it. She threatened to go to Jimmy." She looked at Luke. "Or you."

"Your own sister," I went on. "She was interfering, screwing everything up. Everything your father waited for all those years. You couldn't let that happen, could you, Kim?"

She looked at Luke again. "We couldn't let her. And then when she met with you at the Lodge, well, I was sure she was going to warn you."

"That was the last straw, wasn't it?" I inched forward, more of a lean than a step.

Kim gave a helpless shrug. "You can understand why I couldn't trust her."

"Of course." I took another tiny step forward.

"Daria always got everything she wanted. She was everyone's darling. Prettier, smarter, more ambitious. My father liked her better. Mother thought she was going to be a star."

"It was you she was apologizing to on the phone at the rest stop."

A muscle in her jaw twitched. "We'd been fighting. But it was too little, too late."

I heard a swish of tires outside. Kim didn't pick up on it. "So you and your father had to kill her." It took all my concentration to keep my tone conversational.

"No. It was me."

"You?"

"I called Fred. Told him Daria wouldn't be able to meet him. A family emergency had come up." She grimaced. "He wasn't happy. He'd made all those pastries."

Where the hell was Jimmy? I kept going. "And you knew Daria would call you back and ask you to pick her up after the catering gig fell apart."

She nodded. "She couldn't afford to get her car fixed."

"You'd already gotten Watkins to steal the green pickup by then."

She looked surprised. "How do you know about him?"

"He left fingerprints on the bed of the truck. So…." I picked up the thread of the story. "You called Fred and told him the gig was off. Then you dropped Daria at the rest stop, met Watkins, ditched the car for the pickup, and doubled back to kill her."

She threw me a glance of grudging respect.

"How'd you get Watkins to be your triggerman?"

"He was dealing, and I busted him. He was desperate to stay out of jail."

"But afterward, he became a problem, didn't he?" I paused. "So you killed him, too."

"I had no choice." She grabbed the gun with her other hand and aimed it at my chest. "Just like you."

Shit. Time was running out.

"You should never have gotten involved." She smiled toler-
antly.

"It was you who came to my house," I reminded her. "You
and your mother."

It was strangely silent outside. No car door opening. Or closing. Had I imagined it?

"Kim," Luke cut in. "You can't blame Ellie. She didn't want
any of this to happen."

"But it did." Her eyes skittered with anger. "And now she's
in the way. Like Daria. Taking what was mine." She paused.
"Including you."

"It was never going to be."

I nudged forward another inch.

"I never promised you anything," He kept his eyes on her,
but I could tell he knew what I was doing.

She tilted her head, as if she didn't quite understand. "It
happened. You can't deny it. We were a couple."

My eyes strayed to the doorway behind Kim. Jimmy was
crouching in the hall with Luke's shotgun in his hand. It was
aimed at Kim. Her pistol was trained on me. Whatever was going
down would happen in the next few seconds. Light streamed in
from outside. For a bizarre moment, I imagined us all in a still
life by some past master: Kim's gun on me, Jimmy's gun on her,
all of us frozen on a horrific canvas.

"But I'm not surprised." The corners of her mouth stretched
into a grimace. "No one ever keeps their promises to me. Not
you. Or Daria. Or her." She steadied the gun and squinted.

Jimmy cut in before Luke could answer. "Kim, put the gun
down."

She whirled around. Her voice spiked. "Jimmy, get out. This
isn't your concern."

"Oh, but it is, Kim," he replied quietly. "I can't let you do
this."

I was pretty sure Jimmy had a clear shot. Why didn't he shoot?
Luke started to edge forward.

"Kim," Jimmy repeated. "This is your last chance. Put the gun down."

Kim wavered and turned back to us. When she realized Luke was coming toward her, her eyes widened. I lunged. She pulled back the slide on the pistol. The blast of a shotgun roiled the air. I fell a foot short of Kim. She staggered back, her feet twitching like a marionette's. I went temporarily deaf. Her body collapsed, and she dropped to the floor. Eddies of air swirled around us.

Jimmy lowered the gun. His hands were shaking.

Chapter Forty-four

"It was inevitable."

"What do you mean?" Susan asked. We were hiking down the bike path a week later. The path was stippled with the clear light of evening, the leaves rustling in the breeze.

"The shoe print turned out to be Chip's."

"He killed Herbert Flynn?"

I nodded. "He probably thought he was doing what his father should have done thirty years ago."

"Do you think his father put him up to it?"

I thought about it. "It's an interesting question."

"There was a precedent."

"In both families."

Susan's eyebrows lifted.

"Two families. Two murders. Two siblings. But in the Flynns' case, Daria discovered what they were up to."

"She wasn't in on it?"

I shook my head. "Apparently, she went ballistic when she found out. But Kim was desperate. Especially after she suspected Daria was seeing Luke."

"You're not saying she killed her sister over a man she slept with thirty years ago."

"No. Money and revenge were at the root of it. But I'm sure the rumors about Luke and Daria didn't help."

"How did she arrange it? It had to take a lot of planning."

"It wasn't that hard. After she enlisted Watkins, she got him to steal a green pickup, waited until she knew Daria would be heading to the oasis, then called the guy Daria was planning to meet and canceled it on Daria's behalf." I shrugged. "For all we know, she could have tampered with Daria's car to begin with, so it would be out of commission."

"All that just to stage a sniper attack?" Susan turned a shocked face to me. "And Herbert didn't know?"

"Kim claimed he didn't."

"I guess I believe her," Susan said. "I mean, how does a parent let one of their children kill the other?"

"That's a question I'd like to ask Chuck Sutton."

Susan pressed her lips together. "Has Chip confessed?"

I shook my head. "He's all lawyered up, but if Luke testifies against him, it should be a done deal."

"Will he?"

"He's given statements to that effect."

"So what really did happen that night?"

"From what I can gather, Chip saw Annie getting ready to go out. When she told him she was going to the airstrip to talk to Luke, he decided it would be one of those nights. It wasn't the first time, you know," I said grimly. "He managed to intercept her in the backyard. This time, though, she fought back. She somehow got his fishing knife—he had it with him all the time—"

"Fishing knife?"

"He bought it in northern Wisconsin. They say Chip still has a scar on his shoulder where she stabbed him. Eventually, though, he overpowered her. Threw the knife in the water, I guess. It's never been found. Then he strangled her. When he realized she was dead, he panicked. He stripped off her clothes and the baseball shirt with his blood on it—"

"Luke's shirt."

"According to Luke, he borrowed Luke's things a lot."

"That's kind of telling right there, don't you think?"

"I guess. Anyway, he threw Annie in the water, folded the clothes, and hid them in the ice house. I guess he thought they'd never be found. The story of the 'intruder' was concocted afterward."

"By his father."

I nodded. "Herbert witnessed the whole thing. He went to Sutton right away and told him. The problem was he wasn't sure which brother it was. Sutton told him if anything ever came out about either brother, he would make sure Herbert's family paid."

"Kim and Daria being the family."

I waved away mosquitoes.

"He turned out to be prescient." Susan marched down the path at a brisk pace. "Did Irene know about the—the scheme?"

"Apparently not."

"But Herbert was already back in Lake Geneva when Irene and Kim showed up at your house."

"He was staying in Delavan at a friend of Kim's."

"Which means they were playing you from the beginning."

"They were."

"Tell me something." Susan looked at me through lidded eyes. "If Watkins was the shooter, who drove the pickup?"

"Kim. She wore a wig and glasses."

"What about the third sniper attack? How does that fit in?"

"The police think the third one was the first guy acting out because someone—Kim and Billy Watkins, specifically—actually had the nerve to copycat him."

"Which means someone is still running around killing people with a high-powered rifle because of a bruised ego."

I paused. "Yes."

We exited the bike path and headed back to Happ Road.

"What's going to happen to Irene?" Susan asked.

"I don't know. Luke wants her to go into an assisted living place, but she's in no shape to make any decisions."

Susan nodded.

"Ellie, how can you have anything more to do with the Suttons?"

"There aren't many of them left. Chip and Chuck will spend the rest of their lives in prison."

"What about the coupler business?"

"I guess it's mostly Luke's now."

"Talk about your reluctant tycoon."

I kept my mouth shut.

"I said, let's talk about your reluctant tycoon," Susan said coolly. "Ellie, he's got more baggage than the carousels at O'Hare. How can you contemplate a future with him?"

I didn't answer.

"Ellie?"

I ran my hand over the top of a bush. "You have a point. Whether he was consciously aware of it or not, he knew something was very wrong."

"And his way of dealing with it was to run away. Fly a plane. Join the army. Hide out in Montana."

"He came back. And he was actually looking for evidence that his brother killed Annie up at the fishing cabin."

"I don't know, Ellie," she said, obviously not convinced. "What does that say about his ability to face other issues? How do you know he won't throw up his hands and run again?" She threw me a look. "Because there's one thing I know. If you get involved with him, there are bound to be issues. Have you thought about that?"

"I've been thinking of little else." I shrugged. "We have a lot to work out once he's back in Chicago."

"He's not staying in Lake Geneva?"

"He's going to sell Monticello. After he finds a place for his mother."

"I see," she said. "And isn't there another nagging issue?"

"What's that?"

"I think his name begins with David."

"Susan, I told you. It's over."

"Are you sure? Or could it be possible you still haven't forgiven him for cheating on you?"

"That was eons ago. I've forgotten all about that."

"It was last year. And how do you know you're not, subconsciously, of course, still punishing him? Getting even for the hurt he caused you?"

I thought about it. Was I somehow—subconsciously or not—suppressing my real feelings for David? It didn't feel like it. Then again, given everything that had happened recently, my reactions could be off. I looked over. "Kim Flynn was a woman who couldn't forgive," I said. "I'm not that petty."

Susan didn't say anything

I thought back to the message David left on my machine a few days ago. I'd never called him back. I owed him that much.

⌖

Rachel and I had a late dinner, and by the time I'd cleaned up, it was dark. I went out to the deck to sit on my glider. Clouds rushed across the moon, refracting light into a brilliant white scrim. In the western horizon, the sky was still vaguely pink from the setting sun.

I swung back and forth. Maybe Susan was right. I could patch things up with David. Life would certainly be easier with him. The history between us was powerful. We knew what to expect from each other; we shared a friendship, if not passion. But the ferocity and raw power that surged through me when I thought about Luke made my body ache. He was the one who filled my thoughts. Still, how long could anyone sustain that kind of passion? The events of this summer had drained me. I was tired. And Luke had a lot of healing to do.

Chatter from the TV drifted out to the deck. Rachel was watching a DVD that contained an entire season of "Friends." I'd sworn to destroy it if I had to listen to its doggedly cheerful theme song again. Tonight, though, its familiarity was soothing.

There were still a few weeks until school started. Maybe Rachel and I should take off for a while. We could rent a place on the Michigan shore. Do some mother-daughter bonding. I'd be losing her soon—she'd have her driver's license in a few months. I could invite Dad, too. He could use the distraction.

A car rolled up the driveway, crackling a few dead leaves that had already lost the battle. A car door opened and closed. The doorbell chimed. Rachel could get it. I didn't have the energy. The sound of the TV was suddenly silenced; I heard Rachel shuffle to the door.

A male voice in a deep register mumbled something. I didn't catch the words.

"She's out on the deck." A pause. "I'll get her."

Rachel's footsteps echoed through the kitchen. The screen door squeaked as she threw it open. "Mom," she whispered theatrically. "For you."

I didn't want to know who it was. "Tell them I'm not available."

"I can't." Rachel peered over her shoulder and stepped aside.

He stood framed in the doorway, the light wreathing him like a halo. "Hello, Ellie."

"I—I didn't expect this," I stammered. "What are you doing here?"

He smiled and held out his hand.

To receive a free catalog of Poisoned Pen Press titles, please contact us in one of the following ways:

Phone: 1-800-421-3976
Facsimile: 1-480-949-1707
Email: info@poisonedpenpress.com
Website: www.poisonedpenpress.com

Poisoned Pen Press
6962 E. First Ave. Ste. 103
Scottsdale, AZ 85251